THE STAR-GLASS

THE STAR-GLASS

DUNCAN THORNTON

COTEAU BOOKS
WWW.COTEAUBOOKS.COM

Edited by Geoffrey Ursell.
Cover image and interior illustrations by Yves Noblet.
Interior map by Malcolm Cullen.
Cover and book design by Duncan Campbell.

Printed and bound in Canada by Gauvin Press.

National Library of Canada Cataloguing in Publication Data

Thornton, Duncan, 1962-
The star-glass / Duncan Thornton.

ISBN 1-55050-269-7

I. Title.
PS8589.H556S83 2003 jC813'.54 C2003-905084-X

10 9 8 7 6 5 4 3 2 1

401-2206 Dewdney Ave.
Regina, Saskatchewan
Canada S4R 1H3

Available in the US and Canada from:
Fitzhenry & Whiteside
195 Allstate Parkway
Markham, Ontario
Canada L3R 4T8

The publisher gratefully acknowledges the financial assistance of the Saskatchewan Arts Board, the Canada Council for the Arts, the Government of Canada through the Book Publishing Industry Development Program (BPIDP), and the City of Regina Arts Commission, for its publishing program.

For my father, who came to a strange, vast land,
and for my mother, who went back with him.

Table of Contents

THE WARDS OF THE SEA

1. The Tempest 1
2. The Tall Seas 18
3. The Mill House 37
4. The Council *of the* Western Shores 47

THE RIVERFOLK

5. Into *the* Wild 61
6. The Fens 78
7. Muskets *in the* Dark 95
8. The Freedom *of the* River 107
9. The Leather Stockings 121
10. Noises *in the* Dark 134

THE EALDA

11. The Council Under *the* Moon 149
12. Above *the* Falls 161
13. A Tinker Tale 176
14. The Chain *of* Falls 197
15. Eena Culgach 215
16. The Dark Night 229

THE TINKERS

17. The Long Dream *of* Falling 235
18. Edge-Gleamer 252
19. The Escape 271
20. Winter *in the* Stony Hall 287
21. The Camp *at the* Edge *of the* Wild 304
22. The Turning *of the* Year 317

SOME COLD NORTH THING

23. The Moon *of the* Lazy Sun 327
24. None More Brave 341
25. The Frozen Heart 357
26. The Battle *of the* Thin Moon 372
27. The End *of the* Exploration 388

EPILOGUE

28. What Happened After 397

List of Illustrations

1. *A small, dark bird flew into the room* ii

2. *The Master stared covetously at Tom's Star-Glass* 36

3. *Broe-stach!* 60

4. *A cottonwood, come to life* 94

5. *A hairy, walking house* .120

6. *It was a hard carry* 148

7. *Eena Culgach, The Terrible Claw* 214

8. *Falling and falling* 234

9. *They put their backs against the great tree* 270

10. *They saw Lynx eyes, glowing* 326

11. *The morning light revealed the monster* 356

The Land
Where no people
Live

The Frozen Sea

The Gap

Rockmarch
Camp

The Wild

River Roaring

Eena Culgach

Drumrath

The Hidden
Sea

The Steppes

Meeltacn
Aws

Cold Lake
Country

Lshca
Lunrach

Buffles

The
Shining
Mountains

The Cruel and
Dusty South

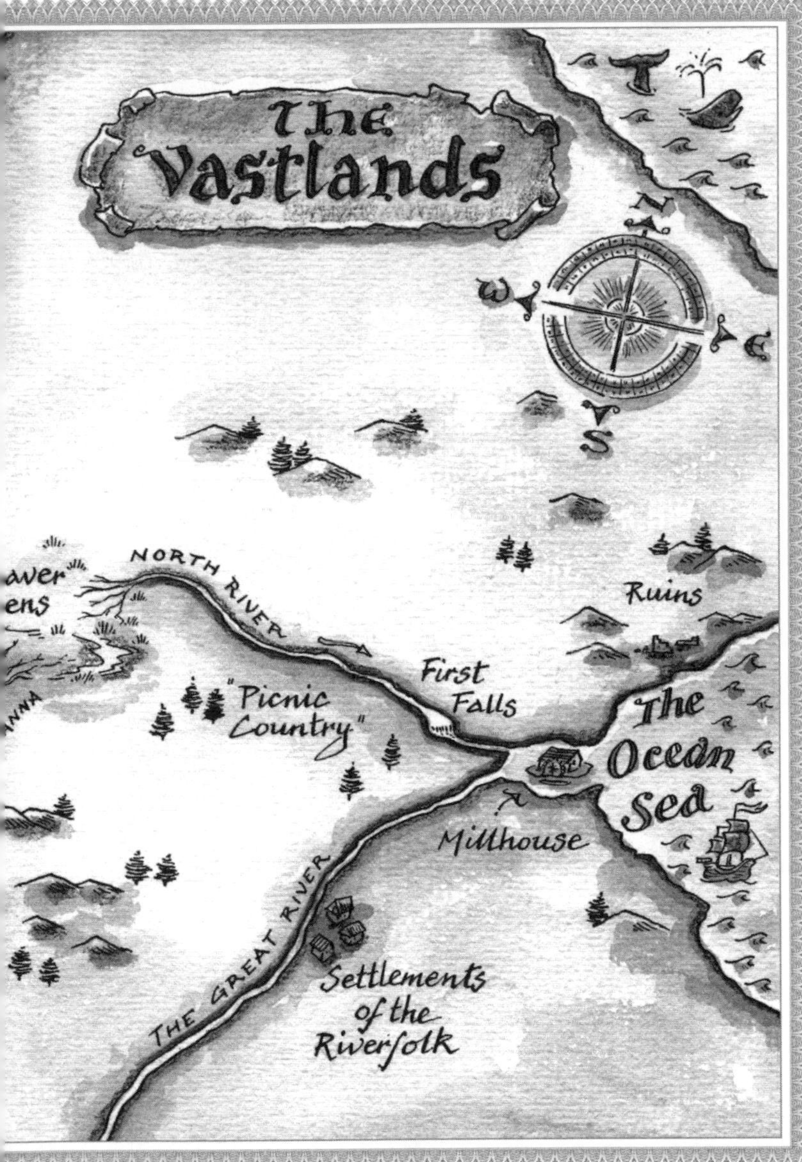
The Vastlands
N
W
E
S
NORTH RIVER
Ruins
First Falls
"Picnic Country"
The Ocean Sea
Millhouse
THE GREAT RIVER
Settlements of the Riverfolk

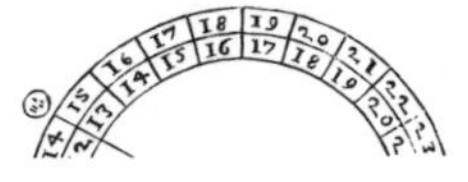

A NOTE TO THE READER

THE LANGUAGE OF THE EALDA AND the Riverfolk may be pronounced in any way that sounds pleasant, but they themselves almost always stress the first syllable, and use "ch" as in *Loch Ness,* rather than as in *peach*.

THE WARDS OF THE SEA

A small, dark bird flew into the room

Chapter One:
THE TEMPEST

– a great storm – disorder in the study – a tower looking West – the hut in the woods – a wet boy – the Storm Petrels –

It was a spring night, but not a pleasant spring night. This night still remembered the black, bleak Winter; this night, the wind whipped chill spray from the tossing sea.

There had been a storm from the West, rolling in warm and itching damp, heavy with gathering half the weight of the sea in its clouds. And there had been a storm from the East, rushing down cold and prickling ice from the mountains, dark and bitter from the trouble it had found along the way. Either storm would have been miserable enough, but now they met at last, and together they were a Tempest – a prodigy of foul weather – for like many unhappy things, each storm wanted at least to be alone in its misery.

And so the storms roared and fought and tore at one another. They spat rain and sleet and hail, and hurled thunder and lightning across the night to crash against the rocky coast. Thunder and lightning over and over again; until the homes and houses that looked West across the sea trembled in the grasp of the black night's weather, and the people who sheltered in them wondered.

In the tall house where Tom lived with his father, even the walls shuddered in that terrible wind. Books tumbled from the shelves and scattered over the floor. Charts and manuscripts rose in the draft and flapped like bats about the room. Countless slips of paper blew out of their pigeonholes and swirled madly in the air. And the roof leaked in seven different spots.

Tom and his father fought nobly to keep some order amidst the turmoil. They heaped fallen books in sturdy piles. They grabbed scattered charts and manuscripts and wedged them under table legs. They caught at slips of paper in the air and held them down with paperweights. When one thick manuscript began to blow apart, Tom's Dad gasped, but Tom caught the pages and pulled a heavy ball of glass from his pocket. Once that glass had been a present from Grandfather Frost; once Tom had used it to find his way through a field of ice, for in it he could see the stars, and the way to the North – but now he only used it like rock, to weigh down his father's book.

But at last the growing mess began to overwhelm them. From the barrel where he liked to hide, Tom's dog Sparky began to howl.

"It's no use," Tom's father said. He had to raise his voice over the storm. "No use any more."

Tom looked at his Dad. "I'm sorry," Tom said. "What a terrible setback for your Great Work."

For Tom's father was a lore-master and a mighty scholar, and spent his life arranging material for a book he meant to call *The Universal Encyclopaedia Comprising All Things Worth Knowing: Practical, Historical, and Mythological, As Well As Useful, Useless, Interesting, and Quaint.*

Tom's father peeled off a map of the Old Sea that had blown against the back of his head. "The storm might *not* have come solely to keep me from finishing the *Encyclopaedia,"* he said. "I think it is a sign, another dire portent."

Just then a shutter banged open, and a small, dark bird flew into the room. Sparky put his head out of his barrel and barked once, in case he was the only one who had noticed.

Still, the bird was not panicked, but flew twice around the ceiling before lighting upon the tallest bookshelf.

In the firelight, the bird seemed coal-black. His father squinted thoughtfully. "Do you know the bird?" he asked.

"It is a Storm Petrel," Tom said. "They fear no wind or weather."

Tom's Dad nodded. "There is a legend that they are the Wards of the Salt Sea," he said.

And because Tom helped his father with the Great Work, he knew about the Wards of the Salt Sea too.

Tom's Dad looked at the bird, and then he looked down for a moment. "It is another portent. I think you are to be called to sea again at last."

Once, when Tom was even younger, he had sailed with the crew of the *Volantix*, North through the Eaves of the World. It had been a cold and terrible voyage, but even

though his father's face and words were grim, Tom felt his heart stir. The sea-longing was rising in him once more.

"Plague and turmoil rise in the East," his father said. "War and hunger slip towards our home. Not this year, not next year, but soon it will come even to Landsend, worse than any storm.

"So there's word the Captain of the *Volantix* means to sail again, West, to the Vastlands, for he means to test the curse against Strangers there, and find some Homely Country we might settle before the Long Night falls."

"Settle there?" Tom asked. For Strangers visited the Vastlands to carry out the business of trading for fur and skins, but for long years none had dared to settle there.

His Dad nodded. "You brought the Captain luck once before," he said. "Luck he'll need again, I think."

"Sail West like the Elves before us," Tom said, with fear and with excitement. "And find out how they vanished."

"Perhaps," his father said. "It was on a voyage West your mother was lost. And with her Jenny's parents."

"I know," Tom said.

And then for a while they stood quiet among the ruin of the Great Work, his father's *Universal Encyclopaedia.* The rain lashed through the open shutter, and the wind howled, and the house shook, and more books fell onto the floor. For one sharp instant Tom saw Sparky's frightened eyes as bright lightning unclosed the darkness. Then the terrible crackling thunder came.

When Tom and his father could see and hear once

more, they looked out and saw a rider on a white horse waiting at their gate, as if the storm had brought him.

Sparky, a timid dog, began to bark wildly then, fur rising along his spine – the way he raged at the mailman while the door was closed.

"Come so soon," Tom's Dad said, and he sat heavily on a footstool.

Tom felt his heart begin to hammer. "Who is it?"

"A messenger from the Captain of the *Volantix,*" his father said, quiet beneath Sparky's barking. Then he carefully sat on his manuscript and gave the glass that had saved it back. In Tom's hand, it showed a glimmer of stars. "You'll need that to find your way there, and back."

Tom tucked the Star-Glass safely in his jacket. Then his father looked helplessly at the slips of paper he held in one hand. "Be as careful as you can. And record the strange things you see and hear, for the sake of our *Encyclopaedia.*"

A Storm Petrel went to visit Tom's friend Jenny too that night.

Jenny was only a Fisher-Girl, but she lived in a tall tower that looked West across the sea, a tower she had built with treasure from her own explorations. And of all the buildings the small bird saw that night, Jenny's Tower withstood the tempest most bravely. The rain swept down, but the ceiling never dripped. The wind roared, but the shutters hardly rattled.

The Wards of the Sea

But because Jenny's Tower stood tall on the edge of the sea, the lightning found it quickly. The bright forks cracked the mortar, sent stone chips flying, and left black, pitted marks that smoked briefly in the rain.

If Jenny had been at home she would at least have cursed the storm, for she was a proud and wordy girl, and Fisher-Girls can utter oaths most fluently. But that night the grey cat Pawlikins had come through the rain to fetch her away, for Jenny's Godmother, the Wise Woman of the Woods Nearby, was ailing.

So Jenny spent the night of the storm in her old Godmother's little cottage in the woods and only heard distant thunder, and didn't know it struck upon her tower. If even in the woods the wind bent tree and branch, and the rain beat hard upon the cottage, she paid the storm no attention.

Jenny's Godmother had watched over her from a child, so now Jenny tended to her most gently. She put cool cloths on the Wise Woman's brow, and made strong teas with added spirits.

"I am *not* worried this illness will persist," Jenny said to her Godmother. "Or overcome you and otherwise leave me here to take care of myself without your further guidance."

The Wise Woman only looked at her with eyes that were bright with fever, so Jenny went on talking: "Rather, you will rally, I think, and perhaps then even command this wretched storm to leave, or otherwise exert your strange and awful powers."

At last, her Godmother reached out. And Jenny felt the old woman's touch was hot, and quivered like a candle flame, so even she fell silent.

"This Tempest is no storm such as I command," the Wise Woman said, and her voice was hoarse and awful. "But a sign the dark Long Night begins to fall at last."

"Already?" Jenny whispered.

"Not this year," her Godmother said. "Not next year." Then she gripped Jenny's hand tight with her burning fingers.

"But soon!" the Wise Woman said. Now she almost hissed the words, more terrible than the storm outside. Even Pawlikins arched up from where he lay by fire and raised his damp fur.

"I see it – *soon!"* she said. "Already in the East soldiers drum the streets, waving banners under torchlight. Already plague and famine and pestilence are on the march. This trouble has no plan, has no leader, no head, no eyes, but it moves from East to West like the sun, regardless – and slowly it comes this way."

Jenny looked into her Godmother's burning eyes. "So I knew when I built my tower," Jenny said. "But I thought we had more time."

"Such a time is not ours to choose," her Godmother said. "So you must sail West, my Fisher-Girl. You must see if the Vastlands are open to us now, and seek for some safe haven there."

Jenny shivered. "I am not afraid," she said, "even

though the Law of the Sea has been that the Vastlands are closed to Strangers."

"Yes," her Godmother whispered, more gently now. "That has been the Law of the Sea, the rule of the World."

"One entire settlement was devoured by bears," Jenny recalled, "and another ruined by tornadoes." Her Godmother nodded.

"And the fate of the third was even stranger," Jenny said, not because she was frightened, but only to lay it all out plainly for consideration. "For it was two years after they set out before another ship came to see how they fared. And that second ship strangely found homes and streets and desks and chairs, and food in the pantry, but no people there to meet them. Only there was a sign nailed to one great tree. Which sign read –"

"It read, 'Gone to the Place of No Return,'" the Wise Woman croaked, "'for the Vastlands are closed to Strangers.'"

Then Jenny's Godmother sat up in her bed, and stared far off, as if she was looking even beyond the Cracks of the World. "The black Long Night comes again," she whispered. "But I think the rules are all stopped at last! And this time some refuge, some Homely Country, might be found among the Vastlands."

Of course, it went against Jenny's nature to run from trouble in any case. But now a thought cheered her: "It will be a hard voyage," she said. "The great salt sea itself might resist our purpose. But that's not to daunt a proper Explorer!"

The Wards of the Sea

The Wise Woman turned from her vision, and looked at Jenny herself again. "It might be found, I say. It might."

"As stories say the Elves once found," Jenny said. "Though Tom says their final fate is hidden –"

And she might have discussed the matter further, but the rumble of the storm grew loud, and suddenly her Godmother shivered. "A blanket, child!" she said. "Put a blanket over me, I feel the chill again."

So Jenny tucked a quilt round the old woman, and bent to build the fire up.

Then there was beating at the door and Jenny felt her heart begin to hammer. Through the little window she saw a storm-cloaked figure at the door, and farther off, a pale horse and its rider waiting.

Jenny grabbed the poker like a sword, but when the door opened, it was Tom who stood there.

As Tom bent under the low lintel, the wind and the rain came into the little cottage with him. He heard Pawlikins complain about the draft, and he shut the door and wiped his boots.

The small room was thick with peat smoke from the fire, but Tom saw Jenny's Godmother lying there, and he touched his hat to her and put it under his arm. For if the Wise Woman frightened him, he tried to mind his manners.

"A messenger from the Captain of the *Volantix* brought me here," Tom began. "But he is too afraid to enter."

"And so he ought to be," Jenny said at once, while her Godmother made a cackle that turned into a huge, long cough.

Tom nodded. "To be fair, ma'am, I think you have daunted braver souls than his."

"Oh yes," the Wise Woman said. "Oh yes, I have –"

And while she was making a longer cackle still, Tom turned to Jenny. "Is your duffel bag ready?

"My duffel bag is always ready," Jenny said at once. "As you well know."

"For the Captain of the *Volantix* has asked us to come aboard as his Ensigns," Tom told her. "He intends –"

"He intends to find some Homely Country, deep in the Vastlands," Jenny finished, and Tom saw her eyes glint, and she gripped the poker tighter. "*If* we survive the crossing, and *if* it is not still closed to Strangers."

Tom looked at the Wise Woman. She had finished her cackling, but not yet the cough that followed. "I thought you might know," he said.

"Which Exploration," Jenny continued, "would be daring, glorious, and yet also – in a strange sense – prudent at such a time!" Then the Wise Woman had finished her coughing too, and Jenny tried to tuck the quilt close around her. "Only my Godmother is – she is not feeling entirely comfortable, and so requires my attention."

The Wise Woman pushed the quilt away. "Nonsense!" she said, and to Tom even her words seemed to burn with fever. "Don't be a fool and worry about one old woman, when the Long Night falls!" She was shaking now, but her voice was sharp: "Go on this expedition; seek some Homely Country, and don't look back until you've found it."

Now Tom saw that Jenny trembled too, though she didn't speak at once. For her Godmother was the only person who could make her quiet.

Jenny put the poker back in its place by the fire, and fiddled with the teapot hanging in the inglenook. "But who will take care of you, in your illness, and with the darkness falling?" she asked at last.

Her Godmother waited until Jenny turned around again. Then she spoke gently. "It will comfort me to know you are exploring, as you were meant to. And I have several other teas and spirits for my fever." Then her voice rose once more. "And I have terrible powers, and can pronounce maledictions to frighten any intruder – and Pawlikins the cat is here to watch after me."

For a while the old woman's heavy breathing blended in with the sounds of the storm, with the beating wind, and the breaking branches, and the washing rain. Jenny nodded.

"Now bend close, for I shall pronounce a *rede* for each of you," the Wise Woman said. "And with that guidance, hurry to your storm-summoned business."

THE TEMPEST THAT NIGHT WAS VAST, and raged even South of Landsend, across the narrow Ocean channel, and over the country of the Corner-by-the-Sea.

The Wards of the Sea

There too the thunder and lightning almost broke the tumbled black sky open. Beasts of the field huddled together, and men and women and children wrapped themselves up against the rain and blowing dark and hid in their homes.

There too only fell creatures were out: goblins and nightmares; jack-o-lanterns and sea-things that reached out with sucking arms; dogs who would have no masters; and wild and solitary cats of the most disagreeable sort. Those creatures welcomed that night, and rejoiced in strange circles.

So of all the people and all the good beasts and fell creatures, only one didn't notice the storm, and he was a boy in a weather-beaten tricorne hat, named Gimlet.

YOUNG GIMLET SAT ALONE by the fire in the hall of the Deputy for Reason Seventeen. Long ago, the Deputy had been a Duke, but then someone told the people of the Corner by the Sea that it would be more reasonable to have a Deputy instead, and certainly the Deputy was always as reasonable as possible. "Considering," as he often said, "the unreasonable circumstances which one often finds."

The night of the Tempest, Gimlet might have called his own circumstances unreasonable, if he had felt like speaking. But he was dumb with misery, and his hat streamed water, and his cloak dripped from the storm, and tears rolled from his eyes, and his nose was running.

So Gimlet sat in the hall while the great fire made him itchy and warm, and a puddle grew round his feet. And he didn't notice the storm, for his other miseries were manifold.

When the old Deputy appeared at last, he carried a tray with hot chocolate, which Gimlet drank from habit, and without caring that he liked it. The Deputy sat across from him on a low chair.

"Wise women say a night like this bodes ill," the Deputy said at last. "But I think you have seen the worst already."

"Grandmother is gone," the boy said.

The Deputy nodded. "Although she lived to a great age," he said, "for she wanted to watch over you, I think." And then they were quiet, except for Gimlet's sniffles.

After a while the Deputy spoke softly: "And your parents were taken by a storm too, years ago."

"So I'm told," said Gimlet. "But I hate them anyway."

The Deputy stared into the fire for a while. Its flames rose and fell strangely in time with the gusts of the storm. "Where are your brothers, in whose care you ought to be?" he asked.

"They're gone for soldiers," Gimlet said. "They won't come back. I hate them too."

"And what else do you hate?" asked the Deputy.

"I hate the blacksmith," said Gimlet. "And I hate my house, and I hate the sky, and I hate the birds, and I hate trees, and I hate the village, and I hate bath-time, and I hate singing, and I hate porridge, and I hate everything in the village." Gimlet stopped for a moment, and then he smiled, because he had just thought of something else. "And I hate this hall, and I hate you," he added.

"Indeed, it would be an insult not to be included in so comprehensive a list," the Deputy said. "And last year, when you sailed the Old Sea, under the command of the girl Jenny, did you hate that too?"

"No," the boy said at once. "For they gave me the rank and honour of a Seahand, Ordinary, and my hat too." And for a moment, miserable as he was, even Gimlet felt the sea-longing rise in him; a sort of melancholy distraction from the rest.

"It's a fine hat, of the best beaver," Gimlet said. "Nobody else has one, just me. Everybody else has a stupid hat." Gimlet stared down at his hot chocolate then, while the winds argued at top of their lungs. "Everybody else is stupid," he finished. "I hate them."

The tempest lashed and pounded the windows of the hall. Suddenly one of them broke its catch open with a great crash. It began to knock against its frame, but inside there was a bird flying in the rafters of the hall now, small and sooty.

"Do you know that bird?" the Deputy asked. Gimlet shook his head without looking up, for he had never bothered with birds, and he hated them. "It is a Storm Petrel," the Deputy said, "the bird that braves the tempests; a Ward of the Salt Sea."

"Birds are stupid," Gimlet said, out of habit. But then he asked, "What's a Ward of the Sea?"

"Long ago," the Deputy said, "when the Elves lived here, they too began to fear tidings from the East. And the bravest Elves sailed West, for the Vastlands that stretch beneath the sunset.

"But the King Beneath the Sea is jealous of that place, and gated it even then by mazy, misted seas; by icebergs and dream tempests. When at last one brave Elf ship, the *Telenix,* surmounted all those perils, the King grew angry, and sent a storm that wrecked the fair *Telenix,* and its crew perished, and were gathered to the bosom of the waves."

"Did they have children at home?" Gimlet asked. "The same age as me?"

The Deputy nodded. "And those Elf-children wept and lamented until the King Beneath the Sea regretted his deed, and took up the children of the *Telenix*, and gave them wings, and taught them the ways of wind and weather. 'I cannot un-make my deeds,' he said, 'But now I will be your foster father. Doom may come to you, but not at my hand. Wind and wave on my broad salt sea shall guide you to your fortune, such as it may be.'

"And ever since," the Deputy finished, "wind and wave have been like friends to the Storm Petrel; like brother and sister to that dark bird."

Then the little dark bird took wing and swept through the rafters like a shadow, and disappeared.

"LISTEN TO ME, GIMLET," the Deputy said at last, more firmly. "You have lost much to the spirits of the sea, I know: first your parents, when you were small, and even your Grandmother tonight, as the seas let loose this storm.

"But the girl Jenny, she had lost her parents to the waves as well. And her friend Tom, who sailed North to the Roof of the World with the crew of the *Volantix,* he had lost his mother to the Ocean too.

"So I think that those whom the salt sea orphans still also become its wards, and may claim some fortune in its arms. For like Tom and Jenny, even you have felt the grace of the Ocean's King, and the protection perhaps of the Maid of Saltwaters."

"Why are you telling me this?" Gimlet asked.

Then the Deputy spoke with strange intensity, with the authority of the Duke he once had been: "Because the Long Night grows closer!" he said.

And now the wind gusted hard, and in the hall the fire rose suddenly, as if the storm was drawing it out of the chimney, and their shadows grew sharper.

"Because yours is not the only family that will be afflicted by war or pestilence, by turmoil or destruction! Because as Duke and Deputy both I must find some place they can shelter better!"

And those words recalled Gimlet at last from his present sorrows. "Why are you telling me this?" he asked again.

The Deputy drew a letter from his pocket. "The Captain of the *Volantix* is to sail again," he said. "He looks to find some Homely Country in the West, across the sea, and deep within the Vastlands."

"I thought that place was closed to Strangers," Gimlet said. "And cursed all who tried to live there."

"The Captain means to try if that rule is broken now," the Deputy said. "Like so many others since the Lost City sank again beneath the waves."

Gimlet felt his heart beat faster. "Could I sail again," he asked, "and have a place and rank aboard a ship once more, and not just stay here lonely?"

The Deputy nodded. "You would bring the luck of another Ward of the Sea aboard," he said. "And be both the Emissary of the Corner by the Sea on this Expedition, and once more a Seahand, Ordinary."

Chapter Two:
THE TALL SEAS

– dire prognostications – looking forward to camels – spotted dog – Gimlet the Very High Up – the challenge –

After the tempest finished, troubled skies remained, and the seas still tossed in rough disorder.

But the *Volantix* had braved rough seas before, had sailed the icy eaves of the world in fact, and its Captain was undaunted. "Rough seas are the least of the dangers we'll face," the Captain told his crew. "We'll sail as soon as we are ready." So the great work of preparing a tall ship like the *Volantix* was done in blowing, wet, wild weather.

Along with Tom and Jenny, the Captain had nineteen crack sailors in his crew, rated Able Hands at least – some grizzled with vast experience. And Gimlet had come aboard as well, although he was small and only rated Ordinary. But there was work for them all to do: hard stowing, and hauling, and rigging to be done.

Harder were the various final arrangements, and the sombre farewell dinners. For everyone knew the *Volantix* sailed on a desperate hope, to find some Homely Country in the West where they might live, because the Long Night was coming.

Then finally came the last goodbyes, which are a sailor's greatest burden. From the wharf, Tom's Dad gave Tom and Jenny each a waterproof notebook, to record their observations. Jenny's Godmother had her fever still, but she came too, wrapped up against the weather. At the last, she had them each bend close, and repeated the *redes* for their instruction.

And slowly at first, but faster as the sails learned to manage the wind, the *Volantix* left the safety of the harbour.

WHEN LANDSEND was almost out of sight in the mist and rain, Tom and Jenny found a small moment to stand at the stern rail, a privilege they had as Ensigns, a privilege like their swords and their bicorne beaver-felt hats. In the East the land grew small; became a dim and cloud-wrapped vista. Tom's dog Sparky was with them there, and even he seemed melancholy.

"How long before we see our home again?" Tom asked, but for a long time Jenny fiddled with the brass button on her beaver hat, and wouldn't meet his eyes or answer.

When she spoke it was of something else: "I much approve of your bringing Sparky along," she said.

Tom nodded. "He's a good sailor, for a dog," he said, "and would have been too lonely without us both."

"Sparky should receive his own commission," Jenny said. "As Gimlet is representative of the Corner by the Sea and a Seahand, Ordinary both. Sparky could be rated 'Ship's Dog and Canine Emissary'."

Tom's dog seemed oblivious to these honours, but he knew they were discussing him, so Tom reached down to scratch him behind the collar.

Now the land was hidden at last in the misty distance, and the *Volantix* seemed to sail alone on the pitching, grey-clad sea. The waves seemed tall now, far from land, but the two Ensigns knew they'd soon grow taller.

"Was the *rede* my Godmother pronounced for you hopeful, ominous, or merely impenetrable?" Jenny asked.

Tom smiled thinly, for in fact the words had troubled him. "My *rede* was only this: 'A missed dinner tastes the best.'"

"Oh-ho!" Jenny crowed. "That exceeds even her general standards of obscurity!" Then she looked at him shrewdly. "Or have you smoked its meaning yet?"

Tom looked down and shook his head, "Snow-Goblins tried to eat us all once in the North," he only said. "But I don't think they meant it personally."

But in fact, once something else had seemed to stalk Tom alone across the cold, dark ice. Sometimes it stalked him still in his worst dreams, with long and loping stride, but he didn't want to talk of it and bring his dreams into the daylight. So instead he asked Jenny what *rede* she was given.

Then Jenny too was quiet, and the ship pitched strangely in the still-disordered sea, and she gripped the stern rail tightly.

"I was pronounced a riddle for my *rede*," Jenny said. "'How does every Exploration end?' The words seemed simple at first, but the more I think on it, the less I comprehend." Then she smiled. "It is the price of having such a strange Godmother."

After that they talked more idly for a while, until they heard the big Bosun blow his whistle.

"Gather the sailors in your watch," Tom said at once. "Right away quick! It's one of the Captain's speeches."

AS ENSIGNS, Tom and Jenny were young sea-officers in training. And the real training of an Ensign was not how to bend ropes and sheet sails (which they were already fairly expert at regardless), or even how to read a chart or set a course (and they were better at that than you might expect), but How to Be in Command.

Now, except for Gimlet, the crew of the *Volantix* was crack, and full of grizzled sailors of vast experience, so they actually needed little commanding. They were the crew Tom had sailed with through the icy Eaves of the World, after all, in the course of a great circumnavigation.

And in the extraordinary circumstances of the summer before, Jenny herself had commanded that same crew in a succession of unusual ships that sailed through the Old Sea to find the Lost City that sank beneath the waves.

Which is not to mention their several victories in battle against Snow-Goblins, the dread Corsairs, and the Boogey Pirates (twice).

So while the crew of the *Volantix* needed little command, still they knew and admired their two young Ensigns, and watched over them too. And of course, they were glad to have three Wards of the Salt Sea aboard – the boy Gimlet, and Tom, and Jenny.

But if they might sometimes have gone so far as to mutter hopeful words about "good luck" or "almost certain preservation against the Ocean's hazards" to one another, none of the crew – not even the two sailors on the poop deck – would ever have spoken such things openly. For sailors are a superstitious lot, and well-mannered in their own way besides.

"Remember what fortune these Wards of the Salt Seas have paid for in bereavements," the First Mate had said. And it was bereavement of a sort all sailors understood well enough themselves.

THE SAILORS had gathered in two rows on the deck, for inspection by the Captain. Fifteen Able Hands and the boy Gimlet, and Tom and Jenny stood beside them.

"We'll hear one of the Captain's fine speeches now," one of the sailors said.

And, "He'll encourage us," added another.

But, "He'll tell us how hard the task will be," a third one declared. "So we'll be ready for the challenge."

A few older sailors who had some special duties stood in the front. There was the grizzled First Mate on his peg leg of course, with an eye-patch he wore for the decoration. And the Bosun next, the biggest, fattest sailor, responsible for practical supervision. Then the Carpenter, nicknamed Chips, a steady old hand, with a fondness for stars and calculations.

Once the gloomy old Cook would have stood there too, but in the Old Sea he had found his doom at last. And of all the other sailors, it had been the most nearly cheerful one who had wanted to take his place, whom they now called Cookie.

Though the Captain knew them all, he looked each one up and down, to know the weight of his command, and then he started speaking:

"The Long Night comes," he said, first off. "So say all signs and prognostications. Plagues are rising in the East; crows increase; Wise Women and astrologers all agree – and soon the darkness will fall over all our people."

"There *are* more crows," the First Mate muttered, for he hadn't thought of it before. "And what could them black-beaked things be hoping?"

And then the Carpenter said something about comets and conjunctions of the stars, and then the whole crew joined in, and discussed all the various bleak tidings.

"Yes," the Captain said. He said it loud, in his great quarter-deck voice, and the others all fell quiet. "Yes, by all signs and prognostications the Long Night comes. But we sail to find some hope," he said, for he thought it should all be laid out properly now, at the beginning of the Expedition. "We sail –" he continued, but Gimlet interrupted.

"Blah-blah, some Homely Country in the Vastlands across the sea," Gimlet said. "Dire prognostications. Blah-blah. We've all already heard that."

Everyone fell quiet. Even Jenny had forgotten Gimlet's capacity for disrespect.

Then the First Mate recovered himself with a terrible oath, and the big Bosun grabbed for the boy, meaning to thrash him with whatever he found handy. But Gimlet ducked underneath the Bosun's arm, and fled up along the rigging.

"I'll fetch him," Tom said, and he began to chase the boy up the ratlines.

Jenny turned red at the Captain's glance, for in the Old Sea she had been Gimlet's first commander. "I don't deny the boy's a foolish larrikin," she said. "In fact, we found him as a stowaway. But I gave him that tricorne hat in the end, for he raised his incorrigibility to a kind of virtue."

The Captain nodded, and they watched the chase up above, over and across the swaying rigging. Gimlet was at the crow's nest before Tom caught him. Then the Captain smiled at last. "Tom was our lookout at that age," the Captain said. "This boy is different, but he'll do fine, if he can already brave the crow's nest."

The Wards of the Sea

So THE *Volantix* SET OUT across the dark and storm-disordered sea.

Strange, shifting winds blew in the aftermath of the Tempest, and great swells followed them. As soon as the sails were set, a different wind would rise, and tall waves would run in some new line; great waves that hid the sky and broke in froth and thunder, and pitched the *Volantix* between them like a toy.

For days the *Volantix* sailed among those confused, tall seas. And the crew might have accommodated themselves to the danger, but the heavy skies rained so hard too; not in long downpours they might have grown accustomed to, but in frequent, yet irregular, chilling showers.

When the sailors weren't sleeping or taking a watch – or practising their musketry – they huddled below-decks by the stove.

"Never you mind," Cookie would tell them, as their clothes steamed in the galley. "It can't rain forever," he'd say, as he poured hot grog into their tin mugs. "And think how glad you'll be to feel warm again. Think about the summer sun, how it'll bake you dry. Think about our landfall and, and –" and here Cookie had to pause, for he was unsure himself about the overland route the Captain meant to follow.

"Think about how you'll sweat in the Vastlands," he went on at last. "Sweat buckets as we march our camels across the great glaring dunes of sand...."

"You're getting your geography mixed up," the First Mate corrected Cookie, "for we're sailing West now, not

South, and will more likely meet Bugbears and wild Buffles rather than camels. Look at your map, sometimes."

The Carpenter looked at the First Mate as if he were measuring out some problem. "These camels we won't see," he said, "would they be one-humped, or two?"

Now the Carpenter was a steady old hand, whom the First Mate felt he usually could rely on. But now the old sailor drew himself up, switched his eye-patch about to look at the Carpenter with his other eye. "Chips," he said, "it would more befit a sailor to say '*bactrian* or *dromedary* camels,' rather than use such plain and lumpish expression. 'One-humped or two,'" he repeated, shaking his head, for he felt fine language and extravagant turns of phrase befit a sailor as much as bright bandannas and striped shirts.

But then the First Mate realized that the abstractions of the debate had made Cookie and some of the younger sailors lose track of the real expedition entirely. "No camels of neither kind!" the old sailor said. "Nor sand dunes neither. We'll travel the Vastlands by boat and stream most likely. (Assuming we is allowed to travel there at all)."

Then Cookie nodded happily. "A pleasant sort of journey, then," he said, drifting off into a kind of reverie. "A summer voyage over cool lakes and down shady streams, and our paddles will lift water to dazzle in the sunlight. Isn't that right?" he asked the First Mate.

"I've never been to the Vastlands yet," the First Mate said. "And you hasn't neither. But it does sound pleasant when you puts it that way."

And by the help of such discussion, and the hot grog, of course, the crew of the *Volantix* kept their minds fixed hopefully on their goal, rather than on their present cold and damp discomfort – something they had learned from long experience, rather than any lack of skill at grumbling.

For Tom, the situation was more difficult. For when he had sailed on the *Volantix* before, he had been one of the crew – a very junior member of the crew; so junior that little had been expected of him except good humour and a sharp lookout from the crow's nest.

But now he was an Ensign, and took his turn in command along with Jenny, and he found it was more of a lonely post, and he missed the easy camaraderie with the crew. Of course, Jenny had known this sort of loneliness aboard a crowded ship, and more, when she had led the Exploration to find the Lost City, and the two young Ensigns could always talk with one another. Except that that they were on different watches, now the ship was sailing in the tall, dark seas; and had little time in common.

One morning Tom tossed in his bunk, shivering. Even as he dreamt, he knew it would be cold when he woke up – but he dreamt that some long loping thing chased him across the frozen North, so his sleep was even colder. So it was only slowly, and with mixed feelings, that Tom woke and realized he was not in the North, but only had to brave dinner with his Captain.

The Wards of the Sea

Every few days, the Captain invited one of the Ensigns to dinner. For Tom, at least, that meant awkward conversations. Once he had talked with the Captain easily, about Grandfather Frost, and model ships, and other boyish topics. But now Tom was an Ensign, and he felt that they should have more adult conversations.

"That's fine spotted dog, sir," he said once – although in fact, like most dishes made at sea, Cookie's spotted dog (really a sort of pudding) had turned out badly. "It has a novel taste."

Then suddenly Tom felt his remark had been foolish rather than properly sociable, and he felt his face go red. "Would you like more biscuit?" he asked quickly. "It's well-toasted this time, I think, and has few weevils in it. Really, the dinner is fine, altogether, I mean. Thank you for inviting me."

With each word Tom felt more foolish, but, "That's all right, Tom," the Captain said. "The dinner is as fine as might be hoped at sea. I think that's why the old Cook was so gloomy, because all his fine soufflés, figees, and calabashes were bound to turn out badly. Do you remember his blobsterdis?"

Tom nodded. "He served it the night the sledges set out in the North," Tom said, "in honour of our doom coming to fruition. It quivered on our plates, and none of us knew how to eat it."

"Or his lemon pies?" the Captain said. "The night of the Turning of the Year?"

"That was fine and unexpected both," Tom laughed. "And when we dined with Grandfather Frost, the Cook was most impressed by the raisin dumplings."

The Captain gave Tom a curious look. "Do you still remember that? I wrote in my memoirs, but it seemed like a dream I had, and not something that happened truly. But whether it was a dream or not, I know the Cook was there. And he was a fine peg-legged sailor, and was fond of you.

"They all were," the Captain said. "Is it strange having them under your command?"

"I only command them in name," Tom said. "They all know their work better than I could tell them, except for the boy Gimlet, and he's in Jenny's watch."

"It's an odd thing," the Captain said. "For commanders don't know the most; it's just they're the ones responsible. When a pudding turns out badly, Cookie feels the worst, though everyone has to eat it."

Tom nodded, and tried to think of something wise to say. But the Captain saved him by pouring out some grog – a tricky thing in those rough seas – and resuming his observations. "When I was an Ensign, dinners with my captain were an awful trial," he said. "But a captain has to know how to speak at even more boring tables."

Tom blinked, for it was hard to imagine the Captain taking someone else's orders. "What was your captain like?" he asked.

"He was terrible," the Captain said. "He brooked no impertinence. He knew everything about wind and wave, and demanded we learn it too. He was grizzled and fierce and roared like thunder."

"Was it hard to serve under such a man?" Tom asked.

"Yes," the Captain said. "We loved him."

Later, at the changing of the watch, Tom discussed those dinners with Jenny. "I just sit awkwardly," Tom said. "And then say something foolish."

"I talk easily," Jenny replied. Which was true enough, of course, for Jenny was proud and wordy, and rarely at a loss for speech. "But then I doubt myself and suddenly fall silent."

ALL THIS TIME, as the *Volantix* sailed West across the Ocean sea, Gimlet kept watch from the crow's nest. In fact, there was little to watch in that forest-dark sea, but he didn't bother the others there, and it kept him out of most kinds of trouble.

Gimlet even enjoyed how the little platform swung with the rolling waves, and thought it fitting that he was stationed so high, above almost all the sails and rigging. Sometimes he watched the crew down below at musket drill, as they practised firing together in a blasts of noise and smoke that thundered more loudly than the tallest waves, or one after the other in great *cracks!* that hammered steadily and hard – hard like the heartbeat of the Heavens.

But once the roll of musket fire was done, and his ears stopped ringing, Gimlet's mind drifted once more to other matters, to his own impressiveness.

Why, he considered one evening, did he have so few official powers, when he had such an exceptional character? Then he wondered also what new honours and accolades this Expedition would bring? Or how –

But the shifting, uncertain wind fell, all at once, and Gimlet saw a sudden mist rise up even as the sails grew slack around him.

In only a few moments the cloud grew so thick the deck below was hidden. "Hey, down there!" Gimlet cried, but even his voice seemed to be lost, muffled in the mist. And then a strange, rusty groaning rose from the sea, and suddenly Gimlet imagined some kind of iron monster straining to reach up, up – "Hey!" he cried again. "I'm alone up here! Someone come and help me."

But no one answered him, and Gimlet became frightened. He was alone, and an odd and terrible idea came into his head: perhaps the whole world beyond the mist had gone. Perhaps there was only him, in the crow's nest in the mist, and somewhere, the sound of iron groaning.

"I am Gimlet, the Very High Up," he said to the warm fog, for he thought he should make it known that he was special, that he shouldn't disappear like the others. "I am Gimlet, Seahand, Ordinary, and envoy to the Deputy," he said, more timidly. Suddenly a small, dark bird fluttered out of the fog, and Gimlet jumped to see it. But he remembered the story the Deputy had told, and, "I am Gimlet, Ward of the Salt Sea," he whispered.

Then the ship's bell rang loudly from the deck hidden down below, and Gimlet heard the Captain's great voice calling:

"Mist-shrouded spirits!" the Captain cried. "The Ensigns Tom and Jenny sail aboard this ship, and the young boy Gimlet! They are Wards of the Salt Sea all! They have already paid in sorrow to the waves before, and are owed not wrath, but indulgence!"

Then there was only quiet again, with no iron groans or creaking.

Gimlet looked at the Storm Petrel. "The Captain angered the fog with his proud words," he told the bird. "So it swallowed them all and I am left alone."

The petrel ruffled its feathers and disappeared in the mist. For a horrible moment, Gimlet felt more alone than ever.

But then Jenny was climbing up from the fog, already talking:

"This was a strange interlude in our voyage. But I think the Captain knows how to talk to Great and Awful things. He took a high hand with the mist just now – but note how he still spoke with due respect."

To Gimlet, it felt like the world had just begun again, and he clung quietly to Jenny as she led him down the rigging.

"You are strangely, uncharacteristically, subdued," Jenny said. But the boy remained silent while the East wind began to rise again, and blew the cloud first to tatters and then away.

"I wasn't afraid," Gimlet finally explained, although Jenny didn't understand him. "Even when the bird left."

By the time they reached the deck, the *Volantix* was making steady for the West once more. West for the Vastlands, through the night.

They had almost crossed the Ocean. Sea and sky were settled at last, and high above the stars were shining.

IN THE BRIGHT MORNING, the *Volantix* reached a great bay, the Mouth of the Vastlands.

In the North, two lone, barren mountains stood on the shore like broken teeth; a few ruined houses sat tumbled in the valley between them.

"Strangers tried to settle in that valley once," the First Mate said.

"There?" Tom asked, for the place seemed so inhospitable.

"Which of the several curses disastered them?" asked Jenny.

"Devoured by mountain bears, I think," one of the sailors from the poop deck said. "But all the trees are gone too," the other pointed out. "They must have been the ones swept away by a tornado."

"Neither," the Captain said, and he spoke quite firmly. "Once those valleys were lush and soft. But the Vastlands were closed and cursed to Strangers."

Then, away in the South, they saw green, pine-clad

hills, and fair meadows patched with snow. And in the West, still far ahead, they saw other tall ships moored out in that wide harbour.

Gulls were in the air now, not just long-winged seabirds, and the breath of Spring, and Sparky began barking madly.

Jenny put down her prize expanding telescope. "Already some great enterprise bustles under a rooftop gleaming in the morning sun," she said.

"The Mill House," the Captain said. "Where Strangers come to trade for skins and furs. We sail on different business, but the Master of the Mill House is like chief of all the Strangers here, and he must know our purpose."

Then he broke off and stood beside the First Mate at the wheel. "We have been weeks crossing the wide Ocean," the Captain said. "But now we're close I'm most impatient."

WHEN THE *Volantix* finally bumped against the wharf, its crew were all decked in finery, as sailors understood it: freshly washed shirts, newly braided pigtails, ribbons in their caps.

As they stepped off the ship at last, and stood on the threshold of the Vastlands, the crew met the moment, and the prospect of all the trials to come, with a mixture of relief, doubt, and bravado.

For whether it was cursed to them or not, they meant to find some Homely Country to settle there, the Captain and his whole Expedition.

And at the touch of the Captain's foot, the land itself, and all the creatures that walked within it, for good and ill, began to stir at the challenge.

The Master stared covetously at Tom's Star-Glass

Chapter Three:
THE MILL HOUSE

– the Warden of the Western Shores – a great unlading – Sudden Green Rot – the marthambles – the comfort of the pelts – singing on the water – a guide through the Wild –

THE MILL HOUSE STOOD ON AN ISLAND IN THE mouth of the Great River. On its side a great wheel creaked and worried, turned by the water that rushed around the island towards the sea.

The Master of the Mill House welcomed the crew of the *Volantix*, and gave them board and room. But the Master worked and worried as steadily as his wheel, and he did not say he was glad to see them.

"Trouble is come to our home across the sea," the Captain told him. "The easy time, the time of gentle folk, is passing, and the hard time, the time of scoundrels and heroes is near."

"Scoundrels," the Master repeated with a thin smile. "Yes, even those of us who labour here can smell troubles rising in the East. But shouldn't you be home to prepare against them?"

"This is not just trouble," the Captain said, and Tom saw his brow grow clouded. "It is the Long Night falling. Plague and famine, and death by sword and spear. Not this year, not the next, but soon. Perhaps before these my Ensigns are full-grown. The winds, the Wise Women, the stars and birds tell us these things."

"There are always dark signs and portents, if you look for them," the Master said. "But maybe you read these back to front."

The Captain gave him a long and steady look. "We mean to find some new Homely Country for our folk," he said. "I hoped you would aid us."

"There is some curse in the Vastlands," the Master said. "No Strangers have ever settled who found more than doom and sorrow. You would do better to stay home and marshal your courage if the Long Night is truly coming."

Jenny had worked to hold her peace, a thing which was not her nature, but now she burst out: "Perhaps you imagine you speak with tact," she said. "While in fact, you have given us an insult that cuts two ways, suggesting as it does that we are –" and here she held up her fingers as she enumerated her points, *"first,* fools for believing in such signs and portents – despite the diverse proofs and warranties issued by several fine authorities" (and here Jenny was thinking of her Godmother of course, though she was too modest to mention it). "And *second,"* she continued, "that we are at the same time *cowards* for not facing those same dangers you hold imaginary."

And Jenny would have had much more to say, for she was properly roused, but the Captain held his hand up to her, and turned back to the Master. "In fact," he said, "we are not cowards, for we mean to test that rule against Strangers in the Vastlands. We mean to break it if we have to. For the Long Night is coming, and we mean at least to find our own doom here, rather than merely wait for it to fall upon us."

The Master of the Mill House looked at the Captain, with his two Ensigns beside him. For a while no one spoke. All Tom heard were the sounds of the river, the creaking of the great wheel as it turned, and his own heart, beating harder all the time. He thought the wheel must have turned twice around before the Master said: "We will call a Council, then. The first Council of these Western Shores. You and your crew must stay and rest while they are gathered – the officers of this house, and the wise among the Ealda and the Riverfolk."

"I don't like to wait here overlong, not in the Vastlands where the Winter comes so quick and fierce," the Captain said. "I would be off exploring with my crew and not wait for this palaver."

The Master nodded and smiled again. "Hurried decisions mean savoured regret," he said. "The Spring convoys of the Riverfolk, who have measured this land most, have already left and are scattered in their work of gathering furs. But there is one greybeard paddler – don't call him so to his face, for the Riverfolk are most proud people – one greybeard who did not leave this year, for he has grown lame at last.

"His house is hardly a day from here," the Master said. "I will send for him. And we will have your Council by the first night of Summer."

As THEY WAITED for the arrival of the Council, the crew of the *Volantix* laboured, taking out all the gear for the Expedition and packing it in bales for easier transport.

Only Gimlet found himself without proper employment. Since each bale weighed as much as the boy himself, he couldn't help with the shifting. And things Gimlet would have liked to do instead (disassembling camp-desks, or over-winding clockworks) were discouraged by all those who outranked him (everyone from the ship, except for Sparky).

So when it seemed there was no one nearby, Gimlet would sneak into the great storehouse that held the goods brought from the East to trade with the Ealda. These rooms were mostly empty now, for the brigades of the Riverfolk had already left for the year, but in the corners there were still things left behind – blankets and beads, pots and pans, axes and knives, and tinderboxes and trinkets. So Gimlet would look at some little thing he wanted to possess and contemplate whether to steal it.

"The Master has too many of these things," he would tell himself, "so many that he has lost track. But I am only a poor orphaned sailor-boy, and deserve his pity."

More than once, Jenny or the First Mate noticed some clanking as Gimlet walked by, and confiscated the things he had purloined. But neither of them ever reported the boy, for they too felt the Master had too many of these things, whereas Gimlet was only a poor orphaned sailor-boy, who deserved their pity.

The Wards of the Sea

But Gimlet's favourite idle pastime had nothing to do with pilfering tools or trinkets. For the Mill House also kept the pelts received from the Ealda in trade, waiting to be carried East across the broad Ocean, and in those strange, waiting days, Gimlet most liked to creep into those dim, mysterious rooms and breath the wild, musky scent.

He never bothered with what kinds of furs and skins they were (muskrat or otter often enough, but beaver most of all), but Gimlet liked to lean against the bales, and run his fingertips along the soft edges of the pelt, and keep very quiet.

Perhaps it was because he was only a poor orphaned sailor-boy, but often Gimlet slept that way, and though he didn't know why, he felt content.

FINALLY, on the first night of Summer, someone came to collect him from the storeroom.

"We have found you out at last," Tom said.

Gimlet sat up from his doze and took off his tricorne hat. "I didn't know I wasn't supposed to be here."

Tom looked like he had been working hard, but he spoke easily enough. "I didn't know you weren't supposed to be here either." And now Gimlet was awake enough to realize they must have finished the unloading at last.

"I haven't been stealing anything," he said.

"Good, for stealing is wrong," Tom told him. "But now rouse yourself and come with me and Jenny as we take Sparky for his walk."

Together they struck out for the West end of the island, Tom and Jenny in front, with Gimlet and Sparky sporting behind them. Gimlet saw three black birds among the grass, crows that did not fly away at their approach, but only looked at them, disdainfully.

"All this waiting feels like a new tooth is coming in," Gimlet heard Tom say. "I try not to, but I worry the spot impatiently."

"Yes," Jenny replied. "For while old tooth is gone, the new one swells and irritates the gap. And when it comes, it will have a sharp edge."

At the water's edge, they looked across the Great River towards a bend where the pines stood dark against the last rosy light in the West. The current was slow there where the river began to spread, and the evening was still, except for the creaking mill wheel, and somewhere, the older sailors talking quietly after a long day's work.

"I am missing three teeth," Gimlet said. "One fell out, and one was pulled by the blacksmith, and one was lost in a pumpernickel loaf."

"You are a fascinating child," Jenny told him, "and able always to supply information in quantities greater than requested."

"I am not a child," Gimlet said. "For you yourself rated me Seahand, Ordinary."

Tom only picked up a stone then, and threw it skipping across the water. "Four," he said.

Jenny threw a stone after him. "Four."

Gimlet's stone only splunked into the water. "These are stupid stones," he said.

Tom threw a stick for Sparky, and in the hush of the evening they could hear his splashing and barking echoing across the river and back from the Southern bank. In the Mill House, they could see the lanterns had been lit, but there at the water's edge the dusk fell more deeply around them.

"We should go in," Jenny said, as if she had just thought of something. "For the boy hasn't eaten yet, and will soon exhibit, among his other charms, the irritation of the hungry."

"Yes," Tom said. He looked out over the water, and around. He pulled out his Star-Glass to check his bearings. "Yes, I suppose we should. Come on, Gimlet."

Then the crack of a musket broke through the dusk. Sparky set to barking, and then from the scrub along the water a blackbird began making a harsh clatter.

"Is it Corsairs?" Gimlet asked with some alarm.

"Corsairs don't come to these shores," Tom told him. "It is a signal-shot."

"It is the Riverfolk at last," Jenny said. "Come on the first night of Summer, as appointed."

AT THE MILL HOUSE, they had heard the signal-shot too, and by the time the Captain and the Master had come down to the riverbank, they could all see a small boat with a lantern on its bow approaching. From it an old man sang loudly:

Softly sing this evening rhyme –

And then a young woman called after him:

Voices tuned and oars in time!

And so they sang alternately as the boat came close, and the strokes of their paddles did keep in time with their song:

To the starry halls we say –
Send a wind to speed our way!

Then both voices sang the chorus together:

Brothers, sisters, paddle fast –
Rapids near, and daylight's past.

"It is Bawdoear, the great old man of the Riverfolk, come as I asked," the Master said.

Now they could see there were lanterns at both ends of the boat, and between the two singers a passenger sat in the middle. The paddlers began a new verse:

River rocks and rushing stream,
Serve for us as sleep and dream.
Stars are out; the night is long,
Hear, O hosts, our greeting song!

The Wards of the Sea

Then, *"Sisters, brothers, paddle fast –"* they sang again. *"Rapids near and daylight's past!"*

Jenny had decided she did not like the Master the first day they arrived, but for a moment she seemed to put that aside, out of a sort of professional curiosity. "What manner of boat is it they drive so skilfully?" Jenny asked.

"It is a *curach,"* the Master told her. "The river-horse of this country. And the Riverfolk would rather ride it than walk or swim, which indeed they only do imperfectly –" Then he broke off and stared covetously at Tom's Star-Glass.

But now the curach was at the bank, and even before it properly stopped, a grey-haired man leapt from the bow. The jump seemed to hurt him, but he straightened himself quickly, and a moment later a young woman followed. Her long hair was black, but otherwise they looked much the same: proud, and broad-shouldered, and dressed in plumed hats and bright sashes and beaded leather stockings.

"They must be related," Gimlet whispered. "They have the same nose and the same hat."

"She is Bawdoear's daughter, Bonawyn," the Master told them.

"She carries herself most brave," Jenny whispered.

"Yes," said Gimlet. "She is full of herself like you, but bigger."

And as they spoke, Bawdoear and Bonawyn lifted an old woman out of their curach with great care, and set her carefully on her feet. The old woman wore a cloak of rabbit skin, and she inspected the Strangers carefully.

"She must be some great Wise Woman or commander of the Ealda," said Tom. "Look how she stands, as confident as the Captain."

But only after they had unloaded the boat and lifted it onto the bank did the two Riverfolk acknowledge the Captain and the Master.

Gimlet and the two Ensigns stood off as the formal greetings began – and continued for what Gimlet considered an unnecessary length. At some point, the Captain must have mentioned the three Wards of the Sea, for the young woman looked in their direction for a moment. Then she turned away, as the Captain and the Master led them back towards the Mill House.

"She has measured you, Gimlet," Jenny said. "And found you short of the mark."

"I am short of dinner," Gimlet said.

"That will come at the Council, where the Captain wants us," Tom said. "Let's go in."

CHAPTER FOUR:
THE COUNCIL OF THE WESTERN SHORES

– dining hugely – the Captain's request – banging fists – the Shawnachan – the Rockmarch – a meeting in the Fall – even Gimlet – Bonnie Bonawyn –

BUT FOR ALL HE WANTED DINNER, GIMLET ARRIVED late at the First Council of the West. For he had first to wash up to Jenny's satisfaction, whereas the Riverfolk had paddled a long day and night without a break, and intended to dine hugely, and at once, before suffering any long talk.

The dinner might even have happened without Gimlet at all except that, as Jenny explained while ensuring that he scrubbed behind his ears, he was wanted that night not only in his usual capacity, "as ship's boy and general nuisance," but rather, "as special emissary from the good Deputy and representative of the people of the Corner by the Sea."

By the time they finally took their places with Tom at the end of the table, they had missed the introductions. No one seemed to pay him any heed, so Gimlet began eating bun after bun as quickly as could, while he studied the candlelit faces around the table.

The Captain and the older sailors were there, of course; and the Master of the Mill House and his officers. Sitting apart from the others, as if they shared some private irony, were Bonawyn, the young River-woman, and Bawdoear, her father. And at the head of the table, by the Master and the Captain, the old woman who had arrived with the Riverfolk sat quietly, with her hood pulled low.

The Captain seemed to have been speaking for some time, and the faces of the Council were grim as he told them that the troubles from the East were come not only to Landsend, but to Gimlet's people as well.

"And so we crossed the sea for help," he told the Council. "So we seek some Homely Country where we might live untroubled, where young ones like the boy and these my Ensigns might come of age before they know war, before they see slaughter.

"These Vastlands are wide," he finished. "Tell us there is some place we might live."

Then they were all quiet for some time, and Gimlet realized that they waited for the old woman to speak first. But she only sat with her head bowed, her dark face hidden in the shadows of her cloak.

"Why doesn't she talk?" Gimlet said at last. "Why are her clothes strange?"

Then Bawdoear the River-man banged his fist on the table. "Be quiet, boy!" he shouted, and under his grey hair, Bawdoear's face was flushed. "This is the Shawnachan, whom you should call Great-Grandmother. Her robes and feathers may seem strange to you, but at least she knows better than to speak until she has something to say."

Gimlet shrank back before Bawdoear's outburst. But then he remembered himself. "Is your face always red and sweaty?" he asked.

And the First Mate, Jenny, the Master of Mill House, and even Bonawyn the young River-woman all began to shout at him for that.

But the Shawnachan herself pulled back her cowl to show that she had marked her face with red and white paint. When she spoke, softly, the others fell silent.

"Surely the boy will only learn by watching you," the Shawnachan told them. "As he sees wise ones talking, so he will learn to talk wisely. And surely I must look strange to him, for he looks strange enough to me." Then she looked right at Gimlet. "We name you all Strangers, you know," she said. "Strange clothes, strange ways, strange tales.

"Now this tale –" the Shawnachan said to all of them. "Isn't it the strangest yet? For you say trouble comes from the East, and look! Haven't you sailed from the East yourselves, and haven't you brought trouble? I think that's funny, though you might not see it." She stopped then, and looked at all the Strangers carefully, from the Captain and the First Mate to Gimlet himself.

"Now I've listened to your tale all this long dinner," she told them. "And I've talked with my people, and done my own share of thinking too. So I'll tell you my mind on the matter, if you're ready to hear it."

Even before she spoke, Gimlet felt a sudden wild affection for this strange old woman who had set the Master of the Mill House right. "I like you," he said. "You speak well. I am ready to listen."

"Hush," said Jenny beside him. "Hush, now just listen."

"There is no land for you here," the Shawnachan said, simply. "This is no refuge."

FOR A MOMENT everyone fell quiet again.

Then out of the silence, Tom cried, "What's to become of us, then?" He looked around at the others. "Have we crossed the Ocean and survived its storms and spirits for nothing?" And as he considered the situation, his voice grew more quiet. "Are we to just go home and wait for the Long Night coming?" he asked the Captain.

But the Captain said nothing, and only sat still and looked at the Shawnachan. "There is no land here," she repeated. "Not near the Mill House, for my people have villages here, and the Riverfolk have made their homes and cabins along the banks of the Great River. And farther upstream, into the Wild – well, that is the Hunting Ground of my people, and there is no place for you there either." She stopped then, and looked at the Captain closely.

"But that isn't where you hoped to find your Homely Country," the Shawnachan said. "You've known this already."

"Yes," said the Captain, hoarsely, and he looked around at his crew. "But I hoped I was wrong. We must go farther into the Wild," he said. "Farther, until we find some empty place."

"My cousin Ahgeneh's people live far in the West," she said. "Far by rock and stream, in the Cold Lake Country; and only the Riverfolk would ever make the trip from here to there unless they were compelled. But they talk of an empty place farther still," the Shawnachan said. "The Rockmarch, on the very edge of the Wild; almost as far as the Hidden Sea."

"I like the sound of the sea," the First Mate said. "For if nothing else, we knows how to manage wind and wave. But why's it empty, is what I'd like to know. For you seem awful tight with these wide spaces." He looked around the table suspiciously. "Thorny bog-land, I suppose, or flush with Bugbears and wildcats?"

"Or both," Bawdoear said, roughly. "And worst of all in Winter. But more than that, it's empty, for it's so far into the Wild. Too far for you to go."

"That's what it should be," the Captain said. "Some place too far and too rough for others, that we'll make a Homely Country from our toil."

The Shawnachan nodded. "Ahgeneh is the Marshal of his people," she said. "And this year they will gather at the top of Meeltach Aws, the great falls, at the Last Moon of Summer, or the First Moon of Fall, before they make their Winter camp. If you can meet them there, you have my blessing," the old woman said. "If that's what you're wanting. Or a friendly word with the Riverfolk, who alone might guide you."

Now Bawdoear the River-man stood, and steadied himself on his daughter's shoulder, and addressed the Captain. "And the blessings of the Shawnachan you have," he said with some heat. "For she's none the worse if you go stumbling through the Wild until you find some gnat-bit, bear-chewed, frozen end. But apparently it's us she thinks should travel with you and your scruffy lot of sailors, because it's us who know the way."

But the old First Mate, who'd listened quietly all the time the Shawnachan spoke, boiled up then. "'*Scruffy*' is strong words from a little puddle-paddler," he said. "For this is the crew of the *Volantix* you're seeing. What's triumphed in sword-play against Snow-Goblins and Corsairs, not to mention the Boogey Pirates (twice)."

"Easy, Mate," the Captain said. "For we have called this council to ask for help, and they have come to it."

Bawdoear nodded at that. "Let me lay it out to all of you brave sailors from the *Volantix,*" he said, carefully. "First, this place you're going is no good land, but a rough height overlooking the barren, wind-swept Steppes. None but the Riverfolk ever go that far, and that's only to trade. And the Winters that blow down from the icy North, there's no reckoning how terrible they are."

"There's no Winter worse than what we've seen, for we was locked in those dark, icy seas," the First Mate said, shortly. "What's your next objection?"

Now the grey-haired River-man looked at his daughter, but she only raised an eyebrow. He stopped and looked at the Captain, and the First Mate, and then Gimlet and the two Ensigns, as if he were measuring even them.

"It is cold, this place you're going," Bawdoear told them.

"We have been to colder," the Captain said.

"It is long, this journey you're taking," the River-man said.

"We has fared on travels longer," said the First Mate. "Circumnavigated the globe, in fact."

"Let me speak plainly," Bawdoear said. "You are like to die."

"Let me speak plainer still," the Captain said. "We have been near death already, my crew and I. We have entered without fear into that cold sleep that has no waking, and yet our eyes have opened, so we count the chance as a little price to find the place we need, for our whole land is like to die."

"The Wild has other hazards too," Bawdoear went on. "Marsh and marsh-lights, woods and Forest-Goblins, waterfalls and the hissing things that guard them. You may not mind these deaths, but to guide you would likely be our deaths too. And then beyond all else there is still the Winter waiting. You say you escaped it once before, but I say that just makes Winter hungrier.

"And what no one has had the heart to say is this: the Vastlands are cursed and closed to Strangers! But you come anyway, even after the Winter-things have your scent –"

The Shawnachan clapped her hand against the table then. "Bawdoear!" she said. "Loon-Son, you are the wisest of the Riverfolk, and have wintered many times in the Wild. Warn these Strangers, but do not name those evil things until evil times have come."

Bawdoear looked at the old woman, and Gimlet was surprised to see that for all his fierce words, the River-man only nodded meekly. "My Aunt, I am sorry," he said, and resumed his seat.

But his daughter Bonawyn stood in his place. "Listen to my father, the mighty Bawdoear," she said in a large, strong voice. She made a wide, wide sweep with her arm. "Are you iron-sinewed?" She looked towards Gimlet and the two Ensigns. "Have you reached your full-grown years?" Then she stared at the First Mate. "Are your limbs whole and healthy? Or do you use peg legs to steer?"

"Why does she speak in rhymes?" Gimlet asked Jenny, loudly enough for everyone to hear.

"'Cause she has the trick of it, and wants to impress," the First Mate told him. Then suddenly he burst out again: "Not full-grown?" he demanded of the River-woman. "These three are young, perhaps, but has done brave deeds what's sung up and down our coasts. For Tom himself saved the *Volantix* when we was attacked by Goblins – and look at the scar on his forehead what proves it. And Jenny – she led me and the others through the Old Sea, and at the last, she stood on the pinnacle of the Lost City and oversaw its ruination."

Then he put his hand on Gimlet's shoulder. "Why even Gimlet," he began, and then he paused as he tried to remember something even Gimlet had done admirably. "Why even Gimlet – foolish as he seems – slew the dread Corsair captain, despite the handicap of being, at the time in question, a goat," the First Mate finished.

Gimlet smiled with satisfaction. "Foolish as I seem," he said.

And at that, Bonawyn turned and spoke quietly to Tom and Jenny, just as if they weren't all arguing. "Does he become a goat according to a schedule, or only as needed?" she asked.

"Neither," Tom told her. "I understand it was a singular misfortune."

"I counted it my fault at the time, and bad luck indeed," said Jenny. "But it all turned out well in the end."

"I liked being a goat," Gimlet said. "There was more to eat."

THE CAPTAIN STOOD AT LAST and looked around at the Council, at Bawdoear and Bonawyn, and at the Shawnachan and the Master too. "You have given us good cautions, both in verse and prose," he said. "Which any mindful hosts would do. For we are not only Strangers in these Vastlands, but your guests still, and under your protection. And as Bawdoear reminds us, the Vastlands have been closed to Strangers – and we know that has been the rule. But the Elves too came here once, and they stayed a while at least – before they left for Story."

"The Elves," said Bawdoear. "That's a desperate hope."

"And we are desperate," the Captain said, simply. "You say we are like to die, but by sign and omen, by *rede* and star, we believe it is the only hope for our people to live. You say *you* are like to die if you guide us, and I say we will go alone if we must, if the Master of this house will lend us boats – *curachs* I should say – for the voyage.

"But if you choose not to lend us your curachs," the Captain said to the Master, "then we will build our own river-boats, clumsy though they might be, and travel West as best we can to meet this Ahgeneh. And if Ahgeneh will not help us, we will follow the scent of the Hidden Sea and seek the Edge of the Wild ourselves. And if our boats are insufficient, we will walk, and if that fails us, we will crawl.

"So we will go meet Ahgeneh at the Great Falls for the First Moon in Autumn. And with or without your help or his, in time we will find some Homely Country in the West," he said. "Alive if we can, or perhaps in death, if it is true that spirits come at last to a home beyond the sunset. But by sign and omen," the Captain repeated, "by *rede* and star, this is the hope for our people, and we will make the trial."

For a long while, the whole Council fell quiet. Shadows flickered in the torchlight, and outside the millwheel still creaked and splashed.

Then farther off, they heard a loon call, and the

Shawnachan spoke at last: "We hear the words the loon sings," she said. "They sing, 'I am lonely, don't abandon me!'" Then the old woman looked around the table. "If dreams have led these Strangers to this terrible journey, it should not be said they died alone."

"I will give you three curachs, and wish you luck," the Master said.

Finally, Bawdoear held up his hand and watched it tremble. He sighed greatly, and wiped his eyes. "If you had come ten years ago, I would have taken you," he said. "Even five. But now I am grown too old to travel the Wild at last."

At that the Captain bowed his head. But Bonawayn spoke again. "I will guide you, then," she said. "Instead of Bawdoear. Let us speak no more on it, but honour my father's tears."

"Bonnie Bonawyn," her father said quietly. And Gimlet had to listen very hard for what the River-man said next. "Watch yourself. Unease has come to the beaver-country. Even there East winds blow."

"I will watch myself," Bonawyn told him. "And those in my care."

THE RIVERFOLK

Broe-stach!

CHAPTER FIVE: INTO THE WILD

– an early start – riding the river – the first carry – the Wild itself – a two-pipe story – poor wood –

JENNY WAS A FISHER-GIRL, SO SHE WAS USED TO waking early, waking before sunrise to be on the water before the fish rose to the dawn.

But even Jenny was still asleep when Bonawyn began calling for the sailors to bestir themselves. Before she knew it, before she was even properly awake, Jenny was standing with Tom in the cold, black water, supervising the fiddly business of packing the three curachs.

The Captain meant to take the lead boat of course, though Bonawyn would guide it from the bow. And Tom and Jenny each had a curach in their charge as well. Then, after a spell of miserable, wet work, something occurred to Jenny about her new command. "It would be both fitting and propitious to name our craft," she called, her breath misting in the morning chill. "For all tales recount the names of the Explorers and their vessels both."

The Captain decided his curach would be the *Dauntless,* and Tom called his the *Adventure.* "And mine shall be the *Fortitude,"* Jenny said. "But we should entitle them according to some more proper ceremony, which –"

Just then Bonawyn stepped into the water and poured some of her tea onto the bow of each boat. *"Dauntless – Adventure – Fortitude,"* she said, shortly. "Now will you hurry? For we should be on Awyn Huaith, on the North River, before the sun is up." Then she gestured to all of them, and used a word in her own language that they would all hear many times when she wanted haste. *"Broe-stach!"*

At that, the First Mate couldn't keep quiet any longer. "Was I sleeping when it happened," he said to Bonawyn, rather dangerously, "or when exactly was it you was put in charge?"

"You might have been sleeping," Bonawyn said, with a coolness Jenny found both irritating and impressive. "For you are slug-a-beds compared to Riverfolk. *Broe-stach, broe-stach!"*

Whether Bonawyn's harrying helped or not, the little brigade of boats was ready before the mist had risen. The River-woman twirled her paddle over her head, and then she dug it into the water, and began to lead them away from the Mill House and the island, West against the flow of the wide water.

They moved slowly at first; clumsily, for the curachs and paddles were strange to them. But the crew of the *Volantix* were sailors of vast experience with both oar and sail, and nothing that floated was foreign to them.

Gradually they gained speed in those frail, bark-skinned boats, and before the sun had risen they had turned into the mouth of Awyn Huaith, the North River. For Awyn Huaith would be the first long stage in their journey.

Now the curachs travelled more quickly; now they cast waves from their bows; now the morning sun dazzled in the spray.

"This is a brave adventure!" Jenny cried at last, and hearing her, Bonawyn began to sing from the bow of the Captain's *Dauntless:*

A River-man had a daughter
–who was his only kin
Bawdoear wondered what to call her
–and named her Bonawyn!
Bonnie Bonawyn! River champion!

Then she turned and reproached the others: "Proper paddlers repeat the chorus, even if they haven't learned the rest," she said. And then she sang again:

She paddles even faster
–than any otter swims
The only one can match her
–he named her Bonawyn
Bonnie Bonawyn! River champion!

And Jenny and the sailors from the *Volantix* did learn to join in the chorus, for Bonawyn seemed to have many achievements, and her song enumerated all of them.

ALL DAY, Jenny and Tom watched Bonawyn, carefully studying how she managed her curach, how she used her paddle, or sometimes a long pole in fast water.

By the time they set out early the next morning, Jenny felt they already understood much of the art. So she paddled confidently through the morning mist, working the stiffness from her muscles, until a bend in the river suddenly revealed a rocky rush of water. Jenny just had time to watch Bonawyn take the Captain's *Dauntless* quickly towards the slower inside current before her curach disappeared from sight.

Tom's *Adventure* was next, and Jenny saw him hesitate before he followed. He looked back at her, but she could only hold up her paddle and shrug.

Then Tom dug his own paddle in and gave a shout, and his crew dug hard, and Jenny followed with the *Fortitude*. They made short, fast strokes, first outside the rocks as Bonawyn had done, then striking hard for the calmer water inside.

Then Jenny saw that Tom had missed his turn. The North River heeled the *Adventure* over, and swept it sideways towards Jenny's boat. She yelled and tried to turn the *Fortitude*, and behind her in the stern the First Mate struck the water hard, but it wasn't enough. In a moment the curachs knocked together in a rushing tangle.

Jenny heard Gimlet scream behind her as the river pushed them against the rocks. The *Adventure* and the *Fortitude* struck with a sickening shock that tore their frail skins of bark. Then the current began swirling the flooding curachs downstream, back the way they had come.

FINALLY, Jenny and Tom found a sheltered bank, and their sailors were able to jump into the water and guide the torn curachs to rest.

Tom looked white, but he said, "It was my fault."

"The turn was obscure," Jenny told him. "Bonawyn used some undisclosed mark, as if she wanted to lead us into trouble."

But by the time they had unpacked their boats and then gently lifted them onto the grass, Bonawyn had brought the *Dauntless* back around to find them.

She leapt out of the curach and splashed up onto the bank at once. "Hm, ho!" she said. "I have seen that passage travelled with more skill."

"Enough, Bonawyn!" the Captain shouted. "Do you mean to drown my crew and then mock them for it?"

The River-woman turned. "Do you think that was a bad rapid?" she asked, coolly. "For you shall see worse, if you mean to enter the Wild."

"But our boats are ruined now!" Jenny cried. "You have led us to their destruction."

"These are curachs," Bonawyn said. "They do not travel despite this country, but are born from it."

"She's right," said the Carpenter, calmly, for he was a steady old hand. "Mending a broken galley in the Old Sea, that was tricky work. But here we have bark for patching, and spruce gum for the seams. We could even make new ribs from cedar if we had to."

"A Stranger with sense," Bonawyn said. "You might survive after all."

When they were back in the water at last, Bonawyn showed Tom and Jenny the marks they had missed, and explained how to read the river better. Still, Jenny could not keep from grousing to the First Mate, who sat in the stern of her curach and managed the steering.

"I admire Bonawyn," she called over her shoulder. "But she galls me at the same time. For watch how tirelessly she paddles, even while singing heartily, yet her songs are most concerned with her own excellence."

"Well, she extemporizes," said the First Mate. "Makes up, like," he explained for the benefit of Gimlet and the junior sailors. "And so draws heavily from her best-loved subject."

"I like her songs," said Gimlet. "They bobble like the river."

"They are obnoxious," Jenny said.

"Still, the singing keeps time, and we move faster through the water for it," said the First Mate. "Credit where credit is due."

IN A FEW DAYS, the Expedition came to where the North River pooled under the foot of a rapids that coursed down from West. The curachs gathered in the shelter of the North bank, and then Bonawyn and all the sailors leapt out to start unloading the boats.

"We must begin without delay," the River-woman told the others. "For these hissing rapids mean bad luck by our measure." Along the bank, seven pines stood bare, stripped of their bark. Bonawyn gestured at them. "Each tree marks one of the Riverfolk who have died here, on the rapids, or even on the trail, worn and dispirited from the toil."

Tom looked at the boiling water. "Died on the rapids!" he exclaimed. "But no boat could come down those waters safely."

"I have taken a curach down these more than once, and fully laden too," said Bonawyn. "But it is true some cat-like spirit hides in such places, and catches who it can. And not even Bawdowear could lead a boat *up* this stream."

So they got ready for a *carry,* which meant just that: every pack on the boats – each as heavy as Gimlet – and the curachs themselves, would have to be carried by stages to a point above the rapids. It looked like a steep hike, and probably two or three trips for each of them, not counting the boats, which would be the most awkward loads of all.

"Well," the First Mate said, spitting on his palms. "There's hard work to be done, but we're the crew for that!"

"We are indeed," said Cookie. "For think of the work we did dragging sledges in the icy North, and we all came back safe."

But Bonawyn had already swung one of the pieces onto her back, pulled a strap down over her forehead to steady the load, and then set a second pack atop it. Now she cried *"Broe-stach!"* and started trotting up the trail.

The Captain and his crew stared as she disappeared into the pinewood. Then the Captain laughed. "Well, it is her trade," he said. He swung first one pack, then a second onto his back, and followed after the River-woman.

"Broe-stach, broe-stach!" said Gimlet. "I can't carry a pack by myself."

"Walk by me," said the big Bosun. "I will carry one for you as well as two of my own."

So the sailors headed off, one by one, and if none of them trotted so quickly as Bonawyn, they all took their two packs. At last only Tom and Jenny and Sparky were left by the boats and the remaining pieces.

Jenny swung a pack onto her back. For a moment she staggered. "I cannot take two," she said. "I am not full-grown like Bonawyn."

"She seems as strong as she is dashing," Tom said. Then he lifted a piece and put the strap over his forehead. Tom stood for a moment, straining under the weight. "I cannot take two, either," he said. "Not yet."

Before they were halfway to the first stage, Bonawyn met them on her way back down. Tom and Jenny were already sweating hard, for it was a was a hot day, and gnats had been biting them on the hands and face. But Bonawyn only laughed at the sight of them.

"A paddler's life is finest of all," she called as she ran past them, almost dainty in her buskins, in her beaded leather stockings. "Now hurry, children, hurry!"

THAT NIGHT, they made camp at the top of the trail. A tall cairn of stones stood there, for that spot marked the real beginning of the Wild, according to Bonawyn.

Soon the sailors had a fire going, and like a reward for the warm afternoon's work, a breeze came up. It carried the gnats away at last, and sighed among the pines and willows.

Cookie served out a salt pork stew made from their provisions, and a sweet burble made from berries he had found along the trail. As the evening darkened, he made hot chocolate too, and the sailors stretched out their sore limbs with some satisfaction. For they had paddled and carried hard, and now they were in the Wild at last.

"How long will we be in the Wild yet before we reach Meeltach Aws, where we are to meet Ahgeneh?" the Captain asked Bonawyn.

"Yet?" she said. "We have only started. For before the first long carry, travel on the river is hardly work at all. Riverfolk count the land you have crossed picnic country."

The Captain laughed. "Do you think we would we ever make Riverfolk?"

"In time, perhaps – if the toil didn't kill you," said Bonawyn. "But my father, he would carry three packs, not two, when he was a young man, and sing as he ran with them."

"But the Bosun carried three pieces," said Gimlet. "And I sat on top of them, so that makes four."

Bonawyn nodded, and spat approvingly into the fire. "That was well done," she said. "That was like a River-man."

Tom looked at her closely. At last he asked the question he'd been pondering since the Council. "Bonawyn," he said, "what are the Riverfolk? For you are not Strangers, like us, nor yet are you Ealda, though you know their tongue."

"Ah," said Bonawyn. "That is a story. That is a two-pipe story."

"IT WAS LONG AGO," Bonawyn began, after she had filled her pipe, "when the first Strangers were testing their coracles against the Great Ocean."

"Long ago, but was it after the Elves had left?" Tom asked, and she stared at him.

"After the Elves," Bonawyn said. "No Riverfolk ever knew them."

"Was it even before the paddling saints?" one of the sailors asked.

"No one can say that," said the First Mate. "For they paddle into stories and out again before you can catch 'em."

And that remark in itself raised so many philosophical questions from the junior sailors that Bonawyn's story was almost undone before she began. But she made a mighty, crackling spit into the fire to recall them.

"It was long ago," she repeated, severely. "And a ship of Strangers had almost crossed the great Ocean when some monster of the salt sea attacked it from a fog, so that almost all aboard were drowned."

"Such was almost our fate," the Captain said.

"All but one were drowned," Bonawyn went on. "For somehow the Vastlands do not welcome Strangers yet. And that one was a sailor named Ferren, and Ferren washes ashore on the rocky coast, and he is weak already, weak already from the sickness of sailors."

The others looked at the First Mate and he nodded. "It comes on long voyages," he said. "As some might recall. But lemon pies wards it off."

Bonawyn nodded. "So Ferren, who at sea is a great commander, stumbles over the land," she said. "He is wasting away from illness and hunger both, and still wounded from the monster in the fog. And he comes to a forest, and his clothes are torn by the trees, and he calls for help, and none comes; and he cries for a sign, and none is sent.

"And then at last he hears bubbling water through the dark of the woods, and he runs towards it, but just as he sees the river through the trees, he falls, and he cannot rise again. But he is a sailor, so raises his eyes at least, and he sees the stars of the Hunter; and then he sees someone bending over him: A Wood-Nymph," Bonawyn said, "and she is lovely, and her eyes are deep like toffee. But she is terrible too, for Wood-Nymphs stand at the Cracks of the World, and they can see this life and the places beyond it all at once.

"Only this sailor is brave," Bonawyn said, "or he is so near death the Cracks of the World seem close to him too, and its terrors are familiar. So, 'Help me,' he whispers. But she is unsure, this Wood-Nymph, for this sailor is not one of the Ealda, who have dark eyes like hers, but a Stranger with blue eyes, and to her the eyes seem pale and ghostly, as though she can see through them and into Ferren's soul.

"So the Nymph begins to go, but Ferren weeps as he reaches for her. 'Stay, Wood-Nymph,' he says in a whisper, for he doesn't know what to call her. Then, 'Autumn Eyes,' he names her, 'Stay.' And his weakness touches her heart, for the Wood-Nymphs know sorrows too, in their own way.

"'If you are not an evil spirit, get up,' she says. 'Or you will perish, here, now. For this is the lair of the Bugbears, and besides the Forest-Goblins walk tonight, and look for blood of mortal men.'

"But Ferren, he laughs bitterly. 'I am a commander of ships in the sea,' he says, 'but now I cannot even rule my own limbs. I could no more get up than you could fly across that river.'

"Then this autumn-eyed Wood-Nymph laughs, for a narrow branch, no thicker than her thumb, has fallen over the water, and she runs up to it and calls back, 'If I can cross, you must get up,' she says.

"'And if I get up, you must help me,' the great sailor tells her.

"Then the Wood-Nymph looks at him and trips up the branch so nimbly she might have been flying. And then she turns and looks back at Ferren. And he gets to his knees, first, and he is shaking. And he leans against a tree then, and pulls himself up to his feet, and his legs are trembling like smoke, but he stands so he can see her.

"The Wood-Nymph, she weeps to see him so, for he is weak and brave at once. But then she hears a noise like the scatter of leaves in the wind, and she know that noise is the noise of hunting Forest-Goblins."

Bonawyn paused to refill her pipe. It was then that the two sailors with blue hoods looked across the black water, for there was no moon that night, and they began to worry. "Were they eaten by the Forest-Goblins?" one of them asked. "Did the Wood-Nymph ever help the sailor?" asked the other.

But Bonawyn took her time getting her pipe working. "If they were eaten by Forest-Goblins, it is bad news for us now," she said. "For all my story happened just at this spot, at the start of the Wild." And the two sailors leaned in closer then, frightened and fascinated both.

The River-woman smiled. "So the Wood-Nymph runs back to Ferren, and holds him up, and leads him by the hand to her forest bower, and she makes him tea from pine needles. And when he wakes again he is frightened, but he sees her beside him still. 'What are you called?' he says, 'For you have brought the World back to me.'

"And 'I am Autumn-Eyes,' she says. 'For that is the best name anyone has ever called me.'

"Then each day she helps him stand, and they walk a little farther, and he grows stronger, until she leads him at last as far as a village of the Ealda where she is known. 'Here you are among friends,' she says.

"And he says to her, 'Don't leave me.'

"And the Wood-Nymph says to him, 'You will leave me, for you are mortal and doomed to die.'

"But for a while Autumn-Eyes lives with him, and they have children, and live as friends beside the Ealda, along the river. And those children were the first Riverfolk, and that is why we seem like Ealda and Strangers both," Bonawyn finished.

"That is a pretty tale," the Captain said.

Bonawyn looked at him a long time. "We count it history," she said, and spat into the fire.

The First Mate nodded and thought it over for a while. "You say she stayed with him some whiles," he said. "But what was the end of that story?"

"The Wood-Nymphs are wild," Bonawyn said. "And in time Autumn-Eyes left him, for her heart was in the forest. But the end of the story is this: Ferren had learned the art of the curach from the Ealda, and he becomes a River-man, and he searches up and down the river-ways, always looking.

"Finally he comes to the Cracks of the World, which she can cross, but not him, and he sees her on the other side, for now he is near to dying again, and can see across the divide. And 'Autumn-Eyes,' he calls to her; 'I am lonely here,' he calls; 'don't abandon me.'

"And the Wood-Nymph calls to the Queen of the Trees, 'Have pity on us,' she calls, 'for he is a mortal and we are sundered by the Cracks of the World.' And she calls to the Maid of Freshwaters, 'Have pity on us, for I am not a mortal and can shed no salt tears.'

"And the Queen of the Trees and the Maid of Freshwaters bend their heads together, and they raise the sailor Ferren and Autumn-Eyes, the Wood-Nymph who loves him, up together as loons. So the loons call still, *'I am lonely; don't abandon me,'* but now it is just a song, for the loons have one another, and they and their children have the river."

Tom had been listening more closely that the others. "Is that where the word 'lonely' comes from?" he asked. "Does it mean we are 'loon-ly'?"

Bonawyn nodded. "Just so," she said. "But not many people know it."

Tom opened his waterproof notebook. "I will write it down," he said. "And include it in my father's Great Work."

JENNY AND BONAWYN SHARED A TENT, and that night Jenny woke from the chill and saw that the River-woman was not there. So Jenny wrapped her wool blanket around her like a shawl and crept out.

The fire was burning low and unattended, except for Sparky, who huddled by it shivering. As Jenny sat by the dog and warmed herself, she tried to remember who was supposed to be on watch.

There was no moon that night, and the Bears were low in the North and hidden behind the tall, dark pines. But right above her, Jenny could see the Champion of Heaven, and somehow those familiar stars reassured her.

But then she saw that to the South, by the riverbank, someone crouched by the night-black water, murmuring more softly than the current. Then one of the glowing logs popped in the fire. Jenny heard a sudden slap and splash from the water, and then she saw Bonawyn stand up from the river's edge.

The River-woman wrapped her own blanket around herself more tightly, and came to the fire. Jenny kicked the wood into a hotter pile, and added some of the sticks and stumps the sailors had left there. "I had forgot you were on watch," Jenny said.

"This fire will never burn well," Bonawyn told her. "The wood was poorly chosen."

Jenny bent and blew hard at the fire, and in fact the new wood did not burn easily. "It was gathered from a stand of drowned, dead poplar," she said. "Which was chosen for it being more combustible than any green pine."

"So Forest-Goblins seem when they are killed," Bonawyn said, "returning to the rotten wood that made them."

Jenny didn't know whether to believe those words, but she looked into the forest then, and she saw the shadows like grasping arms.

"Goblin-wood makes the poorest fires," the River-woman said: "For it is cursed and soon expires."

"You rhyme most competently," said Jenny. Then she looked Bonawyn in the eye. "And you speak the tongue of the Ealda. But only now did I see you can talk with beavers."

Bonawyn's gaze didn't waver. "I am a River-woman," she said. "I speak with beavers as you a Fisher-Girl talk to Tom's dog. So we gather our thoughts."

Jenny nodded. "Sparky and I will take this watch," she said, "and gather our thoughts. And keep the fire burning high."

Bonawyn shrugged and went back to the tent. Jenny sat facing the woods, and then she moved around the fire to have the trees at her back. So she stayed, though she found in fact she didn't know what to tell Sparky about what she had seen. And whether because of creeping damp or because it was cursed goblin-wood, Jenny never did get the fire to burn high.

But when the thin light of dawn began to spread at last, Cookie came out to begin making porridge, and he had better luck.

CHAPTER SIX:
THE FENS

– gnats manifold and infinitesimal – an island in the bog – where is Bonawyn? – pulled under the water – kits and goblins –

SO THE CAPTAIN'S EXPEDITION KEPT ON UP AWYN Huaith, the North River, heading West – more or less. West through the Wild for the Great Falls, to meet Ahgeneh's people by the First Moon of Autumn.

Tom knelt at the bow of the *Adventure* while the big Bosun steered, and followed Bonawyn in the Captain's *Dauntless*, through the strange, rocky country, with its deep pools and tall stands of evergreen and tamarack.

By now Tom was used to the work of paddling, to the dip and bubble of each stroke, and his mind generally ran ahead of the curachs, around the next bend in the river, beyond the tree-clad islands, through the vast Wild, and even as far as the unknown end of the Expedition.

After the first long, awful carries, he had become used to the weight, but carrying two packs as the full-grown sailors did was still beyond him. He and Jenny ended those days more sore and tired than they had ever been, but all the same Tom liked the work, and liked to try his growing strength against the steep and narrow trails. Sparky generally ran with him, of course, and if Tom fell too far behind, would encourage him with barking.

But as they moved deeper into the Wild, the skies grew heavier, and rain fell more often, in warm, heavy drops. When thunder rolled, and the clouds began to flash, Bonawyn made them take shelter on the shore, "For lightning is strangely fond of a curach on water," she said.

So they had to wait out the storms from some muddy shelter, which made them all grumpy and impatient, except for Cookie, who pointed out that the rain did at least keep off the gnats.

Jenny snorted at that. "The gnats remain miseries both manifold and infinitesimal," she said. And in truth, the gnats did seem to like Jenny best, and her face was generally swollen and blotchy. "But still I would rather be bitten while travelling than be stuck here without any occupation other than the counting and scratching of my bites."

Still the skies grew greyer and the water of Awyn Huaith seemed to slow and widen into fens where dead trees stood drowned in the high water. No matter what channel they took, they always found some beaver dams built across their route, and each one meant another carry; short, perhaps, but boggy and gnat-ridden.

"Bonawyn," Tom heard the Captain say one afternoon, "we don't mind the work, so long as this way takes us quickest to the Great Falls. But we seem to move slower now, every day."

The River-woman only nodded. "The route has changed since I was here," she said. "The beaver have been busy. But soon we will come to an end, I think."

BUT IN FACT, there seemed no end to that route, or any beginning, either. As the two sailors with blue hoods pointed out, there seemed to be no path at all.

Then one dark night when the clouds covered the full and pearly moon, the best place they could find for their camp was a small island in the river. A thick bush of poplar stood against the Southern bank, with trunks that bent, and grew sideways, and tangled up with one another. At the island's heart, a small stand of tamarack stood among a damp carpet of moss and brown needles. The rest of it was stony and bare.

So the sailors made a little fire from the few sticks they could find worth burning, and as the smoke and night-mist rose around them, they slapped at gnats, and argued about what path to take.

"We goes upstream, that's plain enough," the First Mate said.

"That's what's not plain," said the Carpenter. "For we don't know what stream this is any more. We poked our boats through three inlets to this fen, and each ran a short way and then another dam, and fen once more –" And then the Carpenter broke off with an oath, for the big Bosun had slapped him across the nose.

Now, the Carpenter was a steady old hand, but that was too much for even him to take, and he got to his feet and readied his fists.

"Calmly, now," said the Captain.

For his part, the Bosun didn't get up, but only said, somewhat sadly, "There was a gnat biting your nose, Chips." And when the Carpenter felt his nose, there *was* blood, but whether it was from the gnat or the knock the Bosun had given him, he couldn't tell.

So he began slapping himself then, for the gnats smelled blood and began swarming over him, whining terribly, until he tore off his hood and beat the air around him. Finally the Carpenter sank back down and pulled the hood low over his face, and almost moaned with frustration.

"That's a pitiable sight," said the First Mate. "We is all reduced to a pitiable sight."

And that's what Tom felt too, and he noted that even Cookie was cheerless, while Jenny only slapped glumly at the gnats still biting her face and hands.

"Enough," said the Captain. "For we *have* a guide to lead us through this murky maze. Bonawyn, what marks must we watch for to lead us upstream?"

But Bonawyn never answered, and in the smoke and mist she was not to be seen. The sailors began to call the River-woman's name loudly, but she was not to be heard either. "She is drowned!" one of the sailors with blue hoods moaned. "The mist has drowned her!" the other added.

"Nonsense," the Captain said. "Who saw her last?" But no one could remember that either. So, to find her with a minimum of confusion in the fog, the First Mate alone stood, on his only one good leg, and after uttering a few elaborate and extraordinary curses, stumped off into the mist to find her.

The others waited miserably, and listened to the old sailor's clockwise progress around the island: to the thumps and splashes of his peg leg, to his muttered oaths and fulminations.

"He is like some rude, well-travelled wraith with a surprising talent for invective," Jenny observed.

"My father says there are spirits embodying water, air, earth, and fire," said Tom. "Perhaps the First Mate embodies foul language."

Then the First Mate roared an oath so loud that, across the fen, startled ducks and geese took wing; so awful that no one would explain it to Gimlet.

And when the First Mate finally returned in a tatter of mist, his face was fell and terrible.

"She has stolen the *Dauntless* and slipped away," the old sailor said. "Snuck away and left us lost." He dashed his cap against the ground.

The Captain's face was hidden to Tom, but he heard his words clearly enough: "So we are lost and benighted here," the Captain said.

The night grew; they uncovered their lanterns, but gnats swarmed over them, leaving only strange blobs of light in the smoky mist.

After a while Tom heard Gimlet whisper in the darkness: *"I am lonely,"* the boy said. *"Don't abandon me."*

That night the air was warm, but still the sailors wrapped themselves in wool blankets against the bugs, and tried to sleep that way: itchy and stifled and miserable.

When Tom took his turn at watch, he draped his blanket over himself and sat in the smoke of the fire, with Sparky tucked between his legs. And from that little shelter they could hear the sailors snore and mutter, and make muffled curses as they slept, or tried to. And there were other night noises from the fen around them: chirping bugs or the high, swooping chitter of bats. And the call of frogs, and the small splashes of muskrats and other hidden water-things.

They had been on watch a long time already when Sparky suddenly got up, twitching his tail against the bugs. Then Tom heard it too: the rumble of far-off thunder. "Do you want to go to your barrel?" Tom asked – for they had brought Sparky's special Dog-Preserving Barrel along as a kind of portable kennel.

But Gimlet must have heard the rumble too, for he had crawled out of his bedding and crept over to join Tom at the fire. The bugs whined around the boy, but by now Gimlet didn't bother to wave them off.

"I hate the Wild," he told Tom. "Grandmother made me wash every day, but at least I didn't have to sleep in a bog and be bitten ten hundred drousand times an hour."

Tom nodded sympathetically. "'Drousand' is not a word," he pointed out. "Likely you mean, 'a thousand thousand,' a sum which may be more conveniently named, a 'million.'"

"Drousands are bigger than millions," Gimlet said. "I know because I made them up. There are seventeen millions in a drousand, so ten hundred drousand is the biggest number in the world."

Then Tom almost asked Gimlet what would happen if he took that biggest number and added *one* to it (for Tom's Dad certainly took every chance to teach about such abstract matters). But Gimlet was spared that instruction, for just as Tom raised his head from the shelter of the blanket, he saw a small blue light off in the mist.

"Hist!" Tom whispered. *"That* is not one of our lanterns."

"Maybe it's Bonawyn, come back," said Gimlet, hopefully. But the light was gone already.

"Perhaps it is some wicked jack-o-lantern trying to tempt us into the bog," Tom said.

But now Gimlet pointed off to the left. "There!"

Tom stood, and looked into his Star-Glass to find the direction. "North-East now," he said, but the boy was already running away in the mist.

"Bonawyn!" Gimlet called, and this time he shouted the words: "We are lonely! Don't abandon us!"

Gimlet ran after the blue light, for suddenly it seemed like it held an end to the gnat-ridden, lonely darkness.

Each time the light appeared, Gimlet saw that he had lost the track again, and he chased off in the new direction, stumbling over roots and rocks in the dark.

And all the time someone chased *him* too, and called his name and demanded he come back. At first, Gimlet understood it was Tom's voice that called, but the deeper he ran through that strange night, the more he shared its dark confusion.

He knew the blue light was ahead of him; he could see it sometimes. But everything else was hidden by the night, and with every unseen sound he became more frightened.

So the night-terror grew in Gimlet, until he no longer knew Tom's voice. Now he only understood that something cried after him from the shadows, and he ran after the blue light more desperately.

Gimlet ran across stone and earth and mud, ran this way and that, until he stumbled into the poplar bush. All he knew was that now there were things, things blacker than the night, and things that scratched and tripped him. Horrible things, that must not catch him.

Then he saw the light again, and Gimlet followed it out of the bush at last, and found he was splashing through cold black water.

Gimlet gasped. For on that muggy night the water seemed very cold, and the shock of it brought Gimlet back to himself.

Then he knew he heard Sparky, and that Tom was calling. Gimlet turned back towards the shore and waved his hat. "Ahoy!" he meant to call, but it came out as a whisper: *"Over here! Ahoy!"*

TOM HAD ALMOST CAUGHT GIMLET more than once, just because he was bigger and faster. But every time he was nearly close enough, the boy made some sudden, unexpected turn. And in the bush, Tom's size only made him slower.

So he and Sparky had just emerged from the trees when Tom saw Gimlet's dimly waving shape.

"I'm coming!" Tom yelled. "But stay put! I don't want to chase you any more."

But just as Tom began to pull his boots off before he waded into the water, there was a mighty splash. Then something seemed to pull Gimlet under, and he was gone.

Tom threw off his hat. *"Stay,"* he told Sparky. Then he ran two steps and dove after the boy.

And though he was a timid dog, Sparky did *not* stay. Instead, he splashed into the water too, and looked around to see his master reappear.

After a moment, he barked once or twice, and then more, and loudly. Sparky ran back onto the shore, and barked and barked so that someone would come and find them.

Tom's dog barked until lightning split the sky at last, and thunder crashed. Sparky howled in terror, and then the rain began to pour.

The Riverfolk

Tom would later count it as one of the three great shocks of his life. For he had caught at Gimlet's heel, and so been pulled down after him through the cold black water. Just for an instant, Tom wondered what could pull them both so strongly; then he could only think about holding his breath, and not letting go.

Two or three times they swerved back up to the rain-bubbled surface, and he saw that some large, dark shape had Gimlet by the collar. But there was only time to take one gasp of air before they were pulled below again.

Then there was one last, long, deep dive in the darkness. Tom's chest grew tight before his free hand felt smooth stones below him. They were in some underwater tunnel now, and Gimlet kicked free from his grasp. When the tunnel began to slope upwards, Tom half-swam, half-crawled up the rock, until all of a sudden he could breathe again.

Wherever he was, the air was thick and musty. Only his head and shoulders were out of the water, but for a moment he stayed on his hands and knees, and just breathed.

There was a little light here, and when Tom finally shook the water from his eyes, he found himself nose-to-nose with some dark, enormous creature. It was hunched up like an old man, but still enormous, and it peered at him closely with sharp, brown eyes.

Tom heard Gimlet panting, but he was transfixed by those eyes. "Come in," the creature said at last, in a strange, humming voice. "Shake yourself dry here on my porch, and climb into my lodge. There is none finer, not on this side of the Cracks of the World."

But Tom only stared at its broad face, at its long front teeth. Then he asked, "Are you some Father of the Beavers, come down from the Hall of Stars?"

"I *am* the Father of the Beavers," the creature told him. "My lodge in the starry halls is small, for I am a modest creature, but I built it well. But on earth, this is my home, and you and your friends have spent these last days paddling lost in my kingdom, in Tearnan Behowar; lost in beaver-land."

"You have very big teeth!" Gimlet said. The boy was crouched in the corner.

Then the big creature bent towards him and made a strange noise. *"Heem, heam,"* he said. "Did I hurt you, kitten?"

"No," said Gimlet. "Although tugging so hard on my collar almost choked me." He put his hands around his neck and stuck out his tongue to demonstrate. "And I lost my tricorne hat when you grabbed me," he added. "It is a fine hat, of the best beaver."

Then the creature turned away. Huge and heavy and round, it climbed slowly up wide stairs, deeper and higher into the stony lodge, dragging its broad tail behind it.

Tom pulled himself onto the smooth ledge and tried to slap the water from his clothing. "I think you shouldn't boast of your beaver hat in this place," he whispered. "It is bad manners."

But Gimlet didn't bother about his dripping clothes. "I think it was bad manners for Mr. Waddling Big-Teeth to kidnap me," he said.

Tom and Gimlet followed the great beaver up the shallow steps into a broad, wood-lined chamber. It had a low ceiling, not big enough for the creature to stand. Around the walls there were ledges set close to the floor, and in the middle a low table fashioned of peeled logs.

At the far end, someone was crouching low over a small fire set in a wide stone hearth, but their host paid no attention and moved slowly onto a seat behind the table.

"You *may* call me 'Big-Teeth,'" said the beaver, "and indeed, that is one of my names. Or Thunder-tail, or Dam-Raiser, or Beaver-Father."

But then the figure by the fire rose and turned to Tom and Gimlet. It was Bonawyn. "Our host is modest," the River-Woman said. "But he likes best of all to be called Oak-Biter."

Tom had grown used to Bonawyn's assurance on the river, but now her calm seemed even more impressive. She brought over a pot of tea, and poured some for each of them, as though it were some normal gathering.

"Are you frightened?" Bonawyn asked.

"No," said Gimlet, while Tom said, "Yes."

"You should be," Bonawyn told them.

Tom took a few sips of the strange, barky tea, and tried

to collect himself. "Master Oak-Biter," he asked at last. "Why are we here?"

"You are here because you held onto the little one's foot," the great beaver said. *"He* is here because I wanted to know why the Strangers had brought one of their kits to my Tamarack Island. It makes a difference as to how I regard you." He stopped and drank tea from his wooden bowl. "Now, Bonawayn, she is here because she had asked for my help; for the Riverfolk have many dealings with beavers."

Oak-Biter looked at Bonawayn closely. "They deal with us living and dead," he said. "Share our rivers and deal our flesh and skin." Then he drummed his claws on the table a while, and made some more of his strange humming.

Now Tom liked Bonawyn's poise a little less. "What help did you ask him for?" he demanded. "To lose us in this foggy maze?"

She looked him in the eye. "Yes, to lose you here," she said. "For a while. For this Homely Country your Captain hopes to find – that stands in the way to our own Hinterland, where Riverfolk travel to trap and trade."

"Heem, heam," said Oak-Biter. "To me, Bonawyn says, 'The Strangers will drain your ponds, will break your dams.' To you, Bonawyn says, 'Strangers will keep Riverfolk from trapping beavers!' "

"Grandfather," Bonawyn said. "We thank each beaver who helps to warm and feed us. You and your kin are our patrons, and we honour you."

"Yes," said Oak-Biter, "and that is the way of this World. Beavers cut down trees for the bark, to the distress of the Wood-Nymphs who love them. Then men and women come and eat us, or wear our fur."

"We make you into hats too," Gimlet said. But at a look from Oak-Biter, the boy fell silent.

"Then other things eat *you,*" the great beaver said. "Bug-bears and the Forest-Goblins who hunt tonight. But at least they will not roll your skins into bales and count your value by the hundred-weight."

"Are there really Forest-Goblins tonight?" asked Gimlet.

"Yes," said Bonawyn. "For the twisted poplars on the island are the very place the goblins like to nest. So although I doubt your case, I came to plead it for you. For I never asked for that."

"And she told me there were young ones too," Oak-Biter added. "I hadn't known about you kits."

"Master Oak-Biter," said Tom. "I left my beaver hat on shore. But receiving it from the Captain was the most honour I have ever received. The same is true for the hat of young Gimlet, whom you call a kitten."

Then Tom told the great beaver the whole tale of the Long Night coming: about the foul winds from the East, about the signs and dreams and portents, and about the Captain's plans and expedition. "And if the Captain can bring us to the great falls in time to meet this Ahgeneh, and so find some Homely Country," Tom said – and he

spoke desperately now – "If he can, my people will not stop treasuring our gifts from the beavers. We will honour you better, make sure there are always ponds for your people, and leave your kits untroubled, in honour of your care for Gimlet."

Oak-Biter looked at him. "Perhaps," he said. "Perhaps." But then he turned to Bonawyn. "When you sent a messenger you didn't say there were kits among the Strangers," he said. "You didn't say they meant to visit Ahgeneh, who is one of my sons among the Ealda."

"But Grandfather, what are we to do?" said Bonawyn. "How will we live if the Strangers stand in the way of our Hinterlands? Our fine life on the rivers might disappear."

Oak-Biter looked at her sadly. "I said much the same to the other princes of the animals when first we saw the Elves," he told her. "And the Elves said it when they found the Ealda – before the Elves fled the Vastlands altogether. And so said the Ealda when the Riverfolk began to grow and flourish."

"And were any of you wrong?" asked Bonawyn.

"Bonawyn," the great beaver said. "Loon-Daughter," he called her. "There was a Wood-Nymph who pitied a Stranger once."

"I know the tale," whispered Bonawyn.

"And she suffered for it too," Oak-Biter said. "But what is there to do except show pity to those who need it, and suffer the changes that come with the turning of the World?"

The Riverfolk

Then amidst all the rumbles of thunder, they heard a great *crack!* come over the water, sharp and loud as a beaver tail.

"It's a musket shot!" said Tom. "The Forest-Goblins do hunt tonight!"

"Please, Grandfather," said Bonawyn. "I cannot abandon these strangers. So I must keep my word."

Then Gimlet surprised them all. "But can I stay here?" he asked. "Your lodge is cozy, and I could be your grandson."

Oak-Biter looked at the boy and smoothed his whiskers for a moment. "You must live your life on the other side of the Cracks of the World," he said. "But you may count yourself as one of my sons, like Ahgeneh."

Then they heard another *crack!* and another, more; muskets firing over and over.

"Quickly!" said Oak-Biter, "Through my back door."

A cottonwood, come to life

Chapter Seven: MUSKETS IN THE DARK

– where is Tom? – susurrations – misfires and wounds – a last and humble ship – the shutting of the doors –

JENNY HAD BEEN WOKEN BY THE SUDDEN THUNDER. At first she looked for the River-woman beside her in the tent, but then she remembered Bonawyn had left them.

Jenny put her head outside. The junior sailors (who only slept on the ground) had stirred as well, and by the firelight their faces seemed to shine with confusion. "What was that big noise?" they called, and "Why is it so dark?" they called, and similar things, and so began to distress themselves into a lather.

So Jenny stepped out, and clapped her hat upon her head. "Steady now!" she called, loudly enough to get their attention. "Steady," she said again. "Now, now get some lanterns lit, and become busy, and – and generally conduct yourselves like proper sailors!"

In a moment the Captain and the older sailors had joined her. "Well done," the Captain said, for his crew was already in some kind of order.

"It's the loud voice and the hat *together,*" the First Mate said. "Half the trick of command right there."

But Jenny had been counting the sailors, and the number was wrong. "Where is Tom?" she asked suddenly. "Or Sparky? – or even Gimlet?"

"I thought Bonawyn had run off," the Captain said. "But Tom would never leave."

Then, Jenny heard that somewhere a dog was howling. "Sparky!" she cried, and she would have followed the sound, but the Captain held up his hand.

"Wait," he said. "Bonawyn, Tom, even Gimlet – there's something in this night that hunts us."

"But it's Tom's dog!" Jenny said. And then, because she was touchy about such things herself, she added, "Tom's dog, *sir,* I mean, and we must find them!"

"No, not alone," The Captain said.

Then the First Mate spoke up, too slowly, Jenny thought: "What if we *all* goes –" the old sailor began.

"Yes!" Jenny interrupted, for somewhere Sparky still howled, and she couldn't bear to hear it. "And so share one, rather than several fates and find our doom or glory together!"

"Ensign," the Captain said, quite seriously, and Jenny stopped, for it was the first real reproach he had given her. "Jenny," he said. "We have come here for a purpose more important than glory."

So they stood in the rain a moment, and struggled over what to do, until the Carpenter cried in rare excitement: "Look there! Lights moving, like the stars come down to walk among us!"

And there were lights in the rainy dark; lights like

Gimlet had seen, but more: a dozen bright blue lights that appeared, and went out, and moved, and showed again. And then, even through the rain, they heard a sound like the scatter of old leaves.

"Not stars," the Captain said – for the crew of the *Volantix* had seen such things before. "Not stars, but goblinry!"

Jenny heard the First Mate sigh. "And so yet once more," he said, "we is just about to get et." Then he adjusted his eye-patch. "Quick and careful now!" he called out. "But look to your swords and muskets."

THE LIGHTS SEEMED TO GATHER only slowly in the mist, with a tree-like patience.

So the sailors had time to form up in a circle, with the tamaracks as a kind of eastern anchor; and then still time enough to grow nervous. The Captain put Jenny where the trees would guard her left, and had the First Mate stand beside her. "I've been in battles before," she had said.

"None like this," the Captain told her.

Jenny stood by the trees, facing South, and fumbled with her musket. She'd practised often enough before, but still it was a heavy, clumsy thing – and now with the rain and the dark, and Sparky's howls, everything was harder. She kept up as the others charged their muskets with powder; and rammed the ball down almost as quick, but now her ramrod jammed in the barrel.

She wrenched at it once or twice, but she saw the goblin

lights had grown still at last. Jenny tugged harder. "I calls that an inauspicious pause," the First Mate said. "How's the musket coming?"

Jenny shook her head. Somehow she was out of breath. "I'll have to use my sword," she said.

Just then, around the other side, there was a sudden scatter. "Stand firm!" the Captain called. "For we've met worse." Then some crooked shadow darted towards him from the mist, and the Captain stepped forward with his pistol. "Always daunt the first one!" he cried as he pulled the trigger.

But the damp had got into his pistol. There was only a sort of fizzing flash that lit the monster brightly. It had a sharp, rude spear and horrible, axe-carved features, and it was almost on the Captain. Suddenly, Cookie's musket cracked, and the goblin toppled like so much dead wood.

"Thank you," the Captain said.

Cookie glanced at the splintery remains as he began reloading. "Now the *Snow*-Goblins," he said, cheerfully, "they were terrible."

Jenny was almost ready to set her own musket aside when the Carpenter appeared behind her. "Here," he said calmly, for he was a steady hand, "switch with mine."

"Chips –" Jenny said, but then in front of her a shadow rose from the mist. She had just put the new musket to her shoulder when the First Mate fired. There was a terrible *crack!* and then there was a kind of hollow noise in her ears, and something awful fell broken at her feet.

The Carpenter gave it a brief, professional, glance.

"That one looks like a willow."

Then there was a lull, and Jenny heard the two sailors with blue hoods wailing. For they shook with fright, and hadn't been able to manage their powder: "We're for it now!" one moaned. "This will be our last battle," said the other.

At that the Carpenter called "Nonsense!" and hurried around to help them.

Now, just to Jenny's left, there was something creaking through the trees. She saw some small and wicked thing, and the sharp rude spear it carried. There was a terrible *crack!* and the shock of the musket-stock hard against her shoulder. And then the thing was gone.

For a moment there was only a kind of empty sound in Jenny's ears, but then faintly she began to hear some thin and awful noise. There were more goblins now, more and more; dozens of them, in a rush of crooked shadows. Somewhere the Captain yelled *"Woe!"* as a kind of battle cry, and the others took it up: *"Woe!"*

Then Jenny heard firing, like a string of firecrackers amidst the thunder. And smoke rose with every shot, and the air grew even dimmer.

Beside her, the First Mate said something Jenny couldn't hear, but she saw some of the twisted shapes coming through the tamaracks. She didn't have time to be nervous then, and she reloaded, and she and the First Mate fired again; and then the goblins came too fast for Jenny to load, or even draw a sword – she could only swing her musket like a club, and knock the spears away.

That wouldn't have been enough to keep the monsters off, but beside her the First Mate had his cutlass out. The old sailor stuck his peg leg hard in the mucky ground, and he chopped down goblins right and left, like a woodsman in a frenzy. And even as Jenny fought to stay alive, some part of her expected to hear the two sailors with blue hoods begin to wail.

But those two timid sailors did *not* wail, for the Carpenter had exchanged muskets with them both as well. "Thank you!" they had said, and "Thank you!" and they felt easier then, although their line was becoming ragged now, and they weren't sure where to aim.

The Carpenter had turned aside to load a weapon for himself at last, when by the chance of battle a gap opened in the line. Then the storm grew loud, and with the muskets firing, and the various cries of the sailors, there was no way he could hear the rustle of one great monster's approach.

He had just finished priming his musket – the fourth musket he had charged in a row – when he saw something from the corner of his eye.

Chips was steady as always then. He only had an instant, but it was time enough to turn and shoot. But of all the muskets he had loaded that damp night, his was the one that misfired.

There was only a pop and a flash, and for an instant he saw the monster very well: saw its rough black hide; its brown, splintery teeth; the bare point of its rude spear. *A cottonwood, come to life,* he thought, and then the goblin was upon him, and began to tear at him at him with tooth and spear.

The Riverfolk

It was only then that the two timid sailors with blue hoods understood what the shadow was, and they both fired, and the goblin fell grey and broken.

So the battle raged in the dark, among the thunder.

The crew of the *Volantix* did many heroic things, but Jenny only found a new and terrible kind of confusion. Books and stories explained how battles ran, but there was no order to this kind of fighting. She struggled to stay alive, and around her muskets cracked, and sailors roared when they were hurt, and when their swords struck home goblins fell with the sound of snapping branches.

To Jenny the battle seemed to go on and on, and she wondered how long she could survive it.

Then suddenly a noise broke over the water: a noise louder than any crack of thunder; a noise sharper than any musket.

Now a wind came up, and as the rain was swept away and the fog blew to tatters, the sailors and goblins saw a great dark shape to the North, standing at the water's edge. And they could hear its weird call: *"Heem, heam!"*

Then Oak-Biter came closer, and if Gimlet had thought he looked comic once, no one saw him that way now. The Beaver-Prince strode into the battleground slowly and heavily, like some doom advancing from beyond the Cracks of the World. And he was tall and wide, and towered even over the Bosun.

His voice swept over the rocks and water like a bassoon:

"What night-creatures have come to my country without asking leave? Goblins, I know the twisted stands of scrub where you were born; I know the rough, black bark of your mothers, and I know the words that made you –

"Goblins, my teeth are itching tonight!" he called. "If you linger here I shall eat your bark. I will un-speak the words of your birth. I will gnaw you to shavings."

And with a noise like the scattering of leaves, like the creak of branches in the wind, the goblins rushed South. Their crooked shadows blended into the bush, and they were gone.

This strange and sudden end to the battle left the sailors dazed. For a moment they only stood and looked at one another, and then stared in wonder at the great beaver who stood above them, and at Bonawyn and Tom and Gimlet who had now returned.

Even Sparky appeared from the trees then, barking for joy; and all around the fallen goblins were turned to tree shapes, like drowned poplars, crooked and withered and broken. But the two sailors with blue hoods were crouched over one tree and they were weeping, for beneath one of the twisted poplars the Carpenter lay dying.

The Captain knelt beside the Carpenter, and all the sailors from the *Volantix* gathered around them.

"Can anything be done?" the First Mate asked quietly, but the Captain only shook his head.

"I'm a practical man," whispered the Carpenter. "And I'm broke beyond mending."

Then a thought struck him, for he was good with figures, and minded the stars and planets. "But look now," he said. "Someone might want to know this: twice we've fought goblins on a full-moon night; how do you calculate that?"

"Bad odds," the First Mate said, "Which has now catched up with us."

"Good odds," the Carpenter whispered. "For twice we've beaten them."

"Chips, you saved us," wept one of the sailors with a blue hood. "Chips, we were frightened and should have been slain instead," cried the other.

"You shouldn't go when you're frightened," the Carpenter said. "That's a horror that can't be mended."

"Aren't you scared?" the two sailors whispered.

But the Carpenter moved his head slowly back and forth. "I know what the numbers show," he said. "All sailors die once."

Then he rolled his head to look up at Oak-Biter. He stared for a moment and then understood. "You built those clever dams," he said. The Beaver-Prince nodded.

"I'm a wood-crafter too," the Carpenter said. "Is this a good place for me to end?"

Oak-Biter made a deep and gentle noise. *"Heuam, heuam,"* he said. "Rest in this place as long as you like," he said. "And labour at the lodges of your dreams."

Then the Captain spoke. "What a steady hand you've been," he said. "What a sailor of great resource."

The Carpenter smiled and nodded, and closed his eyes,

but before it was too late, Jenny bent to kiss him. "You saved me tonight too," she said. Then she had to fight to keep her voice. "And in the Old Sea you built a ship of wonder from scraps and spruce gum once, to pull me from my doom. I still sail it in my dreams."

"I'll have to borrow it back, Jenny girl," the Carpenter whispered. "And sail a while without you."

Then Jenny began sobbing, like the two sailors with blue hoods.

THE MORNING BROKE fair and dry at last, and for the first time the sailors saw the wide extent of Oak-Biter's country, the endless stretch of green water shining in the sun.

They worked hard that morning. First they cut and cleared the strange trees on the battleground. Then, to Oak-Biter's direction, they made a raft of fine birch poles. On it they gently laid the body of the Carpenter, and set his favourite hammer beside him.

Then the Captain said some words: "Chips," he said, "after you have cared so well for so many fine vessels, we entrust you to this humble craft, the best we can make without you."

With that the sailors bore up the raft of birch poles, and set it gently on the pile of goblin-wood. Then they bared their heads. "Will this cursed, damp stuff burn?" the First Mate asked.

But at a word from Oak-Biter, the pyre did begin to

burn. And soon the Carpenter's raft, and all the remains of the battle where he perished, were in flames, and rose as smoke to the sky.

Then the sailors took their curachs out into the water, and followed Oak-Biter quietly across the fen, and down a long canal. In the Captain's boat, the *Dauntless*, Cookie had taken the Carpenter's place, and even his mood was oppressed by the black spirits of the Captain, by the tense set to Bonawyn's figure at the bow.

Some of the sailors had wounds, and all of them were grieved. But they paddled slowly and steadily, and somehow the regular dip and wash of their paddles began to soothe their spirits. Eventually the Captain spoke to Bonawyn: "I thought you had abandoned us in the Wild," he said. "And left me lonely here."

Bonawyn did not turn, but she let her paddle drift in the water a while. "So my father and I meant to do," she said at last. "But after all I am not strong enough."

So they went until the evening began to close in. Once more, pines rose high and strong above rocky hills, and ahead in the darkening West, they heard the sound of quick water again at last.

At the last great dam, the Captain took a moment to admire how tight and well-finished Oak-Biter had built it, and then he turned to the great beaver. "I confirm the promises Tom made to you," he said. "In our Homely

Country, we will honour the gifts we have from your people, and make sure they always have ponds, and leave your kits untroubled."

"Heam," said Oak-Biter. "Bonawyn, you must hurry now, if they are to be at the Great Falls to meet my foster-son Ahgeneh by the Last Moon of Summer. You, too, have promises to keep."

"These Strangers are being tested by the Vastlands now," Bonawyn said. "If they remain undaunted, I will keep my promises."

"None of you are likely to see this place again," Oak-Biter said. "Except you, perhaps," he said to Gimlet. "For I think you were happy in my lodge."

"It is my favourite place," said Gimlet.

"Heem, hueam," the great beaver said, almost sadly, before he called, "Good luck to all of you!" Then there was a sudden splash. When they saw Oak-Biter come up from the water again, he was already far away. They saw the dark flash of his tail, and there was a clap like thunder, and he was gone.

"Quickly now," Bonawyn said. "We must be far West of here by nightfall."

"What's the rush?" asked the First Mate.

"Because Oak-Biter has gone to shut the doors to Tearnan Behowar, to close up beaver-land," Tom told him. "And we do not want to be stranded between dream-land and waking country."

Gimlet looked back at the wide fens, but the Captain called "On, on! For we have our own doom to find."

CHAPTER EIGHT:
THE FREEDOM OF THE RIVER

– downstream at last – Fox Truhanna – the single loudest girl – a broken paddle – the oath of the Riverfolk –

AWYN HUAITH, THE NORTH RIVER, HAD CARRIED them West as well, though its real source was hidden somewhere in the beaver-fens. But from those fens issued lesser streams that followed the high country as it stepped down towards the South-West.

So for some days after they left Tearnan Behowar they travelled more easily, running downstream at last. Sometimes, at night, they were alarmed by the faint sounds of drumming in the distance, but Bonawyn scorned their fear.

"Do you think you are alone in all this Wild?" she asked. "This is the home of many kinds of Ealda."

"Why doesn't they show themselves?" the First Mate asked.

"Yes," said Bonawyn. "For in the dark Wild who wouldn't relish meeting an unknown band of strangers?"

But generally the River-woman calmed them now, and sometimes even allowed them to relax – briefly – and let the current carry them.

One night, after an unusually successful dinner of hot bannock and fresh strawberry jam, Cookie said, "This kind of travel is still hard work, of course, but somehow I think the worst is over."

The others fell silent for a moment. "Cookie," Jenny said at last, "you are cheerful to a degree almost eccentric among sailors."

The First Mate nodded. "Our Cookie shows it more and more," he said, "– though a more sea-worthy term would be 'buoyancy of spirit'."

"Is cheerfulness a bad omen among you?" Bonawyn asked.

"No," Cookie protested. "Tom is cheerful too, and he meant good luck to us in the icy seas of the cold, dark North."

"I am not as cheerful as I was," Tom pointed out, "now that I'm an Ensign."

"Well, it's not natural, anyway," the Bosun told Cookie. "Not natural at all."

Bonawyn laughed at them a while, and then spat into the fire. "My people are the merriest in the world," she said. "Keep all the cheer you can, for tomorrow we have rapids to run –" Then she paused a moment before finishing, "A kind of dangerous fun."

Jenny looked at her. "Was that the rhyme you meant to make?"

Bonawyn laughed. "Don't bother to issue a lampoon upon me. That was a poor effort, and I know it." Then all at once she stopped being merry. "But don't talk late tonight," she said. "For tomorrow we do have bad rapids."

THE NEXT MORNING Bonawyn woke the sailors before dawn, and harried them into their boats.

They paddled for an hour before the sun was up, and an hour more before they felt it shining warm on the cold river. Only then did she let them pause in the water while Cookie passed pieces of bannock around on a paddle, which was what Bonawyn called a working breakfast.

Now the morning sun was strong on the trees that climbed into hills: first poplar and willow along the banks, and then maple and pine, all in their deepest summer greens; and here and there patches of meadow where bright fireweed grew.

"We are come to the Fox Truhanna, the Rushing River," Bonawyn told them. "Wise and cautious travellers take three days and seven carries to reach its end."

At the mention of further carries, the two sailors with blue hoods began groaning. "What if we are not cautious?" they pleaded. "What if we are foolish?"

"Ah!" Bonawyn cried. "If you are foolish? Well, if you are foolish, then you will learn the true art of the Riverfolk, and run your curachs through the rushing stream and wild white water. And we will be through the Fox Truhanna in time to watch the sunset."

"We was almost drowned going *up* the rapids," the First Mate pointed out. "I'm thinking this might be more perilouser than that."

"I missed the turn then," Tom said. "But Bonawyn has taught us better since."

The Captain nodded. "We cannot waste three days carrying our boats down rocks," he said. "The summer is already at its peak, which means it moves towards its end, and by the Last Moon of Summer we must be at the Great Falls if we are to keep our meeting with Ahgeneh."

"Good, for this is how we travel the Wild," said Bonawyn. "This is what you must learn if you are to becomes its intimates, and not always Strangers. You have learned to paddle well, but now you must show you can read the river. Now you must see where the rills and eddies are, and guard against the stones waiting to bite your birchbark."

"We will learn, for we must," the Captain said. " But I think we may always remain Strangers."

Bonawyn looked at him. Then she shrugged, and twirled her paddle over her head. Just before she dug it into the water, Gimlet cried, *"Broe-stach!"*

The River-woman shut her mouth and glared at the boy, but all the sailors began laughing.

Tom turned back to reprimand Gimlet for his rudeness. "Crying *'Broe-stach!'* is Bonawyn's chief pleasure and privilege," he called.

"You laughed," the boy said.

"Yes," Tom said. "But it was rude."

As the curachs moved into the river and resumed their line, in the *Fortitude*, Jenny and the First Mate spoke about the same event. "Although I hesitate to call it wit," Jenny said, quietly, "there is no denying a kind of comedy in the puncturing of such affectation. For after all, she is only a young woman, who has never served as a captain, or even been ranked an Ensign."

Then they were around a bend in the river, and suddenly saw why Fox Truhanna, the Rushing River, had its name. For the current quickened as the riverbed began a long, downward dash through a twisting, boulder-strewn course.

Ahead in the *Dauntless*, Bonawyn quickly changed her paddle for a long pole, and Tom and Jenny followed her. Then, as she came to the head of the rapids, Bonawyn began to call for her paddlers to go faster: *"Moorna! Moorna!"*

Tom looked back at Jenny to be sure she understood, and she gave him a nod. For a boat moving at the same speed as the water hardly steers. To pilot their curachs well, they would have to run them fast through Fox Truhanna.

As the *Dauntless* dipped down the start of the rapids, Tom and Jenny watched how Bonawyn kept her paddlers going hard, while she stood at the bow and used her pole to push away from looming rocks; watched how she made the curach pause where standing waves revealed a rock; and how she suddenly took it plunging through the torrent of a narrow channel, where it was lost from sight in a spray of foam.

"That was thrilling!" cried Jenny. "The curach is a river-horse, and how she makes it leap and turn!"

Whether Tom heard her, Jenny didn't know, for he only nodded one or twice as he looked ahead, and then his curach was entering the white water. "Fast!" Jenny heard him call, and then she heard the familiar wailing of the two sailors with blue hoods; and then Tom was hidden in a spray of white, and it was her turn for the rapids.

Jenny gripped her pole tightly. "We've seen worse, and rocks that was moving too, in the Old Sea," the First Mate reminded her. Jenny nodded, but in fact she hardly heard him.

"Fast!" she yelled. "Fast now!"

Then the water was shooting around her. Behind her in the curach, Gimlet was yelling, *"Broe-stach!"* but Jenny paid no attention. The boulder was looming from the foam, and she pushed away from it hard. The curach had just begun to turn away when her pole snapped.

Jenny reached at once for a new pole from the bottom of the boat, but for a moment, she couldn't guide the *Fortitude* properly or check how quickly it swung. The curach shook as the stern struck against the boulder. Jenny heard something else break, and heard a mighty oath from the First Mate, but she couldn't spare a glance.

"Hard a'port!" Jenny cried. "Hard!" For now they raced towards the great standing wave where Bonawyn had made the *Dauntless* rear and turn magnificently, passing safely to the right of the rocks that hid beneath the water.

But before Jenny could properly set her new pole, the rushing current of Fox Truhanna had caught the *Fortitude*. Now the curach turned without her help. It twisted sideways and turned about, and began to head stern-first down the rapids; backwards through the spray and foam.

Gimlet screamed of course, in fun or in terror, but Jenny yelled louder yet, louder than Gimlet's screams and the rush of the river together. (For although Jenny herself would disdain to boast of it, Tom and the other sailors had speculated more than once that Jenny might be the single loudest girl in the world.) "Hard!" she yelled again.

For they were backwards now, and would never be able to outrun the current. Still, she would be able to steer if they moved against it. "All together! Hard!" So they moved slowly, awkwardly, paddling backwards, towards the tall wave where the rocks hid.

Jenny looked ahead, towards the stern of the curach now, and she saw what had happened when they stuck the boulder. It must have been the First Mate's long paddle she had heard break, for he tossed it into the water now, and grabbed a new one from another sailor, and turned and dug it deep into the water.

Jenny poled hard from the *Fortitude*'s bow, which was now the rear of the boat. Someone stronger might have been able to turn the curach into the channel on the right, as Bonawyn had. That way was clear, she knew, but the best Jenny could manage was to slip to the left and hope.

The First Mate pushed hard off the rocks beneath the water and then the curach almost rolled, but the boat pivoted on the stern, and swung round again in a wash of water.

Then they were head first again, and plunging down a wild torrent. Spray and foam rose all around them, but they were running with the river again, and Jenny's sailors began cheering with delight.

THERE WAS A WELCOME STRETCH of calm river then, and Jenny and the *Fortitude* soon caught up with the others. She twirled her paddle overhead as a signal of their success.

"That was an adventure!" Tom called happily. "That was part of the Wild."

"We broke only a pole and one paddle," Jenny replied. "Which I count as a victory against Fox Truhanna. It was the First Mate who saved us really," she added. "His quick actions, without which the boulder would have wrecked us."

"The young Ensign here steered well," the First Mate said. "Which you must have too, seeing as you have all hands here and still not drowned."

"We were knocked over the side and almost drowned!" one of the two sailors with blue hoods called from the *Adventure*. "But we didn't," the other explained.

"Did the *Fortitude* spring no leak when it struck the rock?" the Captain asked Jenny.

"Look how hard I'm bailing!" Gimlet yelled.

"One moderate-slight leak," Jenny admitted. "But using the sponge makes the boy feel useful, while subduing his exuberance."

For a while Bonawyn let them babble happily, for she remembered the first time she had run those rapids.

They ran three more that day. Each was trickier than the last, and by the time they had passed them all, every paddler in the brigade, and the Captain too, was wet and cold from the splash and spray. All the boats were battered, and even the *Dauntless* where Bonawyn steered was leaking.

But when the brigade gathered at the foot of the last rapids, the sun was just beginning to set, and the clouds had bloomed in red and violet.

THE EXPEDITION paddled slowly now, letting the river carry them until Bonawyn found a spot to draw up on the Western bank.

"Well done," the Captain told his crew. "Today even Bonawyn would say you have travelled like Riverfolk."

But Jenny pointed to a cluster of white poles that stood across the river, where they shone gold in the sunset. "Are those *all* memorial poles?" she asked Bonawyn. "And why are some of them broken?"

The River-woman nodded. "Each a tree stripped bare to

honour a paddler lost," she said. "And the ones broken mark bodies we never found."

The Captain took off his hat. "But there are more than a dozen poles here," he said.

Bonawyn raised an eyebrow. "There are seventeen poles," she said. "Five of them are broken."

"Seventeen!" the Captain cried. "Why didn't you tell us before we decided to run these rapids?"

"Are you really the equal of Riverfolk?" Bonawyn asked him. "For we can name those seventeen paddlers, and their mothers and fathers too, but still we would rather travel white water than waste slow days in carries."

The First Mate took out a new bandanna to wipe his brow. "You counts your lives light," he said.

"Tell me again the reason you come to the Wild," Bonawyn said to them all. "For this is not a place for those who fear for their skins."

After a moment the Captain spoke. "Why do you make us say it again?" he asked. "We come, because soon, when the Long Night falls, our homes will be worse than Wild." His words came out harshly now. "Our lands will no longer be tame and hospitable, but diseased and barren. Death will come, and what lives will face corruption."

Then Cookie said to Bonawyn, "We will take the chances of the Wild and trust our skins to luck and skill – and your good guidance."

The Captain nodded, and then, by the custom of the Riverfolk, they fired one musket in the air for each bare pole.

The Riverfolk

THAT NIGHT they patched their boats, and then made camp in a pine-sheltered nook against a tall rock wall.

After dinner, when the pipes had come out, and the smoke drifted towards the stars, Bonawyn stood in front of the fire. She pronounced herself satisfied at last that they could face both spears and white-water, and had them pronounce the simple oath of the Riverfolk:

"I swear," they repeated after her, *"never to dishonour the River."*

"I swear never to refuse help to a stranger, or carry less than my share."

"I swear never to harm the curach of another, or through carelessness allow a curach to come to harm."

And after each sailor had sworn this oath, and the Captain too, Bonawyn dumped a ladle of water on their head, and granted them the freedom of all the rivers in the Wild.

THEY HAD A REASON TO CELEBRATE that night, for the first time since they had left the battle on the Tamarack Island. The wind blew gentle through the pines, Cookie produced hot chocolate, and the sailors took their ease and pulled out their fifes and fiddles.

At first they improvised a tune, calling it "Gimlet Wants More Chocolate," and took turns carrying the boy on their shoulders while they danced a kind of hornpipe.

Bonawyn had a fiddle of her own, but she stayed back with Tom and Jenny to listen and watch the others dancing.

After a while the music gave Tom a thought, and he turned to her. "The name 'Bonawyn,' has a pleasant roll," he said. "Does it have also have some similar meaning?"

"All our words and names sound pleasantly," Bonawyn said. "Except those for something wicked. And 'Bonawyn' rolls well because it means 'river-woman.'"

"Which name must be an oddly common one," said Jenny. "As it describes so many of your people."

Bonawyn spat into the fire. "It means *the* River-woman," she said. "As I am the daughter of Bawdoear, *the* Boat-man, who is the leader of us all."

Then for a while they sat together more awkwardly, and Tom regretted he had asked the question.

In time the dancing stopped, and the music became more melancholy, as the sailors remembered Chips, and their home that lay across the Ocean, in the Long Night's shadow.

Then they saw the Captain stand among the musicians. He looked in their direction a while, and then turned to the rock wall. He began to sing a long, sad ballad, and after a moment, the fiddlers began to played a low accompaniment. Altogether, Jenny thought it was the most beautiful song she had ever heard.

And when the Captain came to the last lines:

So they grew, as two tall pines
that nestled close for cover
And met at the top, in a true-love's knot;
and so held one another

Well, Jenny wasn't the only one who began sniffling then – for as the First Mate had pointed out more than once, sailors were not just a superstitious lot, but a sentimental one as well.

"I hadn't realized what a fine voice the Captain had," Jenny said to Tom. She wiped her nose on her sleeve. "For things other than bellowing orders in a storm, I mean, where he is most fine."

"Nor did I," Tom said. He didn't look at Jenny as he spoke, but stared up as though he meant to count the stars.

"Does your Captain play no instrument?" Bonawyn asked. "For I had thought he was a man of parts."

"He plays the cello," Tom said. "But it was too big to carry in a curach."

A hairy, walking house

Chapter Nine:
THE LEATHER STOCKINGS

– the Old Woman of the Wind – a huge brown shamble – rules for Bugbears – Bonawyn's general dash – "Back in the Water!" – a hard trade –

Bonawyn hadn't pronounced the Freedom of the River lightly, for by now the sailors in the little brigade of curachs truly had learned much of the craft of the Riverfolk.

The height of the summer had come and gone, but they made good time. Each day they were on the river before sunrise, and they sang as they paddled through the long days. Even when they had to make a carry, they fairly trotted beneath their heavy loads.

After a few days they came to a chain of broad lakes that straggled down towards the South-West. There at last they could jury-rig sails and let the wind begin to do their work for them, and the sailors could rest in the warm sun while their curachs sped through the water and cast waves from the bow. Even Bonawyn was impressed.

In the *Dauntless*, she turned back towards the Captain. "It's not honest work, like paddling," she told him. "But I see your crew is on good terms with Gee Scradach, the Old

Woman of the Wind. No Ealda or Riverfolk can better command the air."

"We don't command the wind," the Captain said. "Though sometimes we imagine we can call it with a whistle."

"Well, the Old Woman will scold even those she likes from time to time," Bonawyn said. "Little things can make her cranky."

From the stern of the *Dauntless*, Cookie overheard Bonawyn's words about Gee Scradach. "She sounds like my old Granny," he said. "She was often cantankerous for no reasons we knew, but mellowed quickly when I gave her some biscuits or short-bread."

"So you should humour Gee Scradach," Bonawyn called back to him. So Cookie crumbled some currant bread he had made, and cast it with thanks into the fair North wind.

By THE AFTERNOON, the wind had begun to fall, and the sailors went back to work. But as they paddled along the Southern shore of one long lake, there was still enough to carry some strange scent from across the water, and Tom was surprised when Sparky suddenly stood alert and trembling.

"Ahoy, ahoy, on the studderboard!" Gimlet cried. He was jumping up and down in Jenny's *Fortitude*. "Look, something is moving. It's a hairy, walking house! Look!"

Tom was the first to see what Gimlet meant, for he still had sharp, young eyes, but was not, like Jenny, preoccupied with teaching Gimlet an important lesson in Sitting Quietly and Not Swamping the Boat.

He saw a kind of huge, brown shamble on the North bank. Not a great moose or deer, but something that moved through the light trees and long grass with a strong and rolling gait.

Tom looked at his Star-Glass to be sure of his bearings, and then called out the creature's position for the Captain. Sparky seemed even more agitated now, and barked wildly. He would have leapt into the water to chase the thing if Tom hadn't put his Star-Glass away and taken his dog by the collar.

In the *Dauntless*, the Captain had been looking through his spyglass. "A bear!" he called. "A large brown bear, almost of a size with the great white bear we saw in the North."

Most of the sailors knit their brows over that, and Tom remembered how the others hardly seemed able to recall the white bear or the time with Grandfather Frost that followed; except late at night, when they were almost dreaming already.

"The great white bear that frightened all the explorers," he reminded them. "When they went on the sledges to find some better refuge. But he helped us in the end."

"And Grandfather Frost," cried the two sailors with blue hoods, for they were best at remembering it. "He helped us too."

But Sparky lunged at the side of the boat again, and Tom thought this bear might not be so kindly. It was several minutes after the thing had shambled out of sight before the little dog could regain his composure.

THAT NIGHT, when they camped under the boughs of a great fir tree, the sailors were still preoccupied with the shambling thing and pestered Bonawyn with questions.

"You saw a Bugbear today," the River-woman told them. "One of the great perils of the Wild."

And her answer only brought many other questions: "Is it a very horrible thing?" some of the sailors wanted to know, and "What does it like to eat?" asked others.

The First Mate's question was more shrewd: "What is their secret vulnerabilities?"

But the two sailors with blue hoods wanted an answer most urgently: "How best might we survive their attack?" they cried.

To all those questions, Bonawyn replied: "A Bugbear is one of the three most horrible things in the Wild, and the other two we may not name. Its hungers are limitless and manifold; it is vulnerable to nothing that walks or swims or flies; and as to surviving its attack, there are three great rules."

Tom watched all the sailors bend forward, for the timid (most of them, though especially the two sailors with blue hoods) were already concerned, while the brave (a few, most audibly Jenny) wanted to be Ready in Case, and

Believed that Fortune Favours the Prepared. Tom didn't know which group he should be numbered among, but he had his notebook in hand. The Bugbears were a topic that should be included in his father's Great Work.

Bonawyn looked at them all, and pulled thoughtfully on her pipe, for she enjoyed an audience, and liked to take her time on such occasions.

"The First Rule," Bonawyn said at last, "is *Do Not Run From a Bugbear.* For a Bugbear is faster than a racehorse, and believes that anything afraid of being eaten must therefore be good to eat."

"I knew it would involved being eaten," said one of the sailors with a blue hood. "And being afraid," said the other. "I knew it would involve that too."

"The Second Rule," Bonawyn continued, "is *Do Not Strike or Hit a Bugbear,* even if it is about to eat you, for that will only inflame its passions, and suggest it should devour you at once, and without further malarkey."

"Does they respond to flattery, or pleas for clemency, mentions of loved ones or children, and so forth?" asked the First Mate.

"Never," said Bonawyn. "Don't forget, they are wild beasts."

"Is it safest to play dead, then?" asked the Captain. "And hope that it grows bored and uninterested in the contest?"

"Not at all," Bonawyn said. "And in fact the Third Rule is, *Do Not Pretend to Be Dead,* for that will only prompt it to swallow you directly, as a Bugbear prefers its dinner fresh."

Then the crew of the *Volantix* counted over the Three Rules for Being Attacked by Bugbears that Bonawyn had described. After a moment they looked up.

"But," said the Bosun, and he looked down at the three big fingers he had used to count off the rules, just to be sure. "But all three rules for surviving an attack are simply ways not to be killed and eaten *at once.*"

Bonawyn nodded. "But what are the ways to not get et at all?" the First Mate demanded. "For that would be more to our purpose."

"If you are not near a Bugbear when it is hungry," Bonawyn said, "then you will not get eaten."

To Tom it seemed that after all the talk of Bugbears, the night became deeper somehow; darker and more strange. The full moon had withered and gone since they left the beaver-fens, and the light from their fire seemed to be swallowed by the boughs of fir overhead, and the crowding forest. In the blackness beyond, or hidden somewhere on the other shore, anything might be hiding.

At the Captain's request, Bonawyn got out her own fiddle that night, and distracted the sailors from their dark considerations. She tried to teach them a particularly long and lively paddling tune of her own composition, which gave Tom and Jenny a chance to talk privately.

As Bonawyn began her twelfth verse (it concerned the

River-woman's particular prowess at knife-throwing) Jenny sighed extravagantly.

"I have supplied a name for this tune," she said to Tom. "For it lacks nothing else save brevity. I would call it: 'Bonawyn, her tedious, several, and unlikely degrees of excellence.' Note, however, that she remains foxed by the proper use of a sail. And when I made some reference to Ola Olagovna, the great privateer of the North, she denied any knowledge of the name!"

Tom nodded, as if he also believed that was a serious deficiency. "Did she know Maxim Tortuca?" he asked, carefully.

Jenny stared at him, for of course the explorer Tortuca was her particular hero. "Bonawyn may be proud, and uncouth from having been raised on the river," Jenny said. "And she might disdain letters, and have no scientific understanding of wind and tide – but it would be an insult to doubt she had heard of Tortuca."

"She is admirable in many ways," Tom agreed. "Appealing – even fascinating in her accomplishments, and her general dash. But she holds some things close."

"Like the character of the beaver-fens," Jenny said. "But she repented of that, and we must not hold a grudge. Certainly not when she is so –" she paused to remember Tom's words. "So, 'admirable, appealing, and even fascinating in her accomplishments and general dash.'"

Tom nodded, oblivious to any satire. "But she holds back small things too," he said. "Consider her buskins, her fine leather stockings."

"Those I am jealous of," said Jenny. "For they are made most neatly and decorated by beads and quills both, and moreover –"

"Moreover, they never wear out," Tom said. "She guards some secret there, for I never see her mending them."

Jenny gave him a conspiring look and leaned in close to speak more privately. "Indeed, she almost discovered their secret to me yesterday while we bathed. For when she pulled her buskins off, there was a small hole appearing on the heel of her right foot."

"Despite her gentle steps," Tom said.

Jenny nodded. "And because she is vain of those stockings, I made a joke, and said, 'It must be worn out from so much excellence.' But Bonawyn only shrugged and said, 'The morrow will mend it.' Now what might that mean?"

"She stood her buskins empty outside your tent last night," said Tom.

"So I've seen her do before," Jenny told him. "But the hole was still there this morning, and note how happy she was to follow the lake all day and not make a carry."

"Let us see how the buskins fare tonight," Tom said.

THAT NIGHT, after Bonawyn and Jenny had retired to the tent they shared, and nearly the whole camp began to sleep, Tom took Sparky out for a walk.

Now, as they walked softly into the edge of the forest, under the arches of great fir trees, the dark was thick around them. Here and there Tom saw a star show through the blackness woven by the branches, brave and bright and lonely. Otherwise the small watch fire was the only bright mark in all the wide night.

Even after Sparky found which trees were best to mark, they stayed in the forest-shadow for a long time, until Tom saw Bonawyn come out of her tent. She had a lantern to do her business by, and the flame was turned down very low, but in that darkness the light seemed almost brilliant.

The River-woman carefully spread a cloth on the ground beside her leather stockings, and laid a few small things on it. A sack of rice, Tom thought, and something else that might be a pot of jam. Then she covered those with one side of the cloth, put her lantern out, and slipped back inside.

It was a queer thing to keep so private, Tom thought, but nothing else transpired for a long time. At last he led Sparky quietly back to bed.

The next morning, when Bonawyn rushed them into their boats as usual, Tom nudged Jenny. For today the River-woman splashed in the water without care for any hole in her buskins. In fact, they looked better than ever.

Even the beads seemed new and bright.

"Make yourselves spruce today," Bonawyn called. "For we will come to a cabin that my people sometimes use. There we might hear word of the Bugbear."

"And you doesn't want us to embarrass you," said the First Mate.

"Just so," said Bonawyn. "For when I say you Strangers have done well in the Wild, they are like to think me eccentric."

Towards the end of the day, they came to a sharp bend in the river, and Bonawyn had them paddle most smartly towards a sandy bank. She twirled her paddle as they arrived, and made a great yell, but no Riverfolk came to meet them.

Then Bonawyn and the Captain led them up a stony path through the trees.

"I feel nervous, somehow," Tom told Jenny. "For we haven't met any other people since the Mill House."

"You fail to maintain your proper self-regard," Jenny said. "Like Bonawyn, you fail to consider perhaps that these Riverfolk should be over-awed, impressed, or made otherwise insecure by the fact of our wide travels and several noted accomplishments."

"Oak-biter was not impressed," Gimlet said.

"Be quiet," Jenny explained. "And straighten your hat."

"They will be impressed by the Captain, at least," said Tom. "For he is a man of many parts."

But when the trail opened onto a clearing, all the sailors fell silent. For there was no cabin in the clearing, but its logs lay broken and scattered like spillikins. If Riverfolk had been there, they had left no sign.

For a moment Bonawyn looked over the ground. Then

she nodded grimly at the Captain, as if they needed no words on this matter.

In that still moment, the Captain didn't need to raise his voice. "The Bugbear," was all he said.

Then the First Mate did yell. "Hurry!" he roared. "Back on the water! All in good order now, but hurry for your lives!"

Even when the dark came over the Wild, Bonawyn did not let them stop that night, but drove them on, trusting to the stars and what they could see by lantern-light.

As they paddled, the sailors felt the dark shapes of the forest closing in. To Tom, the shadows from the shore seemed more troubling than they had the night before when he had crouched among them. "Ghosts!" he heard one of the sailors with blue hoods whisper behind him in the curach. "Shades!" whispered the other. "Shades and un-named things creeping in the forest."

The night was well along before they came to a small lake. In the still and moonless dark, the water was black and glossy. Tom looked down, and for a moment his head spun.

For he was sleepy with the hour, and bone-weary, and suddenly it seemed to him that his curach was not moving beneath the spray of stars, but among them.

Then he wondered if the Queen of the Hall of the Stars herself was watching their progress –

"Tom!" called the Bosun from the stern. "Are you all right?"

Tom shook himself and dug his paddle back in the water. "I'm fine," he said. "Only the stars are dazzling."

At last Bonawyn let them stop at a small island of bare, smooth stone. There they slept fitfully, from the hard ground and the idea that a Bugbear was hunting.

Tom and Sparky woke early the next morning, shivering from their cold, stone bed. Outside, a mist still lay thickly over the lake, and it wasn't until after Tom had taken Sparky for a walk that he saw the pair of tall buskins that stood outside their tent.

Bonawyn was the only other one up so soon. "Where have these come from?" Tom asked her. "Who made them and set them here?"

The River-woman shrugged, and for a moment she only smoked her pipe. Then she said, "I think they are yours if you want them."

Tom looked over the buskins. They were as fine as the ones Bonawyn wore; decorated with lines of beads and porcupine quills. Tom pulled them on, and found they fit him exactly.

By now Jenny had followed Bonawyn from their tent. She looked at Tom standing in his new buskins. "What strange adventure is this?" Jenny asked. "Has the Wild itself given you this present? And why only you, rather than to those ranked Ensign generally?" Then she added, more generously, "But they are fine boots, Tom, and suit you well."

It wasn't until they stopped for breakfast, hours later, that Tom found what his new boots had cost him. "My Star-Glass is gone!" he exclaimed. Then Tom could hardly keep from weeping. "I'm sorry," he said to the Captain. "For that was the finest gift I have ever been given."

"Perhaps you only left it behind on the rocky island," Jenny said. She looked at the Captain. "That chance is worth pursuing."

"I am grieved as much as Tom," the Captain said, and then he looked at Bonawyn. "But I think he has traded it unknowingly."

"The Wild gives no presents," the River-woman said. "But always drives hard bargains."

Tom stared at her, haggard with loss. "The Wild has cost me a treasure," he said. "And it cost the Carpenter his life. I scorn its gifts."

Then he began tugging at his buskins, meaning to cast them in the water, but the Captain put out his hand to stop him.

"That was a hard trade," he said. "The Star-Glass for leather-stocking boots. But to discard these fine things would be scorn indeed. We must learn to live with whatever spirit moves this Wild, and so come to make better bargains."

Chapter Ten:
NOISES IN THE DARK

– curly black hair – the Shining Water – a three-day storm – a salubrious vomit – wishes – a bad dream – alone forever – the waterfall –

NOW THE EXPEDITION PRESSED ON, FASTER through the deep and shadowed Wild. For the height of summer had passed, and the first sliver of the moon was in the sky. The Captain meant to meet Ahgeneh at the great falls of Meeltach Aws by the time it was full, and that was still far ahead of them.

All along, they thought they sensed the Bugbear's heavy following steps. "It will be in no hurry," Bonawyn said, in a way that provided no reassurance. "For it has scented pleasure; and as long as it can follow us, knows it can dine at leisure."

Here and there the deep forest green was already spotted with the yellow of the Fall to come.

"Like the first grey hairs," the First Mate explained to Gimlet as they paddled along in Jenny's *Fortitude*. "What a strong sailor acquires to claim respect, while still hale and hearty."

"All your hairs are grey," said Gimlet. "Even the ones in your nose."

"Are they?" the First Mate asked. Then he called forward to Jenny. "The boy says all my hairs are grey. When did that happen?"

"Father," Jenny called back, "all your hairs were grey before I met you. All your hairs were grey before the boy was born. Before I was born or Tom either." As Jenny warmed to her theme, the First Mate pretended to be astonished, for Gimlet's sake. "No man or woman can remember the sight of a black hair on your head," Jenny told the First Mate. "Not a long-lived whale, or the oldest sea-turtle.

"Was it before the Elves left, father, that you had black hair?" Jenny continued. "Was it before the stars were set in the sky?"

"Why, I doesn't know," the First Mate said, thoughtfully. "I suppose I'm so old I can't remember."

"You are not too old to remember," Gimlet told him. "You are only too old to like to think of it."

The First Mate laughed. "I doesn't mind my age," he said. "But you miss the things what get lost along the way; things that matter more than a fine head of curly black hair.

"Although it was the very kind of hair the Captain still has," he added. "The kind what womenfolk most like to run their fingers through. The kind what most befits a sailor."

Gimlet looked back at the First Mate, who seemed to have grown foolish in his old age. "I would rather buy a comb," he said. "And not have women always fiddling and bothering me about my hair."

Eventually the river curled down to the South-West, and brought them to a wide bright lake: "Ishca Lunrach," Bonawyn called it; "The Shining Water."

For a few days, the sailors made good time, coursing over the clear, green water, West for the great falls, more confident every day.

But perhaps they began to take the friendship of Gee Scradach, the Old Woman of the Winds, for granted, and were not humble enough, and did not scatter enough fine baking in the water. For one day a sudden storm arrived.

With great work, they brought their boats safely to shore, and then they watched as the storm blew the waves into huge, thundering breakers. Waves too great for any curach to survive; waves so high they would have troubled even the stout *Volantix*.

THE STORM BLEW FOR THREE DAYS. The sky stayed dark and grey all that time, and the wind tossed the lake about, bent the trees almost flat, pulled birds off their courses.

All the while the sailors stayed in their shelter, waiting out the storm philosophically, as they had long practise in doing – happy not to be on the lake in that terrible water.

For a while Gimlet thought he was the only one who was bored, and then he saw the Captain was restless too. In fact, the Captain paced like a cat, Gimlet thought, counting out the days left before the full moon over and over as he walked.

Then even as the wind still blew, the Captain had long conferences with Bonawyn, the First Mate, and the two Ensigns, trying to work out how quickly they would be able to travel once the storm had passed.

"We could paddle in shifts," the Captain proposed, "and keep on, day and night."

"We can try," said Tom.

"The Riverfolk do so sometimes," Bonawyn said. "But after two days and two nights, strength fails, and paddlers go faster for having more rest."

"We can rig our curachs with a skill exceeding that of any Riverfolk," Jenny pointed out. "And so might have nights that need but little effort, if the wind favours us."

"For a while I thought you sea-sailors must be the children of the Old Woman of the Winds," Bonawyn said. "But if Gee Scradach still loved you, there would not be this storm. Perhaps she does not approve of your expedition after all."

"We might do many things," the First Mate told his Captain at last. "And you know this crew will work until the pips squeak. But we can't do none of it until we waits out the storm."

On the third night, the storm began to weaken, and when the morning broke clear at last, none of the sailors needed to be harried awake.

But the storm had dragged up the long-hidden secrets

of the lake and cast them on shore. It was littered with dead things: weeds and fish and birds, and broken wood, and strange, waxy stones.

Gimlet picked his way among the waste with an unusual daintiness. "I think the lake was sick from swallowing these things, so threw them up," he said.

The First Mate looked along the shore, considering. "You may become a philosopher yet," he said. "Maybe the storm was only the convulsions needed to spew these things out. A sort of salubrious vomit."

Gimlet made a face. "That's a nice word," he said. "Salubrious vomit. The smell makes me want to have a salubrious vomit too."

AFTER A FEW DAYS of fine sailing, they came to the mouth of a river that poured down from the North, and it was time to leave the shining water of Ishca Lunrach.

They camped on a warm, sandy shore that night, where they could enjoy looking South-West, across the wide, bright lake, and listen to the steady wash of waves.

The silvery moon was only rising as the cloudless sky grew dark, and the sailors could see the changing Wizard Star bright and low across the water. But other stars were falling that night, shooting out across the Eastern sky, and the sailors began making wishes upon them: wishes for the safety of those left at home; wishes for good weather; for luck at darts; for a safe journey and a happy ending.

Gimlet wished for a dessert of berry hubbub, which made Cookie sigh, for of course that was a wish he would have to make come true.

They wished faster and faster, until they gave up, for the stars seemed to fall from the sky without number that night, twinkling and burning and fizzling out into tiny showers.

"There are so many stars I could have wished for two berry hubbubs," Gimlet told Jenny. "But I will not be greedy."

"A fine position," Jenny said. "Which reveals either a new maturity or one you have purposely kept concealed."

"If I had shown it before," Gimlet pointed out, "I couldn't have wished for berry hubbub."

"Then I am glad you have not grown up sooner," said Tom. "For I want some too."

"What was your very mature wish?" Gimlet asked Jenny.

"It was not a wish to make, but only a wish I had," she said. "For I was after remembering how Chips had loved stars, and wished that he could have seen this too. For this is the season for falling stars, but last year, in the Old Sea, the moon was bright, and we were, besides, otherwise engaged."

So they all watched the falling stars, and at Jenny's suggestion, they broke out some grog and toasted the Carpenter's memory. Then they toasted the Captain; and Bonawyn; and Oak-Biter the Beaver-Prince; and then their three curachs by name. Then they were carried away, and began to toast one another, and the tall rocks and trees, and even Gee Scradach, the Old Woman of the Winds.

For once Jenny didn't seem to worry about getting Gimlet to bed, and so he only curled up in his blanket and lay awake for a long time, enjoying the happy talk of the sailors all around him. Gradually the older sailors, and the Ensigns, and then all the rest of the crew drifted away to their beds.

At last only Bonawyn and the Captain were left, and Gimlet watched through half-closed eyes as they talked quietly by the fire. She shoved two driftwood logs together so they popped and sparked, but really, compared to the shooting stars, it was nothing at all. They sat without talking for a long time; and Gimlet wondered what it would be like to have the Captain for a father, or Bonawyn for a mother. Would she make him comb his hair, as Jenny did?

He hadn't intended to fall asleep, but suddenly Gimlet realized that the Captain sat alone now, and smoked his pipe in silence. Half-asleep, half-awake, he watched the Captain tug at his greying beard, then run his fingers through his dark and curly hair, watched a great, black shadow appear from the edge of the woods.

It moved tenderly behind the Captain, quietly around the fire. The waves were beating steadily, there at the shore of wide Ishca Lunrach, and Gimlet heard no sound as the dark shape stopped, and sniffed with its great, flat snout at the upturned curachs, at the sailors who slept on the ground.

It was huge, Gimlet saw. It was still on all fours, but it was as tall as the grown sailors; as tall as the Bosun, even. Gimlet didn't know if he were dreaming or if the Bugbear had come at last. What a patient hunter it was, he thought, to track after the swift curachs and his dreams all these days.

Gimlet wanted to make a noise, but somehow he couldn't. What if this thing heard him? But surely if this wasn't a dream, Sparky would be barking. Sparky wasn't very brave, Gimlet knew, but he did his duty as a dog, and dogs barked at bears. He wouldn't just lie there, quietly.

Now the Bugbear was behind the Captain.

Surely the Captain must feel its breath upon his neck, Gimlet thought.

Then for the first time, the Captain looked at Gimlet, and saw he was awake; and he must have understood something from the look in the boy's eyes, for he set his pipe down very gently. And gently Gimlet nodded at him.

The Captain slowly bent closer to the fire.

Slowly, slowly, Gimlet thought, *everything has turned to slowly.*

Then the Bugbear huffed and the Captain turned and swung one end of a burning log up into the bear's face. Flames and sparks broke over the huge, flat snout, and the bear made one horrible, astonished bark. And then it reared up.

Now the bear was terrible beyond measure.

The Captain showed a pistol in his right hand; but it looked like a pop-gun, like a little toy, and yet the Captain stepped closer. He stepped closer even though the Bugbear stood twice as tall, and now Gimlet thought he would finally scream, for the Captain was going to die. Maybe Gimlet did scream, but he heard only the roar of the Bugbear and then a muffled little *crack!*

The Bugbear knocked the Captain down with one paw, as if it were no trouble at all. His body fell in a heap, limp and bloody.

"Help!" Gimlet screamed at last. "Help!"

The Bugbear turned to look at Gimlet, and its cold dark eyes were as pitiless as the wind. It would eat him now, Gimlet knew.

The boy would have screamed again, but suddenly the bear took one long, lurching step towards him. Then all at once the Bugbear toppled, like some felled tree, and crashed down against the fire.

AFTER THE BEAR FELL, everything turned quick again. There were lights everywhere; flames, and the lanterns of the sailors, and all around Gimlet people ran and shouted. But he could only see the cold eyes of the Bugbear. Amidst all the confusion, Gimlet felt alone and afraid, and so he crawled away and hid under one of the curachs, and he closed his eyes and thought of being in Oak-Biter's lodge, of the quiet and the warm, musky smell.

The lodge was safe, Gimlet knew; nothing could come there without Oak-Biter's leave, and he thought of that over and over: that the lodge was safe, until he fell into some awful kind of sleep.

WHEN GIMLET WOKE AT LAST, he was somewhere else; he was sitting in a tent, and there were blankets piled up all around him, and he gasped for a moment, because he thought he was still alone. But then he saw Jenny sitting there beside him, and he realized that Sparky was with her, and he wondered how much he had dreamt.

"Are we in the Old Sea?" Gimlet asked. "I turned into a goat, and they were going to eat me."

"No one is going to be eaten," said Jenny. "You are in the Wild of the Vastlands, and there have been no horns on your head for a year less two weeks."

Gimlet sat up slowly, recollecting himself. "But the Captain," he said. "The bear..." And then he started shaking.

"Shush, shush," Jenny said, as her Godmother used to say to her. "Don't. The Captain is fine," she said, "or will be fine."

She doesn't even know the Captain is dead, Gimlet thought. He shook his head. "The bear," he said. "The bear with the flat face –" And then Gimlet couldn't help himself, but he shook more and made a terrible kind of gasping sob. He tried to stop, but couldn't; he only wept and trembled helplessly.

For a moment Jenny watched him, unable to think what to do, and then she left him alone with Sparky.

Gimlet clutched at the dog.

It wouldn't stop until everyone had left him alone, he thought. His parents, long before he could remember, and then his Grandmother. And then Oak-Biter had sent him away, and then the Captain was gone, and now even Jenny had left, and would not bother him about his hair ever again.

He held Sparky tighter, and the dog licked his nose, but Gimlet didn't notice, for he was still under the spell of the Bugbear's eyes. He was having a kind of nightmare, one he could not escape by waking.

Gimlet wondered if he was the only one left in the world now. Perhaps the Bugbear had eaten everyone, had eaten the world itself, and only the little canvas tent was left.

He looked at the flap of the tent. He could open it, of course, but what if he looked out and saw no one?

What if he saw nothing, nothing at all, and he would be alone forever?

SUDDENLY GIMLET was in a different dream, for of course Jenny had only left him to fetch the First Mate; and now Jenny and Sparky were back, and the old sailor was lifting him up. The First Mate carried him out into the bright day, with Jenny and Sparky following.

They were still by the shore of Ishca Lunrach, Gimlet saw, and all the crew of the *Volantix* was there: the two timid sailors with blue hoods, Cookie, and the Bosun. And then the First Mate carried him into the big tent, and Tom and Bonawyn were there.

They were tending to the Captain.

"But the bear –" Gimlet said, and he felt as though he weren't in his right mind. He started crying again. "The Bugbear, the bear, it killed you."

"The bear," repeated the Captain, and if he said it a little weakly, Gimlet didn't notice. "The bear you warned me of. It hurt me, Gimlet, but I am alive. Look," he said, "look at the cuts on my face, and see how the First Mate has stitched my scalp. I am hurt, but not dead. Take my hand and you will see. Take my hand."

The Captain spoke softly, but he was so pale, and the wounds on his head so terrible that Gimlet still doubted whether he was alive. So Jenny took Gimlet by the hand then, and held the Captain's hand with the other. Gimlet could feel that *she* was alive, at least, and so he edged towards the Captain. The Captain's hand was rough and hard, but Gimlet felt how it was warm too, and only then did his dreaming begin to drop away.

"Why did the bear fall?" Gimlet whispered. "Is it still here?"

Bonawyn spoke then. "The Bugbear fell because your Captain fired his pistol into its heart," she said. "He killed it himself, which is the work of a hero. So the bear is gone, except that we will dine on it as steaks and stews, and your Captain will have the greatest bearskin cloak; a cloak that by itself would be the fame of a lesser man."

Then Jenny took Gimlet back to the little tent, and Tom sent Sparky along to keep him company.

Now Gimlet could hear the sounds of the sailors about the tent, still talking about the bear, about whose beds its tracks had come closest to; about the Captain's brave shot; about the fine, great cloak it would make.

He could hear the waves of Ishca Lunrach still rolling against the shore; and the next time when he woke, he knew he was in the real world again. He was with the sailors, who were his friends, and with Sparky.

He was with Tom and Jenny, and they had lost parents too. None of them were alone in the Wild, Gimlet thought; for they were Wards of the Sea together.

TWO MORNINGS LATER, the Captain was well enough to move again, and they began their journey up-river.

They paddled hard for two days, then early on the third day, Gimlet heard a sort of broad, terrible hiss.

"What is it?" he asked.

"My ears is too old," the First Mate said. "I doesn't hear it."

But Jenny said, "It is the first faint hint of the roar of the waterfall. We will be at Meeltach Aws, the Great Falls, tonight. We will be in time for the First Moon of Autumn after all."

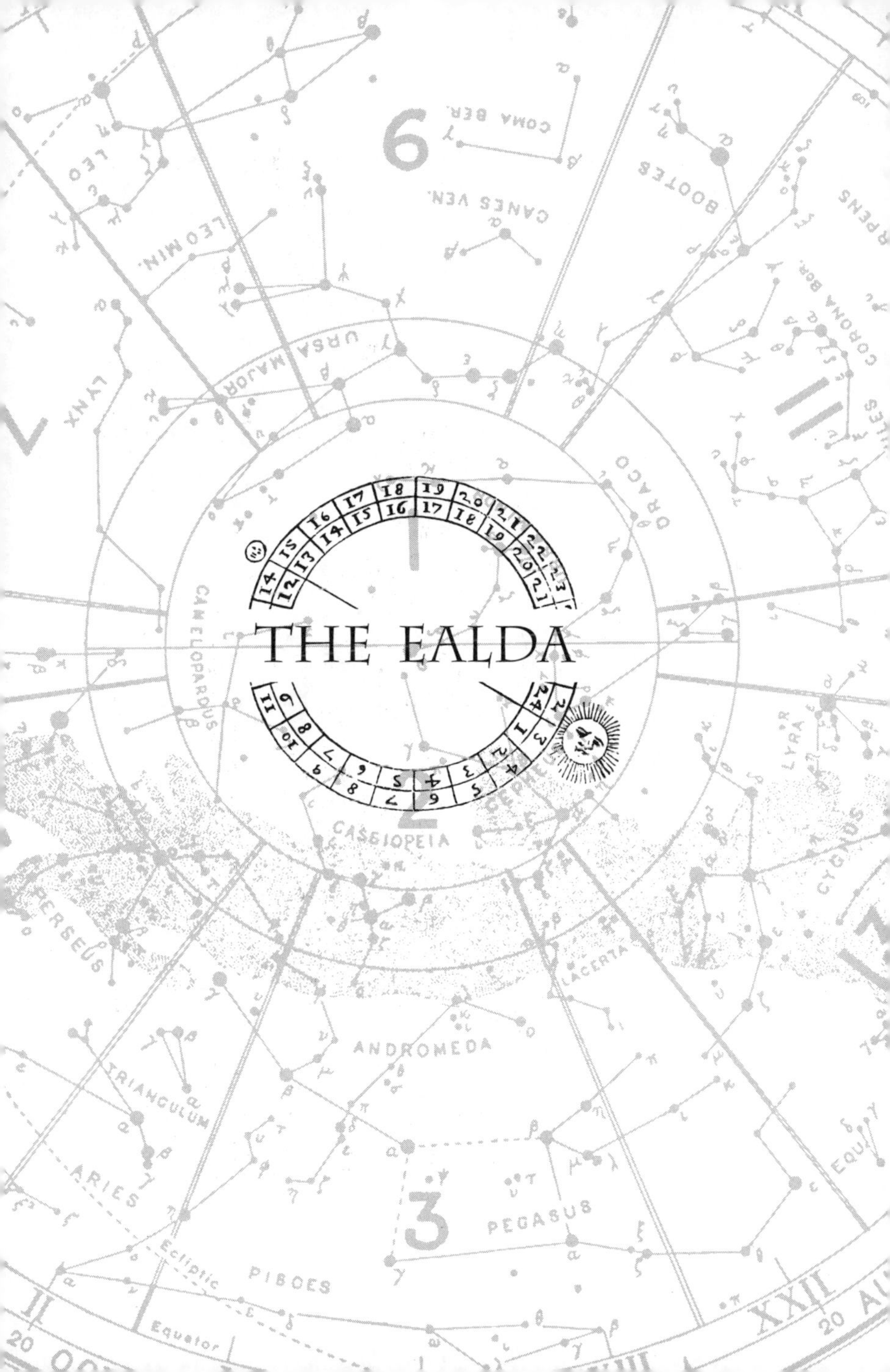

THE EALDA

It was a hard carry

Chapter Eleven:
THE COUNCIL UNDER THE MOON

– a vast silence – entirely lost – kinds of cats
– Gimlet moonstruck – a brave figure
– very nearly respectable
– the greatest rubbaboo in the world –

FROM THE WIDE, SWIRLING WATER AT THE BOTTOM of Meeltach Aws, up the twisting path to the top of the falls was an hour's climb. The spray of falling water shone in the newly risen moon; the misty air glimmered. It was the First Moon of Autumn, and to the sailors with an eye for romance (nearly all of them), they seemed to breathe in silver.

It was a hard carry, though. "Which great exertion will *not* be rewarded at the end," Jenny said to Tom as they hiked along. "Except we will be paid in kind; more work for work. For we will have to climb this steep road a second time, and a third after that before we are done."

Jenny had to speak loudly, over the roar of the great cascade of water. "A kind of vast silence," she described it to Tom, "which drowns out all else, without contributing particular notes of its own. As though the Wild itself rebukes me for too much speech, and attempts to shush me with the water's thunder."

She said a great many other things too as they climbed, but Tom said little back.

After a long while they came to a shelf of rock and stopped to rest. Sparky investigated trees – in case he might scent that another dog, or a bear, or any new strange, strong-smelling thing had been nearby.

"You are quiet tonight," Jenny said. And then a new thought struck her: "Is it that the flow of my speech has stunned, overwhelmed, or otherwise silenced you?"

Tom shook his head slowly. "Tonight I am quiet because I am labouring up this hill with two packs on my back, like the full-grown sailors at last," he said. Then after a moment he added. "But other times the flow of your speech does indeed stun, overwhelm, or –" Here Tom paused for breath. "– Or otherwise silence me. But that is only your nature," Tom said. "You have always talked circles around me – or almost anyone."

Jenny thought it over a while. "Yet I wouldn't talk so much except I have such a quantity of thoughts worth speaking."

They began lifting their packs. "You are used to living and working by yourself," Tom said. "Probably you store up talk, and so it tumbles out quickly in company."

"I hope I do not talk more than my share," Jenny said, earnestly.

"Your share is very large," Tom said. "So that is unlikely."

THEY MADE THEIR CAMP near the top of the falls, among the moon-shadows of a stand of tamarack, that grew green and lush in the damp.

After such a hard carry, after such a long time in the Wild, the sailors took their time over it, and Gimlet grew bored, as he had at the Mill House.

So he searched out a good high place where he could look down on the mighty falls. There Gimlet listened to that wide roar, watched the spills and jets in all their moonlit glory, and breathed in the silver mist, until he became entirely moonstruck. When he left, he gave no thought to his path, but only wandered off into the woods.

As he moved through the wide forest space, the boy would gaze up at the stars again, or follow some trail of moonlight through the shadows. Long before he knew it, he was entirely lost.

"WELL PADDLED, well sailed, well carried, well fought," the Captain told them all. "For we have crossed the Wild against all difficulties – our own ignorance chief among them."

"Yes, it were well done," the First Mate said, loudly, so they all would hear. "As mighty a thing as any voyage on the sea ever was." But then he lowered his voice, and said to the Captain. "*If* the Shawnachan and all them kinds of folk was right. *If* this Ahgeneh hasn't changed his plans, and *if* his people is going to gather here."

The Ealda

"It was well done anyway," Jenny said. "For look what we have explored. And we can always find some Homely Country ourselves, if there is some empty land to West of here."

"Ahgeneh will come," the Captain said. "Sign and omen, *rede* and star, and the advice of the Wise have sent us here, where no Strangers have ever come before, to this fine and majestic place, so deep in the Vastlands. This is the path that fate has given us. Ahgeneh will come."

"Ahgeneh will come," Bonawyn said. "My people know him. And he is the Marshal of all this Land." She turned to Jenny, "So you do need him if you are to find some empty place to live. But I worry this is a poor place to meet, for we count it bad luck to hear the waterfall's hiss, where projects begun are most like to miss."

"Is that some old, wise rhyme based on the Riverfolk's respect for the danger of the falls?" Jenny asked. "Or did you devise it for the occasion, because you are a worry-wart?"

"All my rhymes are wise," Bonawyn told her. "But that is the hiss of the hungry cat we name Pishkeen Mawr. Pishkeen Mawr is not a friendly cat," she pointed out, for the benefit of the two sailors with blue hoods. "But a cat who likes water – itself a thing so strange it is terrible."

"A cat named Pawlikins lives with my Godmother," Jenny said. "And Pawlikins only dislikes water by surprise. And when morally prepared, will sit on the edge of my fishing dory and scoop the minnow from the water himself."

The Ealda

Bonawyn gave Jenny a long look then. "When I speak of Pishkeen Mawr, understand that I discuss a terrible feline spirit, and not the gentle house pet of your old granny."

Then Jenny stood, and stared up into Bonawyn's eyes. "Understand when I speak of Pawlikins I am neither discussing a pet nor anything gentle," she said, rather dangerously. "Rather, he is a wise and crafty beast of high standing. And understand, further, that my Godmother is not to be referred to as an old granny, but is rather the awful Wise Woman of the Woods Nearby, and as such one of the great and powerful personages of our home."

"Now, now," said the First Mate. "Let's keep the talk civil and pleasant-like, after our long and triumphant trip."

"Well said," the Captain told him. "And whether it is good luck or bad, this is where we will wait to meet Ahgeneh."

"Where is Gimlet?" Tom asked.

AND THAT WAS WHAT GIMLET himself was wondering, in the wide pinewood.

"I am moonstruck," he said aloud. "I am bewildered. I am alone again."

Then he heard a drum beating through the moon shadows in the darkness. Not some distant drum, such as Bonawyn had told them not to follow when they were deep in the Wild, but something near and regular. It was like his own heartbeat, Gimlet thought; and as the sound came nearer, his heart beat harder and louder, just like the drum.

Then it was too loud, too close, and Gimlet began to run through the pinewood's wide avenues. As he ran, the shadows seemed to close in and darken, and when he looked up, he saw a cloud covered the moon – pearl-bright and obscure.

That's when he tripped over a root and fell across the soft forest floor. And the drumming stopped. "I hate the moon," he thought.

When he peeked up under his arm, some tall figure was bent over him. It had deep stripes on its face, red and white. "You caught me," Gimlet said.

"Where is Gimlet?" Tom had asked, and when he did, Jenny felt her heart sink.

"That tiresome imp," she said. For somehow, more than a year, and half the world away from first meeting him, the boy was still her problem.

"Well," the Captain said. "Where is he? Who saw him last?"

"He's run off before," the First Mate said. "Usually we finds him according the same principle."

"What would be *the very most and particularly foolish thing to do?"* Jenny explained.

"In this place?" said Bonawyn. "To be tempted by Pishkeen Mawr."

With that, Jenny lost her temper. "Do you have any *practical* advice?" she demanded. "Or will you rather utter only dire words about the feline terrors of Pishkeen Mawr for the whole long rest of this Expedition?"

The River-woman gave Jenny a cool look, but what answer she might have made no one knew, for somewhere off to the South-West, they began to hear a drum beating light and steady, at a walking pace, coming closer. The Captain was on his feet at once, but Bonawyn raised her hand.

"It is the council drum," she said. "A messenger comes from Ahgeneh."

"At last," the Captain said. "At last. Mark this moment, Tom, for it might belong in your father's Great Work."

"Yes, sir," Tom said. "But Gimlet is still missing."

Jenny nodded. "We must still organize parties for the search. Assign them quadrants, name the various signals for possible sightings, fresh tracks, and so forth."

But the drumbeat grew still louder, and before Jenny's plans could get much farther, a young man with a swagger in his step emerged from the trees and stood in the fire-light.

He was one of the Ealda, Jenny could see at once: dark and black-haired, and his jacket was decorated with the finery of the Wild: beads, and porcupine quills, and smooth antler buttons. His face was painted with red and white stripes, just as they had seen the Shawnachan wear at the Mill House so long before.

"What a brave figure he cuts," Jenny whispered to Tom. Then, forgetting their recent quarrel, she leaned in close to Bonawyn. "Is this some prince of their people?"

Bonawyn shook her head, pulled her own dark hair back into a tighter knot, and straightened her plumed hat. "The Ealda have no princes, except those who are revealed by their own character," she said.

The visitor approached slowly, and with a great show of ease, still striking his drum with a flourish at every step. Gimlet walked behind him, also in time to the beat.

The First Mate uttered some long oath at the sight of the boy, but the visitor affected not to notice their surprise. He looked them all over carefully: the sailors and the Ensigns, and Bonawyn. He paused to admire the feathers in their caps, their swords and muskets, even the First Mate's peg leg. Then, with a great rolling of the drum, he stopped in front of the Captain.

"I am Kitchehoar," he began, "the Herald of Ahgeneh, Marshal of the Ealda. Surely you are the Stranger whom Ahgeneh has seen in his dreams?"

The Captain nodded. "Cousin," he began, and Jenny marked how the Captain called the younger man cousin, as though they were the same age. "Cousin, we have come far to meet Ahgeneh. From across the Ocean, even. And survived many dangers." Then, with what Jenny considered a fine sense of drama, the Captain stood, and shrugged the great bear cloak over his shoulders.

"Is it Bear-Killer we should call you?" the Herald asked in amazement. He turned to Gimlet and reproached the boy gently: "Child, next time you meet one of the Ealda by moonlight, isn't that the very kind of thing you should boast of?"

"I don't like to remember it," said Gimlet.

Kitchehoar stepped forward and felt the cloak, and gently touched the wounds on the Captain's face. Then he laughed approvingly. "Well-met in moonlight, Bear-Killer!"

Then as the members of the Expedition stared at the Ealda in turn, Kitchehoar glanced again at Tom's buskins. "Isn't this a fellow on good terms with the Tinkers?" he asked.

Tom remembered to address the Ealda with the dignity of an older man as well: "Uncle, I don't know the Tinkers. But the boots cost me more than I can name."

Kitchehoar looked at Bonawyn then, as if there was something they both understood. "Now Loon-Daughter, you should have warned the boy about the Tinkers' bargains."

"Uncle, it was none of my doing," said Bonawyn. "Only the boy admired my boots out loud." Then she added a few words in the tongue of the Ealda that only Kitchehoar could understand.

The Herald nodded. "That was foolish, true enough," he said. "That's as good as a contract to a Tinker."

Jenny saw that Tom flushed then, for the boots were still a sore spot with him. And Kitchehoar's words had given her a dozen questions about these Tinkers too. But the Captain gave them a warning look, and they stayed silent.

"Thank you for finding the boy," he told Kitchehoar. "Was he very lost?"

"I wasn't lost," Gimlet said. "I found Kitchehoar in the forest."

"He thought he was," the Herald said. "But he has come here, after all, and Ahgeneh my father has dreamt of him too – for Ahgeneh is a Beaver-Son as well."

"I want to meet Ahgeneh," Gimlet said. "Is he nice? Is he a pleasant old gentleman?"

Kitchehoar leaned close and whispered, loudly. "Now I could say he was a terrible old grump, who enjoys frightening children," he said, "and you wouldn't know better. But really he's my father, after all, and has always shown an impatient affection."

While Gimlet thought that over, Kitchehoar stood and looked around at them all again, turned to face the Captain. "As Herald, I pronounce you and your sailors to be the very nearly respectable folk we were expecting." he said. "So it is my honour to ask you to feast with us tomorrow as our guests; guests of the Ealda, here in the West of the Wild."

Then he paused and added, "I only add, from politeness, from concern for your being Strangers, that while presents are not required, they are always welcome."

Then Kitchehoar made a grand flourish with his drum and strode off into the shadows.

After a moment of silence, the Captain laughed. "'Very nearly respectable,'" he said. "That's as strange an invitation as I've ever received."

"Strange, yet dashing," Jenny said.

"The Ealda are mighty orators," said Bonawyn. "But few can speak so well in your tongue as in their own. Kitchehoar must have travelled as far as Mill House. It's no wonder he is their Herald. He could be almost be a River-man."

After the long, hard weeks of travel in the Wild, the prospect of a feast with the Ealda was intoxicating, and the next morning Jenny woke early, along with all the other members of the Expedition. One and all they patched their clothes, combed and tied their hair, made sure they wore their cleanest bandannas.

Then Bonawyn coached them in good manners, as the Ealda understood them.

"Begin by offering your presents," she said. "And then wait a while rather than beginning to speak all in a rush. For these Ealda here in the West of the Wild are not accustomed to Strangers, and it will take a while before they are accustomed to your pale and uncouth faces.

"Finally, share all your food freely, and don't concern yourselves about tomorrow. For the Ealda count it foolish to provide for a day which may never come."

The Captain frowned at that. “Bonawyn,” he said, “that does not sit easily with me. For worrying about tomorrow is perhaps the chief among my duties.”

Bonawyn looked at him. “You could not make your long voyages at sea without husbanding your food. But here in the Wild, life is not so certain. So if the dawn might bring doom, it is foolishness not to feast tonight. Or if the dawn will bring good luck, again it is foolishness not to feast. But if the dawn brings a pale, hungry day, well, that is your fate, and was not to be avoided in any case – or so it seems to the Ealda.”

“And what about you Riverfolk?” the First Mate asked. “For you’re neither Strangers nor Riverfolk, but somewhere in between, by that tale you told us.”

Bonawyn spat thoughtfully.

“When my father, the mighty Bawdoear, was young and strong, he worked harder than any man. And then made merry late in the night, as though the next day might never come. But now at last my father has a little farm, and hopes to end his days in comfort and peace – or so he did, before your ship arrived.

“So we think it is fine to live like the Ealda, and grow old like Strangers.”

“I shall cook the greatest rubbaboo in the World ,” said Cookie. “I shall add all our syrup and raspberries. They are in season now and we can gather as many more as we like.”

CHAPTER TWELVE:
ABOVE THE FALLS

– a parade (without fireworks) – an effort doomed to failure
– a previous claim – masters of oratory
– tedious work to the Ealda – crack! crack! crack! –

AS EVENING CAME, THEY HEARD KITCHEHOAR'S DRUM approach once more, and when the Ealda appeared, Jenny thought he looked more finely tricked-out than ever. He had more and more intricate stripes on his face, and wore a feathered band about his head.

"Children!" he cried. "Is it a feast you're going to? For aren't you all dressed up in finery!"

"You know there's a feast coming," Gimlet pointed out. "You invited us last night."

"So I did," Kitchehoar told him. "I'm remembering now. Well, follow me, then." So they did, in a great procession, walking in time to the Herald's drum. Bonawyn walked with Kitchehoar, and next came the Captain in his bear-cloak, with Gimlet behind carrying the train. Then came the Ensigns, with their jacket and cocked hats brushed clean, and then all the sailors by rank.

"Not a bad parade," the First Mate observed. "Though I always prefers 'em with fireworks if I can."

Kitchehoar led them on a trail through the wide

pinewood, West and South, away from the sound of the falls, until they came to a vast clearing. At its edge they stopped, and Bonawyn had them lay down their swords and muskets. Then they walked into a wide circle made from the lodges of the Ealda.

The lodges were tall tents made from poles and sheets of bark – Bonawyn called them *tawchs* – and in the centre was a bonfire. Around it sat the Ealda, dozens of them, men and women and children, all in their finery. But many of them stood too, as if on guard, and held bows strung and ready.

Kitchehoar ended his drumming with another great flourish, and for a moment it would have been hard to say who was shyer, the sailors or the Ealda.

But at the West end of the circle a man stood up in robes of rabbitskin, with a great crown of black feathers. "Ahgeneh," Tom whispered. "Ahgeneh, at last," Jenny said. "He is like Kitchehoar, but graver."

The old Ealda hailed them in a great, deep voice, speaking in the tongue of his people.

"Who is it come to this camp of the Ealda?" Ahgeneh called.

And Bonawyn answered him in the same tongue: "Bonawyn, a Loon-Daughter come from afar, and Strangers from farther still, from over the sea, mighty mariners, and their Captain." Jenny could tell that the River-woman paused for effect, and indicated the great bear cloak. "Their Captain, who is now called Bear-Killer."

Ahgeneh had known all this from his dreams, and from what his son had reported to him, but he nodded with satisfaction. Then he called out to all his people: "Friends have come from afar! Lay aside your weapons!"

After Ahgeneh had gestured for the Strangers to sit, he walked up to the Captain and touched the scars on his face, just as Kitchehoar had done. He brought the Captain to sit beside him and then turned to Gimlet, who still carried the train.

"Surely you're the one I've seen in dreams," he said. "In Tearnan Behowar."

"Yes," Gimlet said. He paused a moment trying to work out how he was supposed to address an Ealda so old. "Yes," he repeated. "And I wanted to stay there, in beaver-land."

The old Ealda shook his head slowly. "We'll all of us pass beyond the Cracks of the World soon enough. And usually when we don't expect."

"Uncle," the Captain said. "We have brought gifts for your people – gifts we have carried since the Shawnachan told us we would find you here, through rivers and lakes and up steep carries; guided by Bonawyn through many perils."

Then the two sailors with blue hoods came forward carrying boxes full of mirrors and small knives, axes and blankets, and whistles and tops and butterscotch candy.

Not treasures, but things that were hard to come by in the Wild, and the Ealda were greatly pleased by them. The children began at once making loud noises with their whistles. Particularly horrible noises, Jenny thought, though none of their parents tried to stop them.

But Tom pointed out that Gimlet did not try to play with the tops, or make any terrible racket. For he had been given a place of honour between Ahgeneh and Kitchehoar, as a brother in the Beaver-Clan, and for once the boy kept quiet and tried to wear his tricorne hat with dignity.

"An effort doomed to failure," Jenny observed. "Yet somehow touching and ludicrous both."

After the presents came out, most of the Strangers and the Ealda could only sit awkwardly around the fire and stare at one another, for they had no common language, and their skills at pantomime were limited. And they could only wait to hear what the council would report.

That council gathered around another fire, outside the circle of the lodges: the officers and older sailors on one side, and Ahgeneh and Kitchehoar and a few of the wisest Ealda on the other. Bonawyn sat between them, and interpreted much of what was said.

At first Ahgeneh and his people listened as the Captain and the other sailors told once more about the signs and portents that had sent them from their country, about the Expedition and their long journey through the Wild. "The Shawnachan told us you might know of some empty place, as far as the Hidden Sea," the Captain finished. "Some Homely Country we might have, there at the edge of the Wild."

But when the Captain said his last, Ahgeneh only filled his pipe and lit it with an ember from the fire. After a while he passed his pipe around to the others, and when it came back to him, he sat quietly and looked up at the stars for a long time. But no one said a word, not even Gimlet.

When Ahgeneh set down his pipe, he began merely by laying out all he had heard, stating this more clearly, Jenny thought, than the Captain had done himself, down to the smallest detail and number.

"I have never heard of Strangers that have done so well," Ahgeneh said. "No Strangers that have learned this place so hard, or accommodated themselves to its nature. None save that one, long ago, who become part of this place, who was father to the Loon-Children." He looked at the Captain closely. "Wasn't that a brave thing to try, to test the old rule against Strangers in the Vastlands? And you undertook this terrible journey because of your faith in what the Shawnachan, my cousin, told you months ago, in the Mill House-by-the-Sea, and arrived here in time to meet us at the Last Moon of Summer, the First Moon of Fall."

The Captain nodded, but did not interrupt.

"But was it that the Shawnachan did not tell you why we gathered here?"

The Captain shook his head.

"Well, and we meant to kept our reason quiet," Ahgeneh said, "because we are gathering to move our home. For you may count these Vastlands peaceful, but even here there are foes. Not all of the Ealda love one another, just as the nations of Strangers will march to battle. So there are Ealda from the hot and dusty South whom we count cruel.

"Meeltach Aws is the beginning of the Cold Lake Country. And many find it too hard to live here, except for us and our neighbours the Bone-Faces, whom we count as friends.

"But even here the land grows more crowded," Ahgeneh said, "and game is scarce more often. So in lean years we sometimes move farther North-West in the Fall, even as far as the Rockmarch, the land at the End of the Wild. And if the hunting is poor even in the Rockmarch, still it looks over the great Steppes, almost as far as the Hidden Sea, and the great hairy Buffles walk there."

The Captain leaned forward, then, and his eyes were bright, almost feverish. "By the Hidden Sea," he said. "With Buffles – the great hairy cows – nearby." Then he turned to Bonawyn. "Not a hard and barren land, such as Bawdoear suggested." And Jenny knew what hope Ahgeneh's words lit within him; that they could make the Rockmarch their Homely Country, the new home their people needed.

Ahgeneh only nodded at him and continued. "But this year we mean to stay there," he said. "And claim the last high country, the Rockmarch that borders the Steppes and the Hidden Sea, for our own. So we will not come to quarrel with our neighbours the Bone Faces, or suffer from the depredations of others still, of the Ealda from the cruel and dusty South."

FOR A MOMENT, none of the members of the Captain's Expedition believed what they heard, that Ahgeneh meant to claim the Rockmarch for his people.

Then the First Mate leapt up with a terrible oath. Kitchehoar did the same, and then the others were on their feet too: the Bosun, and Cookie, and some of the Ealda, with loud and unpleasant words. Gimlet put his arms over his head. "Ah!" he said. "Ahh!" For he was sure a fight was going to begin. And Jenny was sure there was going to be fighting too, and suddenly she found herself on her feet.

Both the Captain and Ahgeneh held up their hands then, and slowly the others seemed to recover themselves.

When they were all quiet, the Captain turned to Bonawyn and said, quietly, and fiercely: "Did you really not know this?" he asked. "Was no word of this heard in the Wild? Or have you been leading us still on a fool's errand?"

"Bad luck indeed, to meet by the waters of Meeltach Aws, where the spirit of Pishkeen Mawr hunts happiness," Bonawyn told him. "Which I have told you all along, though I came here without fear of life or limb, so that it might not be said that the Strangers were left to die alone in the Wild. But whether you or the Ealda settle in the Rockmarch, it is only bad news for my people, for that place guards the way to our hinterland, where the Riverfolk trap and trade for skins and furs.

"For the Riverfolk," she continued, "it would be best if the Strangers and the Ealda abandoned their truce and slew one another now, and let us get on with the life we know. But I have sworn oaths to Oak-Biter, and promised you. And look, despite the obstacles, I have brought you this far, farther than any Strangers have been in the Vastlands, and brought you wrapped in a robe of honour."

Then Bonawyn turned to Ahgeneh. "Grandfather," she said, "hesitate to challenge these Strangers. For they do what they say, and if they are as fools and children in the Wild, still they lack no spirit – not when it matters. Kitchehoar named him Bear-Killer, but look at his Captain's robe; look at his scars to see what a bear it was!"

Kitchehoar stood then, and such was his anger that he took his drum and broke it against his knee. "Now I'll tell *you* to hesitate to challenge *us,* the Ealda of the Cold Lake Country," he cried. "Or is it that you think we want the Rockmarch because we are afraid of the Bone Faces? Your fine, brave Captain has slain a bear –"

"A Bugbear," Bonawyn put in, calmly.

"Fair enough," Kitchehoar, said, "we don't deny him that honour. Not a wee brown bear; a Bugbear, one of the three great terrors of the Wild. Terrible beasts they are, terrible. But can you count the beasts that Ahgeneh has killed? The Great Cats that haunt your dreams, Bonawyn – Ahgeneh my father has a necklace of their teeth, and he killed them like a hunter, with knife and spear, not the far-away crack of muskets."

Then Bonawyn stood face-to-face with Kitchehoar, and balled her fists as if she meant to fight after all.

"Enough!" Ahgeneh shouted, and the voice of the Marshal of the Ealda rolled across the darkness, so that even the music and dancing stopped. "The Captain of these Strangers has the scars to show how close he fought the Bugbear, as you yourself reported, Kitchehoar. Whether it was done with a musket, an arrow, or his own front teeth, it was the deed of a champion. We will hear him out."

Then the Captain passed his hand over his wounded face. His voice was ragged now too, as he spoke to Ahgeneh and the Ealda. "Ahgeneh," he began. "Uncle, we have come to find some Homely Country for our people. So we thought this Rockmarch might prove. We have told you why we thought this – the dreams and signs, and well-meant advice. But we will not fight you for this peaceful land."

"We will go on instead," the Captain said, and his voice grew low. "Go on beyond the Rockmarch, North or West or South. Until we find some peaceful place. Some new and empty peaceful place."

Jenny thought she knew what it must cost the Captain to say those words, and her tears began to fall.

Tom had seen the Captain in many moods – bold, grim, despairing, and, a few times, content. But rarely had he seen him so low and defiant at once.

Ahgeneh waited for a long time before he spoke again.

"We Ealda hold ourselves masters of oratory," he began, looking at Kitchehoar. "Because we eschew letters, and make speech our only learning. But this Stranger speaks well, and most gravely."

Then he turned to the Captain and the sailors. "You say you will not fight to gain this peaceful land you seek, and those are welcome words, for word has come to me of your battle with the Forest-Goblins – and doesn't your face itself show the victory you found over a Bugbear? We know you are great champions."

The Captain nodded at the compliment, but his wounded face remained bleak and dark.

"My people, the Ealda of the Cold Lake Country, live from the hunt and gifts of the land," Ahgeneh said. "We mean to trust to the plenty of the Rockmarch, to the skills of our hunters, the respect we give to the princes of the animals." Just for a moment, he looked at Gimlet, and then went on:

"But sometimes even the greatest hunter fails. So we call the last moon of Winter the Thin Moon, but some Winters last longer still."

The Captain looked up then, but the old Marshal continued. "And my people count many of your crafts most tedious – such as labour at the forge, or the herding of sheep or cattle. But we have heard that the Strangers live differently in their own country; that your people build great lodges of stone and timber, fill storehouses with flour and grain, delve deep for water; turn rocks to iron and steel at need. And isn't that all tedious work," he added "– to the Ealda?"

Now Tom saw the other Ealda were looking at Ahgeneh most warily. But it was the Captain of the *Volantix* who nodded, as if somehow, wordlessly, he and the Marshal had come to an accord.

The Captain touched the wounds on his face, and his voice rose: "And who would stand against us if we fought together?"

Ahgeneh turned to the other Ealda then. "Should we travel together?" he asked. "And share the Rockmarch with these Strangers?"

KITCHEHOAR STOOD. *"Who would stand against us?"* he said to the Captain. "For you are so terrible, you mean, and your muskets crack and roar, and frighten children – but even the Bone Faces can put five arrows in the air while a Stranger loads a musket, and we do not count them as true archers."

And once more the First Mate stood to face him. "Cousin Kitchehoar," he said. "I've been wounded by bow and arrow twice, once in the Spice Islands by a lucky shot from a jealous suitor, and once in the Great Desert, when

I got stuck in the backside by a teak arrow with a poison tip." With those words, the First Mate's eyes got a dreamy look. "And that's an odd story by itself, which –"

Tom was keen to hear what he would have said next, for although he had heard most of the First Mate's stories, this one was new to him. But the Captain stopped him with a word. "Mate," he said.

The old sailor thought for a moment. "Fair enough," he said. "It's a fine yarn, but I sees your point.

"Well, anyway," he went on, "The point is, I know I can't out-run an arrow, and I know even a poor archer can fire 'em faster than I can load any musket. And if a bow lacks the terror of a musket's thunder, still, when I hears the *whish* of a close shot, it unnerves me more."

Then the First Mate paused and looked around at the Ealda. "But that's not what makes a musket terrible," he said. "Not one musket, not one shot; that's not what you is remembering when you wakes up from a bad dream of a battle that went wrong, a battle when you lost your leg."

He shook his head. "No, it's all of 'em together. Dozens of 'em, all at once, and the sound makes an empty space between your ears, and a cloud of smoke rises all around them. And you know that in that cloud they're preparing another round just as bad.

"Or even worse," he continued, "is when there's a long roll of 'em. First one musket cracks, and then before your ears are clear, one more, and then a third, one after another other another, like that: *crack! crack! crack!* – and any one of 'em hard enough to snap your shin-bone like an old twig. *Crack! crack! crack!"* he repeated.

"And then, when there's been twenty shots in a row, you might think that's it, that's enough, for it's got to stop sometime – but twenty shots means the first one's loaded again. That's if they're any good, if they practise with them like we do on the *Volantix*. Then they start again, one after another, so you know it'll never stop; just a long roll of musketry, beating like your drum, cousin Kitchehoar, only every boom might kill you."

The First Mate stopped for a moment, and mopped his brow with a bandanna. "Face that and come back for more and you're a champion indeed," he said. "I'm not saying our sailors is the bravest crew in the world – I'm not saying it, though we've prevailed against Corsairs and goblins, and even the Boogey Pirates (twice). But we've all been served that musketry before. Even young Tom and Jenny have braved those battles. We've had it served to us – and we've dished it out, too."

The First Mate looked at Ahgeneh. "I'm not trying to scare you," he said, "for I doesn't think you scare easy, and the Captain said we'll walk away – somewhere – before we fights you people anyway. Our folk needs a place they can live without trouble. But it don't mean we're soft. And if you want good friends in a fight, that's us," he finished. "That's all I mean."

Then Kitchehoar looked at Bonawyn. "Is that the way it is with a troop of the Strangers?" he asked. *"Crack-crack-crack?"*

Bonawyn nodded at him calmly. “An Ealda hunter has a better eye,” she said. “The Riverfolk are quicker shots with a musket. But these Strangers train and drill to load and fire in order, and so they shoot, *crack-crack-crack.* They are terrible together.” She looked at Jenny. “Unless it rains,” she added. “Then they would better trust to the long blades of their swords.”

For a moment the Ealda looked at her gravely. Among them was a young woman named Buccaneen, who had kept almost silent through the whole council. “Crack-crack-crack!” she said, suddenly. “I think we shall be friends!” Then they all began laughing – a long, happy laugh. The sound of it lightened Tom’s heart, even though he knew how carefully the sailors had been weighed before the laughter began.

Ahgeneh nodded. “We shall share the Rockmarch,” he said.

Then Gimlet, who hadn’t said a word all this long council, stood in front of Ahgeneh. “Will you really be my family now?” he asked. “For I am also a foster-son of Oak-Biter, the Prince of all Beavers.”

Ahgeneh looked at the Captain, and when he saw him nod, he smiled at the boy. “You are not released from your duties to the Captain,” he said. “But I shall call you my own foster-son too, for love of Oak-Biter, and in honour of the great peace we have made today.”

Then the council rose and returned to the circle among the tawchs, and proclaimed to the sailors and the Ealda both the peace they had made.

Drumming took the place of speech then, and dancing broke out upon the news. The Ealda and Strangers danced in lines and circles. Tom danced, Jenny danced, the First Mate performed a hornpipe. Kitchehoar danced with Bonawyn, and the River-woman danced even with the Captain.

At last Cookie served out tea and hot chocolate, served it freely, remembering Bonawyn's advice about manners as the Ealda understood them. And then he presented his raspberry rubbaboo, an enormous rubbaboo, the biggest in all the world.

So there was general merriment and joy, there under the spreading stars and the bright full moon; by the Great Falls at the beginning of the Cold Lake Country; under the Last Moon of Summer and the First Moon of Fall.

Chapter Thirteen: A TINKER TALE

– squidges and squiggles – not sufficiently superstitious – a picnic – spirits in the rock – fleet Feeahy – cruel but fair – happy at last – too much open space –

AND IN THE MIDDLE OF THE NIGHT, TOM AND Jenny took their tin mugs and walked with Sparky through the trees. The country above the falls was high and rocky, but it was damp too, and overgrown with cedars and poplars. Here and there boulders pushed up through the mossy ground, but Jenny walked on, following some hazy path until they found a tall rock that faced South, towards the moon.

Then Jenny cast the dregs of their tea against it, for she remembered what her Godmother, the Wise Woman of the Woods Nearby, had taught her about casting divinations on full moon nights. For a moment they stood and gazed at the dark marks against the mottled red rock.

"I see squidges and squiggles," Tom said. But he thought Jenny might see more.

And Jenny did stare at the black shapes for a long time, and chewed her lip thoughtfully. But when she looked at Tom again she only shook her head. "This is a poor night for a divination," she said.

"But your Godmother says full moon nights are best for a divination," said Tom.

"At home, but not here in the Wild," Jenny said. "It is all distorted. I cannot see. I have led you on a wild goose chase."

"That's all right," Tom said. "For Sparky needed the exercise. And after such a day, a good walk clears the head."

Jenny only nodded silently, something so out of character that Tom began to wonder whether she had seen something after all. And he thought of her Godmother's *rede*, and remembered his awful dream of pursuit in the cold.

So THEY HAD A FEW DAYS, the Captain's Expedition and the hunters of Ahgeneh's people, before they set out for the Rockmarch. Warm fall days, by fresh water, among tall cedars, and maples just beginning to yellow. The fish agreed to be caught, the berries were easy to find, and the sailors found their first real rest since the early days of summer, since they had left the Mill House.

One day, as the morning passed and the sun grew warm, Tom and Jenny were lying on their backs, staring up at the blue fall sky and the swift, grey clouds. (Sparky was with them, but he lay on his stomach, and watched the trees in case a chipmunk, bear, or rough Ealda dog might suddenly appear.)

"Now we seem to have passed all the obstacles," Tom said, easily. "There is only some travel left, and then we can judge the fitness of the place, and find at least some fine place for the Winter."

"You are not sufficiently superstitious for a sailor," Jenny told him. "Here we are, still in the Wild, and you are counting your salmon before they spawn. Doubtless you are making plans for the party to be held on your return, and committing numerous other transgressions that can only be called tempting fate."

"I am being *hopeful,"* Tom replied, "which you taught me was the chief merit of great Explorers, such as Maxim Tortuca. You have given me dozens of instructional examples about Tortuca alone, and how he maintained hopes which should have seemed ludicrous, and now you are carping because I utter one which is entirely reasonable."

"Firstly," replied Jenny, "I mis-doubt that I have given you *dozens* of examples –"

"Dozens," repeated Tom. "Or perhaps only two or three, but each repeated dozens of times."

"And second," Jenny repeated, as if he hadn't spoken, "it is not having hope, but *uttering it aloud* as a certainty, that is judged bad luck, and which I am trying to caution you against. And I could give you example of this too, from the careers of several famous explorers – not only Maxim Tortuca."

She paused then. "Although in fact, Tortuca *did* leave an account of one ill-judged remark he made, and the unlikely, but well-documented, chain of dismal circumstances – by turns dire, tedious, and mortally terrifying – which resulted."

Tom knew better than anyone that Jenny herself had been wont to utter the most boastful declarations of hope all her life. Still, he didn't argue further, but tolerantly prepared for a particularly long story about Tortuca.

But Jenny was hardly even warming to her tale (something that involved giant ravens, a sack of magic beans, and – of course – a shipwreck) when Sparky got up and gave a bark.

Jenny frowned, for she had just been about to describe the first of Tortuca's ill-fated declarations of hope, when Tom rolled over to see Gimlet marching up with a basket of fish. Kitchehoar was beside him, and today he wore scarlet leggings and had bound his hair in brass wire.

"Yesterday my new brother Kitchehoar taught me how to make a weir in the river," Gimlet said. "And today I caught a whole drousand of pickerel. Look!"

"'*Drousand*' must be not only a large number, but a strangely flexible one," Jenny said. "For it is only four fish I see."

"My father says there is a name for such a varying number," Tom said. "And that it is of much use to astrologers and other labourers in philosophy."

Beside him, Jenny gave the dashing Ealda an apologetic look. "My friend Tom is a lore-child of all manner of arcane knowledge," she explained. "And forgets it may only bore those of a more practical nature."

Kitchehoar smiled. "Now even heralds and philosophers must eat," he said. "So haven't my little brother and I come to invite you to a picnic?"

"Thank you," said Jenny. "We would be most honoured."

Something occurred to Tom as he got up. "We could call it a pickerel-nic," he said, but no one paid him any attention.

Kitchehoar led them through the trees along the river to a low hill of rock that bulged from the ground as if some giant hand had run over it, East to West, and smoothed it down.

There on the wide, warm stone, Tom and Jenny made a quick fire from broken branches, while Kitchehoar bent some green willow to make a kind of grill. The Herald split the fish along the back, and in a few minutes had them broiled and served on their own skin, fresh and hot.

Kitchehoar seemed pleased to show these Strangers one of the pleasures of his country, and Gimlet acted proud that the fish had been caught in his weir. Tom and Jenny were simply happy about the new prospects for their Expedition, and by the fine dinner under the mid-day sun; a hot dinner in the cool Western breeze.

"Wrap the last of your fish in its skin and tuck it in the cracks of the rock," Kitchehoar said. "For it might encourage the spirits of the place."

Tom and Jenny exchanged a glance. "Uncle," he said to Kitchehoar, "Uncle, which spirits are these?"

"Now, I know you're Strangers," Kitchehoar told them. "But that's not the same as being blind. Aren't the spirits all around us here as we sit?"

"I see them," Gimlet said. "Drousands of them."

Jenny looked at the Herald carefully, in case he might be having sport with them.

Then Tom and Jenny looked closer at the veined, old rock beneath them. "Uncle Kitchehoar," Jenny said at last, "Do those lines reveal faces to you?"

The Ealda drew himself back. "A greater wonder is that I even see faces when I look at you pale Strangers. Now, you don't look like proper people either, but don't I give you the benefit of the doubt? Look here!" Kitchehoar pointed at a group of lines. He dipped his finger in the tea and drew damp marks to emphasize them: "Don't you see its mouth and eyes?"

Jenny went quiet, and Tom knew she must be wondering what her Godmother would make of those lines. He looked at the marks more carefully.

"It could be a twisted face," he said. "A twisted face that's yelling."

Kitchehoar nodded, as if that proved his point. "And so you were yelling when you were born," he said. "Don't you remember? Or have you never seen a new-born child? Scrunched and tiny they are, but you don't think less of them for it. And these are trying to be born from far down in the rock, and you wonder why they seem contorted, the poor things."

Tom and Jenny looked at the marks again. But Kitchehoar kept talking, as if their doubts offended him.

"Maybe Strangers are different when they're babies," the Ealda said. "Maybe you come sauntering from the womb and bow and nod to your mothers, dressed in your best robes and hats, and say, 'How do you do, ma'am, might I introduce myself? I am your newest child. Is it that dinner will be served soon, for ooh, I am sharp with hunger.'"

"'Ooh, I am sharp with hunger, I am a very well-mannered child,'" Gimlet said after the Herald. "'My name is Tom,'" he added.

Then Kitchehoar began a good-natured laugh, and Tom found himself joining along, even after so much unexpected sarcasm.

"Well," the Ealda said at last. "So they seem spirits to us, at least."

"Perhaps it is so," Tom said. "For there are spirits of the trees, Wood-Nymphs and Forest-Goblins both."

"And there are Water-Nymphs, kindly spirits of the water too," Jenny added.

"Likewise, Pishkeen Mawr, the great cat, whom the Riverfolk dread, for that is an unkindly spirit of the water," Kitchehoar said.

Then Tom looked at Jenny, for suddenly he felt that they were coming close to an understanding of the world

– and of what lay beyond the Cracks of the World – in a way that had been growing their whole lives.

Jenny nodded. "And of course, there are spirits of the ice and snow," she began, thinking out loud, but that only reminded Tom of his dreadful dream of the North again, and Jenny stopped at once when she saw his face.

Kitchehoar watched them both closely. "We believe all things are born of Spirit," he said. "But the Queen of the Hall of the Stars and the King of the Winds are masters of them all."

Tom nodded and suddenly he knew something no one had ever told him. "But there is Spirit above even the King and Queen," he said quietly. "Only that is too deep a mystery to name."

And when he met Jenny's eyes, Tom saw that she knew it too.

KITCHEHOAR LOOKED at the two Ensigns seriously. "The Ealda also know of this mystery," he said, his voice low. "But you come too close to naming it even now."

Tom flushed, but he nodded. Then he looked up. "Uncle, you marked my buskins before, and knew at once they had come from the Tinkers. Perhaps that story is not too terrible and mysterious to tell."

Kitchehoar laughed. "Tinkers are not so terrible," he said. "They avoid tedious work, like gathering food, when they can, but that's only good sense. And aren't they the finest cooks and crafters, after all? But think twice before you bargain with a Tinker!"

"I know already they are thieves and not to be trusted," Tom said.

The Herald looked at him. "Speak kindly of the Forgotten Folk!" he said. "For they name their true home as West of West, West beyond the Rockmarch, West beyond the Steppes and Hidden Sea, and then even West beyond the Shining Mountains that are as far as any know. But here they live in many of the hidden places of the Wild – and are so stealthy they might always be nearby." Kitchehoar looked around, and lowered his voice. "And in truth," he said. "In truth, no one can be more of a stickler for keeping a bargain than a Tinker. You can trust them to keep a contract too well, that's the problem, even a bargain you hadn't known you'd made."

"As they traded me these buskins for my Star-Glass," Tom said. "I don't call that fair."

"The Tinkers believe their real home is lost in the West," Kitchehoar repeated. "West even beyond the Shining Mountains. But in the meantime they live in hidden places, not only in deep glens in the forest, but in fathomless caves and behind secret doors in the Earth. So they believe all gems and precious stones are theirs by right, since they were all mined once, and taken from the houses of the Tinkers."

"I still call it thievery," Tom said, boldly. "I don't care what hiding Tinker might overhear it."

"If it's thieves they are, sure it must be the well-mannered sort, to leave you those fine buskins in trade," Kitchehoar said. "But I will tell you a tale of a harder bargain with the Forgotten Folk."

"IT WAS IN THE NEW LEAF MOON," Kitchehoar began, "or after Spring-Day, to name it in the fashion of the Strangers. And there was a great hunter of the Ealda, and her name was Feeahy, fleet Feeahy, they called her. Still young she was, but Feeahy was silent as a goblin when she tracked her prey; and her arrows flew fast and sure with eagle-feathers.

"She was often away in the hunt, and she always came back with fine game, with elk and moose and reindeer. And then her wee, young brother Bawg would clap, and she would catch him up and sing, *'Bawg, Bawg, little-bitty Bawg, stay always young and happy.'*

"So when Feeahy grew old enough to marry, many a young man came to her mother's lodge to ask for her hand. But fleet Feeahy always sent them away, for she wanted wee, young Bawg to always have first choice from her hunting.

"A young man of the Ealda would come and say, *'I could marry you, for I am strong and brave,'* But Feeahy would laugh and say, *'Not as strong or brave as I myself, nor half so fine a dancer!'*

"Or a young man of the Riverfolk would come calling and say, *'I could marry you, for I can paddle and carry most excellently.'* But fleet Feeahy would laugh and say, *'Not as fast or as well as I myself, nor half so fine a dancer!'*

"And once there was even young man of the Strangers who came to say, *'I could marry you, for I can hunt so well with my long musket.'* But Feeahy only laughed and said, *'Not half so well as I myself, nor near as fine a dancer!'*

"At last even fleet Feeahy's mother thought that she should wed, *'For Feeahy, child,'* she said, *'what if I were gone, and little Bawg would only have you for family?'*

But Feeahy only caught her brother up and sang, *'Bawg, bawg, little bitty Bawg, stay always young and happy. And never fear I won't be here, for I'd only go off with some finer dancer.'"*

Kitchehoar paused then, and Tom and Jenny knew the Herald of the Ealda was about to come to the point of his story. But Gimlet spoke up regardless:

"I am an excellent dancer. Particularly to the tune called, 'Gimlet Wants More Chocolate.' But I don't want to be married."

"Shush," Jenny told him. "For now you can hear the sound of hearts breaking." And she would have further lampooned the boy, but Kitchehoar only laughed and picked Gimlet up.

"Little brother," he said. "Who is it would want to be married at your young years? But it's in your old age you might want a companion."

"When I am old I will go and live in Tearnan Behowar," Gimlet said. "I will have Ahgeneh and Oak-Biter for company."

"But what happened to fleet Feeahy, the mighty hunter?" Tom asked. "Did the Tinkers become involved?"

Kitchehoar set Gimlet down. "And why wouldn't they?" he demanded. "After issuing such a bargain! *'I'll only marry a finer dancer!'* she said. For fleet Feeahy could dance most fine, of course, but who are the finest dancers in all the world except the Tinkers?"

Neither Tom nor Jenny had an answer to that, but Gimlet spoke up, just as if he'd known about the Tinkers all his life. "No one is the finest dancers except the Tinkers," he said. "Everybody knows that."

"I'm glad to hear it," Kitchehoar said. "for I was beginning to think they were unknown in the lands of the Strangers." For a moment the Ealda ran his finger along the beads in his jacket, as if he were counting off the parts of his story, and then he began again:

"So it was that Feeahy was gone the next night, and her mother wondered if she had gone hunting, but in the morning fleet Feeahy was back in her bed and didn't she sleep soundly till the day was warm? *'Mother, I dreamt a man gave me fine new slippers,'* she said when she awoke.

"*'Those are the very ones on your feet,'* Feeahy's mother said. But then she pulled one of her daughter's fine new slippers off and found a hole with her finger. *'But you have worn them out with all your dancing.'*

"Feeahy's eyes opened in wonder. *'I thought that was a dream, too,'* she declared. *'He was not the strongest or the fastest, nor the greatest hunter, but he danced fleet circles around me.'*

"'*That was no man, but a Tinker you danced with,'* her mother said. *'And that's the very one you shouldn't be dancing with again, not if you want to stay to tend to me in my older years, or watch Bawg your bitty brother grow.'*

"But fleet Feeahy was a mighty hunter, and she was not afraid. *'I'll dance one long night more,' she said, loud enough for anyone to hear. 'But not if he'll leave me with worn slippers.'*

"And that night wasn't fleet Feeahy gone once more, and didn't her mother wait again? Only this time Feeahy did not come back in the morning."

Kitchehoar stopped then, and for a few moments he slowly ran his finger over the beads again, as if he were considering whether there was anything else to tell. At last Tom could wait no longer. "What had the Tinkers done with fleet Feeahy?" he asked.

"Nothing at all but the bargain she proposed," said the Herald. "She said one long night, but when that night was over, and Feeahy came back to find the camp of her people, all the bark-walled lodges were gone, and the hearth was cold – so she ran through the woods, ran lightly in her fine new slippers, quick as a deer, silent as a goblin, and calling for her mother."

"She was a mighty hunter, Feeahy was, remember, and the finest tracker in all the world, but there was no trail left; there was no sign at all that her people had ever been there.

"At last, when she had run so long she had worn her fine new slippers to tatters again, fleet Feeahy came upon a camp, and she was frightened, for here the lodges were painted with familiar signs, with the marks of her people, but there was no one she knew: not her mother, not her cousins, not Bawg her wee, bitty brother. And Feeahy wondered if they had been done away with by some spell, if it was all the work of some wicked sorcerer."

"Not even Bawg, her bitty, wee, young brother?" Gimlet asked. "What happened to him?"

"Shush," Jenny said again, but this time because she was intent on Kitchehoar's tale.

But Kitchehoar only smiled at the boy. "And didn't Feeahy wonder the same? And so she looked at all the men and women and the children there in the camp marked with the signs of her people, and she called her mother again, and she called her cousins, and she called Bawg, her wee, bitty brother: *'Bawg, Bawg, little-bitty Bawg,'* she cried.

"And then an old, old man looked at her, and he said. *'Bawg was my name when I was small, and so my sister would call me: Bawg, Bawg, little-bitty Bawg.'*

"'And who would that sister have been?' fleet Feeahy asked the old man, but even as she asked, she could feel the hairs rise on her neck. The way a hunter feels, when they realize that it's something else that's hunting them."

"I know!" said Gimlet. "I know who his sister was!"

"Do you?" asked Kitchehoar quietly.

"It was *Bonawyn!*" the boy called.

Tom groaned then, but it was Jenny who spoke, rather sharply. "No, it was *not* Bonawyn. Pay attention, child, or think before you speak, or – though this seems unlikely – do both concurrently."

"Maybe it wasn't your bonnie River-woman," Kitchehoar said. "But do you know who the old man's sister was?"

"It was fleet Feeahy herself," said Tom. "And this was her brother grown old after many years."

The Ealda nodded. "So it was. Many years to him, but one long night to her, according to the counting of the Tinkers. So Feeahy wept and sang, *'Bawg, Bawg, little-bitty Bawg, stay always young and happy,'* as she had when he was small. And then she stayed to tend her old, old brother, until he failed at last and passed away, beyond the Cracks of the World.

"And then there was no one left in all the world who still remembered fleet Feeahy, the mighty hunter. So she went out and found a tall rock crest, and drew hard on her bow, and then Feeahy shot an eagle-feathered arrow towards the sky. And some say it fell back at last and pierced her breast, so that she left this world too. But others say it was then the Tinker who'd made the bargain came back. And the Tinker caught the arrow from the air, and then spirited her away to some secret place, and married fleet Feeahy – all according to the contract."

Then Kitchehoar was done at last, and he looked at

Gimlet and the two Ensigns. "We count that one of the saddest stories of the Ealda," he said. "And a great warning about any bargaining with the Tinkers."

"Then the Tinkers are fair, but cruel," Tom said.

"Like the Wild itself," Kitchehoar agreed.

"Uncle Kitchehoar, you know much about the Tinkers," Jenny said. "Do you have any similarly detailed and insightful accounts of the Elves to tell?"

"The Elves were fair as well, we hear," said Kitchehoar. "Fair, but much too gentle to want this land."

A FEW DAYS LATER, they were on the move again at last – the three curachs of the Strangers, and another that carried Ahgeneh and some of the chief hunters of the Ealda.

Gimlet sat there, behind Ahgeneh, for the Marshal seemed to enjoy his company, which was a new experience for the boy, and Jenny had made no objection to him leaving her boat.

Ahgeneh's curach had the mark of the Beaver-clan painted on the bow, and Gimlet asked him if that gave some authority over the water. "For your boat moves more easily along the river than Jenny's does," he said. "And all the sailors from the *Volantix* work harder when they paddle."

"The friendship of the Beaver-Prince is a fine and noble thing," the old man said. "But we Ealda wouldn't cut such fine figures in the tall ships of the Strangers – not at first, we wouldn't. Your friends paddle well enough. But haven't we grown up in curachs, and the Riverfolk too? Practise makes the difference. As Bonawyn says your sailors practise to fire their muskets: *crack! crack! crack!*"

"They do," Gimlet said. "We do, I mean. It sounds like the hammer of the heartbeat of the Heavens."

"And I'm glad to hear it," said Ahgeneh. "See what practise can do."

Gimlet could have learned this principle, and much else too from the friendship of Ahgeneh, but in fact the boy paid little attention. He just liked listening to his foster-father talk, and to the strange, rolling sound of the language the Ealda spoke among themselves – and to the steady dip and wash of the paddles.

Often he just lolled back and looked at the vast clouds drifting high across the sky, driven by some unseen paddlers, or watched the sharp grey and red faces of rock creep slowly by. Still, without even realizing it, Gimlet was learning the speech of the Ealda faster than any of the other sailors.

And something even stranger began happening to Gimlet as he was carried along the lakes and rivers up towards the divide where the waters of the Cold Lake Country began to flow West. For he was a foster son to both Oak-Biter the Beaver-Prince and wise Ahgeneh now; and bold Kitchehoar called him brother. There was work to do, bailing as they paddled, or putting the camp up every night and packing it again in the morning, but

Gimlet knew how to do it now, and knew what they expected of him.

Little by little, Gimlet was becoming happy at last.

In time they came to a long lake – the last lake, Ahgeneh and Bonawyn said, before the terrible chain of rapids that was the quickest route to the Rockmarch.

There was tricky work on that lake, for the West wind blew the water high, and they had to keep close to the shore for safety. The brigade of curachs traced a long and roundabout course, never striking across from one point of land to another, but following the curve of each bay, in and out a dozen times between breakfast and dinner.

The sky was grey those days, and there were flights of ducks and geese calling in the autumn air and gathering on the choppy water before their long journey South.

Something about the noise made Gimlet's heart swell with excitement. He wanted to be on his way too, travelling far like them – and then he remembered he *was* travelling. His home was already half a world away; so far and so long ago that he was forgetting it.

But then there would be another clatter from the skies, and Gimlet would feel his heart lift again. Perhaps he wanted to be turned to a bird after all, like the first Wards of the Sea that the Duke had told him about, and take wing in a great, spreading armada that chased across the sky.

Then Gimlet would spot a beaver again and remember Oak-Biter, and that he was destined to travel at last to Tearnan Behowar.

One morning, after a night spent sheltering from a last, warm, summer storm, the brigade of curachs came to the end of the Long Lake. While most of the sailors had a late breakfast on shore, Bonawyn and Ahgeneh led the officers and the wisest of the Hunters along a path, over high, rocky ground, and through thick stands of spruce.

They walked that way for an hour or more, always tending South, until they found a change in the air.

Sparky noticed it first, and became very jumpy and excitable. But soon they all did; a new warm smell in the air, strange and good, like the first scent of land after weeks at sea. "It's ripe hay we smell, or near enough," said the First Mate.

Through the trees the sailors saw vistas of bright sky, and now the sailors began to hurry, and Sparky broke into a run. Tom and Jenny followed him, with Gimlet chasing after them. They ran ahead of their guides, faster and faster along the narrow track, until they emerged from the forest at last.

Suddenly, after so many weeks among the trees, they were looking out from a great height of land, over a vast and open country.

High above their heads, a circling falcon cried, and to their right, away to the North, the course of the River Roaring sparkled as it moved in and out of the dark woods towards some lower stretch of woodland that reached towards a gleam of wide water in the North-West. That land was the Rockmarch, which Bonawyn and Kitchehoar had brought them to see, yet the sailors hardly looked.

For ahead of them, to the West, the land stepped down in great shadowed shelves of rock and tree – until far off, but bright in the morning sun, they saw waves of tall grass. Endless plains of tall grass that seemed to roll on to the edge of the world.

The three Wards of the Sea stood silent, overwhelmed at the sight of so much space, but Sparky went on barking as the others caught up. When Kitchehoar emerged from the trees, he had to step back. Though he had been at that ridge before, the sight of so much open space seemed to make him dizzy. "Careful, little brother," he told Gimlet.

But Gimlet was not dizzy; none of the sailors were. After so many weeks cooped up among the tree-pillared spaces of the Wild, seeing that open country was almost more than some of them could bear. Some wept and some cheered, and some were incapable of speech.

The Captain only turned towards Bonawyn. "What is that place?" he asked, hoarsely.

"The Steppes. Or the Blank-Lands, or the Flat-Lands," she said, scornfully. "An odd and eerie sight, isn't it? So wide you can't hold it in your mind, stretching out even as far the Shining Mountains on the edge of the West."

"Enough to drive you mad," Kitchehoar said. "And where would you hide?"

"Hide from what?" asked Gimlet.

Ahgeneh put his hand on the boy's shoulder. "It is enough to know that it is a perilous place," he said. "But look, do you see those dark shapes?"

"What are they?" asked the Captain. "Is it a great family of Bugbears?"

Kitchehoar laughed. "Bigger than Bugbears, even," he said. "They are the wild Buffles, the great hairy cows of the Steppes. You might want to hide from Buffles when they run, though they are not the worst danger in the Steppes. But they are a fine thing to hunt in lean years, or when we need warm robes."

Whether Sparky could see or smell the Buffles, he kept barking, barking over and over, and his voice did not fail him. He was mad with excitement, for on the Steppes he saw land enough to run forever.

"Do not be distracted by the empty Steppes," Kitchehoar said. "We must follow the River Roaring, run with it quickly North-West, to the Rockmarch. Winter is coming soon, and we must start our camp well, if we are all to shelter for the season."

"This season," the Captain said. "Then if we find a way our people could live there, some of us will go back, through the Wild and back across the Sea in the Spring."

"So two years before the first of our people is here, if it all works out," the First Mate said. "And all the while the shadows growing."

"We must hurry to the Rockmarch now," the Captain said. "I am jealous of every day and hour."

Chapter Fourteen:
THE CHAIN OF FALLS

– the edge of the Wild – water and warnings
– Prince Admiral – grown old on Ishca Fadras
– only a name! – swept sideways –

"You may not hurry now," Bonawyn told them, when they returned to their curachs. "For the River Roaring is fast enough, but it makes seven great falls in its rush down the Rockmarch, before it runs out towards the Hidden Sea."

"Are all of them carries?" asked the Captain. "Are none of them rapids that we could shoot? For we know how to manage our curachs now."

Bonawyn shook her head. "The Riverfolk, or even the Ealda, might shoot two or three of them."

Gimlet could see that Ahgeneh disputed that, and for a moment, they discussed the matter with Kitchehoar and the other Hunters in their own language, naming the falls: *Ishca Fadras; Eena Culgach; Corrach Grehm.* They were words of biting and clawing, Gimlet knew; terrible names. But the Captain could not follow the rush of their speech and only looked on, frustrated.

"This is our Expedition too," he said at last. "So it would

be fitting to include us in the decision."

Kitchehoar looked at him for a moment. "It's only that Bonawyn worries about you Strangers in so much white water," he explained. "For doesn't all the skill the Riverfolk have at running rapids only make them more suspicious? She worries about the wicked spirits in the water, and feels you have run through your share of good luck already."

Ahgeneh nodded. "I think you handle your curachs well enough," he said. "If we are to have sufficient for the rest of our people to eat when they arrive, we must arrive in time for the fall hunt."

"Bonawyn," the Captain said, "my crew have survived watery perils from here to Wanda-ling, and rowed galleys through the Old Sea like the ancient heroes. You, yourself, granted us the Freedom of the River."

"Hunters seek free game," Bonawyn said. "And even from here you can hear the hissing of Pishkeen Mawr, the great cat. Her great delight is in devouring cocksure sailors."

Ahgeneh held up his hand then. "Don't be courting misfortune," he told the River-woman. "Don't be naming an evil not yet come."

Bonawyn looked away before she said, "Yes, Grandfather. But listen to me," she went on. "The first rapids – Ishca Fadras – they can be run, I remember. But quickly after it comes a worse, comes Eena Culgach, the great claw; and no one can shoot that fall: not unless they have wings. We must not stay on the water to celebrate surviving Ishca Fadras," she said. "But land directly, and begin the carry."

"We have run this water more than once," Kitchehoar told her. "This is almost our home, still in the Cold Lake Country."

"The two longest rapids are also the easiest to run," Ahgeneh said. "So we will take them in the water and save two days at least."

Bonawyn nodded, reluctantly. Before they started into the water, she directed Kitchehoar to guide Tom's *Adventure*, and had the quiet, young huntress Buccaneen go with Jenny. "We must land directly after surviving Ishca Fadras," Bonawyn said again. "For no one would survive Eena Culgach."

AT FIRST, Gimlet thought Tom might be angry that Bonawyn had put Kitchehoar in his place at the bow of the *Adventure*. For Gimlet himself was likely to sulk or complain if any of the few privileges accorded to him were neglected.

Of course, no matter how he sulked or complained, Gimlet was still only a small boy on a difficult Expedition, and so he usually had no more than miscellaneous token responsibilities, such as bailing out a curach. But now and then – often when there was a great deal of packing or unpacking to be done – one of the Officers, or even the older hunters, would remember that someone had to be put in charge of looking for Sudden Green Rot.

Gimlet was glad to be given important work, but Sudden

Green Rot inspection was even more tedious than bailing, and his thoughts would drift and he would begin counting over the titles and honours he had already earned.

In the Old Sea, Jenny had given him the rank of Seahand, Ordinary (and his tricorne hat to go with it), and then the Good Duke had named him a Ward of the Sea, and made him special emissary of the people of District Seventeen. And he had become a foster-son of Oak-Biter the Beaver-Prince, and now he could call himself a son too of Ahgeneh, the Marshal of the Cold Lake Ealda.

Sometimes when he counted over these honours – even though he was supposed to be watching for signs of Sudden Green Rot – Gimlet would be struck by the notion that he might be the single most extraordinary boy in history.

In time, he thought, he was likely to become an Admiral, or a Prince, or perhaps a Prince-Admiral. *Prince-Admiral Gimlet,* he thought, and it sounded well to him.

And as Prince-Admiral Gimlet, he would have ten hats, and as much butterscotch as he liked, and the potentates of other kingdoms, principalities, and dukedoms would ask him to inspect their fleets for signs of Sudden Green Rot, and put on parades in his honour, and bands and orchestras would mass together to play "Gimlet Wants More Jam" with all due pomp and ceremony –

Then something as simple as the splash of a muskrat sliding down a mud-bank would recall Gimlet to the here and now, and to his present, and unfittingly tedious, duties.

So it seemed strange to Gimlet that even though Tom

was an Ensign, and for now still substantially higher in rank, he didn't seem to mind that Kitchehoar had taken over the guiding of the *Adventure*, but only watched carefully for every detail of how the Ealda handled the curach. Even Jenny – who Gimlet did not believe was a modest person – seemed content to watch how the young Buccaneen handled her curach, the *Fortitude*.

Perhaps Tom and Jenny both knew they would never become at last Prince-Admirals, Gimlet thought. Perhaps that was why they didn't get the sulks.

THE AFTERNOON WAS DONE and dusk was settling, warm and sticky, by the time the river-way turned West and ran, more quickly now, under the shelter of a high wall of granite stretching across the North, towards Ishca Fadras, the first falls.

Bonawyn had the curachs pause there long enough to repeat her warnings about the even more dangerous falls to come. "Ishca Fadras, the Long Water, will be hard," she called. "But if you let it carry you to Eena Culgach, you will die."

"Oh, we are always about to die," Gimlet said to Ahgeneh. "What's the point of being a River-woman if you are so frightened of the water?"

"The Riverfolk know they might die on the water better than anyone," the Marshal told him. "And they are *not* frightened by great risks, but only try to avoid bad luck. I think your bonnie River-woman has come to be worried about the Strangers in her care. She has brought you here already, and isn't that all you could ask of a guide? But still she travels with you."

"I think," said Gimlet, "she likes being the boss."

And then Bonawyn gave a cry, twirled her paddle over her head, and took the Captain's *Dauntless* plunging down into a great spray of foam. Gimlet heard her shouting orders as she pushed with her long paddle. Behind her the sailors dug hard into the water, and soon the *Dauntless* had rounded the first tight corner and swept out of sight.

"Hold tight, my son," said Ahgeneh. And now their curach was rushing down the same course: down one fall, round a tight corner, past a high wave, then plunging down again, so that Gimlet felt his heart in his mouth. Foam and swirling water and curlicues of spray were all around them, and while Ahgeneh shouted out orders and pushed and steered with his long oar, Gimlet screamed with pleasure, for nothing gave him such joy or such terror as the dash of an open boat.

There was one pause in the run, where the curach entered an eddy, before working around to the right of an ominous standing wave, and while the hunters strained at their paddles, digging with short, fast strokes, Gimlet looked up from the rocks and roiling water, at the great shelf of stone that ran along the North side of the rapids.

He saw something very strange there, but Ahgeneh and the hunters were so busy managing the turn that for once

Gimlet kept quiet. In a moment, they were around the tall wave – and the rock beneath it – and were racing the river once more.

Gimlet never knew how long it took them to shoot Ishca Fadras. Only a few minutes, perhaps, for the curachs seemed to swoop through the rock-strewn water. But counting all the perils they survived, as the water surged around boulders or cascaded down sharp, thrilling drops, Gimlet might have lived through a whole saga of close calls; a lifetime's worth of daring escapes.

And when at last the rapids swept them into a wide, foam-flecked pool, Gimlet felt he was years and years older. As old as Tom or Jenny, he thought. Even as old as the two sailors with blue hoods.

THE POOL AT THE FOOT OF ISHCA FADRAS was calm water, but the rapids cast a spreading lace of foam across its surface, foam that was being drawn hard for the West, towards the narrow falls of Eena Culgach.

Ahgeneh let the hunters in his curach take a few quick breaths and then he called for them to paddle hard for the South bank, where Bonawyn had already guided the Captain's *Dauntless*.

The sailors from the *Dauntless* gave a great cheer at the sight of Ahgeneh's curach, for they were giddy with the pleasure of having survived long Ishca Fadras.

And Gimlet felt giddy himself, but as the curach crossed

the water, he saw how quickly the foam was being pulled to the West. There the pool narrowed, and water boiled up around a huge point of rock, black and ominous against the setting sun.

Eena Culgach meant the Terrible Claw, Gimlet knew, and the rock that guarded the falls was the claw itself; beyond it the water dropped some unfathomable distance before rising again as mist, thick like wine against the sunset light.

Ahgeneh's hunters were already unpacking the boat by the time Jenny's *Fortitude* appeared at the end of the long falls, with the young hunter Buccaneen guiding it from the bow. The *Fortitude* got a cheer too, of course, but then they saw that Jenny was shouting. Not even Jenny could have been heard over the endless roar of Ishca Fadras to the East and Eena Culgach to the West, but then Gimlet remembered what he had seen on the stony bank.

"The Skeleton!" he cried. "Jenny saw the great painting of a skeleton on the rock!"

The other Ealda cried in alarm, but Ahgeneh took Gimlet firmly by the arm. "Where was it you saw such a thing?" he demanded.

Gimlet squirmed. "You're hurting my arm!" he said, but Ahgeneh did not release him.

"Where was it?" the Marshal repeated. "What did it look like?"

By now the *Fortitude* had nosed in beside the other boats, and Jenny leapt out, still shouting.

"The great skeleton facing the eddy," she cried. "What does it portend?"

Ahgeneh let go of Gimlet then. "The Bone-Faces," he said. "It is a message they have come before us."

Gimlet was confused and afraid now, and for the first time in weeks he looked to the Captain instead of Ahgeneh.

"You're fine, lad," the Captain told him. "But this is serious business. Now be our lookout again and get up a tree, quick as you can, for you can climb higher than any of us."

"Wasn't the Bone-Faces your great friends in these parts?" the First Mate asked. "The ones who wasn't much good with bows and arrows?"

"They say the same of us," said Ahgeneh.

Then he looked at the Captain. "A great skeleton!" he repeated. "For there's none can love or hate you half as much as the one that is your brother."

"Wasn't the *Adventure* just behind you?" Bonawyn asked Jenny.

Jenny nodded. "Tom and Kitchehoar between them should have found their way through the rapids by now."

"Get out your powder," the Captain called to his sailors, then. "Charge your muskets!"

Ahgeneh stood with the Captain now. "Brothers, and friends, and rivals," he began bitterly, before he broke off. "But don't be starting trouble," he said. "Don't be deciding for the Bone-Faces that they're become our enemies."

"We won't start trouble," the Captain said. "But we'll end

it if we have to." As he spoke, his sailors were spreading out in a long line across the South bank. They knelt as they finished loading their weapons, and Ahgeneh directed his hunters to stand ready with their bows behind them.

"That's a good line," Bonawyn observed to Jenny. "If there was something to aim at."

But Jenny was tied up in worry and frustration, and paid little attention to the bows and muskets. "But what has happened to Tom?"

Then they heard a great cry echoing down the long rock wall of Ishca Fadras.

It was the sign from the Bone-Faces that had delayed Tom and the *Adventure*. For even though he was now an Ensign, Tom still kept a sharp lookout from habit, and so had spotted the red marks on the North bank even before the *Adventure* had reached the tricky eddy in the middle of Ishca Fadras.

As their curach reached that pause, Tom had tapped Kitchehoar on the shoulder and pointed at the painting on the North wall.

Then Kitchehoar did something few even of the Riverfolk would have dared in those rapids: he called for the sailors to swing the curach backwards, and tucked it into the very corner of the eddy.

The cedar keel scraped over some rock, and the seams began to open, but the Herald took a line from Tom and leapt out onto a shelf of stone. The rock was slick with water, but Kitchehoar was sure-footed in his buskins, and while Tom kept the sailors back-paddling furiously, he took a long, careful look.

The dusk was already gathering, but the fresh red lines he saw glowed deeply in the last light of sunset. The Bone-Faces had been there first, and had painted a skeleton for them to see, tall and forbidding.

The Herald began muttering many things to himself then. He considered the matter from many angles, none of them pleasant. And then he saw the shapes of hunters moving under the shelter of the North Bank.

"Cluhegon!" Kitchehoar called, for Cluhegon was the Marshal of the Bone-Faces, and Kitchehoar knew he would be watching. But there was no answer.

"What is it?" Tom called from the *Adventure*, which still rocked in the water by the shelf of stone. "Uncle Kitchehoar, what do you see?"

"It is false friends I see!" Kitchehoar called back. And then he formed his hands into a trumpet and yelled the same to the hunters across the water: "Cluhegon, *fawltoear!*" he yelled. If Gimlet had been there he would have known what Kitchehoar was saying – *Cluhegon, the Betrayer.*

As an answer, some figure on the bank beneath the great skeleton loosed a black arrow. It struck deep into the prow of the *Adventure*, piercing the skin of bark as though it were rotting fruit.

"Jump in!" Tom called up to Kitchehoar. "They're

shooting now, jump in!"

But Kitchehoar tossed his line back into the *Adventure*. "Go!" he shouted. "Paddle hard, Strangers! Go!"

Tom took a quick glance back at the stern and saw the big Bosun give him a nod. He scrambled forward into Kitchehoar's place in the bow. "Hard!" he yelled, and dug his paddle into the water.

An arrow hissed past Tom's head. Then the two sailors with blue hoods shouted as another arrow buried itself in one of the packs by their feet. But the Bosun never stopped yelling "Stroke! Stroke! Stroke!" In a moment they had made the turn around the standing wave and were rushing down the length of Ishca Fadras once more.

Tom spared one glance for Kitchehoar, who still stood on the bank of stone. *"Mawta Cluhegon!"* Tom heard. And Gimlet would have known that the Herald was naming Cluhegon a coward.

Then, as the *Adventure* sped away on wings of white water, Kitchehoar made the greatest and loudest oration of his life: "False friend and cowardly Cluhegon, you resent our path, but you still fear the oaths we have sworn together, and you only attack these helpless Strangers!

"Isn't that is the work of a coward – like kicking a dog rather than settle a quarrel with its master. We go to the Rockmarch with these Strangers. Now, if that doesn't please you, speak to us as friends."

Three more arrows rattled against the wet rock, right by Kitchehoar's feet.

Then came the voice of Cluhegon, speaking from some crevice in the rock, so that his voice rolled across the water, and over Kitchehoar's seat of stone, and echoed down the whole valley of Ishca Fadras, so that even Ahgeneh and the hunters and sailors who waited by the wide pool above Eena Culgach could hear him:

"But now you have sworn new oaths to new friends!" Cluhegon called.

Ahgeneh and his hunters understood Cluhegon's cry, of course, though they would not let it show that they were troubled. But even the sailors from the *Volantix* knew those strange words couldn't bode well.

"Tom!" Jenny cried again. "Where is Tom?"

And back in the rapids, when Kitchehoar heard those words from his shelf of stone, he leapt up onto the South bank. He began running down the path that followed alongside Ishca Fadras, even to the pool of Eena Culgach.

By the time Gimlet carried a few loops of rope and Tom's old spyglass to the top of the scraggly Jack pine, he had forgotten how Ahgeneh had squeezed his arm. For the wind blew strangely there on the escarpment, and the top of the tree swayed more than the crow's nest on the *Volantix* ever had.

But Gimlet was still a sailor of sorts, and had been atop

masts (and trees) many times before. After a few moments clinging in terror, he began to remember his knots, and with a few bends of his rope he fixed himself more or less securely to the tossing treetop.

Then he checked to make sure the battered tricorne hat Jenny had given him was still firmly on his head, and then he began to look around.

The evening had grown, and now the great billows of mist that rose from Eena Culgach hid the falls in a bright cloud of copper. Beyond the mist, to the West and North, Gimlet could trace the path of the River Roaring in shining lines, through the last woodlands of the Rockmarch, and down in steps until at last it spread into a wide gleam, burnished by the light of the setting sun. *Perhaps the river would take us at last to a great shield of burnished brass,* Gimlet thought. *Or perhaps in the end it would only bring us to a pool of fire.*

To the East, Gimlet could follow the rock face above the long, foaming path of Ishca Fadras until it disappeared in the gloom. With Tom's old spyglass, he looked for the skeleton he had seen on the rocks, but here at the top of the Jack pine, his perch was too unsteady to see anything but a waver of red lines. But at the foot of the rock, he saw a dozen figures hurrying West.

They were dressed like Ealda, and carrying bows, but now and then Gimlet caught a flash of white, and he knew they weren't Ahgeneh's people. He hadn't known what the name Bone-Faces meant, but now he saw, and for a moment he clutched tighter to the rough bark of the tree. He saw something more terrible than any band of Corsairs; more terrible even than any twisted Forest-Goblins.

For beneath their hoods, Gimlet had seen the white gleams, the terrible grins. *Bone-Faces,* he thought, and all at once Gimlet felt as if all the rules had been broken; felt like things that lurked beyond had slipped through the Cracks of the World.

If the boy had been less frightened he would have given a cry in warning, but for a moment he was overcome. *But I thought it was only a name,* he told himself, and then he pressed his face against the bark, eyes closed against what he had seen by the last light of the day.

Gimlet didn't know how long he clutched the swaying tree like that. But when he opened his eyes, he saw something that made him remember all he had learned as lookout aboard the *Volantix*, and he gave a great shout: "Ahoy!" Gimlet cried in terror and excitement. "Ahoy! Curach *Adventure* on the starboard quarter! Ahoy!"

He even forgot to mispronounce "starboard."

WITH KITCHEHOAR GONE from the *Adventure*, Tom had been left to guide the curach through the rapids of Ishca Fadras. For just a moment, he had let himself feel afraid, and then he was too busy.

Now Tom had to use all he had learned from their months on the river, all Bonawyn had tried to teach him, to guide his crew and curach through the perils of Ishca Fadras. The water surged and swung them around boulders; it cascaded and plunged them down sharp, thrilling drops. There was no counting the number of dangers Tom led them through, and him still a boy. But when the rapids swept them into the wide, foam-flecked pool at last, like Jenny and Gimlet before him, Tom felt years older.

More than that, he suddenly understood how it was that Jenny had changed after leading her crew through all their adventures in the Old Sea, and so returned home at last. He understood what the Captain had told him about being an officer.

For Tom had seen more than his share of danger and tight spots already, here in the Wild – and long ago, in the terrible voyage North, when he had been no more than Gimlet's age. But he had never faced such danger in command before; had never had to worry that one small mistake would cost the lives of his crew.

So the *Adventure* emerged from the trial of Ishca Fadras. And for one giddy moment, the sailors caught their breaths and laughed or cheered or wept, according to their individual characters.

Then "They're formed for battle!" the Bosun shouted. But Tom hardly cared how the sailors and hunters stood on the Southern shore. He was watching how quickly the lace of foam was being drawn towards to falls of Eena Culgach.

"Paddle!" Tom cried. Still, he spared one quick look

North, towards whatever danger the lines of bows and muskets were facing.

In that strange evening light, when anything might seem real, Tom suddenly felt his heart in his mouth. For on that North shore he saw a dozen skeletons gathered; skeletons standing like living things. Skeletons armed and threatening, as if they wanted to steal life back from the living.

Tom's paddling paused, but then his sailors looked up too, and they hesitated in turn, and the two sailors with blue hoods screamed. "Skeletons!" they cried. "The walking dead!"

"Damn them!" the big Bosun yelled then. "That's the Bone Faces, damn them! It's just paint, you fools, painted to scare you – just paint! Paddle on! Paddle on!"

Tom shook his head, as if he had been dreaming. "Paddle on!" Tom cried after the Bosun. "Dig hard!"

And Tom tried to do the same. But in those awful moments of fright, the water had pulled at the *Adventure* so that the curach had twisted and slewed against the current. Now they rushed towards the curtain of mist; now the great claw of Eena Culgach loomed over them; now the *Adventure* swept sideways towards the shrouded lip of the falls. Towards its doom, just as Bonawyn had warned.

"The rock!" Tom cried to the Bosun, for he knew that suddenly the awful claw had become their hope. "We must shelter against the rock!"

"Hard!" the Bosun yelled from the stern. "Dig hard for your lives, but hard!"

Eena Culgach, The Terrible Claw

Chapter Fifteen:
Eena Culgach

– the Adventure appears – drawn towards doom – a duel of archers – the best swimmer – a nitwit – terrible equilibrium – pulled from the water – the doom of Eena Culgach –

Even though Ahgeneh's people and the other sailors were in lines for battle, they had cheered as the *Adventure* emerged from the rapids.

"But where is Kitchehoar?" Bonawyn had cried, for it was she who had given the Herald the duty of guiding Tom's curach.

When the waters of the pool began to draw the curach towards the mist-hidden falls, even as its sailors enjoyed their moment of triumph, Bonawyn, like Jenny beside her, began to yell. *"Hard now!"* they called, even though they knew the noise of the white water would drown their voices.

The Captain didn't yell, but he too spoke as if his words could urge the curach on: *"Hard, Tom, take them hard."*

"Paddle, Tom!" Jenny cried.

"Broe-stach!" Bonawyn called. *"Moorna broe-stach!"*

It was then that Kitchehoar himself emerged from the path through the trees. "Cluhegon," was all he said to

Ahgeneh, but the old Marshal nodded, as if he understood all that had happened from that name.

So the watchers on the South bank looked on, helpless, as the Bone Faces gathered under the rock face on the other side of the pool, and as the crew of the *Adventure* were startled by the sight and made their fateful pause.

"No!" the Captain cried, but it was all too late, and the strong current drew the curach towards the mist.

"Tom!" Jenny screamed. "Tom!" But the *Adventure* swept towards the falls regardless; towards the doom of Eena Culgach; towards the realm of the dread spirit of Pishkeen Mawr.

AND IN THOSE NEXT AWFUL MOMENTS, in that unlucky place, many brave and terrible things happened; too many for any one person to understand until long afterwards, when those who were left could gather and knit the strands of the story together.

For there was terror aboard the *Adventure*, where Tom and the Bosun and the rest of the crew fought the pull of the water, until the very claw of Eena Culgach. The curach struck hard, and broke the Bosun's hand against the rock. But there they found a kind of perilous shelter, while the mist rose around them, and the water tugged at them from either side before it began its long fall to the rocks below.

And on the Southern bank there was fear of the Bone-Faces, whose painted skin gleamed like skulls in the dying light. That terrified Gimlet – who had slipped down from his tree to hide behind Ahgeneh – most of all, and the other sailors generally, for they had never seen such a thing, not even among the strange mysteries of the Old Sea.

On the left end of the line, Gimlet saw that Ahgeneh stood tall, and muttered a few things to his son. But Kitchehoar remembered the challenge Cluhegon had given him on the rocks of Ishca Fadras, and gave his father sharp words in return. *"Mor-tash,"* the boy heard, and he knew that meant something about honour.

Then the Herald drew his bow and sent an arrow to land on the rock before the Marshal of the Bone-Faces.

A moment later, Cluhegon loosed an arrow in reply, high across the dusk-shadowed pool, to bury itself in the ground hardly a hunter's length before Kitchehoar. Two armed lines faced each other across the swirling pool, but the rival archers paid them no attention as they began a slow and deadly kind of game. Each careful arrow was a kind of dare: *Can you shoot better than this? Are you brave enough to stand where the next one might land closer?*

It was too terrible to watch, and Gimlet buried his head in Ahgeneh's cloak.

BUT WHILE THIS ARCHERY CONTEST WENT ON, while the sailors and the other Ealda stood ready to fire on one another more generally, Jenny and the Captain stood behind the lines and only saw Tom and the *Adventure*.

"Someone must carry a line out," the Captain said, but Jenny had thought of this too, and was already tugging at her boots.

"No, girl," he said, putting out a hand to stop her, for he couldn't bear the idea of both his young Ensigns in such peril. Now he began to pull his own jacket off.

But Jenny pushed him away. "My swimming is more skillful!" she yelled, and finished with her boots. And she had never disobeyed an order before, nor ever dreamed of shouting at the Captain.

"It's true," the First Mate said. "She and Tom isn't as strong as the Bosun, but they's better swimmers than the rest of us –"

"No," the Captain said again, but Jenny looked at Bonawyn.

"I can't swim like you," the River-woman told her. "Go, save them."

"Ensign!" the Captain roared, but Jenny was already running East behind the lines where sailors and hunters stood ready, to the upper end of the pool. For the water would begin to draw her to the West at once, and she needed time to swim out far enough to reach the rock before it pulled her into the mist, and the falls below it.

At the water's edge, Jenny threw off her jacket. Bonawyn had followed her, as Jenny knew she would, and now the River-woman tied one end of cord to her belt.

Jenny dove into the water at once, trusting Bonawyn to manage the rest, heedless of any arrows.

The Ealda

In the *Adventure*, they had come to a terrible equilibrium against the rock.

Tom could hardly see either shore from all the mist and spray. As the water parted around the claw of Eena Culgach, it rushed into the billowing fog, and disappeared with an awful roar, tugging at the leaking curach so that it turned first one way and then the other. And with every swing the two sailors with blue hoods gasped, which was hard to hear; and Sparky, hiding in his barrel, wailed, which was worse.

But the current pressed them tight against the tall rock too, and so they bailed water and waited.

"I can't swim against it with my broke hand!" the big Bosun shouted.

Now Tom truly understood the worst of a captain's plight. For there were a dozen foolish things they could have tried, but Tom knew each only meant doom. And if they only struggled to keep the shelter of the rock, they were doomed as well. For the *Adventure* would break under the strain at last, or their strength would fail. But at least that end would be at the hand of fate, Tom thought, and not at his command. At least they might perish together.

So Tom began an awful calculation, there in the shelter of the great claw of Eena Culgach: When his *Adventure*, his first command, began to tip over the falls, and find its doom at last – how should they meet that moment?

Should they shout their defiance, or be nobly stoic. Or should they be singing a shanty or paddling song, as if they were only going off to find some last adventure? Jenny, he thought, would have known how to invest the moment with all its proper significance.

But worst of all was thinking of Sparky's terror, shut up in his barrel. For what consolation could there be for a dog in such a plunge? He would not end his days in old age by the fire, as was fitting for a dog, but in horror and incomprehension.

"Nitwit!" he could hear Jenny shout, as he pondered their end so poorly. And that was what she would say, Tom thought, for Jenny believed above all in never giving up.

And "Nitwit!" Jenny shouted again, and then Tom saw the Bosun lifting her from the water with his good hand, and Jenny was carrying a line, and even hiding in his barrel, Sparky began barking for joy.

ON THE SOUTHERN SHORE, after Gimlet had uncovered his eyes, he realized he was caught between two separate disasters, each unfolding at the same time, careless of the other.

For he stood by Ahgeneh and understood much of what the Ealda said; while his friends were on the curach, half-hidden in the mist, stranded on the rock at the very edge of catastrophe.

So he wept both from the plight of the *Adventure*, and from the terror of the awful contest between Kitchehoar and Cluhegon, the Bone-Face Marshal across the pool.

The Ealda

Each shot came more slowly, for they both meant to show the other a coward, but to actually hit their opponent would be a shame as great as running.

Farther along the shore, the hunters still kept their line, although with every moment they paid less attention to the archers across the water, and more to the duel. Beyond them, Bonawyn bent a stouter rope to the end of the line Jenny had carried to the *Adventure*, and half the sailors – the ones from Jenny's *Fortitude* – had already set their muskets down, and gathered to help with the rescue.

At the same time, the Herald simply stood and stared across at the dim and eerie figure of Cluhegon, and waited for the next arrow. And Gimlet saw Bonawyn's rope being drawn quickly through the water as his friends on the curach pulled for their lives.

There was a noise like tearing cloth, and suddenly an arrow stood in the ground, not a foot's length in front of Kitchehoar.

Ahgeneh roared then. "Foolishness!" Gimlet heard him cry. "Surely you have both shown enough courage to inspire the stories of your children and your grandchildren yet to come!"

But Kitchehoar hardly glanced at the arrow. "If we show any less spirit than the Bone-Faces, what would keep them from loosing a storm of arrows against us? Or is it that you think they have painted on their skulls merely to welcome these Strangers?"

Then there were words, sharp words, between Ahgeneh

the Marshal and Kitchehoar his son; and Gimlet could not follow all of it, and he did not want to hear.

Instead he watched the progress of the rope across the water. While Bonawyn fixed one end around a stout tree, the First Mate paid out the line the crew of the *Adventure* was drawing.

The Captain too ignored the contest of the arrows, and tried to peer through the mist that shrouded the rock. "Can they fix it to their prow?" he asked. "So that we can simply draw the *Adventure* home?"

Bonawyn shook her head. Beside her the First Mate wiped his brow, and then he shook his head too. "It's the angle," he said. "As soon as the curach swings free of the rock, the current will pull it straight, and that'll make slack faster than we could pull. Then they'll slip towards the edge."

"But we could pull tight and catch the boat again," the Captain said.

"We would catch it," Bonawyn said. "But not before it was over the side and dangling into the misty deep. Not before Tom and Jenny and the others are fallen out and swallowed by Pishkeen Mawr."

The Captain stared at the River-woman, still angry that she had let Jenny go, clear against his orders.

"Your crew can live!" said Bonawyn, "If we keep the line tight they can pull themselves along it from the very jaws of that cat. On the little curach, they know already what they must do. Ask your Mate!"

"That's the only way," the First Mate said. "It's their work now." He squinted into the mist. "The first one comes!" he cried.

Now Kitchehoar stepped forward too, for he had ended the debate with his father. The Herald nocked an arrow in his bow, and stood still, peering across the gloom for a long time. Then he drew, and his arrow flew high across the water.

Aboard the mist-hidden *Adventure*, stranded by the current against the great claw of rock, the Bosun had wanted to stay to the end.

"You should go without me," he told Tom, yelling over the huge, blank sound of the falls – "and wee Jenny, here."

Jenny might have protested such a description, but as the Bosun spoke in the heat of the moment, she only said, "Nonsense! You couldn't manage the boat alone with your broke hand."

For his part Tom only said that he was in command and wouldn't leave the curach until the very end. "But no dilly-dallying to make me wait!" he added, as a kind of joke.

Then the first sailor from the *Adventure* leapt into the water and began to pull himself hand over hand towards the shore, against the current.

On the *Adventure*, they fought to keep the rope tight for him even as the parting current knocked and ground the curach against the rock. Then another sailor jumped in, and then a third. As each sailor left, there was one less hand to bail the curach, and one less hand to keep it firm against the rock. Finally the sailors with blue hoods went into the water together. The Bosun paused, even though it had been arranged that the two sailors would help him.

"Leave my boat!" Tom cried. "That's an order."

Then the Bosun cursed, but he left the *Adventure* too. And the two timid sailors began pulling him along the rope.

Then there was only Sparky in his barrel, and the two Ensigns. Tom was as wet as Jenny now, soaked by wave and spray, but in that last moment of calm, he looked at her across the tossing curach.

Jenny nodded at him. "Well managed, Tom!" she called, louder even than the falls. "Most masterful in the face of danger – Ola Olagovna could not have done better!"

Tom laughed then. "What about Tortuca?" he cried.

Jenny shook her head, and her wet hair tossed against her forehead. "All right, even Tortuca! For at last we have come to a predicament that would have taxed even him."

Then they became preoccupied with escaping the stranded curach.

ON SHORE, Bonawyn and Jenny's crew from the *Fortitude* fished Tom's sailors one by one out of the swirling pool.

And like all the rest of the sailors from the *Volantix*, still kneeling in their line, Gimlet had cheered each wet face. But now he heard that faint tearing sound again, and saw an arrow appear, its point right under Kitchehoar's foot. The boy screamed, for he knew that was the last arrow that would not draw blood. "Foolishness!" he heard Ahgeneh cry.

Then the Captain turned his attention to the duel at last.

Kitchehoar stood tall, his chest bared to his rival, and drew another arrow from his quiver.

"Stop it!" the Captain roared. And then in the language of the Ealda, he yelled, *"Aerich!"*

But Kitchehoar turned to him, quite calm. "The Bone-Faces began this quarrel because of you. But they will not win it because of me." Then he raised his bow once more.

"And if you hit him?" Gimlet heard Ahgeneh cry. But the Captain recognized the look in Kitchehoar's eyes, and knew the young Ealda's brave heart had turned as hard and cold as brass. Once his own heart had done the same, long ago, and almost doomed his men in the Battle on the Frozen Sea.

The Captain picked up his musket and handed it to Ahgeneh. The old Marshal lifted the weapon and fired it high in the air, as a signal for the contest to stop.

JENNY HADN'T SPOKEN WITH TOM ABOUT IT, but she knew what the last steps before abandoning the curach would be. First, they would fix Sparky in his barrel to the line. Then she would follow.

Tom would come last off the *Adventure*, because that had been his first command. And as he left the curach it would begin to swing free, and the line would slacken, and they would have to trust the sailors on shore to pull hard, to pull very fast to bring them safely to the bank.

Now, in the glowing mist, they clipped the rings on Sparky's barrel to the line. For a moment, Tom looked through the little porthole into Sparky's frightened eyes, and then Jenny thumped the tub to reassure the dog.

She nodded at Tom and they swung the barrel over the low side. With only the two of them to manage, the tug of the line on the prow was already beginning to shift the curach. "Hurry!" Tom yelled. "She's beginning to swing off the rock."

Just then they heard the crack of the Captain's musket. Tom only cried, "Now! Into the water!" But on the North bank, out of sight of the two Ensigns, the Bone-Faces loosed arrows without number at that sound, for they meant to show they feared no musket.

Most of the arrows passed over Tom and Jenny unseen, like a rush of birds; but two tore into the water beside the curach.

Only a signal, like the musket, Jenny thought. *They do not mean to hurt us, yet.*

But the Ensigns were pressed against the very claw of Eena Culgach, almost in the realm of Pishkeen Mawr, as Bonawyn had told them. And one arrow did not fall where it was aimed at all; for that wicked spirit took the chance all the black thoughts of those who faced each other across the darkening pool had made.

That arrow fell short, and cut the line that Jenny had brought from the shore, cut it on just the other side of Sparky's barrel; the barrel that Jenny had bought in the Old Sea because it had once belonged to Maxim Tortuca, who had never despaired.

Free in the water, the barrel began to swing out with the current, into the awful mist that rose from Eena Culgach. Jenny cried, "No!" and reached out to catch it. But the barrel was beyond her grasp already. Now the water had it, and drew it towards the edge, and then by the line still attached to the prow, the barrel itself began to pull the curach away from the rock.

So the *Adventure* began to slip out into the current. Tom grabbed at the rock, but the whole weight of the curach, of Jenny and the cargo that still remained, was swinging away, out from under him.

If Tom had only tried to keep himself pressed against the rock, he might have kept his grip. But he tried to brace his knees and legs to keep the curach with him, and not even the Bosun would have been strong enough to manage that. The barrel pulled at the boat, and then the weight of the boat tore Tom's fingers away from the rock; and they were all at the mercy of Eena Culgach.

Through the mist, Jenny saw Sparky's barrel slip away and disappear over the falls. She cried his name. Then she cried, "Tom!"; and then the curach began to tip over the edge, and Jenny only knew that she was falling.

For just an instant she saw Tom almost dangling in the air above her, and then the boat flipped down the falls, stem over stern, and Jenny knew no more.

SO THE WATERS OF EENA CULGACH swallowed the two Ensigns at last, and Tom's dog Sparky.

So the curach *Adventure*, which had been Tom's first command, disappeared, and Tortuca's barrel, which had survived so many perils, beside it. Eena Culgach had swallowed them too. And no living man or woman, and neither bird nor beast, nor even any fish that swam, ever saw either one again.

Chapter Sixteen:
THE DARK NIGHT

– after tragedy – a sailor-like tribute – three bare trees –

IN THE LONG, LAST MOMENTS OF THE FOUNDERING *Adventure*, even Kitchehoar forgot his duel with Cluhegon. All the sailors and the hunters of the Ealda had surged to their feet, had watched as the curach was drawn into the billowing mist, and disappeared at last over the falls.

For just an instant, horror held the Captain fast, but it didn't seem like an instant to him; it felt like time had slowed down, so that he grew older with each awful, awful moment.

First he looked to Bonawyn and the First Mate, to see if they knew of any hope. But the First Mate passed a hand over his face, and Bonawyn wept, even as she said, "We must hurry down this trail, to find and tend to them."

At first the Captain hadn't understood. "Might they have lived, then?" he asked, but Bonawyn only turned away.

The old First Mate had pulled off his hat and twisted it in his hands. "She means we must hurry to find and tend to their mortal remains," he said. "Before they is further broken by this awful Chain of Falls, or swept on and lost forever in the West."

"Both my Ensigns," the Captain said, hoarsely. "Young Tom and Jenny the Fisher-Girl. I led them both to their doom."

"They died not from your hand, but because they were brave and dared to face the Wild," Bonawayn said. "They were like Riverfolk."

Then Kitchehoar spoke, and he still kept his eye on his adversary across the water. His voice shook with anger. "It was the Bone-Faces of Cluhegon that destroyed your young Ensigns, who were under our protection. And now we could destroy them, with your muskets, and our arrows."

But Ahgeneh put his hand on his son's shoulder and pointed across the pool. Although the thunder of Ishca Fadras to the East and the roar of Eena Culgach to the West drowned any words the Bone-Face might have said, they could still see how his dark shape moved on the opposite bank.

Cluhegon walked close to the edge, broke his bow across his knee, and cast it broken in the water.

"He will never use that bow again, from shame," Ahgeneh said. "Cluhegon did not intend it."

Then there was only weeping to be heard from the sailors who had known the two Ensigns.

"Young Tom," some of the sailors mourned. "He was our luck and our lookout in the North."

The Ealda

"And Jenny," others wept. "Who was only a Fisher-Girl, but led us through the Old Sea."

The two sailors with blue hoods could not speak at all for their tears, but at last even the First Mate gave way to lamentation. "I was old enough to be their grandfather," he said. "So it's them what should be speaking words for me. But they was as crack a pair of Seahands as any I ever sailed with. And what's more, they was both uncommon well-spoke." Which was the most complete praise the old sailor knew how to give.

Only Gimlet seemed not to understand. "Won't they be all right?" he asked the First Mate. "Won't they make it to the bottom of the falls?"

"They were Wards of the Sea, like you," he said through his tears. "But here they risked wild river water."

After a moment, Gimlet asked. "But what about Sparky? For he had his stout barrel to preserve him."

And the Captain only shook his head then, and picked the boy up.

So Gimlet understood, and even though he had thought he was finished with grief after he left the Corner by the Sea, now he remembered Tom and his kindness, and how much he had admired him. And Jenny, and how she had watched over him, in her way, from the time he had stowed away aboard her ship.

But before Gimlet's tears fell, he took off the battered tricorne Jenny had given him long ago in the Old Sea, and he threw it into the water. "That was hers," he said, as the current began to draw it away, towards the terrible mist and the roar of the falls. "She should have it again."

"That was fitting, lad," the Captain said.

"A most sailor-like tribute," the First Mate added.

Bonawyn let them have a few more moments for tears, and then she cried *"Broe-stach!"* and began hurrying them along the dark trail that led West and down towards the hidden deeps of Eena Culgach.

But they never found a trace of the two Ensigns that dark night, nor in the light of the day that followed either. And then they had to climb back to the awful pool above Eena Culgach and retrieve their boats and packs, which seemed the most awful carry of all.

After that carry was done, Bonawyn and the Captain came back up the trail together one last time. "No matter what Homely Country we find in the Rockmarch, we will only bring sorrow when we return," the Captain said. "For Tom's Dad, and Jenny's Godmother, will look to see them again."

They stripped three birch trees of their bark, to make memorials for Tom, and Jenny, and Sparky the dog who had loved them both.

Then they broke the poles, after the fashion of the Riverfolk, to mark those who would never be found again.

The Ealda

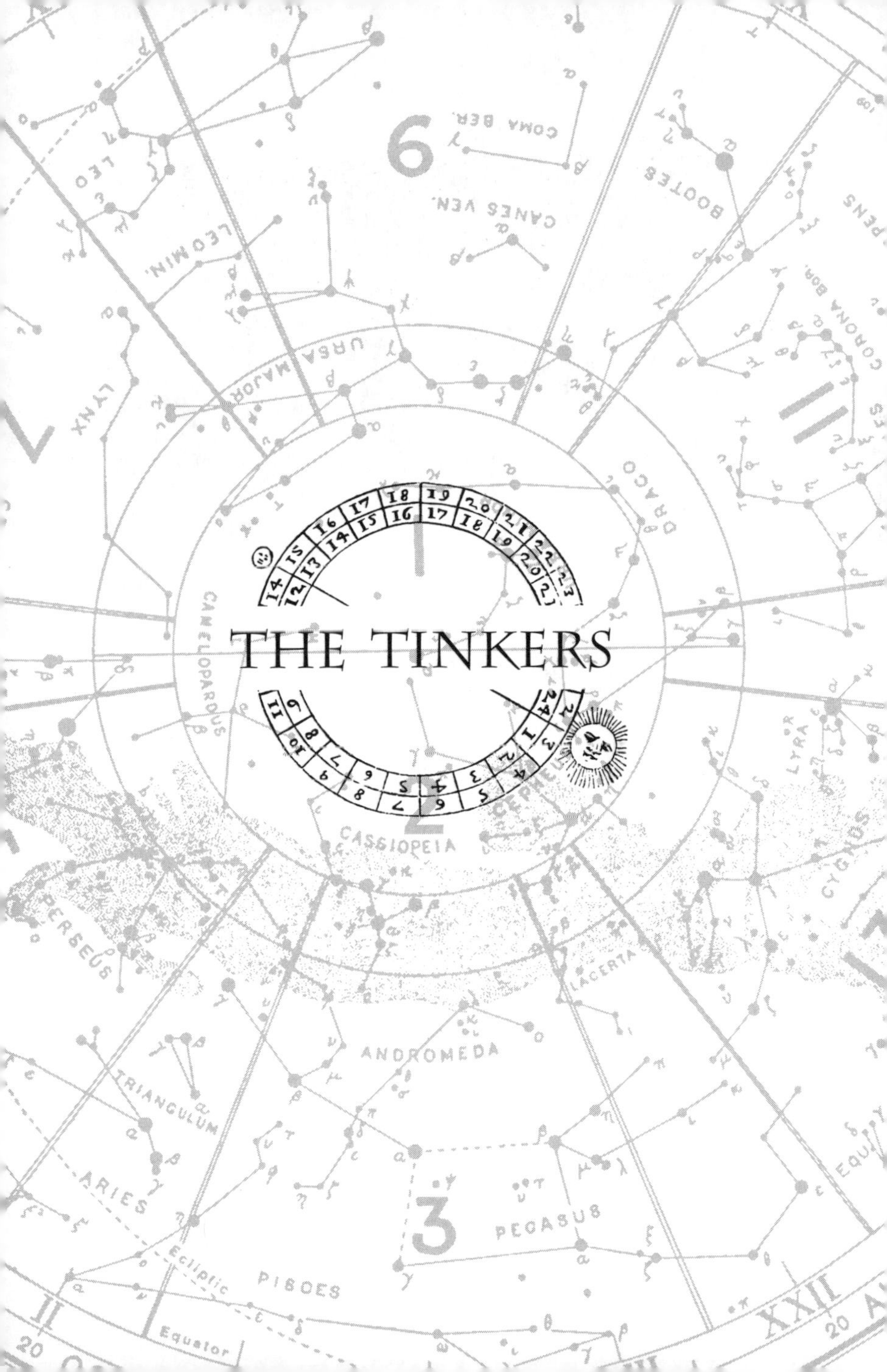

THE TINKERS

Falling and falling

Chapter Seventeen:
THE LONG DREAM OF FALLING

– upbraided by Tortuca – a dim chamber of stone – a two-pipe story – the greed of Pishkeen Mawr – bone and barrel broken – a brave dog – a small and dashing man –

FOR A LONG TIME, TOM DREAMT HE WAS FALLING still.

He would dream first that he was lookout aboard the *Volantix* once more, just a young boy, and that he had tumbled from the crow's nest. His stomach would lurch, and then he would begin the plunge towards the chill and grasping waves.

Then it was Winter, and he was slipping from a great mountain of ice, and as he dropped through the cold sharp air, he knew what terrible, frozen peaks waited below.

But he never stopped falling, and finally he would dream his curach, the *Adventure*, that was his first command, had slipped out from beneath him, and he was falling still, through a torrent of water. Falling and falling while the spray filled his mouth, until he could breathe no longer, and felt himself begin to drown at last.

That's usually when you wake from a dream like that, frightened and grasping. But Tom's dream was worse. For without ever stopping the falling and drowning, he found that he was also on the North bank of Eena Culgach – standing with the Bone-Faces. And there he watched himself tumbling in the falling mist.

Cluhegon would shake his skull-painted head, like one long-familiar with death. "That's a long way to fall," he would tell Tom.

"I should have been more careful," Tom would agree, looking down at the poor figure he cut, falling and choking in the last light of sunset. Falling and choking, but somehow never falling out of sight.

Then Tom's Dad would be there too. "And Sparky and Jenny lost before you," his father would say with a sigh of disappointment. "And all your notebooks too, and so the hope of expanding further the scope of our Great Work."

"How pitifully I struggle," the watching Tom would say, as the falling Tom tried to call out, "Have pity on my struggles! I will be torn on the rocks and drowned!" But his mouth filled with water, and he only made a kind of gargling noise.

And then Cluhegon would nock an arrow on his bow with a sad smile. "It would have been better if they had shot you directly," he would say.

"It would better to perish more quickly," the watching Tom agreed.

Then Jenny's Godmother would appear too, and reproach him: "I gave you a *rede* that warned you of this," she would say.

"No you didn't!" Tom would exclaim, for even in his dreams he remembered that his *rede* had nothing to do with falling or drowning.

"Well, I should have," she would answer. "Look how you suffer, poor thing."

Then Cluhegon would draw back on his bow, and the arrow would fly – and then he himself was only Tom again, falling; and there would be a moment of terror, and then nothing.

But still that wouldn't wake Tom. Only his dreams would drift again, through the places he knew, or the stories his Dad had told him, or Jenny's tales of the Old Sea. Or he would see the strange, soft, ice shapes that had never really left his heart since he had seen them in the North.

And then he would be lookout, in the crow's nest of the *Volantix* once more, and the sea would be pitching, and he would begin to tumble to his doom, and the falling dream would begin again.

Tom didn't know how long his dreams followed this path, falling and drowning. But when he came once more to stand on the bank with Cluhegon, and Jenny's Godmother, and his own Dad – and watched himself tumbling through the spray, and contemplated yet again his inevitable and pathetic doom – at last Jenny stood there with him.

Even in his dreams, Jenny did not tolerate despair, and she spoke sternly: "You have responsibilities as an officer and Ensign," she said. "Among which not least is that of maintaining hope even in unreasonable circumstance."

She exchanged a knowing glance with the man beside her. He wore tall boots and a tasselled smoking cap, an extravagant moustache, and a pair of fierce scars, one on each cheek.

Tom knew the stranger for Maxim Tortuca, for so Jenny had described the great explorer to him on innumerable occasions, not forgetting to mention the scars. (The unfortunate result, Jenny had explained, of a complicated misunderstanding involving an unsympathetic potentate, a set of over-anxious royal guards, and a pair of *almost* perfectly aimed spears.)

Tortuca also shook his head at Tom. "When the Great Owl of the East swooped down one night and seized me in his beak, then I could have given up," Tortuca began, "– *but I did not.*"

And past Tortuca stood another stranger, a stout, fur-clad woman whom Tom believed to be Ola Olagovna, the great Privateer of the North.

Even Olagovna shook her head. "I would keelhaul such officer," she said. "No sailor ever make fortune from despairs."

After Olagovna's scorn, Tom felt he had endured enough disapproval, even in a dream.

He turned to the Captain; he turned to his father; and then Tom looked up at the stars in the sky. "I will stop falling," Tom said then, "and, dead or alive, return to the world at last."

So Tom's DREAM DID END, and he found himself in some tall, dim chamber of stone. He lay on a rough bed of furs spread over a shelf of rock; and Sparky was at his feet.

For a moment he only thought, *This is our death-bed, and so they have laid us out together.* His sword and hat were set at its foot, like memorials in an ancient grave. Beside him, like a curtain, a long-faded tapestry hung: a picture of a hunt. Rough figures with spears stood over some enormous fallen beast that lay dead, or dying. *How long ago did it die?* Tom wondered. *How long have we lain here?*

Then Tom heard a bone-like clatter, and some hook pulled slowly at the edge of the curtain.

Beyond the curtain the light was stronger, and as Tom squinted he saw a pale and wide-eyed face peering in. Even here beyond the Cracks of the World, something had come to trouble them.

But Sparky squirmed at the end of the bed, and then the dog yawned and got to his feet, and barked twice at the face – happily enough, and Tom felt a daze of joy begin to come over him. He blinked, and understood the pale face differently. It was Jenny.

"It is well time you were up," she said, and her voice made husky, bassoon echoes in that stony space. "For the laziness you have shown ill befits your station as an officer and Ensign."

Now Jenny pulled the curtain farther open with the end of her stick. There was real light coming from some chink in the chamber's ceiling, and Tom saw that she was propped up on a rough bed like his. For a moment he didn't know where to begin. Then Sparky began licking his face, and Tom managed to croak, "Good dog."

"I am reassured to hear you utter that opinion," Jenny said. "Or indeed, anything at all. For I had begun to think you deprived of the power of speech."

As soon as Sparky let him, Tom drank, and drank again from a tumbler of water set beside his bed. Then he looked at Jenny with some exasperation. "I am only quiet for the usual reason," he told her. "You talk enough for two, so hardly need my help."

"Ho!" Jenny laughed, and then Tom felt properly awake at last, and saw that she had only been teasing. "That was a fine sally at my expense," she said. "I call that ready wit from someone who has done nothing but sleep and twitch these last five days."

"Five days –" Tom said, and then his waking self began to remember the falls too. "Eena Culgach," he said. "I thought we were drowned."

"And *I* thought we were drowned," Jenny said. "And except that Sparky is a Dog of No Speech, he would tell you *he* thought we were drowned. We tipped over the misty edge of Eena Culgach, after all, and seemed to have little choice about it."

Tom laughed a little. "In my dream, you told me my hopelessness was a failing," he said. For a moment he closed his eyes and chased after the fleeing scraps of his long dream. "In fact, you had Maxim Tortuca and Ola Olagovna there beside you to say the same thing."

"Of course, hopelessness is *usually* a terrible failing in an Explorer," Jenny began, and then Tom saw her mind suddenly change tack. "I stood with Olagovna *and* Tortuca?" she asked. "How were they dressed? Was my hair well-combed at the time, my jacket well-set? I call that a wonderful dream!"

And Tom knew that Tortuca and Olagovna would occupy Jenny's thoughts indefinitely if he didn't set her back on course. "I don't know if it was wonderful," he said, "but it was the longest I have ever dreamt of falling."

Jenny took a moment to regain her bearing, and then she nodded. "My Godmother would ask, 'Where did your fall bring you, and what happened when you arrived?'," said Jenny.

"Your Godmother has told me as much," Tom said. "But I never stopped falling until I awoke here, and now I don't know what will happen – or what *did* happen, or what place I have come to."

Jenny pushed herself up to a sitting position with some difficulty, and then she smiled. "That's a story," she said. "Bonawyn would call that a two-pipe story."

"HAVE YOU TAKEN UP A PIPE at last, then?" Tom asked.

"Bonawyn is admirable in many respects," Jenny said. "But I do not need to imitate her example in order to tell a story well."

Tom nodded blandly. But because he knew Jenny had always been in two minds about the River-woman, he couldn't resist chaffing her further. "When Bonawyn *announces* a two-pipe story," he pointed out, "she does, in fact, use a pipe, and fill it twice. It seems necessary to the endeavour."

Jenny shifted uncomfortably. "She does *not* need the pipe as such. But only uses it as a kind of stage-prop, in just the way your father removes his spectacles to embellish some obscure point regarding cloud formation, hypothetical accounting practices, or, perhaps, the habits and history of bees."

"Or as your Godmother summons thunder-claps for dramatic effect," Tom said.

Jenny frowned. "It is not my Godmother who summons the thunder, but rather the thunder that proves her dreadful assessment of various dire portents," she said. "But perhaps you do not really wish to hear of the plunge down Eena Culgach, and would rather sleep again, perhaps for another five more dull days."

Tom lay back down and stroked Sparky's ears back. "I am done with my sport," he said, quietly.

Then a shiver ran through him. "I remember the slip over the edge in the mist, I think, and after then only a long fall – and then the dream." He paused. "Tell me about Eena Culgach."

Jenny pulled a blanket closer round herself. "We did fall and fall," she said. "Even through the mist I saw Sparky tumbling in Tortuca's barrel, and the poor *Adventure*, that was your first command, tossing end-over-end, and you last of all.

"It's a terrible end," she said. "For you know what will happen, but can do nothing except wait to be broken on the rocks." Then she looked off for a while, not at Tom or Sparky, but only remembering.

"I think it is a worse end than drowning," she said at last, for more than once in her career she had been swallowed by the waves.

"It is worse than freezing, too," Tom said, remembering his long ordeal in the cold.

Jenny nodded. "But then there was a worse terror even than that," she said. "For in the end that tossing spray took a shape like some great cat, like Pishkeen Mawr herself, and she hissed and spoke to us:

"'*Strangers are come to my land at last,*' she said. '*How will they taste?*'"

Jenny shifted again, and looked pale. "And you know even a good cat, even wise Pawlikins, if he has eaten enough already, will catch a mouse for sport at times, and only play with it some while, and bat it back and forth before the end."

Tom nodded. "Dogs are not so cruel."

"And dogs do not hunt so well," Jenny said. "For cats like to practise, although they are lazy beasts." Then she looked up at the small patch of sky they could see through the chimney-shaft. "But Pishkeen Mawr is cruel.

"And she had never found prey like us before, and so she toyed with us. The water poured down, but within it she tossed us up and let us fall again, and then batted us from one side to the other. Even through the mist I could see her green eyes, and they were not hungry, but they liked to see how we twisted and squirmed. She liked to hear us howl, I think; you and me, and Sparky in his barrel most of all."

Tom shuddered, and he found that Sparky was trying to hide beside him in the covers. "But I remember no howling," he said. "I must have been stunned already."

Jenny looked at him for a long time. "Be glad you don't remember," she said. "For I heard you howl. And be glad above all else you don't remember Sparky's howls, for I have heard him terrified, and I have seen him sad, and I have watched him shudder, but I never knew a dog to understand horror before that."

"Dogs have their nightmares, too," Tom said. "And Pishkeen Mawr must be their shape."

"The whole River Roaring became that shape," Jenny said. "And the falls sounded as one great hiss, and the waiting rocks were its teeth and claws. I know why the Riverfolk dread it so, for they must have seen the cat in their dreams at least, and hope never to see it when awake.

"'*What do they taste like?*' it asked.

"*Are they like Ealda or Wood-Nymphs? Are they like Tinkers; or the Elves who are gone forever? Or are they some new things like the Riverfolk? Is their meat light or dark?*'

"So it said, and more too that I can't remember, but it was all much the same: we were to be eaten, but first it wanted us to *know* we would be eaten, to know the dread of Pishkeen Mawr."

"How long did this go on?" Tom asked.

"We were almost beyond the Cracks of the World," Jenny said. "It was dream-time."

Tom nodded. "Heartbeats and hours seem the same in those times. There is no reckoning it."

"Just so," said Jenny. "So we fell in terror, and that Cat-spirit taunted us, and we fell again. And then at last she tossed us onto a ledge of rock in the falls.

"Tortuca's Dog-Preserving Barrel broke apart. It preserved the dog, but itself cracked open like an egg, so Sparky stood bare and trembling before the misty Cat-shape. And you fell, and knocked your head, and lay sprawly on the rock. So I thought you dead, and you never spoke again from that time until you woke, just now."

He looked at her, at the way she sat awkwardly, at her pale face. "But what happened to you?"

"My thigh was broke," Jenny said, shortly. "So I was helpless." Then she saw the look on Tom's face.

"It has been tended well," she added. "But it hurt most grievously. And I think now I will always limp."

Tom wondered about several things, but he only said, “Pishkeen Mawr –”

Jenny nodded. “And I was helpless,” she said again. “And could only slip and sprawl myself on that wet rock. But Sparky tried to stand over us. He was shivering with dread, but he stood and bared his teeth, but what could he do?

“For the shape in the mist loomed over us. But now it hardly hissed. It sighed,” she said. “Like the sigh you make when you sit down at last to dinner.”

TOM STARED AT HER, transfixed, and beside him on the bed he felt Sparky trembling under the covers.

“This is the point,” said Jenny, “when Bonawyn would pause to fill another pipe.”

“I see you are right about the pipe being only a device,” Tom said. “For of course, she could just as easily break off and simply *talk* about a pipe, as you do, and produce the same effect.”

“Just so,” Jenny said, with a kind of relish. “For you know the story *must* turn away from dread at some point, or you would not have lived to hear, or me to tell, its awful course. But any pause, whether produced by the use of pipes, spectacles, or simple digression, increases the suspense felt by the listener as to exactly *how* and *when.*”

“As always,” said Tom, “you are a font of information. Now that you have provided me with understanding of the techniques of story-telling, perhaps you could somehow bring Tortuca into your account as well and thus make me wait a quarter-hour yet before discovering how it is that I am not dead."

"You are not always the centre of the world, Tom, or the hero of every story," Jenny told him. "For with equal aptness you could say, 'Discover how it is my dog Sparky survived,' or, for that matter, 'How the boon friend of my childhood, Jenny the Fisher-Girl, yet breathes.'"

She broke off to think for a moment. "And in fact, there are few kinds of peril whose nature could not be better understood with reference to one of the many adventures of Tortuca. In this case, for example –"

"I am sorry if my words seemed to slight Tortuca," Tom said very quickly, and then his next words came out all in a rush: "For-Tortuca-was-a-great-man-in-all-respects-and-I-admire-him-greatly."

Then he sat up. "Now please tell me how my dog, my boon friend Jenny the Fisher-Girl, and even I myself survived the fall and the depredations of the dread Pishkeen Mawr!"

JENNY NODDED. "So we were on that wettest of rocks. Me helpless, like a flounder on the bottom of a dory, looking up at that awful shape; you lying still, and dead for all I knew; and Sparky barking even in his terror."

"He is a brave dog," said Tom, patting Sparky's head. "After his own fashion."

The Tinkers

"He was as brave as any dog has ever been, then," said Jenny. "For Tortuca's Dog-Preserving Barrel had broken around him, and he was surprised and helpless as some hatchling bird – but still he wanted to protect us from Pishkeen Mawr." She paused, thinking about it. "Perhaps it is that he knew that spirit as one of the great and ancient enemies of all dog-kind."

Tom nodded. "Perhaps he thought that above all it was his duty to defend against a cat."

"But it was awful," Jenny said again. "For it seemed it would have been better had we simply fallen and drowned, or otherwise perished directly in the falls, but at least not be consumed by the spirit of that Cat."

"For that was the most horrible place," she began, but she corrected herself. "For that was as *horrible* a place as any I've known. And so we had come to the end of every hope."

For a moment she looked down, as if even saying such words troubled her, and then she raised her chin again.

"So we were at the end of every hope," Jenny repeated. "Only then we heard the sound of a penny-whistle. Sparky and I heard someone playing a pipe."

She paused then, and Tom kept quiet, and let Jenny collect herself. "That was such a small sound, there among the thunder of the falls, but it skirled in a manner most dashing, and then from the shadows behind the falls someone appeared."

"Who was it?" Tom asked. "Stranger, or Ealda, or –"

"Or Tinker," Jenny finished.

The Tinkers

"And I will tell you what a figure he cut," she said. "This Tinker no bigger than you, but a grown man all the same, and the odd fashion of his dress: the finest buskins, and a sash like the Riverfolk wear, and a jacket like the Captain's, but the felt was red and decorated all over with beads and quills – and a cocked hat besides."

"I will tell you all that in detail later, for I didn't notice it myself. For, as the First Mate says, 'Yet once more, we was just about to get et.' The hissing of the Cat confirmed it," Jenny said. *"'Leave us, Tinker,'* it said. *'This supper is served.'*

"But this Tinker only put down his pipe and laughed, not caring a bit for that terrible Cat, or its awful hiss. He was brave to see!

"'Pishkeen Mawr!' the Tinker called. 'Ye great thrawn cat. Let these go and find some good fish dinner. Or I will find the springs where ye were bornit, and dry them into cinders. I know yer name, and what yer mother hissed to nurse ye.'

"'And if ye still trouble and vex these friends,' he went on, 'I will use that name to curse ye. And if there is trouble still, I will find all Princes of the Animals, and get them to smell you – and they will pull yer fangs, and cut yer claws, and like a house-cat, bell you.'"

"He had Bonawyn's rhyming trick, then," Tom said.

She nodded. "And remembered it while he looked that thing in its green eyes, and bound it with words that would have made my Godmother proud. 'Pishkeen Mawr,' he

said again. 'Ye uggin thing. Go find some good fish dinner.'"

Jenny smiled. "It was brave to see."

Tom only stared, utterly quiet.

"Then the Cat was gone," Jenny continued. "And the Tinker – Edge-Gleamer is his name – bowed to us, and called some of his people. And they bore us out of the mists of Eena Culgach. Some long way they bore us, through great cracks in the rock. But you were insensible, and after a while, so was I, from the pain of my leg, so how we came at last to their warm and hidden snuggery, and to this chamber where they have tended our hurts, I cannot say."

"But our friends –" Tom began.

"Our friends believe us dead," Jenny said.

Tom began to protest, but she looked at him fiercely, and for the first time he saw how much pain Jenny's leg gave her. "For you have been sleeping," she said, "and I can hardly move, and Sparky is a Dog of No Speech, so who was to tell them?"

"The Tinkers," Tom said.

"They are bound to remain secret, I think," said Jenny.

"Is that one of their laws?" Tom said. "Like the one by which they stole my Star-Glass?"

Then down some long stony hall, Tom heard a fair voice singing:

Tinker, tailor – time for sending
Pots or shoes that might need mending

The Tinkers

"They sing so we know they are coming," Jenny said, quietly. "For neither we nor Sparky would ever hear their footfall."

Slowly the song grew louder:

Leave them lying by and by and
Find them fixed by careful tending.

"Tom," Jenny said. "This may not be the most politick moment to be remembering your Star-Glass."

Chapter Eighteen: EDGE-GLEAMER

– an old friend – questions of theft – a matter of honour – scent of the North – the points of the compass – wild revels – fate of Feeahy – an old sword – dreams of the warm old sea –

The tinker made a fine entrance, Jenny thought, managing to whisk in a trencher of meat and drink, while somehow doffing his cocked hat to Tom, and giving her a friendly wink, all at once.

"Good morning to the young, to the waterlogged, and to the recently insensible," he said. "Welcome here to our rocky snuggery. Welcome to our food and drink; to our home and hearth. Stay as guests and leave as friends."

The Tinker made his speech in such an easy and amiable manner that Jenny could not keep from smiling, even though she had heard the same speech before. But, for all that, Tom got unsteadily to his feet, and made a bow, and stood straight again to meet the Tinker's eye. *He stands upon his dignity,* Jenny thought to herself. *After a fashion I don't recall.*

"I am sorry to have only met you now," Tom said. But he gave Edge-Gleamer a keen look. "Though I think we have had dealings before. I am Tom, a scholar's son; Ensign aboard the famed ship *Volantix*, and –" He paused a moment. "And lately commander of the curach *Adventure*."

The Tinker twitched his sharp ears, but his cordiality never waned. "A quare fine introduction," he said. "Where I can only name myself a simple Tinker – though some call that boast enough, here in the fastness of my people. And 'Edge-Gleamer' is what Strangers can call me."

Tom said nothing to these fine words, as if his good humour had been lost with the *Adventure*, so the Tinker kept talking as he laid the food he had brought on the stone ledge that served as a table (not forgetting two fine linen napkins): "But it's fair to see ye awake and talking. Ye have good and worried us all. Not only myself, of course, but this kempie girl, yer fellow Ensign as well."

Kempie, Jenny knew by now, meant that at least the Tinkers thought she was a bold and dashing girlie, so she let it pass.

"Even this creatur Sparky, yer wee wolfie pet, I ken, has been worried," Edge-Gleamer finished.

Tom could keep quiet no longer: "Are you the same Tinker who stole my Star-Glass?"

Edge-Gleamer drew himself as tall as he could. *"Stole?"* he said. "That's no kind of word to address to a proud Tinker, who's defied Pishkeen Mawr to save yer life, who's borne ye from the ledge of Eena Culgach, who's tended ye like a bairn these five days, pate-knocked, stoondit, and insensible as ye were."

"Perhaps, Tom," Jenny began, and then with some pain she shifted herself to look her friend in the face. "Perhaps you are forgetting not only the debt we owe Edge-Gleamer, but even the words of tact I uttered not two moments ago."

"Of course, I am glad to have woken up here," Tom told her. "I am glad to have woken up at all. And I thank you, Sir Tinker, for both our rescue and your careful tending."

Edge-Gleamer gave Tom a small nod at that. *Here they are both upon their dignity,* Jenny thought, *and me with a broken thigh. What tedious conciliations will have to follow?*

"But the Star-Glass was the greatest treasure I have ever been given," Tom went on. "And was restored to me after a trial as terrible as Eena Culgach." Then he gestured at the foot of his bed, where the beaded buskins stood. "So if you call that a fair trade, let's trade back. These are fine buskins, but I'll go barefoot if I must."

Then Tom put his cocked hat on, to show this was serious business. "But you won't trade back," he said. "For it was no trade, but theft."

At that word, the Tinker put his hand to his sword-hilt. Tom's sword was hung by his bed, but he stepped forward, still unsteady, and looked Edge-Gleamer in the eye.

For a moment, the Tinker only rolled his fingers, but then he stepped back and shook his head. "Ye're only a halfling boy, after all," Edge-Gleamer said, softly. "And just recovered from a five-days stunning."

Much as Jenny admired the Tinker's dash and fine language, those words rankled. "You speak with an unwarranted confidence," she told him, "considering that my friend Tom is fully your equal in size. In addition I myself am as large as you. And when we're full-grown, *you'll* seem naught but a half-grown Tinker."

She would have risen herself then, if it had been in her power. "Neither should you think us afraid," she continued, "for we've both seen and fought those that were bigger, uglier, and generally more fearsome in all respects."

Edge-Gleamer only looked at her sadly, untroubled by her boasts. "That's a fine snoot from you, my masterful, wee lassie," he said. "For what plaint do you have? Unless it's that I found ye helpless and am now begrudged yer own fit gratitude?

"As for my size," the Tinker continued, "It's a matter not so easily ment at my age. Can you say as much for yer ill manners? For I'm yer host, and bound to care for ye, and glog all yer insults, rather than defend my honour."

"You named me a halfling boy first," said Tom.

"So I did," Edge-Gleamer told him. His grin might have been friendly, but it revealed a mouth of sharp, pointed teeth. "And so ye are – compared to the tall and feckful man ye will grow to be, after the fashion of yer people."

Then he held out his hands in appeal to Jenny. "Kempie girlie," he said. "What's our quarrel?"

She looked away for a moment. "Tom," she said, "it's

true this Tinker has saved our lives, and Sparky's too. Is that not enough to call it quits between you? Or is this jealous mood some last gift of Pishkeen Mawr?"

Tom looked at her miserably for a moment, but then stepped back.

"Come, my callant," Edge-Gleamer told him. "I'd gain no honour from showing a fledgling how to use a sword. No honour, but some risk to my skin!" he said with a laugh. "For I'll wager ye've scrabbled free from a quare few tight nooks already."

The Tinker held out his hand. "I'll eat your harsh words, if ye'll accept our bargain."

Jenny thought the familiar Tom seemed to break through the shadows then. "Quits," he said. "And perhaps I'm still in your debt, really."

After they shook, Edge-Gleamer said, "But sooth! I understand why ye prize this stone. I'd make any sleek and crafty claim to keep it – so long as it was fair, I mean. But by our law I needn't have given ye the buskins at all, for we count any gem and jewel as ours by right."

"Yours just because they came once from the rock and earth?" Jenny asked.

"Aye, for look around," the Tinker said. "See what we count our oldest hidden home: these hollows in the rock; caverns and tunnels; and even the leads of ore and stones and crystals within."

"But –" Jenny began, and here she gave Tom a warning glance. "But without reference to any past dispute, how can such a thing as the Star-Glass, which is an old, old magic – an enchantment, in fact, from the Lodge of Grandfather Frost himself – how can you claim even that once was yours? For it must have been made a long age before this place."

Edge-Gleamer did not reply, but only pulled the Star-Glass from his pocket. "I knew I smelled the cold North," he said, "upon yer whole wee Expedition. But was it Grandfather Frost himself that gave it to ye?"

"My Captain gave it to me, and he had it from Grandfather Frost," said Tom.

"Aye," Edge-Gleamer said. "And where was it that yer fine, fur-clad Grandfather Frost found the thing?"

"I don't know," Tom said. "I thought he made it."

"A clever one, isn't he?" the Tinker said. "But not so clever as that. I'm not slighting his gift, ye ken – there was naught wrong with it, nor with yer Captain giving it in turn. For there's only three things to do with a gift in the end: break it, or pass it on, or take it with ye to the grave, which we call a muckle-stingy, cheese-paring, close-fisted, tight sort of revenge upon the living –"

"Muckle-stingy," Jenny agreed. "Indeed, and simple, mean parsimony as well. But where did such a thing come from?"

"From the ground, from the rocky deeps, of course," said Edge-Gleamer, and his eyes began to sparkle. "The earth's veins flow with quartz and crystal, and like blood they run purple one place and red another. But they glitter too, with silver and gold. Here in our home. And this is the finest crystal of all, so fine that only the Elves ever learned how to dig or polish it, and they took the secret with them."

He held the glass up. "A beautiful thing," he said. "It holds plummy deeps like the darkit sky, but what do ye reckon it's for?"

"It is my compass," Tom said. "It was my compass, and my Captain's before me. It shows the stars in the sky, and even the Great Mountain that touches to the Peak of the North."

Edge-Gleamer shook his head. "Yet there's naught but the dark to see."

For in the Tinker's hand, the Star-Glass showed none of its familiar glimmering light.

"Have you broken it?" Tom asked hoarsely.

"Look," the Tinker said, and Jenny saw how he passed it to Tom without a pause, without any doubt Tom would honour the bargain.

In Tom's hand, the dark globe shimmered once more with a hundred tiny constellations. He looked at the Tinker strangely, and then he handed the glass to Jenny. It still shone, and for a moment she didn't want to give it up, or ever stop gazing into that miniature, star-strewn sky.

And when Edge-Gleamer took it again, the light went out once more. "It's nae compass," he said. "You fine explorers all, ye see the stars that show yer way, see the Great Mountain that marks the uttermost limit of the World. Do ye ken it yet?"

"Is it that it really only shows what we look for?" asked Jenny.

Tom shook his head. "It shows our fixed dreams."

"Aye," said the Tinker. "Clever lad. Yer Star-Glass was fashioned from the Stone of Heart's Desire, a finer thing than any gold or silver ore."

"But in your hands," Jenny began, "– is it that you desire nothing?"

The Tinker bared his sharp teeth again, in a bitter kind of smile. "My heart's desire is beyond the Cracks of the World," he said, "and not to be seen while I live here. Yer fine Star-Glass – this stone from the deeps of the Earth we call our own, this magic from the North where I once walked – all it can tell me is what I already knew. That our time is past, we Tinkers.

"Lad, those buskins are the finest we ever made," he said. "They won't wear thin, won't fade, won't slip nor tear. Count yerself lucky, for ye got the best of the bargain after all."

Edge-Gleamer tucked the Star-Glass away. "Never mind it," he said.

Then he smiled more broadly, without baring his teeth. "For tonight we will honour yer awakening with a great and merry *birl,* a feast and entertainment – here in our humble Hidlin Hall of stone."

THE HALLS WERE HIDDEN, even to Tom and Jenny within them. Edge-Gleamer had never even told Jenny which way was North or South, so the two Ensigns could only speak of directions as though they were aboard a ship: port and starboard; fore and aft.

But that evening, while they waited for the Tinker to return, and the shaft of light falling down into the rocky hall became a pillar of darkness, they looked up carefully to see what stars might show.

"One bright star," Tom said. "It should be the head of the Great Swan."

"Watch how it moves," Jenny told him. "And learn East from West, and so the other points of the compass."

Tom sighed. "You have known me my whole life, and never yet seen me confused as to the relation of the points of the compass," he said.

Jenny was exasperated in turn. "And you know that I – like fluent speakers generally – often describe things commonly known for rhetorical purpose. Why –"

"Please don't tell me now another tale of Maxim Tortuca," Tom said.

She stared at him. "Did you interrupt me merely on speculation? For in fact, I had no intention of discussing Tortuca –"

"Or Ola Olagovna either," Tom added.

Jenny closed her mouth for a moment, and then *she* rose on her dignity. "Perhaps it is rather that you don't want the benefit of my further conversation," she said. "I will endeavour to hold my peace in future. Silence will become my rule, and reticence my policy."

"I'm sorry," said Tom. "Only I am crusty from having my skull cracked."

"Indeed, that is irksome," Jenny told him. "I was lucky in only having had to lie across this stony chamber and hear you twist and groan obscurely, unable to leave from my thigh-bone being scarfed together like a broken mainmast."

"Didn't Tortuca once break his thigh?" Tom asked.

Jenny stared, for only a moment before Tom had asked her to leave discussing Tortuca. "Tortuca suffered seventeen broken bones," she said. "Including not only each thigh, but his skull, twice, one hideous extruding broken shin, and a minor yet excruciating fracture of his left little toe."

"It's good you've begun at last, then," Tom said. "Although Tortuca is still ahead of you by sixteen breaks."

And they might have bickered so for some time, from the irritation of long acquaintance, but they began to hear the approach of music once more.

FLINT AND WEAVER, the two Tinker women who had helped Jenny tend her leg, bore her slowly on a litter through the crystal-lit tunnels, with Tom and Sparky following.

Flint generally wore a bright, four-pointed cap, while Weaver's hat was a great, black ball of bearskin; otherwise, they had the same small, dark look – like stoats, Jenny had thought more than once. Still, they had always been gentle with her.

The little procession travelled down paved, crystal-lit crevices, around sharp corners, and through odd tunnels, until Tom and Jenny had lost even their notions of port and starboard. Finally, they came into a wide space cleft from the rock, where the walls were striped with shades of raw stone, and veins of ore that glittered in the torchlight.

Flint and Weaver brought them to a rough table laden with platters of venison and bannock, and stone tumblers of fresh spring water. They gave Tom a polished tree stump for a seat, and provided Jenny with a cushioned settee to favour her leg. Then they went off to join other Tinkers moving in the shadows.

All at once, Edge-Gleamer was beside them. Now he had two rings in each ear, and wore a crown of feathers, and a new chain of brass buttons stretched across his fine quilled jacket.

"Welcome proper to our Hidlin Hall!" the Tinker cried. "There are more guests than ye tonight, come for this wild great birl!" He cocked first one ear, then the other, backwards. He gave Tom and Jenny a large, unsettling smile. "Now sit and watch and listen to our Hooley Revels!"

All at once a great shout began to echo through the vast dim cavern. Edge-Gleamer leapt away and the Tinkers began to dance in the torch light. Not in lines or circles, not in pairs hand-in-hand, but all of them together, in strange jumps and shifting figures; all the while playing on pipes, on drums, or the buzzing, reedy shawms.

More and more Tinkers slipped out of the darkness; a good dozen at least, all small and dark; and they danced in weird lines. The music built to eerie chords and then all at once it would drop away to leave a place for a sudden shout.

It was like nothing Jenny had ever heard, and the bent and crouching shadows were stranger than any she had ever dreamt.

As the dance went on, Edge-Gleamer drew his sword, and began to reel it about his head, singing words in the private language of the Tinkers, tossing his blade in the air in time to the shouts of his fellows.

"It is like seeing some strange goblin-dance," Tom whispered. Then Edge-Gleamer looked towards them both and began to sing in words they could understand:

Sing the song of the Tinker's sword;
And crafty and cunning call its lord.
Like lightning are its cuts and lashes –
And fallen foes record its passage.

Sparky, who seemed notably indifferent to the Tinkers, began to howl, somewhat in time, and almost in tune.

Some while later – Jenny couldn't know how long – Flint moved out of the dance and made an odd sort of bow to Tom. "Yer friend is brack," she said, with a gesture to Jenny, and then the Tinker took his hand. "But we count it fit for sich ootlin strangers ta birl in our wild hooley."

Jenny had learned enough to follow the general drift of the Tinker's words, but Tom looked at her, confused.

"You're to join in the dancing," she told him. "To celebrate with them, as I can't. In fact, it would be rude –"

Flint made an unsettling, sharp smile, and began to skip towards the dance, pulling Tom after her. Suddenly Jenny thought of stoats again, and remembered how they danced to mesmerize the rabbits they hunted.

"Tom!" she called. "Remember the fate fleet Feeahy found!"

Tom dropped Flint's hand, and all at once the music stopped, and all the Tinkers' dancing.

Flint looked at Jenny reproachfully. "Nay, kempie girlie," she said. Farther off, among the dancers, Edge-Gleamer's ears twitched. He said something to the others, and the music resumed, but Edge-Gleamer himself came back to Tom and Jenny.

"Fleet Feeahy," the Tinker said. "Now there was a brave and bonnie dancer."

"The Ealda say Tinkers stole her off," Tom said.

"So they would," Edge-Gleamer agreed. "For we like the things they leave us: the rice and sugar and all such things we count it muckle dreary to gather. And the Ealda and the Riverfolk like our clever mending of their odds and ends. But we seldom share our hearts or speech, and so we doubt and misjudge one another."

"I note you still do not speak of Feeahy," Jenny said.

Edge-Gleamer looked her in the eye, and for a moment, Jenny wondered how old the Tinker was. "The Ealda think that sad story is theirs," he said, "and count her stay with us a long time. But we grieve that fair Feeahy, who loved our life and all the wild and hooly birls of our hidden brochs, grew tired of it in the end and left us."

"And how long is it that we will stay with you?" Jenny demanded. For she had a sudden fear that they wouldn't see their friends again until even Gimlet was old and grey.

But at the same time, Tom asked, "Why did you find us?"

Edge-Gleamer answered Tom first. "I might ask the same of you," he said. "But I'll tell ye how it was: we smelled the North on ye. We felt yer Strangers' touch, like all the Wild and the whole of the Vastlands did, but we smelled the North as well. That's a scent the Tinkers haven't smelled for a quare long time. So we watched ye, and of course we desired yer Star-Glass." He gave Tom a hard look. "I dinna apologize for wanting that. For it came from some hoard of the Elves, and they had it from the deeps of the Earth, which are our home now – and after all, it's the Stone of Heart's Desire."

"But you had the Star-Glass already," Tom said. "Why did you rescue us?"

"Och!" the Tinker exclaimed. "Pishkeen Mawr has long been un-friend and foe to me, and when I can I dash that wickit speerit's plans just for sport and pleasement."

"And how long will we stay with you?" Jenny asked again. "How long do you mean to keep us here?"

Edge-Gleamer looked at her, affronted. "Kempie Jenny," he said. "Fisher-Girl. I thought we had been friends again. Ye'll leave in all good time, and we'll escort ye where ye will – taking care only that our hidlin ways remain hidden, and the secrit halls still unknown. But dinna forget, yer leg is broke and mending. When ye're hale and hearty ask again."

"You are careful of our welfare," Tom said, but Jenny knew that really he doubted the Tinker's words.

"I will not cast ye out while yer friend is halt and crippled," Edge-Gleamer said. "For there's one worse reason yet we watched over ye two young sailors."

"Name it," said Jenny. "For we have seen worse already, Tom and I both."

"Ye have not seen worse," the Tinker said. "And I will not name it."

"Perhaps you plan to drive the Captain's Expedition away," Tom said. "As the other Strangers were expelled before us."

Edge-Gleamer smiled, with just a flash of teeth. "The land is hard enough to drive visitors away without our bothering. It's not us, but something else that should concern ye; some cold, North thing that has sniffed and crept yer way since the moment yer bonnie ship *Volantix*, with its fine Elf-name, landed."

Jenny saw Tom go pale.

"I have dreamt this since the beginning," he said.

The wild revels went on, hardly pausing, but in time Tom and Jenny grew weary, and the Tinkers they knew led them away from the music, from the strange leaps and shouts and the shadows of the dancers, and took them by devious ways back to their chamber.

"I thought we would stay to see how the birl was concluded," Tom said.

But Edge-Gleamer leaned close and spoke softly to Tom. "Be careful what you ask for, in this place especially. For that is how guests step out of the paths of time they know and into ours."

When the Tinkers had left and the two Ensigns were alone once more, Tom and Jenny looked up again, through their high window to the sky. But the stars had moved on. Sparky looked up too, but there was no moon to even tempt a howl, no light but their little lantern. Blackness closed around them.

"Did you note Edge-Gleamer's blade?" Tom asked. He spoke low, but the words were strong in the rocky dark.

"It is after being like the Captain's sword," Jenny said.

"The Captain's sword, which the *Volantix* found in the cold, dark North," Tom said. "Found at the resting place of the ancient sailors."

Jenny said. "Now there is something you mistrust more than the chance we will sleep and not wake again for six dozen or a drousand years." Jenny said.

"A sword like the one found by the frozen sea," Tom said, "the Star-Glass from Grandfather Frost – Edge-Gleamer even said he could still smell the cold upon it. Why do they scavenge for these tokens of the icy Eaves of the World, and then warn me of some nameless doom from the North?"

Jenny tried to think of what her Godmother would say. "Bad dreams pursued you in your long sleep," she told Tom. "Now put your fears away for the night. Trust that Edge-Gleamer was right so far: We are safe now, in this hidden broch. Dream about climbing towards the sky, about running with Sparky on a sunny day. Let night-thoughts go." Then she blew out the lantern, and there was no sight left.

After a long while, she heard first Sparky, and then Tom, begin the breath of sleep.

Then she was alone again in the chamber of stone, and for the first time since their rescue, her heart began to race. *Have we been charmed into our tomb already?* Jenny wondered, for now the night-thoughts had found her. Then, no matter how she tried to turn her mind to consoling memories or ideals of fortitude, the horror of enclosure pursued her closely.

Until the chase itself exhausted her, and she finally

slept, despite her broke and splinted thigh. She slept at last in the hidden halls of stone, but in her dreams she swam free again in the warm and open sea.

The Tinkers

They put their backs against the great tree

Chapter Nineteen: THE ESCAPE

– a sudden departure – caught in the storm – the needful fire – howling in the wind – a brave last stand –

Even in the tinkers' rocky snuggery, Tom and Jenny felt the door to Autumn begin to close, while another opened slowly to the pale days of Winter.

One day, Flint presented Jenny with a crutch made as neatly as all the Tinkers' things. And each morning Flint or Weaver would come and lead Jenny hobbling slowly down some different mazy path of stone. Tom and Sparky came along to encourage her, and each day she could walk a little longer.

"Soon she will be well enough to leave this place," Tom said to Flint.

But the Tinker only shook her head and laughed. "Leave and forwandert be?" she asked. "And lost be the secrit of the Hidlin Hall!"

Tom could never understand Flint easily, but he could tell that Jenny chafed at her words. When the Tinker was gone, Jenny explained: "Now that I can move about a bit, I become restive, and yearn to be master of my fate once more. But they want us to remain lest we be lost, and their secrets too."

"So we are to remain their guests still," Tom said.

"Or as one of the treasures they claim and hide," Jenny said. "But for now I can think of nothing else to do."

FROM THE FIRST DAY HE WOKE, though, Tom had found the Tinkers less charming than Jenny did. Often in mid-day, while the Tinkers slept on their beds of stone and Jenny rested from her exercise, he would creep out and explore the rocky maze by himself.

But the Tinkers built all their things with craft and cunning, and they had made their snuggery to confuse. He found countless blind turns and obscure corners, a dozen nearly identical sets of narrow, twisting steps that rose and fell like waves in the sea.

Without his Star-Glass, and with neither sun nor star to guide him, Tom only kept his bearings by scratching a map on a page of the waterproof notebook he still kept for his father. Even then he had to trace a path several times before he could trust that he knew one way from another.

Patience, however, was one of Tom's virtues. So one day early in the Winter – as he and Jenny reckoned it – Tom found his way at last to a stair that only led up.

That evening, Jenny asked him how he thought their friends fared. "Have they found a Homely Country by now, do you think? Did they even survive the Chain of Falls?"

"Bonawyn could bring a herd of sheep down a river," Tom said.

"Failing the intervention of some dread thing such as Pishkeen Mawr," said Jenny. "But I find I often think of Gimlet and the dashing Kitchehoar, his new foster-brother. They were become good friends, I think."

"Do you think the Tinkers will ever lead us to them?" Tom asked.

"They are friendly and proud and hospitable folk," Jenny said. "But most secret too. What do we know of them, even now after all these weeks?"

"Just that," said Tom. "They saved us, but now we are enclosed in this place like one of their stony treasures."

"Edge-Gleamer assures us we have not stepped out of our time," Jenny said. "And I do not believe he lies, about that or any matter of general policy. But still we stay."

"Maybe fleet Feeahy once considered all these things too," Tom said. "For surely she never thought she would stay so long. But every time she asked they put her off, until the hours became days and years, and she had left her time at last."

Jenny shuddered. "In the Old Sea, the Lady of the Isle of No Return was most hospitable too," she said quietly. "And healed my sailors' hurts, and called them guests. Only they were guests of the strange kind that somehow couldn't leave."

"In the middle of the day, while you rest, the Tinkers sleep," Tom said. "An odd thing in itself. But if you can exert yourself to move at noon tomorrow, I think I can show you one way out."

And so the next day he led Jenny and Sparky quietly through the mazy paths of stone and up the long, carved steps. At the top, they found a granite door, and when Tom pushed, it swung open silently to the outside, to the sharp light of a Winter day.

"Close it," Jenny whispered.

Tom nodded. "It would be a great risk," he said. "We have no axe, no map, and can only hope to find some shelter."

"Close it only to come back," Jenny said. "For we have our swords, and we are sailors, and I will not be kept like a pet."

For three days Tom and Jenny made quiet plans, prepared their scant equipment, took what chances they could to hide away odds and ends of food.

Then one noon they pulled the blankets from their beds, led Sparky quietly up the long stair, and slipped out the door onto a mossy shelf of rock. As soon as they emerged from a little overhang of stone, the granite door closed behind them and was lost from sight.

Outside at last, Sparky began to bark from pleasure. For now instead of stern rock, dark clouds roofed the sky, and he could see the tree-pillared Wild before them once more, grey with fog and hoarfrost.

"Now we are back in our own time," Tom said.

Jenny laughed. "Out of the tomb and into the fog." The Winter air was still, but already they felt the cold reach for them. Flakes of snow fell gently, and they wrapped their blankets like cloaks around them and started for the grey shelter of the forest.

The Tinkers had made Jenny buskins to replace the boots she had cast aside at Eena Culgach, so she and Tom both made only gentle tracks in the snow. And Sparky was not a big dog.

Soon the falling snow hid all marks of their passing.

BY THEIR BEST GUESS, the Tinker's snuggery was some way East of the Rockmarch where their friends had planned to go, so all afternoon Tom and Jenny walked West, as a damp North wind rose and blew the snow ever more thickly. They walked hard to get as far as they could before night, and to keep warm.

Even the sheltered paths through the spruce wood were steep and treacherous with the falling snow. They cut staffs to steady themselves, but Tom slipped and fell more than once. And Jenny had her crutch to manage too, and as the hours passed she grew bruised and weary.

"We escape from the Hidlin Hall only to meet a storm," she said once as she paused to rest. "Do you count that as good luck or bad?"

"I have known colder weather," Tom pointed out.

"Oh yes," Jenny said. "Nothing can ever seem properly cold again to all you who sailed the *Volantix* through the icy Eaves of the World. But you were outfitted for that. You had sweaters, and toques with long tails."

"The snow might be good luck," Tom said. "For it will hide our trail."

As the afternoon began to fade, they came to the crest of a long, bare ridge. Now the cold wind had blown the fog away; the snow came in smaller, sharper flakes, and gusts tossed it at them in handfuls.

Tom felt his ears begin to ache with the cold.

"I'm sorry I was so eager," Jenny said. "Perhaps this was folly." Tom saw that she was trembling.

"We will find shelter in the valley," he said. "Do not lose hope."

Jenny made a kind of grin as she leaned on her staff. *"I* do not lose hope," she said. "I am the one who tells you, 'Do not lose hope.' Only this is as far as we can go. We must rest merely as a –" and now Tom saw she had to work to form her words "– as a matter of practicality."

"In the valley," Tom said. Sparky began a sad, comic dance then, lifting his freezing paws from the snow one by one, and Tom picked the dog up and held him in his cloak even as they walked.

Dusk had almost fallen before they stumbled their way into the valley, and found shelter among a grove of small spruce trees.

THERE, AMONG THE TALL SPRUCE, the North wind seemed less cruel. Still the air grew colder as the sun began to fail, and Tom saw Jenny stumbled more often with her crutch and staff. Each time her blanket slipped from around her shoulders.

He knew how perilous it was for Jenny to be shaking in the damp cold, and what it would mean to stop and rest. "Just a little farther," he told her, but when Jenny looked at him, Tom thought he had never seen her so harrowed. *She will not speak again,* he thought, *for she would have to admit despair.*

Now he had begun to tremble with the cold himself, and for a moment he indulged in silent recrimination. *I have led us to disaster,* he thought. *First at Eena Culgach, and now into this Winter storm.*

But he knew what Jenny would have counselled, if she had been capable, so he did *not* give in to despair. Instead they floundered on, numb and wordless, until Tom found what he had been looking for among the frost-furred spruce: a long-dead tree, grey and dry, that stood as thick as his thigh. He shivered as he looked it up and down. "It will have to do," he said.

He led Jenny to one great, thick tree and had her sit against it. Under its wide boughs, the snow had hardly gathered, and its trunk served as a shelter.

Jenny spoke slowly: "What must be done?" she asked. "What should I do?"

Tom set his dog in Jenny's arms so they could cosset one

another. "The first practicality," he said carefully, "is firewood."

For a few moments Tom hopped up and down. He beat his arms against his side. Then at last he began to break off what low, dead boughs and branches he could find on the trees around them.

AFTER HE'D MADE A PILE OF DRY BRANCHES in front of the big spruce, Jenny tried to rouse herself. "What's second?" she said.

Tom put his hands over his ears for a moment. "Kindling," he told her. "Can you gather the old needles and twigs from these?"

She smiled stiffly. "Even with cold and clumsy fingers."

Then Tom went back to the dead tree, grabbed up with both hands, and tried to break it from its stump.

He pulled as hard as he had ever pulled in his life. He tugged until he felt his eyes bulge; until he yelled in frustration. He was almost at the limit of his strength when he heard a thin crack. Tom yelled once more, and finally the tree fell.

It was only when he looked down at his numb hands that he knew they were cut and bleeding.

But one tree wasn't firewood. To feed a fire it had to be broken apart – heavy work that no sword or knife could manage, and Tom had no axe.

"Could you strike a fire?" he called to Jenny. But she only held up her stiff fingers.

Tom would have to strike the fire *and* crack the wood apart. So for a moment, Tom made a grim calculation. If he started the little pile of branches on fire now, would he be able to break up the old spruce in time to keep the fire burning?

But if he began by breaking up the tree with his bare hands, when he was done, would he still be able to start a fire, or would his hands be as stiff and cold as Jenny's?

He looked at Jenny and Sparky huddling together against the tree. *I could fail them either way,* Tom thought. *But at least I can warm them now, for a moment.*

So he went and knelt beside them. For a moment he wrapped his fingers around hers, and under Sparky's coat to feel his dog's warm skin. Then he took out his tinderbox. "You gave this to me lest I find myself shrammed and chill in some dark harbour," he said. "And so I used it on the great mountain of ice."

Jenny smiled vaguely. "A pleasant recollection," she said. "Except that you dropped it there and it was lost."

"I recovered it," Tom said. "In a miraculous fashion. Why do you remind me of its fall?"

"You won't drop it now," Jenny whispered, and she clutched Sparky tightly again. "You will light the fire."

AND TOM DID STRIKE A SPARK in the cold, and make a flame from the tinder – and then the kindling, and then the small pile of branches caught. For a moment he felt the heat wash over him, as fresh and shocking as the first cold wind.

He took his sword and cut viciously at other, thicker branches, and laid them out for Jenny. Then he went back to the old tree he had felled, and wedged one end among the trunks of living spruce, and made the tree a great lever to work against itself. Tom was tired now, but he put his shoulder against the other end, and pushed with his legs until it broke, and broke again.

Then they had fuel to begin a proper fire. Soon the North wind found the flames and blew them hot and high. "A fine blaze," said Jenny. "It begins to revive me."

"It won't last the night," Tom said. But then Tom had an inspiration.

He followed a trail that led down into a creek, and along it he found two beaver-felled birch trees.

Getting them loose from the bush along the water was hard work, but dragging the trees back to the fire was harder. And when Tom had laid them across one another in a sort of thin X, he was at the end of his strength.

"I call that heroic work," Jenny said. "At once steadfast, brawny, and imaginative."

Tom only lay on the ground before the fire. When he could speak, he remembered the inspiration that had led him to the creek. "You should also thank Oak-Biter, the Beaver-Prince," he said.

Through the night the storm blew colder and harder. The trees burned through where they crossed, of course, and then there were four long logs, and so on, and Tom and Jenny took turns adjusting the fire.

After a while they cut down a few saplings – slow work, with only knives and swords – and propped them against a branch of the tall tree that had become their refuge in the storm. When they shingled this shelter with spruce boughs, they had done all they could. The two Ensigns and their dog could only huddle together before the fire, and wait for the blizzard to end.

As dawn approached, their wood was almost gone. But still the North wind blew.

IN THE THIN LIGHT, Tom and Jenny toasted bits of bread and cheese on the waning fire to serve as breakfast. They gave Sparky a few scraps of meat they had kept for him, which he devoured at once. Then they clutched their cloaks tightly around them and considered their chances.

"So the nightmare becomes an awful daydream," Jenny mused. "But without the happy prospect of waking."

"There is no more easy wood to be found," Tom said. He was shaking now all the time, quivering with the cold, and beside him, Jenny was pale and unusually quiet.

"We hiked all day, despite being only thinly clad against such weather," Jenny finally said.

"We fought the blizzard all night," Tom said.

Now the wind gusted through their little shelter, and in the bleakest light before the dawn, they felt the cold air stroke them roughly, like the rasp of a cat's tongue. Swirls of snow blew up around them, and slid cold fingers down their collars.

Soon the sun would rise, but they knew the storm would swallow all its warmth, all its comfort, and that no blue sky would greet them.

"We must comport ourselves to face our doom without flinching," said Jenny, "– or giving up hope."

"There are two ways we could meet it," Tom observed. "We can run through the stormy woods hoping to stumble on some lucky chance, or simply wait for it to find us here."

"Long odds either way," Jenny said. "But we have no chance to find any help here, and will only grow more cold and weary until we sleep and – very possibly – fail to wake."

Tom nodded. "But it would come upon us more gently this way than fighting the storm. And come upon Sparky more gently too."

"Sparky has his own warm coat," Jenny pointed out, as she cradled the dog absently. "Perhaps in the end he would not take that long sleep, but find his luck somewhere in this tree-pillared Wild."

Then they were quiet for a long time.

"Somehow the Winter tempts me to foolish journeys," Tom said. "I am sorry for it."

"We knew we took a gamble, only we have lost," Jenny told him. "But of all the ways we might meet our end, the most ignoble would be as helpless captives, here at what should be the beginning of our careers as Explorers. At least we have fought against the Wild."

And still the North wind blew on, colder and damper, as if the spirit of the place meant to bury them. The snow drifted up higher and higher against their little shelter, even there in the grove in the valley.

A LONG TIME LATER, when the storm was bright with the morning, Tom asked, "Why is Sparky fidgeting?"

Jenny had to rouse herself to answer. "Perhaps he wants to mark a tree," she said.

"No," said Tom. "He hears something. He is nervous."

"What could be abroad in this storm?" Jenny asked.

"Nothing good," said Tom. "The thing which hunts us, perhaps, come at last."

"Foolish thing," said Jenny, as she struggled to her feet. "How much less trouble for all of us if it had only waited an hour or two."

So – from dumb habit, Tom thought – the two Ensigns prepared to make a stand in the blowing snow. They stood over the gusting remains of their fire, and looked out into the storm.

Sparky was noisy now, making little growling barks.

Then Tom and Jenny heard it too. "It is the clamour of wolves," Tom said.

Jenny swallowed. "At least it is not an ignoble end. And every battle brings a chance."

Tom began to laugh at Jenny's unvarying defiance. "It is not the doom I feared," he said. "But I can smell their breath on me already."

"Why do they hunt in the storm?" Jenny asked.

"Bonawyn said the Wild was testing us, once," Tom said. "And Edge-Gleamer said the land itself drove visitors away."

They put their backs against the great tree that had guarded them in the storm. Now the wind tore at them freely, but they hardly minded it.

The wolves were baying like hounds after a fox, and Tom and Jenny drew their swords with numb hands. At least a dozen wolves were giving throat now, Tom thought; great, rough howls coming closer, while Sparky too made terrible noises: barking and crying and snarling, dancing in fear and fury around their feet.

"If we still had muskets they would have served to frighten them better," Tom said.

Jenny nodded. "The first ones will leap for our throats," she said. "But it would be seemly to slash one or two before the others pull us down."

So – not for the first time – they faced their end. "It is easier to be brave, now that I have no strength left for terror," Tom said. But he did feel distress that Jenny and Sparky would find their ends too. Tom took his sword in both hands. "Come on!" he yelled into the wind.

Beside him Jenny leaned against the tree and made herself ready. "Try us if you will!" she shouted.

Now the wolves were loud; now their voices echoed in

the little valley; now they appeared at last, springing down the trail into the grove of spruce; two wolves first, great and shaggy and terrible. Their yellow eyes burned and Sparky screamed – if dogs can scream. Behind them came two more; then two more again – but all in harness, tugging at leather traces.

And the traces pulled a small, covered sleigh, a cariole, and behind it in his fine buskins ran Edge-Gleamer.

When the Tinker cracked an enormous whip above the wolves, they came to a stop, and Edge-Gleamer ran out among them. He called rough words of praise while the animals barked and leapt at him happily, as if they were all great friends.

He looked at Tom and Jenny, at the shelter they had made, at the fire that was dying. He gave them a nod and a fierce, hungry grin. "That was well done," he shouted over the wind. "But think on the work ye put me to! Think on how ye've imposed upon yer hosts."

The wolves jumped and tugged idly at their traces now, and Sparky barked more quietly now – timidly in fact. But in their astonishment, neither of the Ensigns could speak. Tom turned to Jenny, because he knew she would find words first.

"We won't be captives!" she called. "Your wolves or your storm can have us first."

"The storm comes when it will," Edge-Gleamer said, "and not at Tinker's calling. And the wolves are not servants but friends of ours, for we are as wild as they, and hate the dread cat Pishkeen Mawr, and we'll neither know a master."

Then he took a fur cloak from the cariole and put it carefully round Jenny's shoulders. "Kempie girlie," he said. "My mother named me Tornawel. And if I break my word you can use that secrit name to curse me."

Then he put a cloak about Tom. "Fine work, my brave callant," he said. "Few Strangers would have survived this rough night. For I thought I'd find ye dead, but now we can be fools together."

Tom looked at the Tinker. "I thought you were the thing that hunts me, come at last."

"That greater trial still awaits ye," Edge-Gleamer said. "When the Strangers entered the Wild, all creaturs were stirred to see what kind of things ye were. Creaturs both good and wickit, and not all have finished looking."

THE TINKER'S WORDS did not much comfort Tom.

But Edge-Gleamer settled the two Ensigns deep among furs in the cariole, and then gave a great crack of the whip to start the wolves pulling. The Tinker himself ran behind the sleigh, and the steps of his buskins were light, left hardly a mark in the drifting snow.

Then Jenny exclaimed at a strange thing. Sparky ran alongside the wolves, trying to keep pace, while the wild things, with their cheeks back and tongues waggling, seemed to laugh at him in welcome.

"He is in their charge now, in the Wild," Tom said. "As we are guests of the Tinkers."

Chapter Twenty:
WINTER IN THE STONY HALL

– the Blood Promise – clumsy lumps
– a league of Fates and Powers – sword-work
– the exiles from the starry halls –

As the cariole sped along behind the team of wolves, the small Tinker leapt onto the ends of the runners from time to time, and made sure of Tom and Jenny.

"You two caused us a strange calculation," he said once. "For we exposed our Hidlin Hall by seeking ye, and our first law is that of hiding."

Jenny turned and gave him what she believed to be a shrewd look. "Was it that you were worried we might survive and tell the tale?"

He laughed at her then, in the careless manner Jenny considered most annoying. "We had no fear of ye living through the storm," he said. "For ye did well armed only with your swords and some fire-craft, but, in truth, to survive so unprovisioned in that weather, ye would have needed snow-craft too. And I dinna think a Stranger yet has learned the art of making a house of snow."

"I saw one once, in the far North," Tom said. "It glowed from light within."

"Aye, that's how they look," Edge-Gleamer said. "Not dark like stone, but bright like cloud grown thick. And ye hardly need a candle to keep them warm."

As the cariole came to the crest of a small rise, the Tinker broke off to gain the wolves' attention by a mighty crack of his whip. He called for the beasts to turn North along the hill, then he turned back to Tom and Jenny.

"Nay, kempie girlie," he said. "We didn't worry ye'd live to expose us. But we did consider that if we brought ye back like this, ye might know how to find our great hall, which is hidden even from the Ealda." Then he looked at her with a shrewdness Jenny could not match. "But ye don't, do ye? And all that great, cabbling quarrel we had about the matter was for naught."

"We are sailors," Tom said. "And so know our compass points after even the smallest sight of stars. But if we're North or South or East or West of the falls at Eena Culgach, we don't know," said Tom. "Nor even where our friends are."

"Och! Then it was good I came looking," said the Tinker. "Though clear against all our established customs and traditions."

"Why did you, then?" asked Jenny.

"Because ye were guests of ours, and because ye would have died alone in the cold," he said. "And that would have shamed us. So ye see how both debts and error compound.

For if I had only left Pishkeen Mawr be, to swallow the two of ye, we'd never have had to argy the matter."

"Yes," Tom said. "That would have been the end of us, and less trouble all round."

But Jenny had to know one more thing: "If secrecy is the great law of the Tinkers, how will you ever let us go?"

For a moment, Edge-Gleamer cocked an ear as if he were listening to something far away. "Just as we did with fleet Feeahy, who left us when we grew tiresome," he said. "But first, we will ask yer word ye never tell the tale. So when ye are fit and well, and the snow more firm than slushy, we will lead you out through obscure passages and point ye towards yer home."

"Towards our home, or to our shipmates?" Jenny asked, for she knew it was best to be clear even with well-meant bargains.

"It's nae difference," said Edge-Gleamer. "For in the Wild ye count yer friends as home." Then he gave another cry to steer his wolves, and leapt off to begin running behind the cariole once more.

"They do not pull smoothly," Jenny observed to Tom. "For they are wild beasts, don't forget. But still they are most eager."

Edge-Gleamer didn't follow the path Tom and Jenny had taken, so they were surprised when the wolves drew them to a halt before a small hill. At its foot, a small stream still ran open through the snow, and behind the stream, climbing East up the rough and sheltered slope, stood a small stand of pine and maple.

Flint, the Tinker Jenny felt was nearest to being a friend, stood waiting there, even in the blowing storm. She was dressed in hunting gear, and displayed a small stag hanging over her shoulders – small, but still, Jenny thought, almost as heavy as the Tinker herself.

The wolves stood quietly while Edge-Gleamer removed their harness. Then they watched him closely as he called out to them through the wind and snow:

"Ye came at our need," he told the wolves, "as ye've promised; and as we will come at yers." Then he said a few more words in the private language of his people, and a strange stillness grew over the animals. Even Sparky stood still and solemn.

Then Edge-Gleamer cried, "Here is the seal of our Blood-Promise!" The wolves began to tremble, and Sparky came back to stand behind Tom. The Tinker put his hands on the two Ensigns' shoulders, and suddenly Jenny had a terrible fear. But the Tinker only whispered, "Steady."

Now Flint tossed the deer she carried down among the wolves, and all at once the little band began to seem like wolves indeed.

They began to rip at the carcass. First, in order of rank, as dogs and wolves reckoned it – by some mixture of size and seniority – and then more wildly as they leapt and tore at the meat. In their excitement they even bit at one another, and snarled and slavered as they tore flesh from bone.

Tom and Jenny were glad to feel Edge-Gleamer's calm hands on their shoulders. But the sight of the feeding wolves made him bare his teeth. And when Flint finally looked over at the Ensigns and smiled, they saw her teeth were still dark with blood. "Dinna be alarmed!" Edge-Gleamer whispered. "Not by all their snarls and clamour. For don't we eat flesh just like the wolves? – only we have finer table manners."

When the wolves had finished, all that remained of the stag was a bloody mess of scrap and bone and antler, and the wolves seemed to recollect themselves. Then they ran in a circle around the cariole, and back along the trail by which they'd come.

Soon they vanished into the storm; into the tree-pillared shelter of the woods; into the Wild itself.

The Blood Promise had been a terrible sight, but somehow after that the Hidlin Halls seemed brighter to them, and they found their way about more easily.

"The dreamy murk since Eena Culgach seems to lift," Tom said.

"It is still a dream," said Jenny. "But the sharp-edged dream of a real place, and not merely the obscure apprehensions of a nightmare."

Once they had sworn an oath to secrecy, the Tinkers

seemed to trust them more, and with guides, or even on their own, Tom and Jenny began to explore more of the Hidlin Halls.

Sparky followed them happily, up and down narrow stairs cut into the rock, and across the slight stone bridges that spanned deep clefts. The Tinkers themselves seemed to leave few smells, but even a dog could find wonder in their halls. Sparky saw high walls where the water slid down the rock in smooth sheets. He saw chambers that had been opened to display walls streaked by crystal: purple and red amethyst, and quartz that glittered with gold.

Jenny marvelled at those bright hollows. "This is their home," she said. "It is no wonder they believe all gems and jewels are theirs by right."

But sometimes in their explorations they led Sparky not into glimmering chambers, but through tunnels that stretched into profound darkness. Down these the dog was scared to go.

"Never mind, boy," Tom told him once. "For that way is blacker even than the tin mines of the wee, knocking men." Which was something Tom knew from experience.

And, "Never mind, Sparky," Jenny told him another time. "For that's a passage darker even then midnight upon the deepest bosom of the sea." Which was also true. For once upon a midnight, Sparky and Jenny had both been gathered to the deepest bosom of the sea.

Still, there were other darknesses that Sparky liked: great, dark chasms where the air rose from unsoundable depths. If he had had his fill of exploring for the day, and suspected that neither Tom nor Jenny had further need of his dog-talents, he liked to sleep by those.

Now and then they came to spans that neither dog nor Ensign could cross, for the Tinkers had only cast a single rope across. A cat might have considered walking those, but Sparky never even thought to try.

And Tom and Jenny, who'd often run across the rigging and ratlines of a tall ship, were galled to find ropes beyond their daring.

But for the Forgotten Folk, those ropes could have been great high-roads. Once three of them watched Weaver run carelessly over a line stretched across a vast break in the rock before she realized her guests lacked the skill to follow her.

Sparky usually didn't pay much attention to the Tinkers, yet even he barked in surprise.

As they reflected on such feats of the Tinkers, Tom said, "They must think us clumsy lumps."

"They must think *you* a clumsy lump," Jenny agreed. "Whereas I would seem a limping lump and turtle-awkward both. In fact, ever since we came to the Vastlands, the Fates and Powers seem to have been in league to reduce my self-regard."

Tom gave her a curious glance, but Jenny looked away, and pointed her chin upwards as she continued: "For

Bonawyn, as even Gimlet pointed out, is like me, but somehow not so small or young or foolish. And even in the Hidlin Halls, here are Flint and Weaver to make me feel some poorly-knit lummox."

"And *has* your self-regard been reduced?" Tom asked.

She gave him a sharp look. *"No,"* she said. "But I resent the attempt."

"At least the Fates and Powers have a proper concern for your character and special potential," Tom said.

"Yes," said Jenny. "Far worse to be forgotten by them altogether –" but then she realized he was having sport with her and made a long pause. "Tom," she resumed, "you know full well I only spoke of the concern of the various Fates and Powers after a metaphorical fashion. Of course I do not believe I am some special charge of theirs."

She watched for Tom to nod before she added, "Although young Officers and Explorers such as ourselves would not be the worst candidates for their particular concern."

"No," Tom agreed solemnly. "But perhaps the Fates and Powers really mean this voyage for Gimlet's instruction."

"It does you no credit to so mock me, who am your friend," Jenny said. "I have, besides, a broken thigh."

EVEN THERE IN THE HIDLIN HALLS, they could feel Winter deepen.

In the chamber where Tom and Jenny slept, a brazier

kept them warm. But from the tall shaft above them cold winds and small flakes of snow would swirl. And when their breath rose it met cold rock, and furred the walls with frost.

So now as they wandered the Hidlin Halls, they liked to visit most the deep vents where the warm air rose.

The Tinkers, though, hardly seemed to mind the growing cold. And those they saw looked busy now, and quickly slipped away.

"We will have another grand revel soon," Edge-Gleamer explained when they asked him. "So ye see the preparations afoot, and our people go to make secrit trades and fulfil bargains."

"Do they visit Ahgeneh's people?" Tom asked.

"Secrit trades," Edge-Gleamer repeated.

"For wild and hooley dances, as before?" asked Jenny.

The Tinker made an unsettling grin. "Larger, wilder hooleys," he said. "And would ye take a proper part in them now, the both of ye? Now that we have answered even to yer last suspicion?"

Jenny looked at Tom. "We are only awkward Strangers," she said. "And would be mortified by your better grace and all your fine steps and leaping."

"Och, have nae worries aboot yon Hooley," the Tinker said. "For in time the speerit of the thing would come over ye. But there is one step ye might learn now to please me."

It was Tom who understood the Tinker right away. "The sword-dance," he said.

Edge-Gleamer nodded and looked away a moment, the first time Jenny had seen him at a loss for words. "Now I think ye're brave enough," he said. "The both of ye. But – if ye're determined to wander the Wild alone again, well, I saw how low, and awkward, it was ye held yer swords against me."

Jenny flushed. "I've no mind to insult ye," the Tinker said. "Only I've had a long life of practise –"

"All right," Tom said at once. "What do we do wrong?"

Edge-Gleamer drew his odd and ancient blade and saluted them with some swift flourish. Tom and Jenny shared a glance and drew their own swords. *Even our salutes seem slow and plain,* Jenny thought, and her heart began to hammer.

For they had never really had a proper lesson, and now they were about to cross swords – to cross live steel – with this bold Tinker. *He is no goblin made of creaking wood,* she thought, *but will come on us fast as lightning.*

Then Edge-Gleamer leapt forward. Jenny tried to ready herself, but the Tinker's sword flashed twice; and all at once Jenny's blade, like Tom's, flew ringing across the stone floor.

"This is a defect in our education," she said to Tom. "But except the Captain, what sailor knows a sword for more than a steel-edged club?"

"We have also neglected to study the relevant parts in my father's great *Encyclopaedia,"* said Tom.

"Is yer father a sword-master?" asked the Tinker.

"In fact, he is a Scholar," Tom said. "But among his many studies, he has categorized the arts of combat. For example, he has one collection of diagrams named 'Universal Parries'; another, 'Unwardable Thrusts,' and so on."

Edge-Gleamer cocked an ear forward. "And what would be the result," he asked quietly, "if someone were to use such a Universal Parry against a similarly infallible Unwardable Thrust?"

"Ah," Tom said. "You present a paradox of a kind my Dad says philosophers have given a particular name –"

"Tom's father is a lore-master," Jenny said quickly, for she knew that like his father, Tom could lose himself in the contemplation of such topics, "a *great* and *famous* Scholar. Although, as the learned man himself admits, his studies are more concerned with both categories and abstractions, at which he is most adept, than with what could be termed *actual* matters."

The Tinker ran his tongue along the points of his teeth. *"Och,* it's few who live long enough to master both word and deed," he said.

Then he lifted their swords on the point of his own blade and presented their hilts to them. "But perhaps Tom's father would approve that, having first shown ye a practical instance, I'll now give the general maxim it illustrates: *Never hold a blade with yer hand turned in.* For that's how swords are lost most often."

After that, Edge-Gleamer gave them more instruction

when he could, lessons that concerned both the sword-dance itself, and how best to use their blades in earnest. And if Tom and Jenny weren't his students long enough for either to become truly adept, at least he taught them to hold their swords – and to keep their guard up and stand their ground, even in the face of his most furious onslaughts.

"And having learned but those two things," Edge-Gleamer told them, "ye've gained half the art already."

THEY HADN'T SEEN FLINT for some time when Weaver woke them up one night, and had them dress most warmly. Then she led them by some devious way to a lookout atop the hills, where she was keeping vigil.

"Now screenge ye through yon starry sky," she said, "and have a proper lookit through the welkin."

They looked up to see a startling still, clear winter night. Far above, the stars blazed brightly from the black-robed sky, and below, the earth's snowy blanket twinkled. "The kind of night astronomers most favour," Tom said quietly.

"No wonder," said Jenny. "For it is beautiful to a degrec that must be portentous." For a few moments they only stood there, and breathed out sparkling clouds of frost. "Even the cold is curious refreshing," Jenny said. "And helps to wake me up."

Tom nodded, and pulled up the hood on her deerskin coat. "At first it wakes you," he said.

Jenny knew Tom would never think she had enough respect for the Winter. But neither Tom nor the cold disturbed her, and she only took a slow, deep breath.

When Weaver spoke at last, she pointed into the Southern sky. "See where the twa fair ladies stand," she said, "near to yon great Hunter?"

"The Carpenter called those stars the Twins," Jenny said.

Tom nodded. "Twins orphaned from the Hall of the Stars, my Dad says."

"Nay," said the Tinker. "Neither orphaned nor twins, but friends who was forgotten. Did you never ken their story?"

She briefly showed her little, sharp teeth. *Stoats,* Jenny thought again. "I'll tell it to ye," Weaver said. "And whit for did ye think I brung ye to bide my friend's retour and hame-comin – aside from th' pleasure of yer gleg and birkie company?"

"You say *gleg* and *birkie,*" Jenny said. "Or as we would name it, *quick* and *lively.* But why, when we are not half so quick nor lively as any Tinker?"

"Nay," Weaver said, and Jenny was relieved she smiled more gently, and did not bare her teeth. "But ye are childer and we are eldren. Lang, lang-lived eldren by your years. Fleet Feeahy is an auld tale to ye, but I still mind her veesit. So ye seem quick to us, for ye be gane as soon as butterflees." And then she told them a tale, there as they waited in that cold clear night.

The Tinkers

Of course, Weaver's speech was thick with the Tinkers' own strange words, but by now Tom and Jenny knew them well enough, so this is how they understood her story:

"BACK BEFORE THE WORLD AWOKE," Weaver said, "when all was only dream-time, the Powers in the Hall of Stars lived and walked among us.

"They still visit now and then, concealed by stealth and shadow. But then they walked here freely – and made the earth, and found their great adventures.

"There was the Queen of the Hall of the Stars herself, of course, and the King of Wind and Sky beside her. And other powers great and small gathered to their great court, like the two Bears who roam the North together.

"The Champion of Heaven was mightiest of them all, but next was the starry-belted Hunter. The great Hunter coursed the world, chasing wickit things like dragons. And those he found he bounded up, in prisons deeper than the deepest sea – where they could cause no trouble.

"And first among that Hunter's train was fierce, keen-sighted Straikha. That spear-maiden catched the Hunter's awful quarry down; hardly beast nor monster escaped her. Nor eluded Straikha's friend, swift-rushing Terrier, the young, wild huntress.

"All across that dream-time world, keen-sighted Straikha and swift-rushing Terrier chased together. They found no forest too thick for them, no mountain hold unreachable, but pursued their prey into the deepest dens: dark, wickit, slithering things, or furry, fanged, ferocious beasts, and helped the Hunter with their killing. But best of all they liked the great hunt of the dream-time game: the mighty fathers of the deer or moose, or Bugbears or fast foxes.

"But as they settled the world at last, and it began to waken, the Powers departed for their halls; to their starry homes in heaven. So the Hunter recalled his band, for the dream-time was fast fading.

"And keen-eyed Straikha heard the Hunter blow his horn, and began to follow as he summoned. But swift-rushing Terrier was on the trail of a scaly, flying worm, that last one they'd never captured.

"The Hunter's horn rang a second time, for the dream-time spell was ending. And keen-sighted Straikha called to her friend, 'Come quickly, for the Gate is closing!'

"But the Terrier only bared her teeth, for letting such a prize go free went clear against her nature. 'Here I have Quarry Worm,' she cried, 'and won't leave before it's collared.'

"So Straikha paused even at the Gate, and looked for her friend to follow. The Hunter sounded his horn a third, last time, as the divide from dream-time opened.

"Swift-rushing Terrier hardly heard the horn, so intently was she stalking. And the Hunter's spear-maiden, keen-eyed Straikha, leapt back to this world, just as the dream-time sundered.

"Then with the great tumult of that awakening, the Quarry Worm escaped from Terrier. Too late! So, alone of all the starry homes, the hall of those two is always empty.

"Sometimes in the dark woods, or from a great high hill, those two look up to see their house of stars. And sometimes when the curtain thins, the other Powers join them. But mostly those two hunt dark places all alone, still after their hissing Quarry.

"For keen-eyed Straikha and her friend, the swift-rushing Terrier, are almost forgotten by the Hall of Stars, and bound to this waking world forever."

"That's a story I never knew," Tom said. "Not from all the notes for my father's *Encyclopaedia,* or from the Carpenter, who knew so much about the Stars."

"Or from my Godmother," said Jenny, "Who keeps so many secrets."

"The Tinkers count that our ain and faverit tale," Weaver whispered. "For we oursels are so forgotten."

"But you live hidden on purpose, now," Jenny said. "Who was it that forgot you?"

But the small Tinker shook her head, as if she had said too much already.

So Tom and Jenny only looked up again, at the stars by the bright, tall Hunter. And Jenny saw her breath rise twinkling towards the sky, rushing from the cold night weather.

"Ye've been brae company," Weaver said. "And listen well for Strangers. But I forgot yer blood runs thin. Now I'll light ye both a fire."

As Jenny stamped her feet to warm them, she saw how quickly the Tinker got wood burning. "Their every act is smart and neat," she said quietly to Tom. "Down to how they tie their laces."

But Weaver had turned an ear to hear them. "Practise it all ten thoosan times," she said. "And ye'll be as quick as we are."

"You must be very old," Tom said, but they never knew if the Tinker had heard him.

For just then she stood straight, as if she'd heard some signal, and looked down across the slopes of rock and woodland. Somewhere a green light briefly flared, and Weaver made a great shout in her own language.

Then she spun three times before she stopped, facing Tom and Jenny. "Flint brings her gatherings hame at last!" she cried. "How finely ye've helped await her!"

Tom turned to Jenny. "Now I think how our friends would rejoice to see us," he said.

Chapter Twenty-One:
THE CAMP AT THE EDGE OF THE WILD

– rocks and trees – nest like birds – wild Buffles
– Gimlet's dream – a place to set your back
– "is this the worst?"

AFTER THE SORROW AT EENA CULGACH, THE Expedition had continued along the River Roaring. All of them paddled harder then; no one complained about the carries. No other curachs were lost to the Chain of Falls, or sailors swallowed by the water.

So in time they came to the Rockmarch at last; to the last high country at the very edge of the Wild.

THE NIGHT THEY MADE THEIR FIRST CAMP in the Rockmarch, at the edge of a broad lake speckled with little islands, Gimlet made a general inspection while the others did the actual work.

By the time he returned, he found the others gathered around a fire, and Cookie serving a celebratory hot chocolate.

"Well?" the Captain asked the boy. "Does the Rockmarch meet with your approval?"

The First Mate sat with his wooden leg stretched out. "Would it serve for our Homely Country?" he asked. "For don't it seem a pleasant end to so long a journey?"

Kitchehoar was lying on his back and blowing smoke-rings at the first evening stars. "And what would be wrong with the Rockmarch?" he said, idly. "What else would you want?"

Gimlet looked around at all of them. "There's more rocks and trees," he said. "Why did we come all this way North and West to find more rocks and trees?"

"Because these rocks and trees can be ours, with almost no dispute," said Ahgeneh. "These fine lakes and rivers, even the land that runs West to the Hidden Sea, and the wide and eerie Steppes."

"Why didn't you live here before?" Gimlet asked. "Why doesn't anyone else want to live here now?"

After a long silence, Bonawyn spat in the fire. "The Riverfolk have a rule," she said. "Travel North to find deep fur, gentle people, and terrible Winter."

"How terrible do the Winters get?" asked Gimlet.

"That will be the last test the Wild gives the Strangers," said Ahgeneh.

"We know that much already," the Captain said. "But we will hunt with you, and build good shelter, and scout the land. In the Spring we will judge if we have found a Homely Country for our people, and send for them."

"In the Spring we will judge if you can share it with us," Kitchehoar said.

The Tinkers

But before the Winter came, the Rockmarch was an easy place to live. In those last fine weeks of Fall, the waters seemed full of fish, and the woods crowded with game. Two of the hunters even shot a great moose, a beast big enough to feed them all. So there was plenty when the hunters' families arrived at last.

Then, in a small, sheltered valley that ran North from the River Roaring, the Ealda put up their bark-walled lodges, and the sailors built a low log house to the First Mate's instructions. ("Make it like a boat," he said. "Only upside-down.") And so they made a little village there.

To the West, a tall stand of firs stood over the glen, and it looked like eagles had built a nest there, high in the air, where they could guard the whole valley.

One day, after the leaves had turned, and the geese had finished their great, sad clamour, Ahgeneh proposed that Kitchehoar should take the Captain and travel the country about the Rockmarch before the snow came. "For this part suits us well," he said. "But it might be Strangers would rather be closer to the Hidden Sea, where they could clear and till some lower land."

"And they might," said Kitchehoar. "For who's to know where their strangeness ends? Perhaps they would rather live among the tallest pines and nest like birds."

"We might, cousin Kitchehoar," the Captain said. "For we have seen odder ways to live than that, in our travels."

In the days the Captain and Kitchehoar travelled about the Rockmarch, Gimlet found that he and Bonawyn were often cast together and without other company.

"Would you like to go hunting, child?" the River-woman asked, one dull, grey morning. "We could go on our own Expedition."

"Yes," Gimlet said, right away. "No one else will take me because they say I can't keep quiet. But in fact I am an excellent hunter."

"They are probably only jealous," Bonawyn agreed. "But because I am an excellent hunter myself, and a most superb shot, I will be glad to have you along."

Then Gimlet looked at her closely. "But will you be hunting beaver?" he asked. "Wee beaver kits?"

"Not with bird-shot," she said.

After Bonawyn made sure that Gimlet had enough warm clothes, they began to make their way South and West. At a ford in the River Roaring they went across into a light wood that grew on the slopes of the Rockmarch.

They walked for a long time among the bare trees, Gimlet thought, and their buskins made small, muffled sounds on the damp leaves. Even the bird sounds, even the wide, cloudy sky seemed muffled. He would have said something about it to Bonawyn, but there in the shelter of the trees it seemed like the whole Rockmarch had begun to settle into its winter sleep. Even Bonawyn was quiet.

"So far we have been walking, not hunting," Gimlet said at last. "I thought you would kill more things."

"Yes," said Bonawyn. "I am disappointed too, for I thought you would kill more things as well."

"I don't have a musket," Gimlet pointed out.

"That must be the root of the problem," Bonawyn agreed. "For I am sure you are deadly."

"I have stalked lions," Gimlet said. He pulled his hood down low so that it almost hid the world. "And I have slain wild boars, and trapped nasty, red-eyed weasels."

"You are an extraordinary boy," the River-woman said. "Just as everyone has told me."

"I *am* an extraordinary boy," Gimlet agreed. Then he thought for a moment. "At least I think I have greatness of vision," he said. "Which is more important than whether I have actually done any particular extraordinary thing."

Bonawyn gave him a broad smile. "You would make a good River-man," she said. "For you have a fine sense of your own worth."

"Thank you," Gimlet said.

Then they were quiet again a while, until the trail approached a tangle of brush and fallen trees. "Now creep up to that thicket," she said softly. "And when you are amongst it, wave your arms and give great, blathering shouts."

And so he did, waking the drowsy air until a sudden, wild flutter rose up before him.

Bonawyn's musket cracked once. As the black smoke puffed out, the report echoed across the whole great valley, and other birds cried and rose in the air. But close by,

Gimlet saw a grouse lay dead, and stained with blood. He stepped back.

When Bonawyn spoke again, her voice sounded thin through the ringing of his ears. "Pick it up," the River-woman told him. "For we have more hunting before our pot will be full."

IN THE AFTERNOON, they came to a point that let them look out over the valley of the River Roaring, and across the whole land under the Rockmarch. They saw patches of fir and spruce, tan shaggy meadows, and leafless stands of alder trees. Even the river winding through the valley seemed dull.

But, to the West, Gimlet saw a vast, dim stretch of water. "Have you gone there?" he asked.

"The Hidden Sea?" said Bonawyn. "Once, with my father, the mighty Bawdoear. It is dangerous water. Worse than Ishca Lunrach, where the storm kept us waiting on the shore."

"Where else have you gone?" asked Gimlet. "Have you gone everywhere?"

"Most places a curach can bring back furs and skins," the River-woman said, and she gestured as she explained: "To the cruel and dusty South, once. And all through the high country of the Wild back East of us. Northwest across the Hidden Sea, even to the edge of the Land where No People Live. And West over the broad Steppes you saw with your Captain, where the great hairy Buffles thunder, and almost as far as the Shining Mountains."

"Do the Buffles eat you?" the boy asked her.

"No," Bonawyn said. "They are like hairy cows."

"Are they like *bad* hairy cows?" Gimlet asked

"I could tell you a tale," Bonawyn said. "A tale of the greatest herd of Buffles that ever ran, and the boy who stood before them."

"Was he a boy like me?" asked Gimlet. "Did this happen recently, and is it likely to happen again soon?"

"He was like all boys, I guess," said Bonawyn. "And it happened in the dream-time. It happened a long time ago; the Ealda say it happens every autumn; it is always happening."

Gimlet considered that for a moment, and then he nodded. "Tell me the story of the boy like me and the Buffles."

So Bonawyn leaned against a small, gnarled oak and took out her pipe.

"THE STORY BEGINS FAR TO THE WEST," the River-woman said. "Almost as far as the last steppe before the Shining Mountains, that no passes cross.

"And it is Summer, a long, hot, dry Summer, and such grass as there is, is all parched and brown. And the greatest herd of the Buffles that ever was moves across that flat plain, eating the dry grass, and drinking at low and muddy pools, and the dust rises around them.

"For there was a great feast in the Hall of the Stars, and the King of the Winds ate much, and now he sleeps. So the King's Storm Eagles grow restless, and they ride a West wind down from the Shining Mountains and across the Steppes, looking for their master. And they fly fast and sharp, but that is a storm that carries no rain, and only thunder and lightning.

"Now, every animal is afraid of thunder," Bonawyn said. "And the Eagles of the King of the Winds are so great they can carry off even baby Buffles for their prey."

"Eagles built a nest above our glen," Gimlet said. "Could they carry me away?"

"No," said Bonawyn. "For the eagles above our glen are too small, do not enjoy eating children, and have left that nest empty for some time."

"Oh," said Gimlet. "Go on with the story."

Bonawyn nodded. "So when the Great Herd of Buffles hear the thunder in the West, the noise starts them running. As the Eagles chase after them the lightning comes too, and crackles against the grass, and sets it alight. So in the wake of their flight, the Eagles leave behind a bright, wild fire, and the West wind blows that fire after them, so that it too races across the Steppes, and towards the Buffles.

"So the Great Herd flees the fire and the Storm Eagles too, and they charge East, all the Buffles, six and sixty thousand of them."

"What about the boy like me?" Gimlet said. "Was he the one who counted them?"

Bonawyn set down her pipe a moment to consider him. "In fact," she said, "the boy like you *does* see them all, for he and his mother are walking the land, looking for fresh water, but six and sixty thousand is only his estimate.

"But the Buffles make so much dust that first the boy and his mother notice how red the sunset looks. Then in the morning they begin to hear the Herd coming, a whole day away. And they look for shelter, but they are in the most open part of the whole plain, and there is nowhere to hide. But the Buffles keep on; and now their hooves sound like thunder, now the whole sky is black with dust, now the earth shakes."

"Then what happens?" Gimlet whispered.

"The mother of the boy like you holds him tight while the world trembles around them," Bonawyn said, "and the roar of the charging Buffles grows. Closer and louder it comes, and the boy buries his face in his mother's robes from terror."

Then Bonawyn stopped and busied herself with her pipe a while.

"What happened?" Gimlet asked at last. "What happened when the Great Herd came, in all its dust and thunder?"

"The mother of the boy like you stands as steady as an oak," the River-woman said, "and the Buffles begin to part around them. For they have short front legs, and can turn most quickly – for such large beasts."

"So nothing bad happens," Gimlet said.

"The boy and his mother are not trampled," said Bonawyn. "For the Buffles sweep to either side, as the rapids flow around a rock. But this is the Great Herd, the greatest of all the Buffle herds that ever was, and so the Buffles sweep around the boy who clutches his mother; all day and another day, and a whole week and another week, and for a month and another month too. This is the dream-time," Bonawyn repeated, "so in a way they are running still.

"The Buffles run so long that the boy like you is grown before they pass," Bonawyn said. "And when the thunder and the dust stop at last, and the earth ceases to tremble, the boy sees that his mother who held him so long and so stoutly is become an oak, a mighty oak, the greatest oak in all the Steppes, and so sheltered him so well and so long."

Gimlet looked out to the Southwest, where the Steppes were, and stayed quiet for a long time. "Is that story true?" he asked.

"I have seen that oak," said Bonawyn, "days and long days West of here, where it stands lonely and proud on its great plain. And if you travel past that tree, you give it a gift, so it is garlanded in ribbons, and there are tokens and copper rings and gems all around it. For that oak marks a kind of shelter against the terror of the open, even in that widest of lands."

Then Gimlet asked, "What happened to the boy?"

"He becomes both the greatest hunter of the Buffles, and the high chieftain of the Buffle clan," the River-woman said. "For he never forgets how he and his mother were spared."

Then the afternoon had grown late, and Bonawyn made a fire, and they ate their dinner at that lookout. Afterwards, they watched the clouds in the vast sunset.

"It's a long way back to the camp," said Bonawyn. "Should we stay out here tonight?"

Gimlet nodded. "There is a dream of the Steppes I want to have," he said.

In his dream, Gimlet walked along a faint trail across the flat Steppes, through tall, tall grass, in the middle of the day. There were clumps of bush here and there, and patches of fading meadow flowers, but no trees, no hills; only a wide sea of grass.

At first Gimlet felt the terror of the open spaces Ahgeneh had spoken of, but then he found he could hide in the grass itself, and as he walked he heard the scurry of small things that lived in the grass, of the birds and the bugs and the little animals.

No one was near him, no one at all, and Gimlet looked up at the grey Fall clouds high up in the wide sky. Some bird made a wide circle there, wondering what it might find worth eating, but it wouldn't eat him, he knew. As he looked up at the bird, Gimlet began to turn himself, around and around, until the endless nothing all around began to spin.

Almost none of the things he had told the Duke he hated were there; the steppes seemed new and empty, he thought, like a whitewashed wall. He turned and turned, and still he didn't hate anything. He spun until the sky and the grass began to spin on their own, but he went on, faster and dizzier all the time, until he fell into a soft, grassy bed.

His face was pressed against the stalks then, and he studied them from very close. Little bugs walked along the stalks, or crawled down into the shadowed earth. Even the bugs were spinning.

So Gimlet dreamt, until Bonawyn woke him in the morning.

AFTER FIVE DAYS, Kitchehoar returned with the Captain.

"Haven't we been great Explorers?" Kitchehoar cried. "Haven't we been about the whole bounds of the Rockmarch?"

"Did you find what you wanted?" Bonawyn asked the Captain. "Some piece of it that might suit your people best?"

"South of the River Roaring," said the Captain. "Kitchehoar my cousin showed me land that would be good to farm, and on water that runs easily towards the Hidden Sea."

Kitchehoar made a face. "We would hunt, but not live there."

"What's wrong with it, then?" asked the First Mate. "If we'd be happy with it, why wouldn't you want to be there?"

The Ealda laughed. "You must truly be Explorers at heart," Ahgeneh, the old Marshal, said. "If you don't care about having a place to set your back. If you don't worry that some wind or hand from the heavens might sweep across the open space and snatch you away."

"They are Strange," said Bonawyn.

THE DAY AFTER THE CAPTAIN returned with Kitchehoar the weather changed. Even in the shelter of the glen, cold winds came down from the North, and snow fell. In the Fall, the Rockmarch had been a land of plenty, but now the Ealda in their bark-walled lodges and the Strangers in their long log hut prepared for the long test of Winter.

Only Gimlet had never felt such weather before, and each week he asked Ahgeneh the same question: "Will it stop getting colder now? Is this the worst of Winter?" And while the old Marshal tried to answer him gently, any other Ealda who heard him only laughed, as if Gimlet had made a very funny joke.

So every week he went and asked the Captain the same thing, because he didn't believe the answer.

And the next week the snow would grow deeper and the wind blow colder still, and Gimlet would ask again: "Is this the worst?"

Chapter Twenty-Two: THE TURNING OF THE YEAR

– different celebration – a piece of cake – the Hooley ended – presents for the young –

In that camp on the Rockmarch, as the Turning of the Year approached, the weather grew clear and still and bitterly cold.

In the cabin of the Strangers and the lodges of the Ealda, they made their own preparations, and decorated them as best they could, and cooked the best stews, and baked the best bread, and made the best sweets, and brewed the best tea and coffee and hot chocolate they had left.

When the very night of the Turning of the Year arrived, they took turns as hosts, going in groups of three or four to visit, and admired one another's decorations. They played the games they knew (dice and checkers, and rings-and-pins, and spillikins and spinning bones); they sang songs; they played their drums and fiddles; they drank toasts. Finally they all gathered around one great fire, and made a mighty feast; and they wished one another joy on the occasion.

That night, even though there were other children of the Ealda about, Ahgeneh and Kitchehoar took pains to make Gimlet feel welcome. And that night the sailors seemed unusually happy to have him there too.

"I am most popular tonight," Gimlet observed to Cookie. "I am not so much of a nuisance."

"It's good to have young people around at the Turning of the Year," Cookie told him. "You remind us of how we enjoyed this night when we were your age."

"We was all a nuisance once," the First Mate said. "Or so I seems dimly to recall. And then Tom and Jenny is gone," he added more softly. "And you're the only young one left."

When Gimlet began to nod off, Cookie led him into the sailors' long log hut. But late, late in the night, Gimlet tiptoed across the bright snow, half in the world of dreams, where he thought he saw Bonawyn and the Captain standing hand in hand, gazing at the stars together.

And somehow that vision made it easier to dream of Grandfather Frost when Gimlet found a place to curl up, and slept by the hearth of his foster-father Ahgeneh.

IF ONE OF THE GREAT STORM EAGLES had flown across the Rockmarch that night, and over the hidden places of the Cold Lake Country, and looked down into a great, snowy valley, they would have seen another bonfire, and the Forgotten Folk dancing a great wild hooley round it.

The Tinkers

For the Tinkers marked the Turning of the Year too, although they made no reference to Grandfather Frost. "For he is a class of creatur after our time," said Edge-Gleamer. "He does not notice us, and neither do we venerate him."

But the Tinkers had their own ways of marking the great change in the season, and the longest night of the year. So they danced in their strange, shifting figures to the humming music of the pipes and shawms.

This time Tom and Jenny did join in the dancing, and crouched and jumped with their hosts as best they could. Though Tom could still move and leap more easily, somehow it was Jenny who knew better when to whoop or shout. In the hidden, snowy valley, at the bonfire hooley, Jenny felt she had come to a dream place, one she might have known before, and would visit again in her sleep.

When the birl paused at last, the two friends stood together and caught their breath. They watched the Tinkers crown themselves with the masks and horns of beasts: stags and wolves and bears and lynx.

To Tom it looked more eerie than anything else they had seen in the Hidlin Halls. "Is this some old magic forgotten to us?" he asked.

"My Godmother informed me of it once," Jenny whispered. "It is the oldest magic."

"I shall write this down for my father's Great Work," Tom told her.

But all at once, Edge-Gleamer stood beside them. He wore a crown of antlers, the tallest of them all, and strange marks painted on each cheek. "You will not write it down," the Tinker said softly, and Tom felt a chill as if the Tinker were casting a spell.

"By the name of yer father's Great Work, by the tall house where ye were born, by the hopes of yer people, ye will not write it down," Edge-Gleamer said, still softly, but his eyes held Tom fixed in place. "Nor tell any account of this place, not to yer Dad, not to yer fellow sailors. Not to any other Stranger or Ealda; not to any Riverfolk or Wood-Nymph; not to any talking beast or knowledgeable creatur of other kind. For these are our own and Hidlin Halls, where we have given ye sanctuary, and that is the bargain for your return."

Tom nodded. "We will not speak of it."

And beside him Jenny said the same: "We will not speak of it, except to each other –"

"Or to others who have had this dream," Tom finished.

And with that, the music began again, louder than before, and hand-in-hand, one pair of Tinkers after another began taking their turn to leap over the great fire, under the bright winter stars.

Flint, masked like a great lynx, took Tom by the hand as she had once before, and led him in a jump high across the flames. Then Edge-Gleamer himself put his arm around Jenny, and they flew over the fire while the circled dancers made a whoop, and then all of them crouched again, and spun, and so the hooley went on.

Suddenly Edge-Gleamer sang out: *"Now lament the lost and leaving year!"*

And all the Tinkers joined in his song:

Now lament the lost and leaving year!
Then forget its joys and fallen tears
And may its brother born tonight
Lay an end to our forgotten plight!

Even Sparky began to howl in time with the dance. Then somewhere far out in the rocky hills, a wolf joined in, and then another, and more, and the music of the howling chorus echoed strangely through the valley.

It was as if the wolf-music was a kind of signal for the Tinkers, for Weaver appeared then and put a great poppy-seed cake on a table by the fire. The cake had been baked with knobs of dough around its edges, and now each of them, Tinker and guest, took one knobbed piece and dipped it in a cup of wine.

But when Tom bit into his piece, he almost broke a tooth on a silver coin. The music suddenly stopped, as if the dream was coming to an end. The piece of silver had been stamped with some strange, curled mark.

Tom looked at Jenny, but she only shook her head.

The Tinkers gathered near to Tom, and Flint took off her lynx mask and put her arm around him. "What does it mean?" he asked.

"It means ye'll find some great trial in the New Year," Edge-Gleamer said.

"I remember the mark now," said Jenny. "It means some great danger and opportunity both."

Weaver looked at her strangely. "Aye," she said. "Summat like that."

Then the bonfire crackled and sent up a great shower of sparks: blue and green and red.

"The Hooley is ended," Edge-Gleamer announced. "The year has turned at last. And ye young Strangers mun best be sleeping."

IN THE ROCKMARCH, the children of the Ealda woke to find small bells, and clever games made from leather and bone, and carved dolls in their stockings. Gimlet found a tasselled cap like Bonawyn's in his, and a little carved beaver, and butterscotch candy.

But neither Tom nor Jenny found anything in their stockings. Nor did they expect to.

"For we are here in these Hidlin Halls," said Tom. "And I do not think Grandfather Frost looks for any of his children here."

Jenny nodded. "Or perhaps we are only too old at last," she said. "And will soon hardly remember we ever expected him to visit."

Tom looked at the tarnished silver coin in his hand. "But I would have liked some token less dire than this."

The Tinkers

So at the Turning of the Year, on the Rockmarch and in the Hidlin Halls, they had their Yule celebrations, according to their different customs, and received presents by ways both known and obscure.

SOME COLD NORTH THING

They saw Lynx eyes, glowing

Chapter Twenty-Three:
THE MOON OF THE LAZY SUN

– the true test of Winter – to never be alone
– Degrees of Chilly Suffering – a call to wickedness
– the first leaves of a storm – shadows they would not name –

WITH THE NEW YEAR, THE DAYS BEGAN TO GROW longer, but as the weeks passed, the cold grew even deeper. Ice closed even the deepest river channels now.

The snow itself shrank from the cold, and only fell from thin clouds as a kind of glimmer in the air. Days would go by without a successful hunt; no birds sang, and people talked less. *The whole world is frozen,* Gimlet thought.

"It is the Moon of the Lazy Sun," his new brother Kitchehoar told him once. "And we become lazy with it. Patience is the truest test of Winter."

"I will be patient," Gimlet said, "if that will make the Spring come faster."

ONCE, when the Captain took him hunting, just as Bonawyn had, Gimlet pulled down his icy scarf and said, "I want Winter to end now."

"It will end," the Captain said. Then he looked at Gimlet with a rare fondness. "When you are older you will not want time to hurry, even Winter-time. You will like this pause, as the world sleeps under its blanket of snow."

"I will not," Gimlet said. "I am freezing."

But the Captain didn't seem to pay attention. "As the world sleeps, we can dream things that would never be in the daylight world of Summer," he said. And Gimlet thought the Captain might be dreaming then, for he had a strange and almost contented look on his scarred face.

"It is so cold my nose hairs are stuck together," Gimlet said. "That would never happen in Summer."

And several times the Captain and Bonawyn met to take Gimlet out into the cold, black night together, to walk along the river ice and show him the Winter stars in the clear night sky.

"I see the stars turning," Gimlet announced once, when the grown-ups been talking softly too long together. "The big horse is running West."

"The boy is learning," the Captain said to Bonawyn. He clapped a gloved hand on Gimlet's shoulder. "But call it rather the Great Steed of Heaven."

Bonawyn stepped closer. "Run slow," she said. "Run slow, horses of the night." Then the Captain put his other arm around the River-woman.

"If you sail away together, you should take me with you," Gimlet said.

Bonawyn looked down then, and the Captain laughed.

"Well," he said. "But what about your new foster-father Ahgeneh, and your brother Kitchehoar."

"Yes," said Gimlet. "We could all sail away together so I would never be alone."

THERE CAME A DAY when Gimlet visited the sailors in their low cabin, and the boy realized he could hardly remember the warmth of the sun.

"Has it *always* been this cold?" he demanded.

The First Mate set to work to light his pipe as he thought the matter over. "It were warm once, of course," he said. "Though you might be too young to remember. But it ain't always *this* cold, even in Winter. A proper sailor should be able to distinguish the *degrees* of a thing."

"Now he will enumerate the degrees of the cold again," whispered one of the sailors with a blue hood. The other nodded. "He will list the Six Separate Degrees of Chilly Suffering. Again."

But the First Mate overheard them and issued a fierce stare. "There's *seven* kinds of cold," he said. "Any what think otherwise has not paid proper attention." Then he paused to order the matter in his mind.

"The *First* Degree of Chilly Suffering is: Put on a cable-knit sweater cold," he said, rather loudly. "The *Second,* build up the fire cold; the *Third,* wrap a scarf round your nose cold; the *Fourth,* too cold to snow cold; the *Fifth,* when you expectorate –"

Here the First Mate paused until some of the sailors looked confused. “When you spits,” he elaborated, “and it freezes when it hits the ground; the *Sixth,* when your expectorations freeze and crackle *in the air,* and rattles down like hail.”

“That’s the new one,” whispered one of the sailors in a blue hood. “Crackling expectorations is good,” agreed the other.

“And *lastly,”* the First Mate went on with some severity, “lastly, the *Seventh* degree –” He waited to make sure the others were ready (and in fact, they all mouthed the next words with him): “Lastly is the cold that tries to kill you, plain and simple.” Then he looked around with satisfaction for having reached the end of his newly expanded categorization.

But Gimlet looked as unhappy as ever. “Which kind of filthy enumberated degree of chillable sufferifaction is this?” he asked.

The First Mate gave him a steady look, and he rose on his peg leg and stumped out the low door. From inside the cabin they heard a mighty spit.

When the First Mate returned he wiped his mouth with his sleeve. “It’s only number five.” Then he added a few other words, for appropriate colour and emphasis.

So THINGS CONTINUED, until what the Ealda called the Month of the Thin Moon.

"Not for the moon being any thinner," Ahgeneh explained to Gimlet. "But because we are like to be."

Gimlet looked at him in some distress. "Are we running out of food?"

The old Marshal smiled. "Not this Winter," he said. "For didn't we come to this place just so we wouldn't starve? Didn't we make a store of all that fine fish and moose?"

"I am sick of dry fish and old moose," said Gimlet.

Ahgeneh only nodded amiably. "Patience is the true test of Winter," he said.

But somewhere by the Tinkers' Hidlin Hall, the dread Cat-spirit Pishkeen Mawr grew restless too, there in her Winter tomb. For while the waters of the Wild stayed frozen above her, she had no chance for wickedness.

But still she sent a call to all her kind from far and wide: every bobcat and great lynx and cougar. Trapped beneath her icy cover, she could feel some other wickedness coming.

One still, cold night in the little village in the glen, the dogs set to barking, and roused the whole camp.

When the hunters went to see what was the matter, they found an old woman and her daughter, who bore a young baby boy in her fur jacket, and they had travelled some long way in great fear.

When Ahgeneh emerged, with Kitchehoar beside him,

the old woman clasped the Marshal around the knees before he could speak, and begged for their shelter.

"Rise, friend," said Ahgeneh. "For sure you are safe now; only tell us what you are fleeing."

The old woman looked North through the darkness and shook her head. "We are Ealda from the Northlands," she said, "who winter by the Frozen Sea. Others came to us, raving and in terror; and now we flee before them."

Ahgeneh nodded at the woman and her daughter, and the small child they carried. "I know of your people," he said. Then he turned to the others who had started to gather: Strangers and Ealda, and the River-woman Bonawyn. He shouted as Gimlet had heard him shout once before: "Friends have come from afar! Lay aside your weapons!"

Now Kitchehoar spoke to the old woman as gently as he could. "And these others," he said. "What is it they were fleeing?"

Her daughter answered, "Others yet, Snow-People even, who fled screams in the night, who ran from shadows come down from the North. Six great shadows, if they were only shadows."

The Captain stepped forward then, with the First Mate beside him, and even in the dark and torchlit night, the newcomers could see they were no Ealda. The child buried his face in his mother's robes, and she spoke urgently to Kitchehoar – too quickly for Gimlet to follow.

But the other Ealda began laughing then, and

Kitchehoar made some reassuring words, and then he turned to the Captain and the First Mate with a broad smile. “She’s only worried for you look so pale and eerie,” he said.

“She ain’t a calming sight herself,” said the First Mate.

“Ahgeneh, my uncle,” the Captain said, “who are these frightened and bedraggled folk?”

The old Marshal looked out into the black night, and at the eyes of the hunters gathered there. Then he met his son’s gaze. “They look to be the first leaves of a storm,” said Ahgeneh. “Or rabbits who run before the forest fills with fire.”

By daylight, other small groups of fleeing Ealda had arrived from other clans in the Northlands. Some Snow People came, and even a few rough trappers of the Riverfolk who had fled their Winter cabins.

Each brought worse rumours than the last to the little village in the glen: stories of a growing still and deadly cold; of the sight of wild-cats running; and last of all, of the six shadows they would not name, even as they fled them.

Gimlet saw there was something bad that the Ealda understood, and they gathered closely to exchange dark whispers. But for the sailors things were even worse, for they had no name to give their fears, yet felt a growing horror. Even the big Bosun seemed unnerved, while the two sailors with blue hoods could hardly speak.

At last the Captain went to Ahgeneh. "Uncle, you think this thing is best left un-named. But that means our fears can grow in all and every shape, and my crew cannot steel themselves for any actual danger."

And Bonawyn said, "Grandfather Ahgeneh, we have held our tongues to honour you, but the Riverfolk and the Ealda all know what the Strangers do not. Evil times have come at last; now it is right to speak of evil things."

The old Marshal slowly nodded. "It is time to strike the council drum," he told Kitchehoar. "Now all the wise and bravest folk should sit and talk together."

SO THEY GATHERED in the Marshal's birch-walled lodge: the Captain and his oldest sailors, and the wise and brave among both Ahgeneh's people and those exiles who had fled to the Rockmarch for refuge. In the middle of them all, Gimlet tended the fire.

This time, the Captain was the first to light his pipe, and passed it patiently around to the others. When it had come back to him at last, he looked around, and pulled at his beard, and then he began: "We are Strangers here," he said, "and depend on the Ealda for wisdom and advice. So we are glad to speak to you as if you were our aunts and uncles, our grandparents even. But now we need you to speak to us not as children, but as friends and brothers."

Ahgeneh did not reply himself, and only turned to his son. "You see, it's that you're asking us to say a thing that has no name," the Herald said. But then even Kitchehoar had no more words. After a few moments of silence, the First Mate began to shift his peg leg restlessly.

"Names have power," Bonawyn explained. "Sometimes power *over* a thing, and sometimes power to *draw* a thing. And that is an awful chance."

"Well, I'd say that's fair," the First Mate said. "But you *does* converse the matter. We hears your whispers, your covert mutterings. So just tell us what words you uses to *introduce* such a grim and unpleasant topic."

But of all the Ealda, it was the young huntress Buccaneen, who had guided Jenny's *Dauntless* down Ishca Fadras, who stood up, and she almost shouted the answer: "We say they are the icy dead who hunger!"

It seemed to Gimlet that when Buccaneen uttered those words aloud, she broke some bind about the Ealda. They sat more easily now, and for the first time he heard them even laugh about the thing, the way they did about their other troubles. But the sailors only looked more grim.

"Ahgeneh, my uncle," the Captain said, "I will use the Strangers' word for such things." He waited until the old Marshal nodded. "Ice Trolls, we call them. Tall and vicious loping things, the worst kind of Northern horror."

"Ice Trolls," the Bosun said, and swore then like a sailor.

"Ice Trolls," the First Mate said. "Damn their frozen giblets."

And, "Ice Trolls!" Cookie said, but only he seemed undistressed. He turned towards the First Mate. "But when we sailed the frozen North, you declared they only had icicle bones and guts of slush, and so were no real worry."

The big Bosun shook his head. "Cookie, your strangely cheerful nature shows itself again. Think about the matter, about the young and timid in the crew, and how little they needed scaring. And the Ice Trolls were only imagined then, not some imminent horror."

The Captain nodded. "The Mate said words to calm the crew," he said. "Which was what I really asked of him."

"I'd have said more, if we was about to fight," the First Mate said. "And if I'd ever heard a story from those what survived them."

Gimlet felt himself shiver then, even as he kept the fire. "Just you wrap yourself in my rabbit cloak," Ahgeneh told the boy. "For won't I preserve you from any troubles?"

"Now, you call them Ice Trolls," Kitchehoar said, "after ferocious things in the warmer lands you know – but in fact, those trolls are merely monstrous. And we don't fear to name the little monsters that we know, the *worrichoes* you call goblins. But the – the icy dead who hunger, they deserve no proper name, for they have less spirit than the rocks and stones."

Then Ahgeneh spoke again, and his voice became rough and hard like rock: "They are horrible," he said. "For aren't their lips pulled back to bare their teeth like fangs? And aren't their nails long like talons? They have no spirit, for haven't their spirits already flown?

"They are the cold dead who walk, in long and bony strides," he declaimed, "and have no wit left but hunger. They are the icy dead who hunger for living men and women, and hope to gain their spirits."

Now the unattended fire burned low, and the smoke and shadows grew deeper.

"They do this when they are dead," the old Marshal said. "For didn't they do horrible things once – just to try to keep on living?"

The Captain broke his pipe in his hand, and waited until the embers began to burn him. Gimlet thought his scarred face looked grim and awful. "Uncle, we stand together against these awful things," the Captain said. "Now tell us how we will beat them."

"The icy dead have frozen hearts," said Ahgeneh. "And neither knife nor arrow can pierce them."

"Well, what about a musket shot?" the First Mate asked.

Bonawyn spat in the fire. "I think we may test that now," she said.

"So we might, perhaps," said Ahgeneh. "Those are still new weapons in this land. But there is one sure way we know –" and he pulled out his long knife then. "To close with them, to cut out their hearts of ice, and then melt them in some great fire."

"Who has done this before?" the Captain asked.

"It has been a long time since those things have come so near," Ahgeneh said. "But my father, the mighty Shawnatheir, slew one in his youth."

"Was it him what told you the trick of it?" asked the First Mate.

But Ahgeneh shook his head. "My father was the greatest of warriors," he said. "And drove his foes before him like a storm. But it takes a while for a frozen heart to melt, and first that dead thing killed him. It was my mother told me the tale."

"WHY DOES WE WAIT HERE?" the First Mate asked. "Why doesn't we pack our things and run?"

"We have crossed the Ocean already to escape the Long Night," the Captain said. "When will our fleeing stop?"

And Ahgeneh said, "These things – six shadows, we hear – could have done much worse to the settlements in the North than scatter them and send their people running. I think it's our new village they come for. We can face them here or let them catch us running."

But Kitchehoar looked at Bonawyn. "Wasn't it folly to join with them, and bring them here?" he asked. "When we know the Vastlands are cursed to Strangers?"

"Yes," she said. "It would have been wiser to let them die alone in the Wild. But I am a Loon-Daughter. And the Riverfolk are here only because long ago Autumn Eyes would not abandon the sailor Ferren."

"A long time ago, the Riverfolk came," said Kitchehoar, "and took some of our best hunting. But even they didn't lure these dread things here. But look now, Loon-Daughter, what you have brought with these Strangers. Look what caught the scent of them once in the icy seas of the cold, dark North – the journey they always boast of."

All the others fell silent then, and in Ahgeneh's rabbit cloak, Gimlet began to tremble.

"Aren't the icy dead always hungry?" the old Marshal said at last. "And so we've had to fight them. And aren't they nightmares from an Ealda's dream? For these sailors hardly know them.

"And say it were the Strangers' fault, what's to be done? Stake them all out in the cold, and hope they'll sate the monsters' hunger? Wouldn't that do us all an honour?"

Kitchehoar coloured at his father's words, and when he looked at the sailors again, his words were softer:

"I spoke in heat, which I regret," he said. "It doesn't matter why these things have come. It's our task just because we've lived to see it. No one will ever say we left our guests to die alone."

"Well spoken," Bonawyn told him.

"Yes, that's all fair enough," the First Mate said. "And of course, hard times makes for short tempers. So I'm sure any hard words that was recently spoke –" and here he stared at Kitchehoar, "well, I'm sure they has been forgot already. But unless them things what you can't even bear to name is frightened by long talks and argy-bargy, they're still coming this way."

Then the old sailor stared around, stubborn and fierce (with what Gimlet remembered the First Mate called "a proper show of *truculence*"). "What's our plan, I mean? Or ain't that what a council's for?"

Ahgeneh looked at him with some amusement. "You've named our business well enough," he said. "For that's what we must consider."

"We have fighting plans to make," the Captain said. "But my First Mate is right that we should think of escape as well – not for my sailors, or the brave hunters of the Ealda. But for the young and old, the families of the Ealda."

Ahgeneh nodded. "To the South there is the Drumrath, a cave of refuge in the ridge," he said, and so they began to make their plans at last.

BUT HOW COULD THEIR FAMILIES get away to that fastness in time to escape any trouble? The council was still deep in talk when they heard a sharp musket crack. And then shouts came from outside, and a frightened sailor put his head inside the lodge.

"The Bone-Faces have come!" he said. "Painted in their awful colours!"

Chapter Twenty-Four:
NONE MORE BRAVE

– practising grim stares – honour lost
– departure for the Drumrath – screams and howls
– a journey in the rock – lordly cousins
– an open-handed host – stars again –

THEY MET THE BONE-FACES OUTSIDE, UNDER THE cold stars. Ten grim Bone-Faces, hunters who had travelled quickly.

"Who comes to this camp of the Ealda?" asked Ahgeneh.

Cluhegon pushed back his hood, to show his skull-paint. "You know who we are," he said. "Name us friend or foe as you like, but we have come in a time of need."

Then Ahgeneh called, "Friends have come from afar! Old friends, I suppose," he added. "So lay aside your weapons."

Then Kitchehoar said, "Is it a new bow you have, Cluhegon? Well then, what else could you need?"

"All our bows were broken, from shame," the Bone Face said. "But now we come at your need, not ours. For all the Wild knows the hunting cats and even the icy dead who hunger come this way, from the frozen North. Are you ready to meet them now? Have you already sent your families to your shelter?"

For a moment the cold camp was silent. Finally the First Mate shifted his one good foot. "I calls this too frosty a place to stand and glare," he said. "Let's go inside, and practise our grim stares in some better sort of comfort."

By the fire in Ahgeneh's bark-walled lodge, Cluhegon spoke with urgent firmness. He didn't know much of the Stranger's language, of course, but by now they knew much of his, and Kitchehoar and Bonawyn were there to help translate.

"Back in the Cold Lake Country we have made our camp," Cluhegon said. "And we had good hunting in the fall. But even so this Winter has been hard, and this Thin Moon has been the thinnest. That's Winter in the Wild, so we had no cause for complaint, except your lack of friendship."

"We could say the same," Kitchehoar told him.

"Still, you never came to say it," Cluhegon pointed out. "And then we see strange flights of birds, and dreams come to us of wild cats, and worse hunting things, and then we hear word of your trouble. Not long ago," he said. "For we find you still aren't ready. No palisade or line of pickets, and all the defenceless young and old still waiting here."

"It's no easy thing," said Ahgeneh. "For those things run fast. If they didn't stop to trouble the camps they would have already found us."

Cluhegon nodded. "So you could send your families away, but what happens if – those things – sweep around and catch them?"

"But we know the Ice Trolls run on a line this way," the Captain said. "How could we let the families and the exiles from the North wait in this glen to meet them?"

The Bone-Face turned towards him. "Yes, they make for here," he said. "As if even they are troubled by your Strange presence."

"We're not going to be having all that long talk again," said Ahgeneh. "For all we need to know is they've come again, and it's become our task to face them."

"There will be slaughter if the wild-cats catch the families here," Cluhegon said. "Or in the country on the way to your rocky shelter. And worse than slaughter if – if the icy dead who hunger come on them first."

"Is that what you came to tell us?" said Kitchehoar. "And next time you take a long fall, won't I be there to tell you you might hit the ground? But there's risk any way. We don't have time to send the defenceless away; we can't keep them here to wait for attack. And however well we guard the camp, some cats, or things, could catch them as they travel around it."

"What a disaster you face," said Cluhegon. "What a tragedy."

"Did you come to mock us?" Kitchehoar cried in anger.

Cluhegon shook his head. "We came at your need," he said. "And because there are none more brave than the Bone-Faces."

"What is it you mean?" asked Ahgeneh. "How do you mean to help us?"

"We are ten fast hunters here," said Cluhegon. "Who lost honour at Eena Culgach. We will make a stand at the gap in the North, and hold it against the wild-cats, against the icy dead."

The others looked at the small band of Bone-Faces for a long time. "Then you will die there," said the Captain.

Cluhegon shrugged. "We all die once," he said. "But we will give you time to let the families gathered here escape. Then you will have all the other cats, and things, to kill – for we don't need to own all the glory."

"Friends and brothers often quarrel," Kitchehoar said then. "So I have said hard words more than once. But if we survive you, we will watch after all your folk. And we will tell them there are none more brave than the Bone-Faces."

The Bone-Faces set out at once, in the dark, for the gap in the North.

And the young and the old among Ahgeneh's people, and the exiles, and all the families of the hunters, packed their things for the journey to the Drumrath. They wore great Buffle cloaks, or were swaddled in furs, according to their size. Only their dogs had no coverings, but leapt and pulled at their harness, and barked with excitement, for they would warm themselves soon enough by pulling the loads behind them.

Some Cold North Thing

But Gimlet refused to leave. For the boy wanted to stay by the other sailors, and with his foster-father, and Kitchehoar his brother, for that was all he knew of safety.

In the end, neither Ahgeneh nor the Captain could bear to make him go, so at the first light, the families set off from the glen without him. They made for the frozen water of the River Roaring, which would take them towards the fastness of the Drumrath.

Then the hunters and sailors were left alone. They set guards above the glen to watch the trails from the North, and others on the frozen river-ways. They worked hard in the awful cold to build a ring of sharp pickets. And piled wood to keep a great, hot fire burning.

"We have done what we can," the Captain said, when the palisade was finished.

"All that's left is waiting," said Ahgeneh.

NO MORE EXILES CAME THAT DAY, nor did they see wild cats or monsters.

By nightfall those who weren't on watch gathered around the great fire. There Gimlet glumly watched the flames rise tall in that still cold night, saw sparks leap up to join the stars. Finally he opened his hood enough to speak. "Has the wind been frozen too?" he asked.

Cookie pulled the scarf down from his own nose just long enough to speak. "That's a pleasant thought. For more wind's the one thing that could make it colder."

"So this is really as cold as it can be, at last," Gimlet said.

Then the First Mate pulled down his scarf, to try his test of spitting. There was a quick crackle in the air. The old sailor moved his eye-patch back and forth to look carefully where his spittle had fallen.

"We're only at the Sixth Degree," he said. "There's yet the Seventh: the cold what simply kills you."

That night Gimlet slept by the fire in the sailors' hut. But he woke in the darkness and crawled out from under his Buffle robe. The two sailors with blue hoods were the only other ones inside, and they were awake as well, and shaking in the firelight.

"What is it?" Gimlet asked. But then he heard it himself: the dogs left in camp were barking.

"Something bad has come at last," one of the two sailors said. "Something bad," the other added like an echo.

But they only sat in the darkness, the three of them, while the dogs grew more excited.

"We'd go outside," one sailor said, and the other finished, "If we weren't afraid."

"I am not afraid," said Gimlet. But he shivered as he said it. Then the barks grew louder and more fierce, and they heard the horrible screams of wild-cats, of lynx and cougars, somewhere in the trees outside the pickets, and suddenly they didn't want to wait there.

From the packed snow outside the hut's low door, they crawled up towards the campfire.

The dogs sounded terrible now; frightened, or mad with rage, at whatever they heard stalking around the camp.

Then from the trees a quick shadow darted towards the line of pickets; a great lynx with its cat eyes burning yellow. *"Pishkeen,"* Gimlet heard Kitchehoar say. "It is cut and wounded; the Bone-Faces have met them already!"

Then more and more, around the camp, they saw lynx eyes glowing.

The dogs were in a frenzy. The cats screamed in the woods. And now from the frozen river came the howling of beasts; came some new and awful howling.

IN THE TINKERS' HIDLIN HALLS, carved deep into their immense solidity of stone, a day came when Edge-Gleamer appeared looking grim. "Now pack yer things," he said. "For the time has come to end this."

"All our things?" said Tom. "Where are we going?"

The Tinker only said, "Another secrit you alone will ken. The very last one I'll entrust ye."

Then Edge-Gleamer led them silently though a dark way they had never found before, into a rift in the rock, and down stone steps, deep down into the darkness.

The Tinker went first, and tripped down easily with his torch, as if it were no matter. Jenny followed him, still using a cane, but determined not to fall behind. Sparky followed her, his claws clicking on the stone. Last – because less likely to fall – came Tom. All of them kept close to the wall on their left, for the torch-light only showed the cold stone wall and the rough stair; and to the right there was only a gaping darkness.

Down it went, down and down, as the wall of rock bent first one way and then the other. "What is this journey for?" Jenny demanded at last. But in a moment the question came back to her loudly: *What is this journey for?* the rocks echoed. *What for?*

"Silence is the best policy," Tom said, and then he winced when he realized what he had done. For of course those hissing words began echoing too: *Silence is the best policy; silence is best; silence.* And still, though ever more faintly, *What for, what for?*

Hearing the words of both of them repeated like that was too much for Sparky. The dog began barking at the strangeness of it all and then the noises became almost unbearable. Tom leaned against the wall, and remembered his dream of falling. And Jenny almost said words about the unprecedented and severe cacophony, but she stopped herself just in time, and sat down on the stone to collect her wits.

Farther down, Edge-Gleamer turned and looked up at them. The shadows from his torch flickered madly, but he kept silent, and only shook his head.

At least he does not seem angry, Tom thought. Then the Tinker bared his pointed teeth, and raised his fingers to his lips.

A request for silence that seems superfluous, or sarcastic, Jenny thought. But Sparky at least did fall quiet, and so they waited a long while, until the last echoing barks subsided.

Then Edge-Gleamer's sharp ears twitched, like a cat, and they began to hear a noise, faint, but resounding strangely in that stone cleft. They heard wolves howling, and Tom quickly stepped down to hold Sparky and keep him from answering back. And Jenny and Tom both thought the same thing: *The Blood Promise.*

But they were lost in the darkness, and could only follow as the Tinker led them on.

At last they came to a landing, and turned left into a broad tunnel, leaving the great cavern behind. Here the wolves sounded louder, but the echoes less terrible, and now Sparky howled too.

"He thinks they are his friends," said Tom.

"Aye," said Edge-Gleamer. "So they are. The wolves will honour their Blood Promise again, and take ye in a cariole to find yer friends, just as we assured ye."

AHEAD OF THEM, the tunnel mouth opened into further darkness. But before the darkness stood six wolves, and their eyes shone like glowing coals.

Edge-Gleamer fixed their harness, as they jumped and trembled with excitement. Sparky trembled too, as the Tinker offered him a collar with a longer lead than any of the others. "They are courteous beasts too," he explained. "And will let their guest run before them.

"I mistrusted you at first," Tom said. "But you have kept your bargain."

Edge-Gleamer flashed his teeth. "Aye," he said. "Well, don't be too quick to give yer trust to anyone. That's a lesson the Wild will teach ye."

"Will we see any of you again?" Jenny asked.

"Will you see us?" said the Tinker. "For we'll see you at times. The two of ye might see us more easily than most of yer kind. But we are shy, since first we were forgot, and like best to keep ourselves hidden."

"You were forgotten, like keen-eyed Straikha, and her friend the swift-rushing Terrier," Tom said.

Edge-Gleamer gave Tom a keen glance. "Weaver told ye that tale, did she?" he said. "Aye, like them who were left here below, when the long dream-time story ended."

"You saved us three from Pishkeen Mawr," Jenny said quietly. "And though we doubted you, we are in your debt, and owe you more than thanks."

The Tinker nodded. "Most fairly spoke," he said. "But ye had little choice in the matter. For saving yer lives was a gift, of course, so it would have been rude to refuse it."

Edge-Gleamer turned towards the cariole, but Tom spoke once more. "In his lodge in the North, Grandfather Frost told me that the Elves had gone to story, long before his time," he said.

One of the Tinker's ears swivelled back at that. "Well,

and so it happens they did," he said, without turning around.

"Are you Elves?" said Tom. "Was it the Elves who forgot the Tinkers, and left you all behind?"

Then Edge-Gleamer did turn around, and now he had more wrath in his face than Tom or Jenny had ever seen, and he bared his sharp and pointed teeth.

"NOW YE'VE UTTERED A NAME we never speak," the Tinker said. "For that – that was the name of our clever, older cousins. *O*, they were so lordly, so learned and wise, and they built those fine and gull-winged ships, and *O*, their names and stories will live on the lips of the earthly evermore."

Then he smiled less sharply. "We hardly knew our cousins then, but still dwelt in the hidden rocks and woods of old. And we were rough, and we were rude, and we sought neither power nor glory.

"For whatever gifts or grace ye think we possess, they had more, and so they scorned to know us. But when they fled the troubles in the Eastlands long ago, and then found they couldn't bear the rough and troubled Wild, well then they travelled even West of West, and returned to the dream-time land of story.

"Or so we heard, we who they left behind to survive this rough world's troubles. And when we tried to follow them, the gate was closed, and so we sailed and crossed the ice to get this far, and lost many in the voyage.

"So that's why I knew the smell of the North on ye," he said to Tom. "From having once tried that passage."

For the first time the Tinker's small figure didn't make him seen like an ungrown youth. He seemed old instead, shrunken with age.

"How long ago was that?" Tom asked. "For we found ancient sailors resting there, and swords like yours beside them."

"Long ago," Edge-Gleamer said. "And it's my brother's blade yer Captain has, wound round with charms against all Northern perils." He looked at them closely for a moment. "Well, I hope it gives him better luck."

Then Jenny spoke in wonder: "Master Edge-Gleamer," she said. "How long ago was that?"

But the Tinker only held Tom's Star-Glass out to him. "Here. I thought ye'd like this, as a gift again. For my fixed dreams will never be."

Tom looked down into the glass, but he had no words.

Then the Tinker spoke more sharply. "Kempie girlie," he said to Jenny, and held out a proper, brass-bound walking staff. "I'd not have you leave thinking I'm not open-handed either. So throw away yer cane, and here's a staff for all yer future explorations."

Jenny took the staff. "But will we ever see you again?" she asked a second time.

"Will I ever see you?" said Edge-Gleamer. "For do ye know what test awaits ye?"

"The Ice Trolls," Tom said. "I have known all along.

They missed me in the North before, and so they hunger more fiercely."

"Aye," the Tinker said. "Aye. Yer friends will face them now; and that's where the beasts will take ye. So I'll wish ye luck." Then he led them onto the cariole. "That's three secrits of ours ye have: our halls, our old magicks, and now the name of our proud cousins. But I know ye'll never tell em."

Tom shook his head. "Thank you, master Edge-Gleamer," said Jenny.

The Tinker leapt up behind them onto the runners of the sleigh, and made a mighty crack with his whip. The wolves leapt up and began to pull, and followed as Sparky ran lightly before them.

As the cariole began to move faster, the Tinker put the whip into Jenny's hand. Just before they reached the mouth of the cave, he jumped off. "Mind ye keep yer blades up high!" he called.

Then the wolves pulled them away, into a long and twisting tunnel of ice, and the team began to bark and howl with pleasure.

For a long time, the wolves sped them down that icy way. Now Tom took the whip, and then Jenny again, but really Sparky led the wild team without them. Or at least the wolves did him the honour of letting him seem to lead.

But when Sparky tired he would slip back to ride on the cariole with Tom and Jenny, and he seemed as happy as a dog can be. For he not only ran First among that rough, wild pack, but was also still approved by his own and proper master.

Finally they emerged from the ice, and found a wild, cold, Winter night. But in Tom's Star-Glass, like in the sky above, the heavens burned bright again.

IN THE CAMP ON THE ROCKMARCH, beset by wild-cats and terrible sounds, the howls along the river-way resolved into the sound of the wolf team running.

"Don't shoot!" Gimlet called to the hunters watching there. "That's Sparky barking."

In a few moments they had opened a gate in the pickets, and as the cariole swept in, the dogs in camp fell as quiet as the astonished sailors. For the wolves seemed huge, and grey and wild and shaggy.

Jenny jumped down first. "I see we have only just arrived in time," she cried at once. "For here we find you getting ready to fire on all the wrong targets."

Bonawyn was the first to move. For she saw Jenny's fine new clothes, and understood they came from the Tinkers. So she laughed with joy, and made a great deep bow, and kissed her like a sister.

Then Tom stepped down. He walked slowly toward the Captain. "I come to report that I lost the *Adventure*, my first command," he began.

The Captain shook his head. "I lost mine too," he said, and picked Tom up, and held him like a father.

Then Gimlet shrieked with joy, and Sparky jumped and barked as loudly. And all the other sailors began to dance and cheer, and so likewise did the Ealda.

Only the wolves stood still, panting patiently now. For they had run a night and a day and a night, and knew what they had done, and waited proud as princes.

Jenny saw the flash of a lynx looking from the woods, and she cut the traces of the wolves. In a flash, they disappeared into the trees, and the forest filled with snarls. Then the cats made no more sound. The wolves had been paid their Blood Promise.

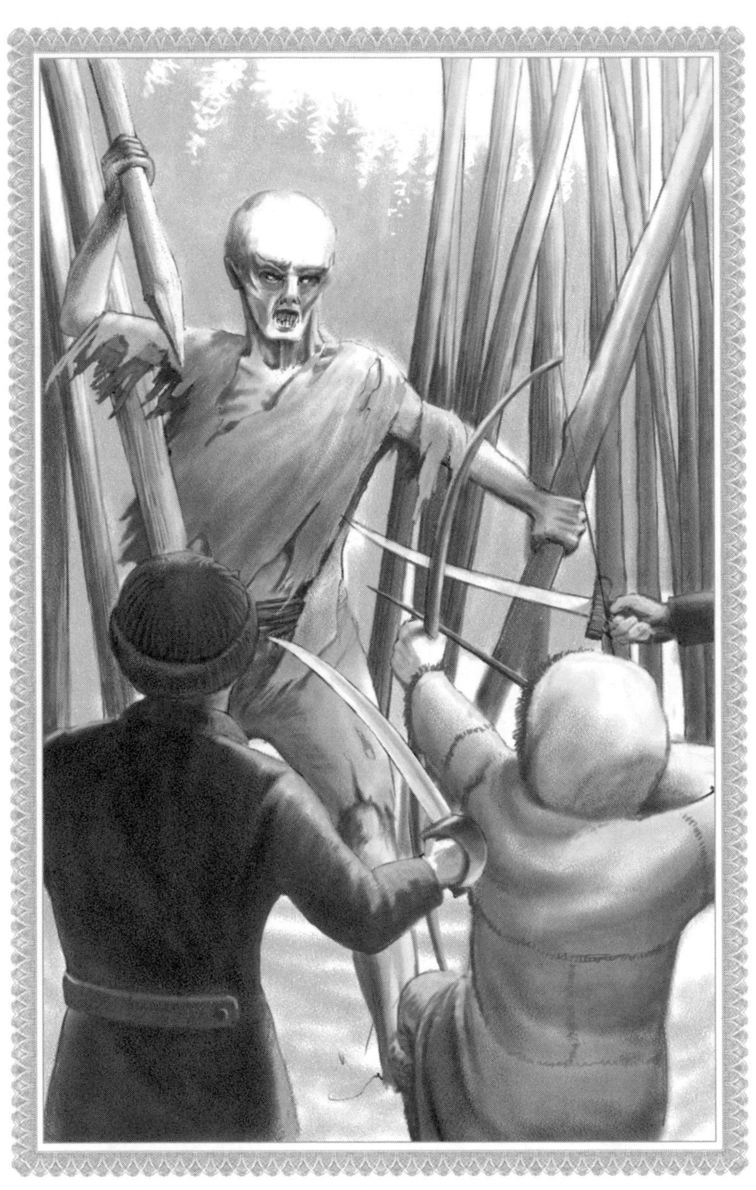

The morning light revealed the monster

Chapter Twenty-Five:
THE FROZEN HEART

– respect for Sparky – old friends – limping closer – talking backwards – none more brave – sent away – a River-man –

The wolves did not leave after their meal, as Tom and Jenny had seen them do before, but sniffed around the dogs in the camp. Then they dug their own shelters in the snow, and generally acted as if they had always lived there, and been animal princes.

The other dogs treated them with awe and fear; and even gave Sparky a strange new respect.

As they waited for things that were even worse to come, the two Ensigns had stories to hear and a few that they could share, huddling in the great cold by the fire.

But as the thin light of dawn began to spread, the First Mate spoke to Jenny quietly. "Likely I'd be proud of all you've done," he said. "But for once you've kept quiet about most of your surprising discoveries and accomplishments."

"You would be even prouder of Tom and me, if you knew all we've seen and done," she said. "And indeed it irks me to keep quiet. But mysteries were revealed to us that we swore to hold as secrets."

"You wouldn't even write 'em in your journal of all your great Explorations?" the old sailor asked. "Nor won't Tom include 'em in his Dad's big book, purely for the preservation of all that strange knowledge?"

"Mate, you wouldn't be asking us to break an oath?" Jenny said. "Which binds us as strongly as any Law of the Sea, which no proper old salt would question."

The First Mate grinned, and pulled up his toque to scratch his itchy forehead. "It's just I'm curious," he said. "For once in the Old Sea I was held in an enchanted place – one with charming company, and quantities of fine dancing. Before you came back and broke the spell, that is, to my general wonder and stupefaction."

Jenny looked at him closely. "Mate, do you regret that?" she asked. "Should we have let you stay there dozing?"

"No," the old sailor said. "I guess there was more work I had to do, though that would have been a fine end for a sailor."

"But you don't think this is how you'll end your days?" Jenny exclaimed. "Shrammed and chilled on the edge of the Wild? That's an end would ill befit a grizzled Seahand of such vast experience."

"I've had my time," the First Mate said. "If those Ice Trolls was to et any of us, rather me than some promising young crew member."

"Don't be uttering such bleak thoughts!" Jenny said.

"We have several good reasons for hope, before we even turn to our reserves of foolish optimism. I will enumerate them –"

"That's all right, girlie," the First Mate said. "But if, well, if something bad was to befall, and you or Tom found me dying –"

"Don't say that," Jenny said.

But the old sailor kept talking. "Well, but could you say it then, share those secrets with an old man who was passing?"

Once it would have been against Jenny's nature to even consider such a moment. But now she only whispered, "We would tell you anything, Tom or I – in such an unlikely, but distressing situation."

BEHIND THOSE FIRST FEW LYNX, an Ice Troll came limping closer.

Once two Ice Trolls had run ahead of the others, swiftly, in their loping way, untroubled by the killing Winter weather. For they no longer lived, nor had for ages past, but only hoped to eat the life of others.

But the Bone-Faces had found them first, and kept their word. They had struck one down, and when this troll had left the bodies of the slain behind, it was cut and lamed and awkward as it loped towards the camp at the Rockmarch at last, and stared down at the ring of sharpened pickets.

It was a stupid, clumsy thing, but when it saw the bloody scraps left in the woods, it knew some wild-cats had been there first, and how badly they had been beaten. Even a goblin might have quailed at that, in all its wicked cunning. But the Ice Troll hungered for the living it had smelled once before in the frozen North, and had no wit or spirit to be daunted.

IN CAMP, within the ring of pickets, in the cold, thin light of morning, they heard the monster come at last.

"I will eat you now," it said. *"But you can choose how quickly."*

No one in the camp had ever heard such a thing speak before, and its voice was loud and terrible.

"Why does it sound so strange?" Gimlet whimpered. "Why does it sound so awful."

"They talk backwards," said Ahgeneh. "That's what my mother told me."

"Backwards?" asked the two sailors with blue hoods.

"Backwards," Kitchehoar explained. "For they're such shabby, dead, unliving things they don't have breath to call their own. We breathe out as we speak, but they can only breathe in."

"You're dead, you great, stupid, clot-headed, cadaverous thing," the First Mate called back. "Come closer and we'll explain it."

"No," said Gimlet. "I don't want it to come closer."

"Stay still, close by the fire, my son," said Ahgeneh. "It's the safest place of all."

Then Tom tried to lick his lips. A foolish thing to do in the Winter, he knew, a sure way to get them chapped and peeling. But he was too frightened to have any spit left. With the Ice Troll, the Seventh Degree of Chilly Suffering had come at last: the cold that simply tries to kill you.

Beside him Jenny cocked her musket with stiff, numb fingers.

Then they heard a hideous, backwards moan, and the morning light revealed the monster at last. Its flesh was ragged and torn, and it was pulling at the sharpened pickets.

TOM SAW how its lips were pulled back and bared. *It died in the cold,* he thought. Jenny saw how its grasping fingers seemed to end in claws. *It died hungry,* she thought. And Gimlet saw how it moved even though its bony limbs were deeply cut. *It still wants to be alive,* he thought.

Then the muskets of the sailors began to roar, and a flight of arrows from the hunters followed. Any living creature would have died at once, but this cold thing took no notice. It tore one picket from the ground and used it, slashing left and right as it came inside the circle.

But the defenders closed with the monster anyway, and a dozen swords and spears began to cut and stab it. Tom and Jenny stood back with Gimlet then, for all the others were grown and stronger.

So with the wolves, the three young Strangers could only watch the terrible battle unfold. For the troll seemed not to notice all its wounds. It cast down its own sharp stake, and began to grab and throw aside the swords and spears of its attackers. Somehow it seemed to make for them, Jenny thought, and its eyes were fixed on Tom.

"Just seize it!" yelled Ahgeneh. And, "Never mind the fencing," cried the Captain.

So the sailors and the hunters closed in, and many were clawed and bit and tossed and wounded in the morning twilight. But when the monster's arms were partly pinned, Kitchehoar stabbed his long knife up from below, and cut its heart of ice out.

EVEN AS GIMLET WATCHED IT FALL, the frozen heart still smoked with cold. The boy began to shake with relief. For no one had died! And his new brother Kitchehoar was a mighty hero!

But then he saw that tearing out the monster's heart only made it all more awful. For the Ice Troll did not fall, but only fought the harder. Now it made a great shrug, and pulled one ragged arm free from the press of all the defenders.

"The heart!" Ahgeneh called to Kitchehoar. But with one sweep of its taloned hand, the monster struck down his son, and pressed once more towards the three young Strangers.

Then Gimlet remembered how Ahgeneh's father had died, after cutting out an Ice Troll's heart. For the thing still moved until its icy heart was destroyed, a heart so frozen hard no stone or steel could break it.

The big Bosun pushed forward holding a ship's axe high; and Ahgeneh drove a spear deep into the Ice Troll's side; and Bonawyn rushed to help the Herald. But Gimlet himself did a strange, brave thing, and darted among the legs of those struggling with the monster.

Gimlet was nearly trampled underfoot, but he saw the pale, smoking, frozen heart still lying amidst the battle, and reached out to grab it. The heart was colder than any frozen steel; colder than the worst degree of chilly suffering. It was as cold as the touch of death itself, so however hard the hunters and sailors roared their battle cries, Gimlet's shriek was louder.

The cold of it burned his hand, and the pain gave him the strength to throw the heart far away, right into the middle of the fire.

But the ice did not melt at once. Instead it make a great hiss of smoke and steam; as if the flames and not the ice were about to disappear. Then the troll broke free of the struggling crowd, and made a great stride towards the fire. Jenny skipped back away, but Tom stayed, transfixed by the monster's eyes. In its awful backwards voice it roared: *"Your life's blood for mine!"*

THAT TERRIBLE CURSE alone made many of the defenders shrink back. And like Tom, the two sailors with blue hoods stood stock-still, as if they too had been frozen.

Jenny fired her musket then, and as the ball struck it made the monster start. With a blow of his axe, the Bosun cut off of one of the Ice Troll's legs. From front and back, Ahgeneh and the young hunter Buccaneen drove their spears through its body to hold it fast, enough for Bonawyn to lift Kitchehoar's body clear of the fight. Still, the monster took another lurching step towards Tom.

And now Tom himself had his sword in hand as he stood beside the hissing ice, and faced the doom he'd long delayed.

But then Captain was at his side, and slashed down at the smoking heart. He used his strange and ancient blade, the one they had found far in the North at the grave of some lost exploring sailor; the sword of Edge-Gleamer's brother.

That blow shattered the monster's frozen heart, and it fell, and was properly dead at last.

So like his grandfather long ago, Kitchehoar had found a way to destroy one of the icy dead who hunger. And Gimlet and the Captain's sword had finished it.

FOR A MOMENT, the defenders could only stand panting. But beyond the fire, the dogs began to howl again, in chord and discord, wild and tame together.

In the pale morning light, Kitchehoar came back to the world at last, in the arms of Ahgeneh his father. He put his hand to his face, torn by the Ice Troll's talons. "I'm thinking this might have been a blow as hard as any from a Bugbear," he said.

"You'll be living to fight again," Ahgeneh told his son. "A fine thing, if more of those are coming."

Others had been wounded too, both Strangers and Ealda. But after his hand was bound, Gimlet only sat there shaking. "That's enough for the boy," Bonawyn told Jenny. "He must be sent away to the others sheltering in the Drumrath, for he is foolish-brave, and will find a way to die if he sees another battle."

"What if the icy dead find him on the way?" Tom asked.

"That would be a terrible chance," the Captain said. "But it's certain those things will come here again."

"I won't go," Gimlet said. "I should stay with the crew, and with my family."

Jenny looked at Tom and off into the bright, still morning.

"Indeed," she told Gimlet. "Or again, it is also true that you should stay with me and Tom, as we three are all Wards of the Sea together."

"Yes," said Gimlet. "And you and Tom are young too."

"Which fact your presence renders strangely easy to forget," Jenny said. She met Bonawyn's gaze before she continued. "So Tom and I will both go with you to that safer place. And leave the battle to those who are full-grown and stronger."

Gimlet had not expected Jenny to take that line. "I won't go," he said. "Ahgeneh will let me stay with him."

But Jenny took him firmly by his unburned hand. *"First,"* she said, "he will not either, as you will soon enough discover. And, *second,* I would take you away regardless, for your foster-father has other things to do. And, *third,* that is ungrateful to me who has saved you from such various perils as: suffocation, drowning, exile, and a terrible, lonely height. And, *fourth,"* Jenny finished, and she was fairly roaring now, "fourth, or *lastly,* you are still under *my* command, who provided both rank and commission when you were still yet a lubberly, tedious urchin."

The Captain smiled. "You have done your part already, you three," he said. "Gimlet in snatching the frozen heart; Tom and Jenny by bringing the wolves to silence the wild-cats."

Tom said, "Only if, if it works out badly when those things return –"

"Then you two would be left to lead a last stand by those who shelter at the Drumrath," the Captain said. "Go now; run down the frozen river with the boy. And at the Drumrath, make sure you keep a hot fire ready."

So they ran down the trail along the glen, and onto the frozen River Roaring, Tom and Jenny and

Gimlet, and Tom's dog Sparky, and soon the camp and its palisades were hidden from them.

Bonawyn and the Captain, and Kitchehoar and Ahgeneh his father, remained behind. The crew of the *Volantix* and the hunters of the Ealda stayed too; almost all the friends they had on this side of the Ocean, waiting to meet more fell North things.

The snow-covered banks were high around them, lined with bush and scrubby oak trees. And beyond the banks, North and South on either side, was the folded country of the Rockmarch edge, where tufts of Jack pine peeked up from the snow.

They ran in a line: Tom, to break the trail; then Gimlet, still sullenly slow; and last, Jenny, sometimes leaning on the Tinker-made, brass-bound staff. Sparky carried a pack with the small things they might need, and ran about the three of them in the snow.

On their first leg along the river, they made good time, for the families of the Ealda had packed the trail only the day before. Yet the cold still snatched at them as they ran. Even the snow sounded different now: high and thin, like a fiddle-string about to break. Their throats were raw from the cold, and their faces burned where they were bare.

They ran till after noon, when the trail turned South off the river at last, and into the mouth of a small ravine. This was the way the Ealda had gone, the way that led to the fastness of the Drumrath.

In the shadowed ravine, bare brush and scrubby trees still showed above the snow. From there the trail led to the shelter of a light pine wood, and so they stopped to rest.

Tom and Jenny hardly spoke a word as they went about the business of starting a small fire, and Gimlet looked on silently.

When the tea was ready, Jenny poured some into the boy's tin cup. "We have a long way yet to go," she said. "Which requires you to be warm and fed."

"I don't care," said Gimlet.

"Listen to Jenny," Tom told him. "Do as you're told. Drink your tea and eat your biscuits."

So Jenny and Tom took it in turns to give Gimlet instruction. For bothering about the boy at least kept them from worrying about the same things themselves: What would happen at the new village in the Rockmarch? What awful things might follow them even to the Drumrath?

When they had stopped long enough to feel the cold again, they meant to put their things back into Sparky's bag, but the dog would not stand still. "Why is Sparky restless?" Gimlet asked.

"Why are you restless?" Tom asked his dog.

Then the three young Strangers saw a shadow had fallen across the trail. A great, tall shape stood against the bright Southern sky, as hairy as a Bugbear.

"A most unexpected ambuscade!" Jenny hissed as she stood and put her hand to her sword. Tom reached for his musket.

"Now, I thought Strangers were friendly with Riverfolk," the shape said. Then they saw it was only a man; a huge and unkempt man, clad in tattered furs, and even bigger than the Bosun. Tom noticed his bright sash and tasselled toque, and knew him for a River-man.

He let his unopened musket-case fall. "We didn't know," Tom said.

"And we are *most* friendly with Riverfolk," Jenny added. "For didn't Bawdoear himself endorse our Exploration? And hasn't Bonawyn his daughter been our guide across the whole wide Wild?"

"Except when she didn't like us yet and tried to lose us in the fens," Gimlet put in.

"An event long forgotten by all involved," Jenny said.

Then Tom and Jenny introduced themselves properly, as Ensigns from the *Volantix*. And Gimlet told the River-man his name, and said he was a Prince-Admiral in Waiting.

"Quiet, boy," Jenny told him.

The big River-man broke into a broad smile. "Strangers of various ranks," he said. "Well met, I think, in this hard time. Call me Awsook."

"Well met, Awsook," said Tom. "But there is harder coming, and we must hurry."

"Harder times?" Awsook said. "For you know, across the Wild the cats have been gathering together, which is an odd thing for those lonely hunters. And they have torn animals from our traps like wolverines, and fought us with tooth and claw." He walked close and showed them his torn and ragged coat.

"We know," said Jenny. "They came to the village last night. Before –"

"Before something even worse," the River-man finished. "And for both of these things I must thank you Strangers. And Ahgeneh, of course. All of you who have unbalanced this land. Even Bonawyn, though I wonder that she helped you."

"She has fallen in love with the Captain," Gimlet explained, to everyone's surprise. "I think they mean to marry."

"I'm so happy that I met you," Awsook said, and he made a smile that Gimlet had seen before. Jenny and Tom felt their blood run cold.

"Is he a Corsair?" Gimlet asked.

But Jenny only stared at the burly River-man. "Mighty warriors crowd that camp," she said. "Any two or three of whom could easily defeat you."

"I've already been clawed by cats, and more frightening things are coming," Awsook said. "I think those will be my new friends."

Suddenly Tom saw how it would work: Awsook would arrive at the camp like the other exiles who'd fled the North. Ahgeneh and the Captain would be glad for the help of such a stout arm, and never think to suspect him – then Jenny stepped in front of Awsook.

"I'll hurt you three – and your dog – if you get in my

way," the River-man said. And when Jenny didn't move, he grabbed her by the collar.

Sparky began snarling in a new way then, as if the wolves had taught him. "Gimlet, Sparky – run!" Jenny cried. And Tom drew his sword.

Awsook tossed Jenny aside straightaway – like a sack of turnips, she thought, just before she tumbled against a tree. "Run!" she shouted again. Gimlet took to his heels at once, and after an instant's doubt, Sparky followed. "Run and warn them!"

Then the River-man had batted Tom's blade aside, and drawn a cutlass of his own. "None of that, my boy," he said with a sigh. "For you know I'll only gut you like a piglet."

Chapter Twenty-Six: THE BATTLE OF THE THIN MOON

– sailors swear worse – first blood – last blood – death on the trail – shouldn't have come back – the ruin of battle – don't look away – Ned and Fred – the departure of the Tinkers –

Tom brought his sword back at once, and Jenny got to her feet and drew her blade too.

Awsook shook his head, and with a great sweep of his cutlass knocked both their swords aside. Then he made as if to start a backhand cut, just to show them what would happen.

But Edge-Gleamer had taught Tom and Jenny better than that, and they both had their swords raised again already.

The big River-man nodded. "That's enough," he told them. "You don't really want to fight me." But he stepped back, to put them both on his right.

"Our friends are meeting worse than this," Tom said. "So you can't frighten us either."

Awsook made a terrible oath, and slashed at Jenny's sword. She felt the shock of it through her arm, but she kept her blade, for she had remembered to keep her hand turned up. "Is that the best curse you know?" she asked. "Sailors swear worse things for a lullaby."

"Stop it," Tom told the River-man. "We don't want to hurt you."

Then Awsook looked at the Ensigns and cursed again. He took another circling step. "No, you don't," he said. "So now you've still got the chance, imagine how this fight will go. You know a little about swordplay, I see that now. Still, you've never cut a man you've spoken to before, and you'll hesitate – you know it as well as I do. But I'm quick and strong... and won't mind to see your blood pour!"

As the River-man's voice rose to a shout, he jumped forward and made a great cut down at Tom, and then another across at Jenny.

It was a near thing that they both parried the blow. And they both knew his words were true. But the clash of swords didn't give them room to think, and they only swept their blades back around as they had been taught, and lunged in turn.

With each clash of steel, every quick exchange of blows, Tom and Jenny fought more in earnest. The fight dodged around trees and in and out of cover. Awsook was strong and fast – but not half so fast as a Tinker. Soon they knew that for all his size and speed, the River-man knew little of sword-science; and there were two of them, and they began to give him trouble.

Still, Tom and Jenny always hesitated before striking home, just as Awsook had foreseen, so as the sword fight went on he began grinning. "You're tiring now," he said. "Drop your swords and we'll call it finished."

They didn't drop their swords. Then Awsook dodged to put a tree in Tom's way, and made a hard cut at Jenny. She turned it aside, but while their swords still rang, he made a second, harder backhand blow that knocked down her guard and slashed across her right shoulder.

"First blood!" the River-man yelled. "Now drop your swords!"

At the start, that might have been enough to end the fight. But now Tom only closed again and he had no more hesitation. He made a cut that Awsook had to turn to block; and when the River-man swung back wildly Tom made an easy parry. And then he put the point of his sword deep into Awsook's thigh. Awsook let his blade flail back in surprise. Then with both hands, Jenny swept her sword around and sent his cutlass flying.

Awsook put a hand against his bleeding thigh, and for a moment the three of them stood panting. Tom felt the sharpncss of the cold in his lungs once more.

"The girl's hurt, and so am I," Awsook said. "Should we call that quits?"

"We won't let you pass," Jenny said, as she clutched her wounded shoulder. The River-man nodded and bowed his head.

We've won, Tom thought. And he began to worry about Jenny's wound, and how far Gimlet had gotten.

Then all at once Awsook had twisted Jenny's sword from her hand; but Tom ran him through to end it.

TOM AND JENNY BACKED AWAY, and staggered down the ravine towards the river.

They sank down on a ledge of snow, and bound their wounds without speaking, as if the fight had made them animals who acted without word or thought.

"My Godmother would say he pronounced his own doom," Jenny said at last.

"We have to leave this place," Tom said. "We have to catch Gimlet. He was right after all; we should never have left the camp."

Jenny pressed a bare hand against the numb spots on her face, where the skin was growing cold and hard. "And perhaps we should never have left our home across the Ocean," she said. "But only stayed to wait for the doom that gathers."

"I think we will meet our doom here, soon enough," Tom said.

But Jenny got up and leaned on her staff. "We have to catch Gimlet."

So they ran through the cold again, along the trail back to the palisaded village. They were tired, and Jenny's limp was slower. But now and then they heard Sparky faintly barking. And after a long time, they heard musket shots, and a great dog chorus howling.

Some Cold North Thing

THEY HURRIED AS THEY COULD, towards the sounds and cries of fighting, but the afternoon light was already growing thin by the time they came upon the first sign of the battle. A great cat lay stretched and twisted, bloody on the snow. Not a pishkeen, as the Ealda called the big lynx, but something worse, with sword-long fangs still bared and silently screaming.

"A sword-fanged tiger," Tom said. "It came from as far as the Shining Mountains to find us here."

"Arrows in its throat," Jenny said. "Some Ealda killed it."

Not much farther, they came on another great cat, sprawled and torn. And beside, an Ealda lay still and dead, and they stopped. The Ealda's face still wore stripes of battle paint, but his throat had been ripped apart, and his stomach laid open by great talons.

"No," said Jenny. "Oh, no. It's Kitchehoar."

The blood was still red and wet on the snow; and the gore on the ground was horribly steaming. But the Herald would never speak again.

"We have to hurry to the camp," Tom said at last.

But a Tinker crept out from the bush along the river-bank. It was Flint, raised up on one hand and holding Gimlet by the scruff of his neck with the other.

Flint bared her bloody, pointed teeth. The boy hung limply in her grip. "Young Strangers," she said. "Ye shouldn't have come back."

Jenny already had her sword out. "What have you done?"

Suddenly Flint sprang. Almost at once she pulled the sword away and grabbed Jenny's collar in her teeth.

"Flint!" Tom shouted, and now his blade was out.

The Tinker's ears twitched and she let Jenny's collar go to turn a fierce, wild gaze upon him. "Oh no," Flint said, and her shoulders rolled under her jacket.

Then she blinked her amber eyes. "Oh no, I didn't mean to fright ye. But my heart is fast from battle." Flint breathed twice, slow and deeply. "No, we came at the summons of the wolves, to help them with these great cats. I came too late to save yon brave fellow hunter, but I stayed when I heard it was you coming."

Now they were near enough to hear more shots, and shouts, and screams from the camp. Jenny shook off the Tinker's grip. "The boy," she said.

"The boy?" Flint blinked again, and looked down at the child in her right hand, as if she'd forgotten him. *"Och,* the Stranger-child is fine, except for what he's seen. It made him fall asleep at once, to find some less awful dream." Then she shook Gimlet by the back of his jacket, and the boy shifted so that Tom and Jenny knew he lived.

"I'll take him," Jenny said. She put away her sword and lifted the boy with an effort.

"The child meant to warn the camp about some wickit River-man," said Flint. "Is that still important business?"

"No," Jenny said, quietly. "That problem is no longer vital."

The Tinker gave them a keen glance. "Such little lives ye have," she said. "It must feel cruel to take them."

"Quiet," Jenny said. "You don't know."

"What about Sparky?" Tom asked. Then he saw his dog crouched in the bush, where the Tinker had emerged, still shaking.

"Yer brave, wee, wolfie creatur," Flint said. "His barking called yon poor Ealda here to save the child. And then, too late, I heard it as well."

Tom picked up his trembling dog. "What's happening in the battle?" he asked.

"Follow me and I'll show ye." Then the Tinker made a terrible smile. "But hurry, or the bloodletting will all be finished."

THE TINKER led Tom and Jenny quickly, by a trail they hadn't known, through the snowy wood towards the sounds of battle. As they came to the fir trees that stood on the West side of the glen, the two Ensigns watched Flint run quickly up one tall fir, as if it were a staircase. Then she looked back down, and returned to help them carry Gimlet and Sparky up to a wide seat, high in the tangled boughs, that looked down upon the glen.

"I had marked this before," Jenny said, "but thought it was an eagle's nest."

"Well," said Flint. "They are also hunters."

From that seat they looked down upon the palisade, down upon a nightmare; looked at the bloody ruin of battle.

Many wild-cats lay dead around the camp: bobcats, lynx and pishkeen, cougars, and more of the awful, sword-fanged ones, the great cats from the mountains, some still in the awful throes of dying. "Look at those," Flint said. "Dead by a spear cast right through them; that's Tinkers' work. How we did our wolf-summoned duty."

Some cats had been shot or fallen as they leapt over the wall of sharp stakes, and died impaled, still clawing for the defenders in the palisade. And many had found a way into the little village, and camp-dogs and great grey wolves had died, some as they ripped a wild-cat's throat out.

"See yon Squint-Eye, the wolf that led yer team, lies there with his stomach open," Flint said. "And Broad-Back with her neck torn. But they died like brave dogs, those two, and fell on a bier of cats they'd slain. Wickit cats who were born to hate them."

But Tom and Jenny hardly cared about the wolves. For more than one Ealda lay dead as well, and a large sailor who clutched a boarding axe. Jenny didn't need to pull out her prize expanding telescope to know who it was. "That's the Bosun," whispered Tom.

"Him?" said Flint. "Aye, then I'll say yer Bosun died well. Stood like an oak-tree, and let the battle break over him, and swung his axe, and cut down any cat who came near him. Even the sword-fanged thing who killed him. A brave end, if that matters to you people."

"So no Tinkers died," said Tom. "You hid in the woods to cast your spears."

Then Flint hissed and blood splattered on Tom's face. "We keep hid in death as well as life," she said. "So Brazier fell and has been carried off, and wasn't he a Tinker? We fought outside yer fine safe wall of stakes, and he died killing the cats that came to slay your people. Yer big Bosun will miss a few dozen years of life, but count how many brave Brazier lost."

"More lives will be lost," Jenny said. "Hear how everything is quiet."

ACROSS THE ICE-BOUND ROCKMARCH, over the brittle snow and down the frozen river, through the still, cold air sparkling with a chill of tiny crystals, the quiet of the dead had come, and time itself seemed smothered. Then the terrible cries rolled out; backward gasping cries, that sucked in air and life to make a scream.

"How many are there?" Jenny whispered, as the noise went on and on, echoing through the wooded river valley. Not a chorus like the howls of wolves, or the discordance of the wild-cats, but one common sound, the unliving moan of the killing wind of winter.

"They were six once," Flint said. "As many as have ever gathered. And two of them loped faster. Yer friends the Bone-Faces slew one in their brave stand, and here ye killed another."

"Then four are come," Tom said. "And one was almost too much for all of us together."

"Aye, four," the Tinker hissed. "And from this seat ye can watch this doom play out. Like entertainment for some wickit tyrant in the East, where the Long Night has already fallen."

"We must go fight with them," Jenny said.

But Flint stared at her scornfully. "Oh, aye," she said. "Ye haven't done enough killing today. And wouldn't that be the dream of any grown warrior, to have two children, two wee, young officers with their own wee swords, help them? Ye've run halfway across the Rockmarch and back today; now what could you do but die in someone else's place?"

"Nothing," Tom said. "We couldn't climb this tree without your help."

"Nothing," said Flint. "Now look and bear witness."

Now they saw them emerge from the pine wood in the North: four tall, pale things in rotting graveyard clothes: the icy dead who hunger.

The monsters screamed and prowled the palisade and here and there tore at the sharpened pickets. The defenders of the village fired bows and muskets many times, but when the dead creatures were struck they only shivered. Even the fire seemed to have more life, as it burned quick and crackling in the centre of the camp, and rushed hot and bright up into the winter sky.

Then one Ice Troll broke through the Eastern gate. While the others still tore at the wall of stakes, this monster knocked away hunters and sailors left and right, and made a hungry noise, and bore down upon the Captain.

"I must look away," said Jenny.

But Flint grabbed Jenny's wrist, and squeezed it tight with her blood-browned nails. "Nay, don't look away," the Tinker said. "For what if the two of ye are the only ones who survive this night; the only witnesses for yer people? Then the fight yer brave Captain makes with his Tinkers' sword will be forever be lost and forgotten."

"We will look," Tom said. And at the gate, the Captain stood his ground; he did more. He shouted *"Woe!"* which was his battle cry, and swept his sword against the monster. He met every slash of the stone knife in the monster's hand; he swung his own blade just as hard. And stroke by stroke he forced the Ice Troll backwards.

With one great slash the Captain took off the troll's left arm, but it fought on regardless. With another he lopped off its head, but even then it moved and cut at him. The Captain opened up the monster's chest, and then struck one last great blow, and shattered the frozen heart, just as the dead thing slashed him. Then they both fell together.

Tom and Jenny were dumb with horror. But Flint whispered urgently. "A brave end. Honour him by watching."

In the North, a second Troll made a way into the palisade, and scattered defenders, and lifted up one sailor and bared its teeth to begin its eating.

"That's Cookie!" Tom said.

But Ahgeneh stepped forward then. The dead thing slashed at him, but the old Marshal blocked the blows with his strong shield of Buffle hide and returned each with a cut from his long knife. Others came to stand with Ahgeneh, but he had the troll's attention. He made tatters of its long-dead flesh, though that was not enough to stop it. Ahgeneh never minded his wounds, but gave them back in kind; he fought as if he had seen enough of life, and didn't care if this would be his last battle.

"I hope Gimlet does not awake," Jenny whispered.

"We should be fighting with them," Tom said.

The longer Ahgeneh stood and made his battle cries, and named Shawnatheir his famous father, the more others gathered round, sustained by his courage. Hunters and sailors both came, and struggled with the Ice Troll. They took wounds too, many of them, but at last they pinned the monster's arms. Only for a moment, but long enough for brave Ahgeneh to stab deep and cut out its frozen heart, and carry it smoking to the fire.

Nearest to them, on the West side of the palisade, another troll had almost torn its way through the pickets. But below them, Edge-Gleamer suddenly stepped out from the long evening shadows. He held his own sword high, and with this chant loudly cursed the monster:

"Hungry ghoul who walks tonight, ye thrawn and foolish creatur. Sleep the long sleep the dead have earned. Or I will find the ground where first ye fell, and fire it till yer bones are burned. I know the secrit name ye were given at yer birth; now fall like dust, or I myself will speak ye back into the earth. And if even that spell dinna suffice, I'll use this blade to cut yer heart, and melt it down, or smash its ice."

"Like the spell he uttered against Pishkeen Mawr," Jenny said.

"Aye," said Flint. "He has the power, and does know the secrit names, and how to speak the magick." The troll took one long stride towards the Tinker, and then, un-spelled, it remembered it was truly dead, and its bones unknit all at once. And then it was ashes, and then it was dust.

But in the palisade one monster's heart still hissed and smoked where Ahgeneh had cast it in the fire. The Ensigns watched in horror as that troll flailed and screamed, like an animal that knows it's burning. Sailors fell then, and hunters died who were close enough to fight it.

And as the winter evening began to close, the last Ice Troll came through the Eastern gate, where the Captain lay fallen. The monster made its awful backwards cries, and tore and beat down more sailors still, but it looked for the Captain, for the North was most strongly in his heart, and that was the smell they followed.

Bonawyn stood over him, and she led the defenders there most fierce and bravely. The River-woman was knocked down more than once, and cut by both stone knife and talon. But she would not leave the Captain's side, no matter how loudly screamed the monster.

"Look who stands by her!" said Jenny. For the two sailors with blue hoods, who feared the Ice Trolls most of all, stood stoutly there.

"Ned and Fred," Tom named then in a whisper. "It is their long-feared doom, and see them bravely face it!" And both of the Ensigns would have turned away, except for the shame that they weren't there to help. Then the Troll cast Bonawyn aside, and bent for the fallen Captain. But the two timid sailors threw themselves over his body, and died then in his stead, for love of him, by the monster's tooth and talon.

In the fire, one frozen heart neared its bubbling end. And at the North of the palisade, that heart's monster picked up the young hunter Buccaneen from those who pressed around it. Ahgeneh himself was there, and tried to pull the dead thing off, but too late. For the troll bit her throat, and killed her just before it fell at last and its un-life finally ended.

Then Edge-Gleamer appeared from the shadows, by the monster who bent to slay the Captain. Three other Tinkers were with him too, and Flint's amber eyes flashed, and she pulled her ears back and made a hissing sound, and dropped from the tall fir tree and rushed after the others, quick as a deer. Tom and Jenny were left high up in the nest, with Gimlet who still slept, and Sparky who could only shudder.

Now there was no time for one of Edge-Gleamer's long spells, but still the Tinker-chief made his battle cry, for he would not attack even such a thing from behind, like some skulking bandit. So the monster turned to face the Tinkers, and struck out with its claws and blade; heavy blows the small Tinkers hardly parried. Edge-Gleamer made a mighty stroke with his ancient sword, and it struck deep into the Ice-Troll's chest and among its ribs was trapped there.

Edge-Gleamer pulled hard at his blade, and Tom and Jenny saw that another Tinker held the right arm of the struggling monster, and Flint herself grabbed hard onto the other.

Now Bonawyn had risen again, and the River-woman cocked her musket, and pressed it against the Ice-Troll's back, while the three Tinkers held him. And Bonawyn fired and the ball burst the monster's frozen heart with a mighty crack.

Then Edge-Gleamer's sword came loose at once, and Flint stepped away, but the other Tinker only fell, for the monster's knife had slain her.

Then the night fell, and the Tinkers melted quickly into the dusk, and Tom and Jenny slowly carried Gimlet down from the tree and stumbled towards the village in the little valley.

As THEY CAME TO THE TRAIL that led to the Eastern gate, the wolves passed them pulling a cariole, and they saw on it lay Weaver, the Tinker who had told them the tale of Straikha and her friend Terrier, the swift, wild huntress. Edge-Gleamer ran behind the cariole, and gave them a quick flourish with his hat as he ran past, as if to bid them goodbye forever, and then came three other blurry Tinker shadows.

Only one of them stumbled, something no Tinker ever did. It was Flint, and when she got to her feet, she looked up at them, and her wild eyes were weeping.

"Where do you go?" Jenny asked.

"They go to our hidden snuggery," Flint said. "But I go to find some way across the Cracks of the World, and follow Weaver's speerit."

"Where?" Tom asked.

"I dinna ken it yet!" the Tinker hissed. "But I will go West and North, and look on great mountains, across the wildest torrents, through the most bitter cold." Then she, too, took a step into the shadows.

"And one way or another I will leave this world," they heard the Tinker say, and then she was lost from sight forever.

"Poor Flint," Jenny said. "And poor Ned and Fred, and all the others lost tonight."

"Keep back some tears," Tom said. "For we will need more before we see the dawn."

Chapter Twenty-Seven:
THE END OF THE EXPLORATION

– farewells – the Homely Country
– the Stone of Heart's Desire – "Don't abandon me"
– all things change – ending in glory –

SOME WARM WIND BEGAN TO BLOW WITH THE END of the battle. And the Captain lay on a bier by the great fire and waited for some dawn-light in the East, for no sailor wanted to end his days closed up against the sky.

His beard looked grey now, and his face bore the terrible scars of the bugbear, but his hair was still full and dark, the kind of hair that most befits a sailor.

Ahgeneh, and the First Mate, and Tom and Jenny, and even Gimlet, had sat with him in one long, last council, and made what arrangements they could about the time to come.

Bonawyn never left his side. But her tears fell, and she stroked her fingers through his hair.

A kind of last light shone from the Captain's eyes, and he said, "This is not our Homely Country after all, not a place to start, after such a wrong beginning."

"But if this land had any curse against Strangers, I lift it now," said Ahgeneh. "For haven't we fought together here, and hasn't our blood mingled as it fell? – red with red upon the snow, and we have become one blood and family."

"Our Homely Country is not in the Wild," the Captain said, "but still West of here, in the open Steppes; and at the mouth of the Hidden Sea, where we can pursue our trade of sailing. Our people would disturb you less.

"You hunt the Buffle there already," the Captain said. "But now hunt and stay and visit us, and our spirits will go into the West together, and be company against the empty spaces."

"Yes," said Ahgeneh. "In honour of my new son, and of Kitchehoar, who will go there with you."

Then the Captain turned in pain, and reached for Jenny's hand.

"Sir, you are my hero and model," Jenny said. "A wise commander; a fine teacher – and a great Explorer."

The Captain smiled. "A fine compliment, from someone who once commanded my crew to such renown," he said. "What a noble Explorer you will grow to be."

"Not as great as you," Jenny whispered. "Not even Tortuca was greater."

He laughed, for the Captain knew that was the highest praise Jenny could conceive. Then he gasped, and looked suddenly away to the West, as the first pale sky of morning hurt him.

Then Tom knelt beside him. "My Captain," Tom said. "I should have stayed here, to help preserve you, as you have preserved us all so often."

But the Captain's eyes flashed at him. "Belay such talk," he called in his great quarter-deck voice. "For you preserved your crew at Eena Culgach, and your bargain with the Tinkers brought us the wolves, the wolves and others I think, who fought in the shadows."

"I should have fought beside you," Tom said. "For you have been like a father to me."

"Belay such talk," the Captain said again, more gently. "For you have been like a son to me, but your own real father waits for you too, in Landsend, across the Ocean. He wants your reports to add to his great work. And then he will bring it here, to this new country, and preserve what might be forgotten as the Long Night falls across the East."

"How shall I remember you?" Tom asked. "What monument should I make? What epic should I write?"

"Mark the names of all you knew who fell here," the Captain whispered. Then he said, "But let me hold the Star-Glass once more."

And when the Captain took the glass in his hand, there were no stars, no icy mountain peak, but some wide and sunlit waves. He smiled, and then he gave it back to Tom. "My sight fails," he said. "But set me in a ship – not in the ground, where the wind and waves are hidden. And when the wind blows West, send it across the Hidden Sea, towards the setting sun. Which shall be my last exploration."

Then the Captain looked about. "Mate!" he cried. "Most fine and faithful Mate!"

"Here, Captain sir!" the First Mate called. And he came

to the Captain's side right away quick. "Aye, here and ready." And Tom saw that the First Mate's hair was all white now, like a bright cloud of snow, nimbus-like, as the old sailor would have said.

"Here, my Captain," the First Mate said again. "Here, my old friend."

"You must lead our people now," the Captain said. "Not just the sailors, of course, but those you call from Landsend, and from the Corner by the Sea. And it will be left to you to settle with Ahgeneh, and even with Bawdoear, Bonawyn's father, all the terms and conditions of sharing the Vastlands."

"Does we even want to stay after this ghastly start?" the Fist Mate asked. "After we's begun with so much pain and sorrow?"

Ahgeneh spoke then. "All things are changing now," he said. "The Ealda will not live as they would have if the Strangers had not come, or the Riverfolk, if we had not come to this place together.

"But the icy dead who hunger are our foes from ancient times, and now we will be free of them for long years. So we should count our losses – and mine are as great as yours, for I have lost my son, my son the fine and dashing Kitchehoar, even though I have gained another.

"And then it will be a good time to make a start," said Ahgeneh. "For this will be a peaceful land, down from the Rockmarch to the Steppes beyond the Hidden Sea; calm and wide and open."

The First Mate nodded. "A good place to live," he said. "Once we learns to like the Winter. But I had thought to retire."

"I had thought to retire once too," the Captain whispered. "But an end comes regardless."

Then the sun rose in the East at last, and Bonawyn brushed his grey hair back from his brow again, and kissed him. "Once I had thought to abandon you in the Wild," she whispered. "But now you are leaving me."

"Bonnie Bonawyn," the Captain whispered again, and those were his last words.

"I am lonely here," she wept. "Don't abandon me."

They stepped away then, to let Bonawyn and the Captain be alone, and Tom felt his tears roll down his own cheeks unstopping; and beside him Jenny even sobbed.

"I grieve mightily," she said. "As befits the occasion."

"Grieve, child, but not without ceasing," Ahgeneh told her. "For the first breath of Spring is in the air, and many heroic things have been done, especially by the fallen.

"Only keep some tears in reserve," the old Marshal said. "For all things will change now, for good and ill, for Ealda and Riverfolk and Strangers. And no one can foresee the tally."

When the families of the Ealda returned from the Drumrath, the shelter on the ridge, they mourned anew.

And then they tended their dead, Ealda and Strangers and Riverfolk alike, each after their fashion.

But when Spring came, and the water began to flow again, the Captain and Kitchehoar the Herald, who was Ahgeneh's son, they laid together in the *Dauntless*, and set their weapons beside them: bow and musket, and long knife and Buffle shield, and ancient sword.

Then they began a procession of boats down the icy waters, as far as the Hidden Sea, and drew the *Dauntless* most gently behind them. Bonawyn paddled quietly in Jenny's *Fortitude*, except that twice she sang the Captain's song about the two tall pines; once strongly, and once much softer.

At last they came to the Hidden Sea, and one afternoon pushed their way to a likely shore, and set the *Dauntless* riding on the water, kept close by a stone anchor.

Towards sunset an East wind arose. Then Tom unfurled the sail of the *Dauntless*, and Bonawyn loosed the anchor, and Gimlet went into the frigid water and pushed the curach ahead.

For a moment the curach moved uncertainly over the waves, as if it was nervous of the ice. And then the wind began to fill the sail, and the little boat's banners flew: one from the *Volantix* for the Captain, and one marked with a crow for Kitchehoar.

So it moved West; West as if the broken ice parted for its coming, or carried it high on rafts of frozen water; West across the shining crests and bright ice; West against the red and gold that poured out of the setting sun, so that the *Dauntless* was dark like a shadow.

Smaller and smaller that shadow grew, as the gold light spread, and the sun moved lower. At last, the sail disappeared in a blaze of red against the darkening sky, as if the boat had changed to fire at the end.

SO THE CAPTAIN'S LAST VOYAGE ended in glory; so Kitchehoar was Herald to the heavens.

And night fell then, and those they left behind were on a cold, dark shore, and they gathered around bright fires.

EPILOGUE

Chapter Twenty-Eight:
WHAT HAPPENED AFTER

– Mill House again – a crown of antlers
– the Long Night falls – uttering maledictions
– a glimmer in the West –

IN THE BROAD, TALL-GRASSED STEPPES, CLOSE BY the Hidden Sea, Cookie and a few other sailors stayed to begin the first houses of their new Homely Country.

But most of them crossed the Wild with Bonawyn again, to the Mill House where the *Volantix* had rested for the Winter. Then there were explanations and accommodations to be made with the Master, with Bonawyn's father Bawdoear the River-man, and even with the Shawnachan, the wise Ealda who had given them their first kind words.

"We has crossed the Wild," the First Mate told the Master of the Mill House. "We has survived the land and weather, and even received the blessings of Ahgeneh, despite all your warnings, threats, and what can only be called general disapprobation. Now what do you think of our hopes and schemes?"

The Master looked at him straight on, and if the Master still looked proud, he was pale and thinner too. "It doesn't matter what I once thought," he said. "More and worse tidings have come here from our homelands, East across the Ocean Sea. The Long Night is falling just as your Captain told us; the signs, *redes*, and dreams that sent you are all coming true. The trade across the sea, which is the business of this House, is almost finished.

"So do as your Captain planned," the Master said. "Take those Strangers who want to return to face that doom, and speed home across the waves; and in Landsend, in the Corner by the Sea, and wherever else you might find them, gather all who will dare to come before the darkness swallows them. And next Spring bring them here, where our people's lives might start again."

WHEN TOM AND JENNY returned with the others to Landsend at last, in the shadow of the Long Night falling, they found that awful rumours had become dread reports. They found that makers of wool sweaters had turned to knitting armour of mail; they found that armies marched close; that plague and pestilence had begun to stalk the land.

So, many of the people of Landsend were ready to hear the call to the West. Tom's father began at once packing dozens of crates with books and notes. "I hope I can find some congenial place for a new library," he said. "But at best this will delay my Great Work by years."

Although Jenny's Godmother had recovered her health, and become once more merely bent and elderly, despite

Jenny's most desperate entreaty she would not leave. "No," she said, "No, I am a Wise Woman of the Woods Nearby, not a Wise Woman of the Unknown West. I will stay here with Pawlikins the cat until the last extremity, and utter maledictions upon the heads of trespassers, and won't that serve them right?"

"But you will die," Jenny said. "And I will never see you again."

"I might," said her Godmother. "And you might do many things, so who knows?"

"Do you have at least one final *rede* for me?" Jenny asked.

"Has your last *rede* finished?" the old woman replied. "Have you smoked its meaning yet – *'How does every Exploration end?'*"

"But I think every Exploration only ends with another beginning," Jenny said.

"Jenny Fisher-Girl," her Godmother said. "I have raised you well. Now keep close; keep this old Wise Woman company; right until the day you must sail West once more."

And Bonawyn helped Gimlet sneak back into the Corner by the Sea, where things had grown darker yet; and they found the Duke no longer in his castle, but only in the moonlit woods, by the standing stones, reigning in a crown of antlers.

"You are an extraordinary boy," the Duke told Gimlet, once he had finished his report as a witness for the Corner by the Sea.

"Yes," said Gimlet.

"Six families hide with me who are ready to follow you West," said the Duke. "Now show them the way."

"Will you come?" Gimlet asked, for he suddenly realized that the Duke, too, had been like a father to him.

But the Duke shook his great, antlered head. "No, for my work will still be here," he said.

"What work is that?" Bonawyn asked.

The Duke smiled grimly. "Loon-Daughter," he said in a low and terrible voice, "My work is to give darkness to those who darkness bring."

Then he disappeared into the forest.

SO SOME OF THE STRANGERS escaped to the West, before the Long Night closed the way.

In time, the Master of the Mill House gave up his place to Tom's father, who made his library there, to try to preserve all that once the East had known.

But most of the Strangers followed the sailors from the *Volantix* back to the Homely Country by the Hidden Sea, and they made a new home there. The First Mate became the mayor, of course, and Cookie was his deputy. Sometimes Gimlet lived there, with his friends from the *Volantix*, and sometimes in the Rockmarch, with Ahgeneh his father, among the Ealda. And Bonawyn looked after him wherever he was, or when he came with her on some business of the Riverfolk.

Tom stayed in the Mill House to help his father, but first, as he had promised the Captain, he wrote a memorial of all those who had sailed in the *Volantix*, and marked the names of those who had fallen.

For a while, Jenny went to try her trade of fishing in the Hidden Sea. But in time she grew restless, and took the staff Edge-Gleamer had given her, and travelled once more.

First she visited Tom, and told him of her plans, and intended Explorations: "Which shall entail extensive travelling," she said. "North and South and West. But now and then always returning to see you here in the Mill House, where you and your Dad preserve the memory of the East we left behind."

ACROSS THE OCEAN, in the Corner by the Sea, the Duke made a fortress of the forests, and became a nightmare to the wicked who had overrun his castle.

And by Landsend, in the Tower Jenny once had built, her Godmother made a great and terrible stand against all the evil things that had trespassed on the Woods Nearby, and uttered her awful maledictions.

So in the East the darkness of the Long Night fell at last, while in the West some small light still glimmered. In the Homely Country by the Hidden Sea, the new houses of the Strangers shone like lanterns. In the cold, still winter, fire still danced in the black night sky. And smallest, but maybe strongest of all, light still burned in the Captain's Star-Glass; hope still shone from the Stone of Heart's Desire.

Appendix: Tom's List

THE ROSTER OF THE *Volantix* AND ASSOCIATED VESSELS:

Those who crossed the Wild in the curach *Dauntless*:

Captain Forril*
Franklin, the Carpenter *(known as Chips)***
Tate, the new Cook *(known as Cookie)*
Able Seahands:
Jack Red-Scarf
Matt
Hackett
Timkin*
Clay
(Bonawyn, the River-woman, guided this ship)

Those who crossed the Wild in the curach *Fortitude*:

Ensign Jenny, a Fisher-Girl *(once Captain of, variously, the Otter, Ruggles, and Nonesuch, in the voyage to the Old Sea)*
Oakes, the First Mate
Able Seahands:
Two-Eye Bob
Bill*
Ralf
Darwin*
Jack *(plain)*
Gimlet, lookout and Seahand, Ordinary *(formerly Ship's Boy, Goat, and Stowaway, in the voyage to the Old Sea)*

Those who crossed the Wild in the curach *Adventure*:

Ensign Tom *(formerly lookout in the voyage to the Frozen North)*
Tucker, the Bosun*
Able Seahands:
Ned*
Fred*
Clay
Willy
Rawlins
One-Eye Bob

* *These fell in the Battle of the Thin Moon*
** *He perished in the Battle on the Tamarack Island*

In the voyage to the Frozen North, Cookie was an Able Seahand only, and Barold served as Cook. For a time Barold also served as Mate and Cook in the Old Sea, before he was gathered to the bosom of the waves.

DUNCAN THORNTON is the author of two juvenile fantasy adventures: *Kalifax*, which was a finalist for the Governor-General's Award for Children's Literature, the Mr. Christie Book Award program, and two Manitoba Book Awards; and *Captain Jenny and the Sea of Wonders*. He has also written radio drama, theatrical drama, and several screenplays, in addition to his fiction and non-fiction prose.

Born at God's Lake Narrows in Manitoba, Duncan Thornton has Honours degrees in English and History. He is currently a new media instructor at Red River College in Winnipeg. He and his wife live and write in Winnipeg.

His e-mail address is *thornton@kalifax.com.*

YVES NOBLET was born and raised in France and attended the Collège des Beaux-Arts in Bordeaux before emigrating to Canada in 1973. He received a Diploma in Visual Communications from the Alberta College of Art (Calgary) in 1977 and worked as a graphic designer and art director before founding Noblet Design Group, his current company, in 1996.

Yves has mastered the traditional and digital mediums with equal success, receiving a long list of awards for his designs and illustrations. He has created covers for the Coteau books *The Blue Field*, *Buffalo Jump: A Woman's Travels*, *Kalifax*, and *Captain Jenny and the Sea of Wonders*. Yves and his wife Brigitte make their home in Regina with their four children.

Acknowledgements

The author wishes to thank the Manitoba Arts Council for its support in the creation of this novel.